ONCE UPON A SCANDAL

BARBARA DAWSON SMITH

St. Martin's Paperbacks

ONCE UPON A SCANDAL

Copyright © 1997 by Barbara Dawson Smith.
Excerpt from *The Venus Touch* copyright © 1997 by Barbara Dawson Smith.

ISBN: 0-312-96277-0

Printed in the United States of America

St. Martin's Paperbacks edition/September 1997

10 9 8 7 6 5 4 3 2 1

Dedicated to Suzannah Davis:
you live on in the hearts of so many friends.

St. Martin's Paperbacks Titles
by Barbara Dawson Smith

A GLIMPSE OF HEAVEN
NEVER A LADY
ONCE UPON A SCANDAL

Acknowledgments

My heartfelt thanks to the finest writing pals in the world:

Joyce Bell
Christina Dodd
Betty Traylor Gyenes
Susan Wiggs

❧ Prologue ❧

*I*t was the perfect night for thievery.

As she climbed out the attic window and onto the third-story ledge, Emma, Lady Wortham, felt blessed by luck. The fog hid her presence high atop the row of elegant town houses. The dense mist also kept her from seeing how far she could fall.

Hugging the brick wall, she inched her way toward the home of her quarry. Only the faintest glow from the lower windows penetrated the darkness. The soup-thick moisture in the air gave the illusion of solidity, as if she could step off her perch and sink into a black featherbed. . . .

Emma shuddered. One false step, and she would break her neck. This narrow shelf was intended as decoration, not as a walkway for the Bond Street Burglar.

She slid one slipper along the ledge, then the other. Right foot, then left. Right foot, then left. These supple soles had once graced ballroom floors in the finest mansions of London. She smiled, thinking of how horrified the *ton* would be to learn the use to which the Marchioness of Wortham now put her dancing slippers.

Not, of course, that she intended to get caught.

A series of robberies had plagued Mayfair over the past few years, the most spectacular of which had been a daring daytime theft on Bond Street, when the Earl of Farleigh had had his jewelry case nipped from his carriage while he visited his tailor. Residents of the exclusive area had raised a hue and cry to apprehend the criminal, but to no avail. They never dreamed the culprit was one of their own. A woman.

Born to privilege and wed to wealth, Emma knew she was above suspicion, in spite of her ruined reputation. Most men had no inkling that she even possessed a brain. After all, her dainty figure made her appear childlike, helpless. And at one time, she *had* been helpless. But never again.

Never again.

Though the damp chill bit through her snug black coat and pantaloons, the heat of determination warmed her. She crept past the connecting wall to the neighboring town house. At last the shadowy square of a window loomed through the fog. Deftly, she inserted a wire into the frame, wriggled the latch, and eased open the casement.

The hinges squawked. Emma froze, listening for sounds of alarm, but she heard only the clopping of horse hooves and the rattle of carriage wheels from the street below. She hoisted herself over the sill and into a small, gloomy chamber. An odor of neglect hung in the air. Apparently, Lord Jasper Putney's taste for luxury did not extend to the attic rooms occupied by his servants.

Emma felt her way through the darkness toward the faint outline of a door in the far wall. She paused to check her mask and the hood that hid her silvery-blond hair. Then she twisted the doorknob and cautiously poked her head out. A guttering candle in a wall sconce illuminated an empty corridor. Silent as a wraith, she stole down a steep staircase and slipped through a door cleverly concealed in the paneling.

In contrast to the barren passage allotted to the servants, this corridor was decorated with sumptuous abandon. Watered green silk adorned the walls, and Greek statuary cluttered the side tables. Gilt moldings edged the ceiling and framed the doorways. Through the eye slits of her black domino, Emma appraised the richness of the decor. Yes, the master of this house could well afford to relinquish his ill-gotten gains. The conniving blackguard.

Voices rose from the dining chamber on the floor below. According to Emma's informant, Lord Jasper was entertaining a large party of friends, and his valet was assisting the footmen in serving the guests. The upstairs should remain deserted for at least another hour.

Her heart pounding with anticipation, Emma found the master bedchamber and entered the adjoining dressing room. The heavy scent of pomade mingled with the smoky odor from the fire that burned low on the hearth. A branch of candles flickered on the dressing table, casting light on a large coffer of studded Morocco leather.

It was unlocked, of course. Despite the previous burglaries, these aristocratic gentlemen seldom considered themselves potential victims. Only their lust for gambling surpassed their arrogance. They thought little of bleeding the pockets of a too-trusting old man.

But tonight, Emma would rectify that wrong.

She lifted the domed lid of the coffer and assessed the contents. On the white velvet lining lay an array of stickpins, jeweled sleeve links, and silver waistcoat buttons. She picked up a ring and examined it in the candlelight. The cabochon ruby glowed a deep, rich red against a figured gold setting. Sold at a certain shop where no questions were asked, the precious stone would yield a tidy sum.

Emma tucked the ring into a special pocket inside her coat, then selected several other items until her booty approximated the amount her grandfather had lost to Lord Jasper a fortnight ago. She never took more than was strictly necessary. She was, after all, a seeker of justice, not a common thief.

Yet this once, she found herself caressing a diamond-encrusted pocketwatch. With the money it would bring, she could restock the larder and pay the account at the butcher. She could properly refurbish Jenny's wardrobe, rather than letting down the hems of her gowns again.

Emma held the watch to her breast and squeezed her eyes

shut. How she ached to see her daughter arrayed in the finest silks and laces, with an ermine muff to keep her small fingers warm in winter and a frivolous bonnet to shade her blue-green eyes in summer. Jenny deserved so much more than Emma could afford to give her. Jenny, who was too sweet and innocent to comprehend the sins of her mother. Jenny, who needed the love of a father.

From the prison of Emma's heart, a rush of bitter despair escaped. Jenny, who would never, ever be accepted—

"I say, who the devil—?"

The raspy voice pierced her anguish. Emma dropped the watch with a clatter and spun around.

A stout gentleman blocked the doorway of the dressing room. He looked like an overstuffed sausage in his broad, brocaded waistcoat and tight gray pantaloons. His pale eyes bugged out in a face crisscrossed by broken red veins.

Lord Jasper Putney.

Emma's heart slammed into her throat. Then the shock of discovery was eclipsed by a new terror as her gaze fixed on his hands. On the fingers that clutched the half-unbuttoned placket of his trousers.

Dear God. *Dear God.* Memory drenched her in a sickening wave. He meant to force himself on her.

A whimper squeezed past her dry lips. Her limbs felt leaden, gripped by horror. Time stretched into an eternity.

"Help!" Putney bellowed. " 'Tis the burglar. The Bond Street Burglar!" He wheeled around and staggered drunkenly away.

Emma snapped to her senses. She had mistaken his intent.

Trembling with relief, she sprinted toward the outer door of the bedchamber. From the corner of her eye, she spied Putney by the bedside table, fumbling in a drawer. He turned, his shaky hands raising an object that glinted in the firelight.

A pistol.

Panic iced her lungs. She was almost to the door when an explosion split the air. A numbing impact struck her left side, and she stumbled.

Lucas. Lucas!

Clutching at the doorjamb, she righted herself. She could not think why her mind cried out to the husband who had abandoned her.

The gabble of voices and the clatter of feet sounded from the main staircase. Spurred by hot pain, she lurched in the opposite direction.

Down the deserted corridor. Up the servants' steps. Into the dark attic room and out the window where the black mist waited.

✑ Chapter 1 ✑

Somewhere off the coast of England
September 1816

As always, her hands worked magic.

Lucas Coulter lay prone on the bunk, lulled both by the rhythmic rocking of the ship and the mesmerizing massage administered by his mistress. With his eyes closed, he was more keenly aware of his other senses. The whisper of silk as Shalimar shifted position over him. The musky-warm scent of the oil she applied to his bare back. The firm pressure of her fingers kneading the tension from his muscles.

He could almost fancy himself back in the cozy houseboat he and Shalimar had shared on Lake Dal in the Vale of Kashmir. He could almost forget the misty shores of England loomed but a half a day's sail away. He could almost believe himself off on another exotic adventure rather than returning home after seven years abroad.

Home. The thought evoked a sweet-sharp joy that verged on pain. When he had exiled himself, he hadn't thought there would ever come a time when he would wish to return. Yet now he found himself looking forward to visiting his two older sisters, to meeting his nieces and nephews, to seeing his mother and assuring himself of her improved health. He wanted to ride in the crisp autumn mornings over his estate in the wild hills of Northumbria. He wanted to view his lands through the eyes of a man, not the untried youth he had been all those years ago.

His travels had taken him across Egypt and Asia and India, through deserts and mountains and jungles, into mud huts and palaces and temples that had never before known the tread of an Englishman. Until at last, he'd come to realize that no matter how far he roamed, he could never escape the anguish of memories. They would always be with him, those events that had shaped him. Only then had he made his peace with the past.

His head pillowed on his folded arms, Lucas concentrated on the gentle rubbing of Shalimar's hands, on the soothing sensations that enveloped his body. Tomorrow night he would sleep at his London house. As the sixth Marquess of Wortham, he needed to reacquaint himself with his holdings and tend to the duties of his title. He grimaced. There had been a time when he would have given it all away for the love of one woman. Emma.

His wife.

Bitterness seeped from a place deep inside his chest, but with the strength of habit, he subdued the sentiment. Years ago, he had sworn not to allow Emma to obsess him. From the letters written by his mother, he knew Emma and her child lived quietly with her grandfather in London.

She was never seen at *ton* functions anymore.

The scandal had clipped her wings, and he could not imagine a more fitting punishment for a social butterfly like Emma. At one time she had teased and flirted with an army of admirers, and he had been among their ranks, the most smitten of them all. . . .

Tempted to plunge into the dark well of memory, Lucas gave a growl of disgust and rolled onto his back. He scowled in an effort to shake off a past that no longer mattered. A single lantern hung from a hook in the low ceiling. The swaying of the ship caused light and shadow to dance across the small stateroom with its plain wooden furnishings bolted to the floor.

Against the dreary setting, Shalimar bloomed like a wild

orchid. To ward off the chill in the air, she wore the traditional Kashmiri *pheran,* a cloaklike garment of indigo blue
cotton, the collar and cuffs rich with silver embroidery. A
length of white silk draped her black hair and framed the
dusky splendor of her features.

She sank into a submissive pose on the floor beside the
bunk. "I do not please you, my lord?"

Her smoky-soft voice wafted over him, easing his ill humor. He no longer tried to change her humble posture; since
the early days of their love affair, he'd come to realize she
was happiest serving him. It was the way of her people, the
training of a woman accustomed to the harsh hands of men.

Touching her satiny cheek, he tilted her face up. "You
always please me."

"Yet I cannot reach the empty place inside you. The part
you keep hidden from the world."

Those dark, sultry eyes regarded him with a timeless wisdom. Restive, he sat up on the bunk, the air brisk against his
naked chest. His reckless, youthful passion for Emma could
not compare to the serenity he'd found with Shalimar.

"Come here," he said, drawing her up onto the mattress.
"It is you who fulfills all my needs. It is you who gave my
life back to me. And now I shall return the favor by finding
your son."

"My lord." Her slim hands clutched at him. "I fear
O'Hara-*sahib* has taken him away from England. I fear I will
never see my Sanjeev again in this lifetime."

Anger flashed through Lucas. The rogue had callously
abandoned Shalimar and had absconded to England with
their ten-year-old son. "Shh. I'll find him."

"May the gods bless you for bringing me to the land of
your birth." Shalimar bowed her head again. "Even should
you choose to stay here with your wife."

The notion jolted him. "Never. Emma could never, ever
take your place." His arms tightened around Shalimar; she
reminded him of a willow, bending, always bending to his
will. Pressing a kiss to her jasmine-scented hair, he muttered
fiercely, "I've no intention of even seeing the bitch."

London
September 1816

Full of righteous resolution, Emma marched up the front steps of her husband's mansion. The imposing entranceway sported a grand pediment and pillars that had been scrubbed clean of London's soot. The brass fittings on the double doors gleamed in the sunlight. A blustery breeze scattered leaves along Wortham Square, but here the marble steps were pristine, as if even the Almighty could not bring Himself to sully the property of his lordship, the Marquess of Wortham.

According to Emma's informant, her husband had returned four days ago from his journeys abroad. Since then, each of her written requests for an audience had been refused with a polite note penned by his secretary.

Blast politeness. Emma intended to speak to Lucas today. It was a matter of life-shattering importance.

She reached for the filigreed knocker. Her gloved hand paused an inch away as cowardice surged out of nowhere. She wanted to turn and run, to abandon her plan to maneuver her husband one last time.

It wasn't that she feared Lucas. His shy, unimposing nature had drawn her to him in the first place. He had been so much easier to gull into a quick marriage than a man of experience.

No, it was her own sense of shame that crippled her confidence. She dreaded the notion of facing the husband she had betrayed. The husband who still did not know the depth of her manipulation of him.

Once he heard her out, she quickly reminded herself, he would understand. Likely he would be grateful to her. And she'd survived worse unpleasantries over the years. Confronting a long-lost husband could be no more horrible than fleeing the Bow Street Runners while bleeding from a bullet wound.

Emma took hold of the knocker and gave three firm raps.

A gust of cold wind tugged at her bonnet and pelisse. The air had turned unseasonably chilly. To save the fare of a short-coach, she had walked the two miles from Cheapside, and she clenched her teeth to keep them from chattering.

The door opened. A tall, white-wigged footman looked down at her in polite disdain. No recognition flickered in his cool gray eyes. She didn't recognize him, either. "Yes, madam?"

"I've come to see Wortham. If you would be so kind as to summon him."

Walking brazenly past the servant, Emma entered an enormous foyer hung with ancestral portraits and tiled in creamy Italian marble. A wave of bittersweet nostalgia inundated her. The last time she'd stood here, she had occupied a position of honor at Lucas's side while accepting the good wishes of the guests at her wedding breakfast.

How naïve she had been to hope that her troubles were over. How blind not to have foreseen that her quiet husband would prove to be the most unforgiving puritan in London.

Yet she had no regrets. She had done her best for Jenny. As she would continue to do now.

Emma unbuttoned her outmoded pelisse and handed it to the footman. "I shall wait in the drawing room."

"I beg your pardon, madam," he said huffily, stepping into her path. "I regret to say his lordship isn't receiving callers today."

"Oh? Tell your master that the Marchioness of Wortham awaits him."

Emma had the brief pleasure of watching comprehension wipe the haughtiness from the servant's pinched face. He bobbed a swift bow. "Yes, m'lady. At once."

As he hurried away down a corridor, she drew a deep, steadying breath and went in search of the drawing room. She found herself tiptoeing as if she were an intruder come to steal the family jewels. How ironic. Of all the grand houses she had burglarized in the name of justice, she had never even been tempted to come here.

Had she demanded her rights, she might now reign over

this splendid house with its high, frescoed ceilings and elegant rosewood chairs against the soaring walls. A tall casement clock marked the genteel passage of time, reminding her how insulated life was here in this aristocratic household. How different her own life might have been.

A knot of guilt ached in her breast, and Emma knew why. She had already taken enough from Lucas. Accordingly, she had demanded no privileges, no money, no favors.

Until today.

Too jittery to sit, she paced the long length of the drawing room. It had been tastefully redecorated in the latest fashion. Who had chosen the sky blue accented by white, the striped silk cushions on the chairs and the gold-fringed draperies at the windows? Who had selected the fine Grecian frieze around the chimneypiece? The intricately embroidered firescreen appeared to be the dowager's handiwork. The richness of it all put Emma's own shabby household to shame.

She caught sight of herself in a gilt-edged mirror and stopped short. Sweet heaven, she looked a fright. The wind had wreaked havoc with her appearance, slapping bright pink color into her cheeks and luring wisps of silvery-blond hair from beneath the edges of her bonnet.

Swiftly she repaired the damage by rewinding the exposed curls around her forefinger into a girlish style. She had grown accustomed to hiding her beauty beneath drab clothing and mobcaps. But today it was imperative that she look her best, and she had spent the previous day refurbishing the single remaining gown from her trousseau, a lilac silk with puffed sleeves and a perky yellow ribbon tied just below her breasts. With the modesty piece tucked into the low-cut bodice and the straw bonnet framing her big blue eyes, she appeared the epitome of the frail female.

The effect always worked on men, and Lucas himself had fallen victim to it once before. Luring him into an impetuous marriage had been as simple as stealing a diamond from an unlocked jewel case. . . .

"My lady." With noiseless steps, the footman entered the drawing room. The faintly haughty smirk was back on his face. "His lordship has a full schedule today. He said perhaps if you might make an appointment for later in the week . . ."

Emma compressed her lips around an exclamation of dismay. Dear God, she couldn't fault Lucas for not wishing to see her. Yet she wanted to settle her future once and for all. Now, more than ever, Jenny needed a father who would give her both material comforts and unquestioning love.

Lucas could never be that man.

She studied the footman through the screen of her lashes. "What is your name, please?"

" 'Tis Stafford, m'lady."

"Stafford," she repeated, lowering her voice to girlish coaxing. "Would you kindly ask my husband if I may return on Thursday afternoon?"

"I'll be happy to relay the message to his lordship's secretary."

"Oh, do ask Wortham now. I cannot leave without having his promise of an audience." Seeing Stafford's hesitation, she turned the full force of her pleading gaze on him. Making her lips quiver, she dabbed at the corner of her eye with a lace handkerchief. "Please, sir, speak to my husband. You would have my undying gratitude."

The severity melted from the servant's face. "As you wish, m'lady."

Emma held her woebegone expression until he vanished out the door. Then she darted after him into the corridor, just in time to see his stiff-shouldered form turn the corner. Her slippers made only the faintest sound on the marble floor. Keeping a circumspect distance, she followed him through a maze of corridors toward the back of the house, where he knocked on a door before entering. The library.

Lucas was in the library.

Armed with that information, she slipped into the nearby conservatory and hid herself behind the drooping fronds of an aspidistra plant. And not a moment too soon. The library door clicked open and shut again; then she heard the tapping of Stafford's returning footsteps.

The damp smells of earth and plants surrounded her. The wind rattled the many panes of glass in the domed roof. She shivered, less from the chill in the air than from the prospect of facing Lucas again.

Especially if he hated her.

A fresh attack of cowardice seized Emma. She wanted to slink out of the house, to handle her business by letter. But that would be unfair of her.

She owed Lucas the courtesy of making her proposal in person.

"I knew it would happen someday. Didn't I, Toby?" Reclining on a chaise in the library, the dowager Lady Wortham addressed the old white terrier curled in her lap, then looked at Lucas. "I knew the chit would come here and demand her rights. I'm only surprised she waited so long. She must be planning to win her way back into your good graces, and you must promise not to allow it to happen."

At one time, Lucas had resented being talked to like a child, but now he merely smiled, bending to give his mother a distracted kiss on her cheek. "Don't fret, Mama. It isn't good for your health."

"Bah, those doctors are a flock of fussy geese. They would have me lying all day in bed like an invalid. I'll have you know, my heart is as hale as a newborn babe's."

"You were overcome by exhaustion on the day of my return. And you will rest accordingly."

She pursed her lips as if to protest. Then a rueful smile brought vivacity to her ghostly pale cheeks. "You've grown autocratic, just like your father. You speak with such confidence now. Ah, Lucas, how good it is to have you home again."

"It's good to *be* back."

It was true. The library had always been his favorite room, his sanctuary, and it looked exactly the same, as if he'd never gone away. A fire crackled on the grate, and leather wing chairs flanked the hearth. Filled with nervous energy, he paced around the room. The walls held row upon row of books collected by his father, who had devoted himself to scholarly historical research. Lucas had spent many a happy hour here, reading about the strange customs of foreign peoples.

He'd feel at peace now were it not for Emma. He sensed her presence like a pall on his good humor. Of course, she would be gone once Stafford relayed the news that her husband had no time for her today.

Was she still the blond temptress? What the devil did the bitch want from him? Money, no doubt.

Lucas forced his attention to the pile of wooden crates that littered the Turkish carpet. Picking up a crowbar, he inserted the pointed end between a crate and its lid. He did not wish to think about Emma. He did not want to know if her appearance had changed, if she still could melt a man with her baby-blue eyes.

Lucas shoved downward, applying pressure to the crowbar. The dry wood gave way with a protesting squawk, and the top of the crate came off. "I've brought you several gifts," he told his mother, tipping the box toward her. "Jade from the Orient, ivory from Africa, jewels from India."

Lady Wortham hardly glanced at the exotic offerings, though Toby watched dolefully from her lap. "I've been thinking," she said. "Perhaps you *should* see Emma. The sooner, the better. Before she has the chance to concoct more of her mischief."

Lucas's fingers tightened on the box. The straw inside the crate prickled his skin and exuded a musty odor. "I'll deal with her in my own way. And in my own time."

As if she hadn't heard, his mother went on. "My dear, you mustn't blame yourself for what happened. Forgive me for speaking so frankly, but when Emma moved back to her grandfather's house and was brought to childbed not five months after the wedding, everyone in society deduced the truth. Rest assured, your peers regard you as an honorable man."

The warmth of love flowed between them, but Lucas also felt the sting of resentment. Damn Emma for driving him away from his family. Over the past seven years, a lacework of lines had aged his mother's patrician features. Noticeably thinner, she had to stop and rest whenever she walked up the stairs. His ill-advised marriage and prolonged absence had affected her deeply, he knew, coming so soon after his brother Andrew's death in battle. Lucas would not permit anyone to upset her further.

Especially not Emma.

He met his mother's gaze. "My only regret is the scandal I brought upon you and my sisters."

"It brought worse upon Emma, and justly so. We became objects of sympathy. *She* became an object of scorn." As she stroked the terrier, Lady Wortham's hand trembled. "Emma herself confessed to her wicked behavior the next day, after you'd gone away. She stood in front of me, as bold as brass, and admitted she'd entrapped you." His mother bent over the dog as if to take comfort from his unconditional devotion. "Isn't that so, Toby?" The animal licked her hand.

"I shouldn't have left you to face her on your own," Lucas said with a shadow of guilt. "It was unforgivable of me."

"You were too kind to recognize her true character. She acted the flirt, luring all the gentlemen to herself, even the married ones. Given her lack of morals, she might even have dallied with a servant." Lady Wortham made a disapproving noise in her throat. "We can be thankful she did not bear a son. A footman's get might have been your legal heir."

That possibility had galled Lucas; and he'd wasted months agonizing over the identity of her lover. But no more. He refused to expend energy on bitterness and regrets. His memories of Emma held no more significance than an old, aching wound.

"There is no point to idle speculation." Lucas bore down on the crowbar and another crate creaked open. "The matter is closed."

His mother sat up straighter, and Toby snuffled a protest in her lap. "But that's where you're wrong," Lady Wortham said. "Have you considered your future? If you were to speak to the archbishop about an annulment . . ."

His jaw muscles clenched, but he spoke calmly. "You know as well as I that the banns were announced. I was not coerced into speaking my vows. The bishop himself presided over the ceremony. There can be no doubt that it was all quite legal and valid."

"Then seek a divorce. There is surely enough proof of her infidelity to win your suit. And you could marry again. I know any number of lovely young ladies who would make you the perfect wife."

Lucas only just stopped himself from snapping out an order to stop interfering. He would not quarrel with his mother. The anxious hope lighting her hazel eyes revealed her good intentions. Having been blessed with a loving marriage before his father's death, she viewed wedlock as the cornerstone to happiness. But Lucas no longer shared her belief.

The thought of divorce had tempted him in the past. He could end Emma's connection to him once and for all. No longer could she claim the distinction of Wortham.

Yet were he free, his mother would make it her mission to introduce him to a succession of well-bred ladies. He would be forced to tell her about Shalimar, that he had already found the only woman who mattered to him. A foreigner who, like Emma, had borne a bastard child by another man.

Christ, he despised the need for deception. He didn't want to hide Shalimar in a discreet house in St. John's Wood as if she were a dirty secret. Yet he could not—he would not—risk his mother's health.

Carefully, he drew a gold jeweled mask from its nest of straw in the crate. "The future can wait for another day," he stated firmly. "Now, I promised to show you what I brought back from my travels. This piece came from a maharajah's palace. It's reputed to bring great luck to its owner."

He crouched beside the chaise and presented the tiger mask to his mother. She raised a thin eyebrow as if to argue further, then lowered her gaze to the mask. In the shape of a tiger's head, it was designed to cover the upper half of the wearer's face. Rows of yellow diamonds alternated with strips of dark brown jasper to form the striped head. Slits framed in tiny emeralds comprised the eyeholes.

Lady Wortham stroked the pointed gold ears, much as she had stroked the old terrier nestled in her lap. "It looks quite valuable. Be sure to lock it up. During your absence, there have been a rash of robberies by a ruffian known as the Bond Street Burglar."

"The mask won't be here long. I plan to donate it—and several other pieces—to the museum at Montague House." His voice warmed. "My hope is to organize an exhibit displaying artifacts from all over the world."

She smiled fondly at him. "Much as I missed you, I'm glad you had the chance to travel. It's always good for a young man to take the grand tour before he settles down."

Her words jolted Lucas. She thought he was home to stay.

Now there was something else he couldn't yet tell her. Eventually she would have to learn he did not intend to remain in England, that he would return abroad after he located Shalimar's kidnapped son. London held too many unhappy memories.

A discreet knocking saved him from answering. Stafford entered the library again, his steps hesitant. "My lord, beg pardon for disturbing you again. But the marchioness"—he looked at Lady Wortham and gulped—"er, the younger marchioness, well, she refuses to leave until you promise her an audience. On Thursday afternoon."

Lucas's stomach clenched. Emma was still here, haranguing his servants.

He might as well find out what she wanted from him. It was childish to play waiting games. "I'll see her in the drawing room in ten minutes."

As the servant left, Lady Wortham swung her feet off the chaise. "I shall go with you. It will give me great pleasure to send that brazen hussy packing."

"No. I'll deal with her myself." Rising, Lucas bore the

priceless mask over to the desk at the far end of the room. He moved a row of books from the shelf behind the desk, revealing a small iron door nestled in the wall. With cool efficiency, he inserted a key and opened the hidden repository, then reached for the tiger mask.

He would use the same cool efficiency with Emma. He would permit her a brief, formal interview, the shorter, the better. Now that he knew her true character, seeing her again would be no different than brushing off an annoying tradesman in the Calcutta bazaar.

Toby loosed an excited yap. Ears perked, the terrier sat up on Lady Wortham's lap, then leaped to the floor. He raced past the heap of crates, short legs pumping, and reached the door just as it opened.

Tail wagging furiously, the dog danced a welcoming jig on its hind feet as a woman stepped into the library.

She glided like a ghost from the past. Slender as a girl, she reached down to pet the dog. "Hullo, Toby. I'm afraid I haven't any treats today."

Then she straightened, spied Lucas, and smiled.

The breath left him as if someone had driven a fist into his stomach. His fingers stiffened around the heavy, jeweled mask. The deep blue of her eyes drew him like magic. His tongue felt thick, and for the first time in years he feared he would stutter if he tried to speak.

Damn Emma and her treacherous beauty.

And damn his reaction to her.

The truth hit him with searing force. He'd still sell his soul to have her legs wrapped around him in bed.

✂ Chapter 2 ✂

The first thing Emma noticed was the startling difference in Lucas. It was more than his physical appearance, although he did look tanned and fit. Beneath the walnut-brown coat, his shoulders had widened, and his legs were long and muscled in buff breeches and shiny Hessians. He seemed to have grown taller, broader, more commanding. His boyishly attractive features had hardened into the arrestingly handsome face of a stranger.

Yet the most disturbing transformation of all was the cold indifference in his dark eyes. Not a flicker of attraction shone there, only a faint annoyance, as if he'd been interrupted by an irksome servant.

Emma held her smile with determined effort. Her heart was beating so fast she felt flushed from her cheeks down to her bosom. There was no reason to feel so overwrought. Now that Lucas was back in England, he surely wished to be rid of her. For good.

"Good morning, my lord. Do excuse me for disturbing you at this early hour." Wanting to spare him a tongue-tied reply, she curtsied to him and then to her mother-in-law. Reclining on a chaise, the elder Lady Wortham looked thinner and her face was unnaturally pale. Fine lines of age framed her eyes and mouth. "Madam," Emma said with perfect courtesy. "I trust you are well?"

"Perfectly so." The dowager's curt tone was just short of rude. "Toby, come here."

With one last worshipful look at Emma, the terrier trudged across the rug. He lay down beside his mistress, his head cradled on his paws and his eyes mournful.

Did the woman begrudge her even a greeting from a dog? Emma stifled the resentful retort. She had not come here to antagonize the Coulters, but to do them a favor.

Accordingly, she flashed another brilliant smile at Lucas. "Well," she said in her sunniest voice. "You must be busy reacquainting yourself with friends and family after your trip abroad. I beg only a few moments of your time."

"As always, I place your needs above all others." He enunciated each word with crisp contempt, unlike the boy who had once stammered out his proposal of marriage. He turned to the dowager. "If you would excuse us, Mother."

Lady Wortham remained stubbornly on the chaise. "My son brought back some fascinating artifacts," she said. "He was showing them to me."

It was a polite way of saying Emma was intruding. Determined to stay, she stepped closer to her husband. "May I see?"

A strange breathlessness came over her. Lucas's long fingers held the piece, and she couldn't help noticing his skin was burnished as if he'd spent many hours in the sun. She forced her gaze to the jeweled replica of a tiger's head. "Why, it's a mask. What marvelous workmanship—it must be priceless. Where is it from?"

His fathomless expression hinted at secrets she could never share. "India."

His movements brisk and self-assured, he placed the tiger mask into the shadowy interior of the safe. How strange to think Lucas had traveled halfway around the globe and seen sights she could only imagine in her dreams. With a pang, Emma remembered the wedding trip they'd planned to the Continent. He'd dreamed of taking her boating on the Seine, drinking wine in a villa near Rome, walking the ancient steps of the Acropolis. He'd set off alone instead, less than twenty-four hours after he had bound himself to her by a vow of everlasting love.

He closed the repository door and locked it, then crossed the library to the desk and tossed the key into a drawer. The essence of him lingered in the air, a faint whiff of musk along with something spicy and exotic, mysterious and masculine.

"Don't you think you ought to keep the key in a less obvious place?" she blurted out without thinking. "Any thief could find it in a moment."

"Thieves are the very least of my son's concerns," the dowager snapped, sitting rigidly upright on the chaise. "Unless, of course, *you've* come to steal from him."

Emma's blood chilled. For the barest moment, she feared both of them knew she was the Bond Street Burglar. But that was absurd. "I wouldn't think of it. You yourself made certain I have no say in his affairs."

Lady Wortham pursed her patrician lips as if composing a retort.

"Mother, I believe you were about to leave," Lucas said.

"It might be wiser if the two of you spoke at the office of our solicitor—"

"I should like to be alone with my wife. Now."

A look passed between the two of them. Then she lowered her eyes and stood up, Toby in her arms. "As you wish."

Emma blinked in surprise. In the past, the dowager had kept a firm rein on her son. How masterfully Lucas behaved now.

Taking his mother's elbow, he led her to the door. "Mind, no overtaxing yourself," he said quietly. "You're to rest before luncheon."

The tender regard he showed to his mother brought a lump to Emma's throat. At one time, he had shown the same loving attention to his fiancée. He had followed her around like an adoring terrier, fetching her drinks, bringing her posies, guarding her from the unwanted attentions of other men. She wondered if a kernel of that regard still existed. . . .

He closed the door and turned to Emma. "Tell me how much you need."

Again, she was struck by his air of command. His hands pushed back his coat and rested at his lean waist, making her uneasily aware of his muscular build. Her palms went damp and cold. He was staring at her, waiting for an answer. And she couldn't remember what he'd said.

"I beg your pardon?" she asked.

"Tell me the amount you require," he repeated in a tone of jaded politeness. "I will inform my secretary to issue a bank draft to you."

Money. He thought she'd come here for money.

Resentment pricked her. If only he knew all the economies she had practiced, the made-over gowns, the times she'd skipped meals so Jenny could eat. But of course Lucas had every reason to think the worst of her. "I don't want an allowance from you—I never have," she said evenly. "There's another matter I wish to discuss with you."

His eyebrow cocked in skepticism. "Go on."

Calling up the words she'd rehearsed, Emma clasped her hands tightly and dipped her chin in a girlish pose. "First, I must humbly offer my apology. I wanted you to know how very sorry I am . . . for deceiving you. I cannot even beg your forgiveness. Rather, I would like to make amends." She paused, absurdly hesitant to finish the rest of her prepared statement.

His eyes were hard, brown mirrors, revealing nothing of his thoughts. Was he reliving the horrible moment when he had walked into her dressing room and had seen the proof of his bride's betrayal?

Emma swallowed the impulse to defend herself, to blurt out that she, too, had been wronged—terribly wronged. But he must never know. She would take that secret to the grave.

"Well, speak up about these amends," he said. "I haven't all day."

She lowered her gaze to her gloved fingers, forcing herself to play the shamefaced wife. "I should like to offer my co-operation to you . . . in procuring a divorce."

There, it was out. She felt as if a great weight had been lifted from her. He would say yes gladly. And then she could give Jenny a real home and a father who loved her.

"No," Lucas said.

"No?"

"You heard me." Smiling coldly, he strolled to a small crate, picked up a metal bar, and used a violent gouge to pry off the lid. Wood splintered with a harshly grating noise. "I will not subject my family to another scandal. If that is all you've come to say, you may go."

Her carefully constructed plans threatened to tumble around Emma. She had braced herself to offer sympathy for his pain, understanding for his anger, gentle persuasion for his reluctance. She had humbled herself, practically groveling at his feet. Never had she expected him to refuse with calm, unshakable conviction.

"You haven't given the matter enough thought," she said, keeping her voice sweet. "You needn't fear I'll ask for an annuity from you, Lucas. I only wish to give you your freedom."

"I've been free enough these past seven years."

What did he mean? That he'd had other women? She swallowed hard. "The scandal will be trifling if the divorce is obtained quietly."

"Quietly?" He chuckled without humor. "There is the small matter of airing one's dirty laundry in a public forum, for all the world to hear. The small matter of securing a Parliamentary bill of divorce."

"You have influence. Use it."

"I don't care to bother myself."

Frustrated by his indifference, she ventured a few steps closer and lowered her voice to a husky murmur. "Don't you wish to marry again? All men want an heir."

"Most men." Lucas searched through the straw inside the crate. He drew forth the small jade figurine of a woman and examined it, turning it over and over in his big hands. "However, I'm fortunate enough to have a cousin to ensure the succession. A sober-minded gentleman with three sons of his own."

"But what of you? Don't you want a real wife? A companion?"

He glanced at Emma, his mouth crooked into the trace of a smile. "If you refer to the attentions of a loving woman, I have that need fulfilled to my satisfaction. By my mistress."

A hectic heat rushed over Emma's skin. He returned his attention to the figurine and carefully brushed off the bits of clinging straw as if caressing his lover.

Was that why he seemed so unaffected, so secretive, so *male*? Because he kept a woman to appease his physical lusts? The notion made her shudder inwardly. Who was his lover? Someone he had met on his travels? Was his mistress responsible for his transformation from stuttering boy to domineering man?

He placed the statue on a bookshelf and then stood back to survey it. There was no reason to feel betrayed, Emma told herself. She should be happy he hadn't pined for her all these years. "Then you'll wish to marry her. I'm offering you that chance."

"How decent of you." He paced slowly past the piles of packing crates and circled around behind her. "However, I am beginning to believe your interest in my welfare is not what brought you here to plead so prettily."

His muted footfalls brought to mind a tiger stalking its prey. She imagined him reaching out to grab her, pinning her to the floor. Standing rigidly still, Emma ignored the prickling of alarm down her spine. "I don't know what you're talking about."

"This sudden kindness of yours has nothing whatever to do with concern for my happiness. Rather, it is *you* who wants freedom from wedlock."

Her heartbeat quivered. She fancied he stood directly behind her, that she could feel his warm breath stirring the fine hairs on the nape of her neck. Forcing herself to keep her head bowed in the guise of a helpless female, she murmured, "Surely we share a common interest in ending the marriage.

That's why I'm here. To spare you the trouble of broaching such a delicate topic.''

"How alluring a heroine you are, my Lady Wortham. I wonder how far you would go to convince me of your sincerity." Then he caressed her.

His fingertips glided over her cheek, brushing against her lips. The shock of it sizzled through her. In an instant, she plunged into a dark river of memory.

She jerked around to face him, backing up against the crates. A splinter drove into her palm, but she was numb to the pain. Her throat knotted so tightly she could scarcely speak. "Don't. *Don't.*"

The fire crackled into the silence. An unreadable emotion flickered in his gold-flecked brown eyes. "Don't what? Don't touch my own wife?"

Maturity had hardened his features, lent him an aura of danger. Yet she could also see traces of the boy he had been. On either side of his firm mouth lay hints of the dimples that showed when he smiled.

He was not smiling now.

She felt like a butterfly pinned to his corkboard. She could only stare mutely at him and pray he would leave her be.

"Were I the dastardly sort," he said, "I would have demanded my rights on our wedding night." Folding his arms in a casual stance, he looked her up and down. "Rest assured, though, I prefer a woman of honor."

"Of course," she whispered. "And I'm willing to set you free for her sake."

He cocked an eyebrow. "Tell me the truth, Emma. What man have you found to gull this time?"

She lowered her gaze to his neckcloth. "Man?" she said on a trill of surprise. "Why do you assume there is a man involved?"

"Because a woman like you is never without a man to maneuver." His fingers roughly nudged her chin up. "Tell me his name. I would know who's been cuckolding me."

"I—"

"Tell me, for the courts will require proof of your adultery."

His forefinger and thumb held her chin firmly in place. She fought the panic his touch inspired. There was no point to concealment, she knew with dismal certainty. In order to obtain a Parliamentary divorce, he would first need to win a civil suit against her lover. Her supposed lover. "I—I have an understanding with Sir Woodrow Hickey."

Lucas frowned. "Andrew's old school chum?"

"Yes. He wishes to marry me."

Releasing her abruptly, Lucas strode to the fireplace. He leaned his forearm on the mantelpiece and gazed at her. "I remember Hickey as an honorable, level-headed gentleman. Not the sort to take up with a fallen woman."

The slur hurt, but she refused to let it show. "*You've* taken a mistress. Why should you deny me the privilege of companionship?"

"Because one spurious child is quite enough for me." A faintly feral glint entered his eyes. "And perhaps Hickey knew you intimately before we were wed. Perhaps *he* is the father of your child."

She stood in frozen denial as fear slithered forth from the dark place inside her. No one would believe what had happened. Least of all, Lucas.

Snatching up the sword of anger, she struck back with a lie. "I haven't the least notion who fathered my Jenny. He could have been any one of a dozen men."

"So you said. On the night of our wedding."

She would not feel guilty. Not for taking the only course of action that benefitted her daughter. "Woodrow loves Jenny. That is all that matters to me. If you won't be a father to her, then I must seek a man who will. A man who can forgive a youthful error and accept a blameless child."

His expression hewn from granite, he studied her with a stranger's hard eyes. "There will be no divorce. That is final. Good day, Lady Wortham."

The bars of the prison closed in on her. Fighting back, she

retorted, "As you wish, Lord Wortham. Only prepare yourself for another scandal."

Lucas watched his wife march toward the door of the library. She moved with her unique brand of sensual dignity, her head held high, the lilac silk gown draping her slender curves. He had forgotten how small she was, how dainty, how angelically fair of face. She exuded an air of innocence that infuriated him. For a moment there, when he'd been standing behind her, he'd felt like that callow lad again, dazzled by her deceptive purity. And he'd been seized by the desire to press her down on the rug and consummate their marriage.

He clenched his fingers. Damn her.

When she reached the doorway, Emma turned her head to glower at him with her beautiful blue eyes. As if *she* were the injured party. Then, with a twitch of her skirts, she vanished into the passageway.

She would go back to Jenny now. The thought squeezed his chest in a vise so tight he could scarcely breathe. Somehow, putting a name to Emma's child made his resentment blaze hotter. And his regrets burn deeper.

If you won't be a father to her, then I must seek a man who will.

He slammed his fist down onto a crate, splintering the wood. Pain speared up his arm. Did she think *he* ought to have accepted her bastard?

No, not a bastard. Under the law, her child bore his name and the distinction of his rank. Lady Jenny Coulter. She would be six by now. Of an age to ask questions about her father. Did Emma tell her the truth? Did Emma admit her own wrongdoing?

To hell with it. What she told her daughter held no interest for him. His emotional turmoil arose only from the fact that he fully realized now the danger of having an untrustworthy wife.

Running restless fingers through his hair, Lucas paced the length of the library. Considering Emma's penchant for toying with men, it was a wonder she had not conceived again. In fact, it was a miracle she hadn't given birth to a boy. By law, the Wortham heir.

The ramifications of such an event struck a grim note. While he'd been away, the issue of the succession had seemed remote, unimportant. Now he faced the fact that he could not permit Emma to hold such power over him.

Yet if he did not divorce her that left him only one choice. His pulse surged as the solution enticed him.

No. He wouldn't even consider such madness. He'd only bring calamity onto himself and his family. On the other hand, perhaps he was underestimating himself. He was no longer the green boy, easily hoodwinked by a pretty smile. He could keep Emma under strict control.

The unthinkable course of action took flame inside him, filling him with dark, damning fire. Yes. He must do it.

He must ensure that Emma bore *his* child.

Emma's thoughts were in such chaos that she walked straight past the man who loitered on the front steps of her house in a seedy neighborhood on the fringes of Cheapside.

She had been reliving each moment of the meeting with Lucas. From the instant she had seen her husband looking every inch the omnipotent lord, she had lost control of the conversation. She had failed to guide him into accepting the only reasonable resolution to their unconventional marriage. Why was he so adamant about not wanting a divorce?

Because he had a mistress, a woman he loved. The notion stung with surprising poignancy. His lover must be unsuited to marrying a man of his high station. Was she a foreigner, then? Or a lower-class Englishwoman he had met overseas?

Whoever she was, she pleasured him in bed. She lifted her gown and submitted to his dominance. She allowed him to perform that painfully degrading act on her. . . .

"Out burgling, m'lady?"

Jolted, Emma found herself standing on her own front steps. Beside her stood a pigeon-breasted man wearing a battered black top hat and the cast-off brown suit of a gentleman. One of his eyelids drooped, lending a sly look to his sallow face.

Clive Youngblood.

Her stomach took a dive. The Bow Street Runner had plagued Emma and her grandfather for months, suspecting one of them was the Bond Street Burglar. He alone had noticed the pattern of the robberies—that in the weeks preceding each theft, her grandfather had lost money to the victim.

Surreptitiously, she glanced up and down the residential street. No one was watching. "I beg your pardon," she said icily. "Did you speak to me?"

"You know I did. It h'ain't polite to ignore an officer of the law."

"Nor is it polite to address an unescorted lady."

"Maybe 'tis a rule fer you top-drawers. But 'ere, in my part of town, we h'ain't so particular."

She gritted her teeth on a retort about self-important little men. Youngblood lacked proof of her crimes, yet he continued to dog her, disappearing for weeks, then reappearing. "If you've something to say, then say it."

"I might at that." A crafty smile curled his lips as he rocked back and forth on his heels. "Yer grandpa's been gamblin' again."

Her feet froze to the step. "You're lying."

"Nay. Saw 'im wid me own eyes. 'Twas last night, comin' outa Chutney's Club." He clucked his tongue. "'E 'ad the look of a bloke oo's lost 'is last farthing."

"Well, I'm sure you're mistaken. Good day, sir."

Grinning, he lifted his top hat with the hauteur of a lord. "I'll be on the lookout fer the Bond Street Burglar."

The warning didn't deserve the dignity of a reply. Leaving him standing out in the cold, Emma went inside and shut the door. Only then did she allow anxiety to wash over her.

Chutney's was a backstreet gaming hell. Where Grandpapa had been wont to go in the sad months after Grandmama's death.

Emma shook her head. Youngblood's accusation could not

be true. Ever since she had come home bleeding from Lord
Jasper Putney's bullet, Grandpapa had stopped gambling. He
would not risk the dice, not ever again. Where would he get
the money for a game, anyway?

The cash box.

Denying her doubts, she walked briskly across the bare
wood floor of the entryway. The downstairs was silent as a
tomb, though she could hear Maggie singing off-key in one
of the bedrooms above. The familiar sound lifted Emma's
spirits. It was Monday, washing day, when fresh linens were
put on the beds. Jenny would be up there, helping Maggie
and chattering instead of doing her lessons. Were it not for
her doomed errand this morning, Emma would be with them,
sweeping the dustballs from beneath the beds or scrubbing
the grates. At one time she would have been appalled to do
the work of a servant. But necessity—and Jenny—made it
all worthwhile.

Entering the small morning room, Emma could not help
but compare it to Wortham House. Here, the blue curtains
were frayed. No fire burned on the hearth, for coal was too
dear to waste. She had placed the furniture in strategic lo-
cations to hide the worn spots in the rug. Yet a pair of windows looked out on a tiny rear garden dominated by a stately
beech tree. And they had a roof over their heads and food
on the table. That was all that mattered.

She went to the tall secrétaire in the corner. Standing on
her tiptoes, she took a chipped porcelain vase off the top
shelf and shook out a key into her palm. She used the key
to open the metal strongbox inside the desk.

And found herself staring down into the empty interior.

Her stomach lurched. Where was the money she had set
aside until the next quarterly payment from her trust fund?
Just yesterday, there had been six pounds, three shillings, and
a few pence. Enough to scrape by with nothing to spare.

Closing her eyes, she pressed her forehead to the oak secrétaire. It took a moment of deep breathing to alleviate her
distress. Youngblood was wrong. He *must* be wrong. Grandpapa would not break his vow.

But he had come in very late last night and gone out early this morning again, leaving the house as she'd come down to breakfast. Had she not been wrapped up in her own troubles, she would have paid more heed to his air of jolly frivolity. *Was* he up to his old tricks again?

The question nagged like a sore tooth. As soon as he returned home, she would get the truth out of him. Agitated, she paced to the front door. If only she could put her financial woes behind her by marrying Sir Woodrow.

Though he wasn't sinfully rich like Lucas, Sir Woodrow Hickey was comfortably settled. He wanted to take care of her and Jenny. Her heart warmed at the thought of his kindness and gallantry, his undemanding and courtly devotion. She had grown exceedingly fond of him over the years, once she'd looked beyond his slight acquaintance with Lucas's family. A trusted friend, Woodrow had stayed at her side during the difficult years of early motherhood. Emma had hoped to repay his regard by making them a family.

She peeked out the front curtains. Almost as if she'd conjured him, Sir Woodrow was marching up the steps. The sunlight shone on his impeccable blue suit with the perfectly tied cravat. Thank heaven, he had a firm hold on her grandfather's arm. She could only pray they'd missed Youngblood.

The moment the two men came inside, she knew her wish had been denied.

"Confounded Runner," Lord Briggs muttered, shaking his fist. "A pox upon him, bothering his betters. Why, in my day, a person of common birth knew his place. He didn't gabble on and make sly remarks."

"Good day, madam," Woodrow said, bowing to Emma before turning back to Viscount Briggs. "I confess, I'm astonished you would be acquainted with such a man. How did you come to meet him?"

Dear God. Woodrow didn't know about her secret life as a burglar. "Grandpapa met him in a gaming hell," Emma said quickly. "He . . . he came by to deliver some interesting news. And I've been wondering if it has to do with my strongbox being empty."

Her grandfather opened and closed his mouth. His gently weathered face took on a sheepish expression, and he tugged at his neckcloth, mussing the starched linen. "I can explain that, my dear."

"I'd hoped so. In the drawing room, then."

"After my nap."

"Now."

He blew out a sigh. "Lead the way, girl."

"Before we talk, I should like a word with Sir Woodrow."

"Take as long as you like." With a benevolent wave of his hand, her grandfather marched past her like a martyr on his way to the lions. "Go on, Hickey. Save me the trouble. You'll tell her everything, anyway."

The baronet removed his hat, revealing wheat-brown hair that receded from his brow. His clear gray eyes were grave. "I don't know quite how to say this, Emma."

"You must tell me," she whispered back. "Where did you find him?"

"At a small club in the Strand. I'm afraid he was . . . er . . ."

"Gambling again." Struck by despair, she struggled to keep her expression calm. On impulse, she reached for Sir Woodrow's hand and squeezed it. His fingers felt warm and comforting, nonthreatening. "Thank you for bringing him home."

The ruddiness of his cheeks deepened, and he withdrew his hand. "Never fear, I shall see to his markers."

"You'll do nothing of the kind," Emma said fiercely. "I've some money put away. Just tell me who he owes this time."

"You know I cannot. It's a debt of honor between gentlemen."

"Nonsense. Grandpapa has always told me in the past."

Woodrow frowned. "He expressly asked me not to reveal the gentleman's name. I cannot betray a confidence."

She bit her lip against another argument. Woodrow wasn't

one to bend his strict principles. "As you wish, then."

"May I visit with Jenny now, until we've time to talk further?"

"Of course." Emma managed a smile though the lump in her stomach grew heavier. She would have to break the bad news about her interview with Lucas. But she could not bear to think of the future. Not yet.

In the drawing room, she found her grandfather standing at the sideboard, hoisting a glass of port. A short, wiry man, he had a perpetual twinkle in his blue eyes. Even now, good humor radiated from him as he drank deeply and grimaced. "Nasty stuff," he said. "Must have a word with Spencer's on the quality of their wine."

"We don't buy from Spencer's anymore," she reminded him. "We can't afford the prices."

His bushy white brows drew together. "Ah, how right you are, my clever girl. The blasted bankers won't let go our money."

Not for the first time, she breathed a prayer of thanks for the trust fund set up by her father before his death. The small quarterly payments had saved them from the poorhouse.

"Speaking of money," she said, "you were going to tell me what happened to our household funds."

"Why, I want to win us a fortune. I'd found a lucky shilling in the roadway, you see."

Emma decided not to ask him what finding a shilling had to do with gambling away their food money. She unfastened her pelisse and dropped it onto a chair. "Just how much did you lose this time?"

"A trifling amount. Never fear, I'll win it back in a trice. Had a streak of luck going when Hickey came to fetch me home—"

"How much?"

"Confound it, girl, must you plague a feeble old man?"

"How much?"

Lord Briggs lifted his glass of port and mumbled into the drink.

Emma stepped closer. "Louder, Grandpapa."

"All right, then, I confess. 'Twas a monkey."

"Pardon? We haven't such an animal here."

"Not an animal." He grimaced. "A monkey, m'dear, is five hundred pounds."

The strength fled her legs. She sank onto a fringed footstool and waited until her throat unclenched. "Dear heaven," she whispered. "How could you?"

The flamboyant confidence left her grandfather's face. His hand trembled as he set down his glass, and his eyes glistened suspiciously bright. That was precisely why he lost at the gaming tables, Emma knew. He showed emotion too readily.

And that was why she loved him in spite of his failings.

Shoulders hunched, he perched himself on the edge of a chair like a pupil awaiting punishment. "I broke my vow to you, girl. But 'tis the first time since April, I swear it. 'Twas my fault you came home that night, bleeding from Putney's bullet."

Emma buried her face in her hands. She didn't want to remember; she wouldn't let herself. Yet in an instant she was back on that ledge, dizzy and shaking, burning with pain. . . .

The fog blinded her. She could see only blackness. Clutching awkwardly at the stone railing, she moved along the ledge. Her left arm hung useless. Hurry. She must hurry. At any moment, the Watch would come. And the Runners. She'd die in prison. What would happen to Jenny?

Jenny.

Panic spurred her. She reached the neighboring town house, the empty one. In her haste, she lost her balance and pitched headfirst into the attic. She landed on her left shoulder. Agony blazed through her. And darkness descended, thick and tempting.

Jenny.

She stumbled to her feet, staggered down the staircase, slipped through the back door. Shouts rang in the distance. Panting, she paused in the foggy yard. The search was on. She'd never reach home.

Jenny.

She fled through the fog. She could not see the hunters, nor could they see her. Sustained by the thought, she kept running. Blood trickled warm and wet down her left breast, soaking her black coat. She forged on through the cold night and the hot pain. . . .

Emma blinked hard, snapping out of the memory, thankful she had survived the ordeal. By some miracle, she'd found the way to her own back door. Her grandfather had been in a dither, hollering for a doctor, but she'd managed to stop him by choking out a confession. Luckily, the bullet had passed through her, and as Maggie bound the wound, Emma had told her grandfather everything.

That was the first he'd known of her midnight exploits as the Bond Street Burglar. Out of desperation, she'd broken into the houses of the men who had fleeced him. She had stolen jewelry in the amount he'd lost and then fenced it. She'd fancied herself invincible, a Seeker of Justice. Instead, she'd found out exactly how vulnerable she was.

Horrified, Lord Briggs had promised to abstain from card playing. He had kept his word.

Until now.

Emma hugged her knees as the jaws of dread closed around her. She would be forced to steal again, and she had lost her nerve. The very thought of clambering on rooftops nauseated her.

"Don't you fret," said Lord Briggs. "I'll recoup the money."

"How?" She rubbed her arms against the chill that surrounded her, both inside and out. She wished she did not have to be the practical one, the one who had lost her ability to dream. "By playing cards again and making your debt all the steeper? Oh, Grandpapa, when will you learn to stay away from the gaming tables?"

He ran his hand over his face. It was the mournful gesture of an old man. "I didn't mean to gamble. I was thinking about your grandmama again, that's all. Didn't know how else to get my mind off her."

Compassion softened Emma. His beloved wife had died

of a fever shortly after Emma's marriage. "Gambling won't bring her back," she said gently. "It will only ruin us."

Her grandfather lowered his hand from his face. To her surprise, his blue eyes sparkled again. "No, we shan't be ruined. I know exactly what I shall do."

"What is that?"

" 'Tis what I wanted to do years ago, had you not stopped me." He grasped the lapels of his coat with a show of resolution. "I shall demand your rightful due from that errant husband of yours."

❧ Chapter 3 ❧

$\mathcal{E}$mma surged to her feet. "Absolutely not."

Lord Briggs sprang up, too. Only an inch taller than Emma, he glowered at her, blue eyes to blue eyes. "For seven years Wortham has neglected you. It's high time he treated you with the respect you deserve."

"In case you've forgotten, he has good reason not to respect me."

"Bother your addlepated pride, girl! Wortham can afford to pay you a handsome allowance. 'Tis rumored he's returned with a shipload of riches from the East." Circling a sadly frayed green chair, her grandfather waved his arms with theatrical extravagance. "Jade figurines from Shanghai! Gold statues from Siam! And the greatest treasure of all is the sacred tiger mask. 'Twas a gift from the maharajah of Jaipur—"

"I know. I've seen it."

"—and 'tis fabled to bring luck to its rightful owner—" Lord Briggs stopped dead and stared at Emma. "You've seen what?"

"The mask."

"Confound it, girl! Where . . . how . . . ?"

"I called on Lucas this morning. I saw him put the mask into the safe in his library."

"Well, hang me for a dog! What did he say? If the blighter dared to insult you . . .''

"He didn't." Unwilling to admit she'd asked for—and had been denied—a divorce, Emma went to the window and looked out on the narrow street as a dray passed by, its wheels clattering over the potholes. In her mind she saw her husband's hostile, sun-browned features, felt the touch of his fingers on her face. Willing away a shudder, she spoke over her shoulder. "Though I can safely say he has not forgiven me."

"A pox upon forgiveness. Wortham shouldn't carry a grudge so long. He should realize you're a decent girl who committed only one mistake."

"That one mistake ruined his life."

"Bosh." Her grandfather stomped closer. "If Wortham's bent on punishing someone, he should track down the rake who seduced you. If only you'd tell us the bastard's name."

She pressed her forehead to the cold glass. Lord Briggs didn't know the whole truth. No one did. And no one ever would.

"We've been through this many times before, Grandpapa. I mentioned my visit to Lucas only so you'll realize the futility of approaching him."

She tried to smile, but clenched her jaw instead. Every muscle in her body quivered. To her dismay, the scene outside went blurry, and she blinked in fierce denial. She would not weep. She had not shed a tear since the night Lucas had discovered her act of desperation.

Her grandfather awkwardly patted her rigid back. "Oh, blast it, girl. Wortham don't know a twenty-four-carat treasure when 'tis right before his nose. I've a good mind to call him out. Pistols at dawn will teach that young pup a lesson—"

"For pity's sake, no!" Emma whirled around to face her grandfather. As with his gambling, he had a knack for acting on impulse without a thought for the consequences. She took hold of his wiry-strong hands. "Please, you know as well as I the wrong I did to Lucas. You will not intercede on my behalf."

"Bah. Should he punish you for the rest of your life?

Someone ought to exact retribution from the scoundrel.'' He pulled his hands free and waved a fist. ''An honorable man provides for his wife.''

''I'm not an honorable wife. And he shan't pay your gaming debts, either. I'll have your promise that you'll not ask him for money.''

Lord Briggs mumbled something under his breath.

''Your promise.''

''All right, then, if you insist.''

The obstinate glint in his eyes troubled her. ''You'll not go begging to Lucas?''

''Confound it, didn't I just give you my word?'' Lord Briggs clapped his hand over his gray and blue striped waistcoat. ''I hereby pledge not to ask Wortham to share his disgusting wealth with his own wife. There, you troublesome minx. May I take my nap now?''

''Of course.'' Emma gave him a peck on his cheek. His prickly skin smelled of shaving soap and tobacco, scents that brought back memories of a time when she had felt safe and cherished. She had grown up expecting to find that same aura of love and security in marriage.

Those romantic dreams had no connection to the brutal realities of adulthood. Her husband cared nothing for her wishes; she had known that with her first glance into his dark, indifferent eyes. It should not hurt to know that Lucas reserved his affections for his mistress.

It should not.

''Never mind the fire,'' Lucas said. ''Tell Mrs. Gurney I want her down here immediately.''

The mobcapped young maid who knelt on the hearth rug darted an awestruck glance up at him. ''Aye, m'lord.'' She snatched up her supplies, nearly tipping over the coal scuttle in the process. Bobbing an awkward curtsy, she ran from the room.

Lucas grimaced. He had been waiting in this godforsaken parlor for nearly a quarter hour already. But he had not meant to frighten the poor child. Ever since his clash with Emma that morning, he had been snappish and brusque.

Ever since he had contemplated the unthinkable.

Removing his gloves, he clenched them in his palm as he prowled the cramped private parlor of the rooming house. There was scarcely enough space to walk between the numerous chairs and chaises. The fire hissed on the hearth, a low angry murmur like the voice of his conscience.

He had the perfect mistress, a pleasing, submissive woman who fulfilled his every need. He should have no interest in consummating his marriage. He should not think about holding Emma's slim, sweetly curved form. He should not dream of knowing the feel of her bare skin against his. He should not imagine hearing her cry out his name in ecstasy.

Damn her seductive body to hell. Like a drunkard who guzzled gin and then flung away the bottle, Emma wished to discard her husband now that she had found another man to gull. Lucas told himself he would be better off divorcing her.

Yet how gratifying it would be to thwart her plans. To show her how it felt to be used.

To take her to bed after years of fantasizing.

Driven by restless energy, he snatched up a candle and touched the wick to the fire. He went around the parlor, lighting other tapers. Emma's dressing room had been ablaze with candles on their wedding night. The image of her was indelibly etched in his mind: the alabaster curves of her naked back, the silvery-blond hair cascading to her waist, the heady glimpse of her full breasts.

And the stark horror on her face as she'd spun around to see him.

At first he had not understood. He'd thought her shy as a maiden, thought himself gauche as a moonstruck pup, so eager for her love that he could not wait the prescribed time for his bride to prepare herself for bed. The blow of his stupidity had struck him with a ferocity he would never forget. For then, he had seen her hands cradling the gentle roundness of her belly. . . .

"My lord marquess," trilled a voice from the doorway. "Do forgive me for keeping you waiting."

A short, plump woman hastened forward and sank into a curtsy at his feet. She took her time rising, no doubt to give him a good look at her voluptuous breasts.

He hid his distaste. "Mrs. Gurney, I presume."

"Yes, m'lord." In a fog of flowery perfume, she sidled closer to him. She wore a daringly cut gown of pale pink that ill suited her brassy auburn hair and aging face. "May I offer you some refreshment? Tea and plum cake? Though our poor fare surely isn't fine enough for a man of your rank—"

"No. I've come to inquire about a man who lived here two years ago. A red-haired Irishman by the name of Patrick O'Hara."

Mrs. Gurney's obsequious smile pinched into a mean line that added years to her face. "What would you want with that rascal, pray?"

"O'Hara had just returned from India. A boy was traveling with him. His son."

"I remember the dark-skinned lad," she said with a sniff. "The little beast was O'Hara's by-blow by some foreign female."

Lucas considered slapping the superiority off her vulgar face. He struck his gloves against his palm instead. "Tell me where they went after they left here."

Mrs. Gurney shrugged. "How should I know? The scoundrel stole away in the middle of the night without paying his bill."

"He must have given you some hint of his destination. Did he speak of any place in particular? Or say how he meant to support himself?"

"It happened so long ago." Mrs. Gurney ran a fleshy fingertip along her décolletage and slanted a smile at him. "Perhaps if you would tarry with me a bit, something will come back to me."

Lucas took a gold piece out of his pocket and let it clink

onto a nearby table. "That should help to jostle your memory."

"Oh, m'lord, how generous of you." Quick as a cat, she snatched up the sovereign and stuffed it into her bodice. "He loved the theater. He spoke of joining a company of play-actors. I'm afraid that's all I remember."

It was little enough to go on, Lucas thought grimly. But at least he had a starting place. "Tell me, how did O'Hara treat his son?"

"Why, the boy fetched and carried to earn his keep. Deserved all the slaps he got for dawdling. I'd've taught him his place in a trice, I would."

Lucas's chest tightened with anger. He had expected the worst of the man who had stolen away Shalimar's beloved son. God only knew what desperate straits the boy might be in now.

A sharp sense of purpose spurred Lucas. He would hire a team of men to search every theater in London. And in the meantime . . .

Another fantasy harried him—luring Emma into his bed. Turning on his bootheel, he strode toward the parlor door.

"Wait!" Mrs. Gurney called. "Can I not be of more service to you, m'lord?"

He glanced back to see the landlady rubbing her hands down the front of her gown. "It seems, madam, that you shall have to service yourself."

Emma floats alone on a vast dark sea. Her body is half submerged in water. Sluggish waves lap in her ears like a rhythmic heartbeat. She's safe here on the surface. Nothing can hurt her so long as she lies very still. So long as she doesn't draw the attention of the beast that lurks in the black, bottomless depths. . . .

Something snatches at her sleeve. It's him!

Her lips part in a silent scream. Fingers close around her arm and drag her down, down, down. . . .

"Wake up, Mama. Wake up."

Emma blinked at the bright morning sunshine that poured

past the lacy bedhangings. The linens lay in a jumbled heap all around her. The terror slid away as she found herself gazing into her daughter's sweet, solemn face. Jenny was dressed and ready for the day, her wavy, chestnut-brown hair drawn up with a blue-green ribbon that exactly matched her eyes.

"Gracious," Emma said, half groggy. "What time is it?"

"It's nine o'clock, and you mustn't be a lazybones to-day." Jenny tugged on her mother's arm again. "Uncle Woodrow has promised to take us to the park to feed the swans, remember? I saved my bread crusts from breakfast and made Maggie do the same. So we shan't have to use our last loaf before baking day tomorrow."

The little girl placed a crumpled white handkerchief beside her mother on the pillow and unfolded it to display a hill of squashed crusts. Earnest pride glowed on her delicate features.

A rush of love inundated Emma, washing away the lingering darkness of the nightmare. Smiling, she sat up in bed. "You are the most amazingly resourceful girl in London," she said. "Perhaps in all of England. Or even the entire world."

Jenny giggled. "How silly, Mama. It's only crusts."

"Yes, but you thought of it all on your own, and that's what makes you especially wonderful."

Emma gathered Jenny close. The feel of her daughter's small, sturdy form, the rainwater fragrance of her skin, filled her heart to aching fullness. Jenny shouldn't be worrying about using up the last of their bread. It wasn't right for a little girl to practice economies. She should be serving tea to a party of dolls instead of collecting scraps off the breakfast plates.

And she would have that life if—*when*—Emma married Sir Woodrow.

The memory of her interview with Lucas the previous day crept out to taunt her. It was no wonder she had a dull headache from oversleeping; she had lain awake half the night, pondering what course of action to take next.

Prepare yourself for another scandal.

Brash, boastful words. In truth, she had no wish to cause more trouble for Lucas. It was her fault he had become a cold, aloof stranger. The crushing realization weighed upon her. She had destroyed his soft-hearted innocence, just as her own innocence had been destroyed. In truth, she was hardly better than the man who had—

Emma slammed the door on that memory. It was useless to bemoan the past. Better she should contemplate her new plan to enlist the aid of Lucas's mother. Although the dowager had once sent Emma away in disgrace, she might agree to join forces now. Together, they could make Lucas realize the necessity of a divorce.

Yes. The scheme had merit.

Emma threw back the covers. The bare floorboards chilled her feet as she went to the dressing table, where she sat down on the stool and unbraided her hair. Her mind grappled with the problem of how to approach the elder Lady Wortham without being tossed out on her ear.

Jenny took up the old tortoiseshell brush and began to groom her mother's hair with the sober concentration that made her seem older than her years. Six going on twenty, Maggie often said fondly. Emma agreed, though with less enthusiasm.

"Mama, when I grow up, I should like to work as an abigail. But Maggie says I cannot be a servant. I must be a lady."

"Mm-hmm. You were born a lady." Smiling, Emma poked through the jumble of ribbons and cosmetic pots in the drawer. "My own Lady Jenny."

"Maggie says my papa is the Marquess of Wortham. He has just come back from a long trip to heathen lands."

Emma's heart lurched. Dropping a handful of hairpins back into the drawer, she looked up to see her daughter's gravely curious eyes reflected in the age-speckled mirror. Seldom had Jenny expressed more than a passing interest in her father; she had been satisfied with the vague explanation that he had gone away on an extended journey. "Yes, lamb-kin, he's returned."

"Why has he not come to live with us, then? Doesn't he know where to find us?"

"Lord Wortham and I quarreled a very long time ago—before you were even born," Emma said carefully. "We decided it was best if we lived apart."

"Agnes Pickett says I should hang my head in shame, for I haven't any father at all." Jenny's voice lowered to a for-lorn whisper. "She says that's why his lordship doesn't come to see me. Because he is not really my papa."

The words plunged like a red-hot lance into Emma's breast, and the pain of it spawned an unreasoning anger. Curse Lucas! How could he hurt this dear child?

Swiveling on the stool, she gently clasped her daughter's arms. The time to explain things had finally come. Did she have the right words? She had rehearsed them many times, but now they flew out of her mind.

She spoke with motherly fervor. "Agnes Pickett is a cruel, thoughtless girl. You've done nothing to be ashamed of. Nothing whatsoever."

"Then who is my papa? Don't I have one?"

Her fingers trembling, Emma stroked a springy chestnut curl off Jenny's brow. Silently begging God's forgiveness for the lie, Emma said, "I loved someone else before I wed Lord Wortham. That man is your true father. He died before we could marry."

"Did he love me?"

"He didn't even know you existed." That much at least was true. Swallowing hard, Emma forced her lips into a re-assuring smile. "But I'm certain he would have been proud to have you for a daughter. How could anyone resist a sweet girl who saves her bread crusts for the swans?"

She tickled Jenny, who dropped the brush and lapsed into a fit of giggling. Then, while Emma dressed, Jenny chattered about their outing, choosing a serviceable gown of garter-blue from the clothes press and imploring her mother to make haste.

To Emma's relief, the little girl asked no more difficult questions.

Blast the gossips, Emma thought fiercely, as she searched the drawers of a highboy for her only decent pair of kid gloves. Seven years had passed and still people spoke of the scandal as if it were yesterday. She cringed to think of Jenny fending off callous remarks about her birth.

How many more times would she endure taunts and teasing? Emma couldn't protect her forever. The thought rendered Emma breathless with despair, and she leaned against the opened drawer, the edge pressing into her abdomen.

She must remarry. With Sir Woodrow, she and Jenny could find a quiet, respectable life away from London, in a rural district where no one had heard of the scandal. A place where she could keep her grandfather away from the gaming tables, too.

And there was still the matter of the five hundred pounds he had lost. The mere thought of resuming her masquerade as the Bond Street Burglar made her blood run cold. The risks were too great, considering the danger of leaving Jenny an orphan.

Perhaps, Emma thought, she could bend her pride and negotiate a settlement after all. Five hundred pounds for accepting the blame for the divorce. She would call on the dowager today and make the arrangements.

And if Lucas didn't agree?

Recalling his implacable brown eyes, Emma resisted a shiver of misgivings. Yesterday he had been angry, unwilling to listen to reason. Once he had time to think on the matter, he might reconsider. Yes. He would see the benefit of ending their mockery of a marriage.

"Here, Mama!" Jenny waved the gloves in triumph. "I found them behind the bedside table. You forgot to put them in the drawer again."

"Ah." Smiling, Emma took the gloves. "Whatever would I do without you to look after me?"

Jenny glowed at the praise. Arm in arm, they went out into the passageway, and Emma found herself looking forward to an outing in the sunshine, to a morning when her plans again held the promise of success.

Lord Briggs hailed them from the bottom of the narrow staircase. "Hurry on down here, my two pretty treasures. I've a surprise for you."

Rubbing his hands in fidgety glee, he fairly danced with impatience by the newel post. He wore a drab black suit and no cravat, and his white hair was disheveled as if he hadn't bothered to comb it. Suspicion niggled at Emma. She had not seen him so excited since the time he'd won a hundred pounds and had brought home a fancy carriage that had cost two hundred.

Jenny skipped down the stairs, her slippers kicking up the back of her blue-green skirt. "What is it, Great-grandpapa?"

"Go into the drawing room and see for yourself. 'Tis a present."

"A present! Hooray!" Jenny flew across the foyer and threw open the drawing room doors.

Emma descended at a more sedate pace. As she passed Lord Briggs, she whispered, "I trust this has nothing to do with the breaking of certain vows."

"A pox upon your distrustful mind," he said, grinning. "I've done nothing, young lady, but follow in your own fine footsteps. And solved all of our problems in the process."

Emma had but a moment to ponder his puzzling words when Jenny stuck her head out of the drawing room. "Mama, come look! It's a tiger."

A tiger?

Confused, Emma hastened across the foyer, her shoes tapping on the wood floor. Sunlight poured past the opened draperies of the drawing room and accented the shabby state of the furnishings. In the middle of the threadbare carpet, she came to a halt, frozen by the sight of Jenny touching a head-shaped object that lay upon the faded cushions of a chaise.

In the morning sunshine, the diamonds glinted a cold, hard yellow in between stripes of brown jasper. The emerald-rimmed eyes glowed like an omen of disaster.

Her grandfather had done the unforgivable. He had stolen the priceless tiger mask from Lucas.

ᴄᴏ Chapter 4 ᴄᴏ

*I*t was a dreadful night for thievery.

Not, of course, that she had robbery in mind, Emma grimly reminded herself. Quite the opposite, in fact.

Balancing on a ledge high above the ground, she gritted her teeth and kept her eyes trained on her destination at the end of the row of town houses. Silvery moonlight painted the rooftops in stark detail, the chimneypots and iron railings and dormer windows. And a ledge so narrow it would give pause to a cat.

Fear froze her muscles to the verge of paralysis. The black domino over her face limited her vision. The scar on her shoulder ached, reminding her of the last time she had played the Burglar.

The thought was enough to make her shudder. By sheer strength of will, she inched her slipper-clad feet along the slim projection.

She must do this. She *had* to do this. Breaking into Lucas's house in the middle of the night was the only way to return the tiger mask with no one the wiser.

The black pouch holding the artifact was belted securely to her waist. With each step she took, the heavy mask thudded against her thigh as if it were a live thing that struggled to get free.

A chill wind moaned through the treetops, wafting coal smoke that stung her eyes. There was no fog to hide her tonight. She imagined her small, black-clad form silhouetted against the eaves, and her skin prickled. At any moment, someone might shout from below, a servant perhaps, or a resident of one of the elegant homes that lined Wortham Square.

Or worse, Clive Youngblood.

God help her if she were caught in the act, for she'd get no help from Lucas. He'd grown so coldhearted he might give her straight into the custody of the magistrate at the Bow Street Station. The scandal-hungry public would clamor for a conviction. Her shady reputation would seal her fate. Grandpapa might end up in prison himself. Jenny would be left alone.

Her heart wrenched. What would become of her little girl?

Emma's fury at her grandfather had erupted like lava, then cooled to bleak resolution. He couldn't seem to accept that she had stolen enough from her husband already. And to take the tiger mask! With all the luck he lacked at the gaming tables, Lord Briggs had found an unlocked window and slipped into the library the previous night. A window which had now been secured—she had ascertained that much for herself.

At last she reached the scrolled ironwork along the rooftop of Wortham House. For all their locking of doors and windows on the ground floor, residents of London seldom barred the upper-story windows. Of course, people might have become more cautious in the five months since the wounded Bond Street Burglar had fled along the rooftops.

She hoped not. Earlier in the day, Emma's faithful footman, George, had taken up a spy post in the mews. He had reported the arrival of a party of guests from the country—Lucas's eldest sister, Olivia, her husband, and their three children. Remembering her friendship with the outspoken Olivia, Emma felt an ache in her chest, which she immediately banished. Emotion made a person careless. She needed to concentrate.

Gripping the stone coping, she sidled past a chimney. By this hour, the family should be fast asleep. Except for Lucas,

who was gone from the house. George had reported seeing
the marquess's carriage drive away in late evening.

Where had Lucas gone? To his mistress? Was he even
now lifting her skirts and subjecting her to his lust? Did some
women like it?

Emma's foot slipped, and the bottom dropped out of her
stomach. Catching a dizzying view of the moonlit garden
below, she clutched at the dormer window and willed her
heart to slow its pounding.

Enough, she told herself. *Don't let yourself get distracted.
Think only of putting the mask back where it belongs.*

Confidence trickled back into her. She would tiptoe
through the darkened house, replace the mask in the safe,
and then retrace her steps. Her husband would never know
the mask was missing. Tomorrow, with the incriminating evidence out of her possession, she would seek the cooperation
of the dowager. Lucas would come to his senses and agree
to the divorce.

Emma went to work on one of the attic windows. The
latch gave way to the wire she inserted, and the casement
swung outward on well-oiled hinges. She hoisted herself over
the sill, careful of the sack hanging at her side, and dropped
lightly to the floor.

She stayed in a crouch, listening. The darkness seethed
with silence. She could hear no snoring to indicate a sleeping
servant. With any luck, the room was unoccupied.

Peering through the domino that concealed the upper half
of her face, Emma crept deeper into the shadows, skirting
the black lumps of furniture. There was nothing to be afraid
of. She had done this many times before. She had only to
take her time and move quietly—

Something squeaked nearby.

She swung toward the sound, the mask clanging against a
chair. Dear God. *Dear God.* A gunman could be hiding here,
watching her. She would never know until the bullet exploded—

Then came the scratch of tiny, running feet.

A mouse.

She melted against the wall in relief. *What a craven ninny you've become, Emma Wortham.*

Scoffing at herself, she felt her way across the bare floorboards. A lamp or candle had been left burning in the passageway outside. The faint yellow light showed the rectangular shape of the door.

Her hand closed around the cold knob. As she turned it, another sound surged from the darkness. The deep, throaty noise raised the hairs on the back of her neck.

It was a human groan.

In a leased house miles from Mayfair, Lucas lay beside his mistress. His body was sated, yet a relentless shame gnawed at him. He clenched a handful of bed linens. Christ, he owed Emma nothing, least of all faithfulness to vows made under false pretenses. He would honor the woman who cherished him.

Not a lying bitch.

In a whisper of movement, Shalimar rose from the bed, donned her *pheran,* and padded to the fireplace. As if they were back in the mountains of Kashmir, she squatted before the hearth and brewed tea in a samovar. Lucas forced himself to relax. He had everything he wanted. A mistress who satisfied his every physical whim, who never made unreasonable demands. A companion he could trust.

Her silver earrings and bangles clinking musically, Shalimar served him a cup of cinnamon-scented green tea. Then she fetched another cup, sat cross-legged on the floor beside the bed, and blew at the hot liquid. If she guessed at his torment, she showed no sign of it. Her serenity was one of the qualities that had drawn him to her. There was nothing artificial about her, no false smiles or helpless pretense. An inscrutable calm smoothed her face, and no one but he would have detected the hint of sadness in her gaze.

He had been so caught up in his own troubles he had nearly forgotten the sorrow that ruled her life. Setting down his teacup, Lucas drew her onto the bed. "Have faith," he murmured. "I've three men searching every theater in London. We'll find your son soon."

"Tomorrow, I must search, too. Lest I go mad."

"We'll look together, then."

Taking his hand, she lowered her forehead to the back of it. "My lord, you have another destiny. You must answer the call of the tiger god."

He frowned at her bowed head. "What is that supposed to mean?"

She straightened up, and her eyes shone like dark diamonds in the glow of the fire. "The mask bestows fertility upon its owner. I realize now it was not meant for you and me. It belongs to you and your English wife."

Her words hit him like a fist in his gut. Jerking his hand free, he leapt off the bed. "That is superstitious nonsense. I've no intention of keeping the mask. It will go in a museum where many people can appreciate its beauty."

"You cannot!" Shalimar blurted out in rare reproach. "The mask is sacred. A gift of the gods."

"It was a gift to me by the maharajah, to do with as I will."

He stalked to the heap of his clothing and snatched up his breeches. To his disgust, he had emerged from his mistress's bed still burning with the dark, driving need to possess Emma. He yearned to lie naked with her, to sink into her heat, to feel her soft and submissive body accept the essence of himself. He wanted to impregnate his wife.

Damn her heartless soul to hell.

Shalimar sank to the floor in front of him. "Master, I beg a thousand pardons for offending you. I wish only to make you happy."

Her long, black hair fanned out on the rug and framed her willowy body. Unaccountably annoyed by her servile posture, he lifted Shalimar to her feet. "For God's sake, I *am* happy."

To prove it, he pulled her into his arms. She felt familiar and comfortable, her almond scent evoking a pleasant warmth in him. He pictured himself introducing her to his mother and his sisters, and his mouth twisted bitterly. They would sooner welcome Emma back into the family fold than accept his attachment to a lowly foreigner.

Did he want Shalimar to share the English part of his life, anyway?

Guilt nagged at him. His ambivalence was due to no fault in her. Even if he were free, he did not wish to marry again. Emma had cured him of that particular craving.

He finished dressing and bade Shalimar good-bye. Outside, he motioned to his coachman. "Return to Wortham House. I've decided to walk."

The servant doffed his black top hat. "Beggin' yer pardon, but the streets can be dangerous."

"I appreciate the warning," Lucas said dismissively.

"Aye, m'lord." The burly man flicked the reins, and the pair of matched bays drew the coach down the road, hooves clopping and harness jingling until the sound disappeared into the night.

Lucas strode through the quiet neighborhood, a new development of small brick houses with cottage-type gardens. It must be well past midnight. The moonlight cast a pearly sheen over the pavement, making the shadows beneath the trees denser. As black as his thoughts.

He despised Emma for more than the unforgivable trick she'd played on him. He hated remembering the lovestruck boy who had once believed in miracles. She had made him feel tongue-tied and gauche, as if he did not suit her sophisticated tastes.

Even at eighteen, Emma had favored the wild bucks, the aristocrats who lived on the edge of society. He himself had never possessed a ready wit or an interest in wagering. He had trouble conversing with strangers. That was why he'd been astonished when she had chosen him from her many suitors.

He had been awestruck by her beauty, her air of fragile femininity, and he had walked straight into her spider's web. She'd spun the silk of her charm around him, and he'd only realized her deadly intent when she had sucked the blood from his heart.

Emma had never desired him. Her skittish reaction to him two days ago had proven he still disgusted her.

He took in a lungful of bracing night air. Her opinion of him shouldn't hurt. He wouldn't let it. His affection for her was long dead, buried beneath the dirt of her deceit. To hell with the tiger mask and its reputed powers. He didn't want a son from Emma. A child would only bind them together.

Though it rankled him to agree with her, divorce was the next logical step. The matter could be resolved with a suit to establish her infidelity, then a petition to Parliament. No peer in the House of Lords would stand in his way. An immoral wife posed too great a threat to the succession of his title. Then Emma would be gone from his life. Forever.

Yet as he crossed a deserted side road, he pictured her in bed, her fair hair loose on the pillows. She'd be wearing a sheer gown that revealed her womanly curves. She would be smiling, holding out her arms to . . .

To her latest lover. Surely a siren like Emma didn't sleep alone.

I haven't the least notion who fathered my Jenny. He could have been any one of a dozen men.

God knew how many times she had cuckolded him. She must have learned some method of birth prevention, else she would have spawned many more bastards. Her latest conquest was Sir Woodrow Hickey. Did the enraptured fool lie beside her at this very moment?

A violent resentment throbbed in Lucas. If ever he saw Emma again, he wouldn't trust himself in her presence. He'd be tempted to show her exactly how a wife should behave. He'd take her to bed, take what she'd given freely to a succession of lovers. And he'd make damned certain she forgot all men but her husband.

Emma stood stock-still. A moment ago, the groan had nearly scared her out of her skin. She waited, straining to see into the gloom.

A snuffling snore came from the left. Bed ropes creaked heavily. A manservant was asleep in the attic room, that was all.

Step by careful step, she edged out the door. The mask bumped against her thigh as if to remind her of her mission. Without awakening the servant, she slipped into the corridor.

Emma allowed herself a sigh of relief. Now to complete her errand.

Praying her luck would hold, she nipped a candle from a wall sconce and then crept down the servants' staircase to the ground floor. A door loomed at the bottom, and she cautiously peered out. The grand passageway was deserted, lit by a single oil lamp that flickered outside the conservatory.

As she tiptoed toward the library, the scents of damp loam and flowering plants drifted to her. She recalled hiding there two days ago while Stafford gave her message to Lucas. Her throat tightened. She might as well never have bothered to finagle a meeting with him. Her husband was convinced of her mercenary nature. The bitter irony was, she truly meant the divorce to be an atonement for her sins as much as a chance for Jenny to have a real father.

Well, with any luck, she need never see Lucas again. Their sham marriage would be over quickly once she enlisted the aid of the dowager.

Emma had no time to fathom the melancholy inside herself. Taking another swift look up and down the corridor, she stole into the library.

The house was dark and quiet when Lucas let himself in the front door. He stopped in the dining room and poured himself a drink. The French brandy was as smooth as silk and as warm as a willing woman. The perfect tonic for his troubled thoughts.

Crystal decanter in one hand and a glass in the other, he stood in the silent, shadowed room, aware of how alone he was. His mother would be asleep upstairs. As would Livvie and her husband and their children. Tomorrow, with the arrival of his other married sister and her family, no doubt he would long for such a moment of peace. He would not feel so lonely then, so starved for companionship. And so reluctant to go to his empty bed.

He strode out into the passageway and paused there, hesitating. For some strange reason, the tiger mask lured him. *You must answer the call of the tiger god.* Nonsense. It had no magical powers. Yet he felt the fanciful urge to see it, to hold it and know it was nothing more than gold and gemstones, a masterpiece crafted by human hands.

He proceeded through the darkened house, his way lit by an occasional oil lamp burning low, casting long shadows over the walls. How odd to feel so at home here, as if he'd never left. He took quiet pride in knowing he was master of this grand house. It had been built by his great-grandfather in the time of the first King George, and passed on through each generation to Lucas. By all rights, his own son ought to play and laugh in these halls.

But the line of descent would be broken. Unless he sired an heir.

Rancor consumed him. He took a long, burning gulp from the glass in his hand. To hell with Emma. He'd wasted enough time brooding about his amoral wife.

Turning his mind to the mask, he walked toward the open door of the library.

Emma was glad for the meager light of her candle. The library was dark and spooky. The scent of leather-bound books perfumed the chilly air. Resisting the temptation to poke around her husband's retreat, she wended her way past the chairs and chaises, around the wooden crates that littered the center of the room. At the mahogany desk, she opened the drawer and plucked out the key.

An inexplicable exasperation flared in her. How careless of Lucas. Even her grandfather had managed to locate the key.

She set down the candle, removed the books from the appropriate shelf, and unlocked the safe. Within the dark mouth of the repository, jewels glinted like a pirate's treasure trove. Under ordinary circumstances, she would have been eager to calculate the worth of the gemstones.

Yet the notion of coveting her husband's wealth sickened her. Briefly she closed her eyes beneath the ebony domino. She had stolen something from him more precious than jewels. She had robbed Lucas of the chance to have a family and a loving wife.

But now was no time to torture herself.

Untying the black scarf she'd used as a pouch, she drew out the tiger mask. The piece weighed heavy in her hands, and she gazed down at it a moment, wondering what Lucas meant to do with the mask. Perhaps wear it to a costume ball? That struck her as out of character for a man so reserved, yet he had changed considerably during his journeys abroad.

He exuded an aura of mastery now. He spoke with sharp precision. He kept a mistress.

Heat prickled over Emma's skin. The yellow diamonds picked up the candlelight, and the emerald eyes seemed to watch her. She stared back. The tiger mask glowed with a strange, almost erotic energy. It was like an enchantment cast by a sorcerer, a seductive charm that repulsed her even as she felt the pull of fascination. . . .

"What the deuce—?"

A harsh male voice broke the spell. She spun around to see a dark form silhouetted in the faint light of the doorway. The man loomed big and powerful and threatening, a tiger about to pounce.

Her fingers clenched around the mask. Dear God.

Dear God, save her.

It was her husband.

An intruder clad entirely in black stood before the opened safe. The light of a single candle illuminated his small, wiry form and the black domino that concealed his features. He was holding the tiger mask.

Rage exploded in Lucas. His fingers tightened around the

decanter and glass. Without further thought, he surged into the long, shadowy room.

The robber let out a muffled gasp. Then he dashed around the large desk and skirted the pile of crates. Lucas expected him to run for a window. Instead, he pounded straight for the door.

Dropping his drink, Lucas lunged at the fugitive. Brandy splashed his trouser leg as he leaped over the chaise. Chairs went crashing to the floor. He reached out to seize the man. The robber hurled something through the darkness. The heavy object hit Lucas in the abdomen, knocking the breath out of him.

The tiger mask. It landed with a *thunk* on the carpet and skated under a chair.

Lucas reeled backward and gulped in brandy-scented air. He recovered himself in time to see the burglar dart into the passageway.

"Come back, you thieving bastard!"

He rushed in pursuit. The black figure raced toward a door in the paneling and disappeared into the servants' staircase.

Lucas entered the narrow shaft. Darkness hung thick in the air, but above him he could hear the patter of the man's fast footfalls. Where the hell was he going?

Fear gripped Lucas. His family slept on the second floor.

He took the steps three at a time, grimly hoping his long legs gave him the advantage. By the time he reached the second floor, he had closed the distance to a bare yard. He snatched at the villain and caught a handful of his cloak.

The robber loosed a guttural cry. Wrenching open a door, he plunged headlong down the corridor.

Lucas flung the empty cloak aside. "Stop, thief!" he bellowed.

He hoped to rouse the servants who slumbered in the attic directly above the family bedchambers. How dare this footpad invade his domain and attempt to plunder his property. The tiger mask was priceless, the keystone in his dream of opening a new wing in the museum.

As Lucas sped down the dim-lit corridor, the robber skidded around a corner and crashed into a table and vase. Porcelain cracked; water and flowers went flying. With a final surge of speed, Lucas brought down his quarry against the mahogany railing of the grand staircase.

Panting, his captive wriggled and squirmed like a madman. Gloved hands battered Lucas's face and chest. On a burst of angry triumph, Lucas wrestled him to the carpet. The man was skinny, almost dainty. Looking for a hidden weapon, Lucas slid his hand over legs and arms slender enough to belong to a child.

Bedroom doors opened, and the buzzing of voices rose in the corridor. Her nightrobe rustling, his mother hastened to his side. "For the love of God, whatever has happened?" She caught sight of his black-clad captive and gasped. "Dear heavens! It's the Bond Street Burglar!"

She staggered back into the arms of her elder daughter, Olivia, who watched with rounded blue-green eyes, her rusty-red braid draped over her shoulder. "That ruffian broke into the house?" Olivia said in a rage, her hand resting on her pregnant belly. "We might have been murdered in our beds!"

"Don't be dramatic, Livvie," Lucas said. "He doesn't even have a weapon. Now give me the belt from your dressing gown."

"But why—? Oh."

She untied the gold silk cord and handed it to him. He rolled the struggling thief over, yanked his arms behind his back, and secured the wrists together. The restraint seemed to sap the strength from the man, and he went stiff and still, except for the rapid rising and falling of his chest.

"Thank goodness you came home," the dowager said, half swooning against Lucas's sister. "We might have been robbed of all of our jewels."

"He went after the tiger mask down in the library. I chased him up here." Lucas glanced up at her wan face. With the wisps of gray hair peeking out from her nightcap, she looked old and weary and utterly shaken. "Go on back to bed," he said gently. "I'll send Stafford for the Watch and have this riffraff carted off to jail."

"Can you manage him?" Olivia asked. "Hugh's asleep—he could sleep through a tempest—but if I shake him hard, I'm sure I can rouse him—"

"Let your husband rest. Now, Mother's on the verge of collapse. Escort her back to her chamber. And stay with her."

Olivia raised a doubtful eyebrow, as if he were still the gangly, ineffectual adolescent and she the all-knowing big sister. Then she nodded primly and guided the dowager away.

Lucas returned his attention to his prisoner, who lay as rigid as a mannequin. Easing himself off the scoundrel, he discerned a light, pleasing scent that stirred a faint recognition in him. For the first time he noticed that the lips beneath the black demimask were soft and pouty. There was an almost feminine roundness to the robber's form, a curvaceousness . . .

A snake of heat bit Lucas's groin. He felt the unexpected urge to press himself into the cradle of those shapely hips.

The instinctive response of his body appalled him, but his self-disgust lasted for only an instant. Seized by suspicion, he moved his hand to the robber's black shirt. And found himself caressing the fullness of a womanly breast.

Before he could react to his amazing discovery, his captive gave a violent shudder. In a blur of motion, she lunged up off the carpet. Her teeth clamped down hard on his forearm.

Lucas jerked backward, more from surprise than from pain, for his coat sleeve protected him. "Damn you!"

Already she was rolling away, struggling to stand up, though hindered by her tied hands. Before she could scramble to her feet, he slammed his body over hers and pinned her to the floor again.

"Not so fast," he growled. "So the Bond Street Burglar is a woman. I'll have a look at you." He yanked off her domino, taking her close-fitting, black cap along with it.

Silvery-blond hair spilled like moonbeams across the dark

carpet. Impossibly blue eyes stared up at him. Astonished, he found himself gazing into a face so pale, so lovely, that the breath left his lungs.

No wonder her body seemed so sinfully familiar—it had been the subject of his adolescent dreams. And he felt like that boy again, thick-witted and struck mute, able to voice only one hoarse word.

"Emma."

↶ **Chapter 5** ↷

*H*is stone-cold expression froze Emma. She couldn't move, she couldn't speak. She could only stare up at her husband as the moment of recognition stretched into an eternity.

Lucas exuded a raw animal power that terrified her. He smelled of brandy and male anger. As he straddled her on the floor, she could feel every muscle in his brawny body. Struggling was useless against his superior strength. With her hands secured behind her back, she was caught as neatly as a rabbit in a trap.

No longer the amenable boy, Lucas had become a stranger, a savage man with impenetrable dark eyes. She was defenseless to stop him from punishing her. As defenseless as she had been against another man, another time. . . .

Panic rushed through her like a great wind, snatching away her breath, plunging her into mindless terror. She couldn't bear the suffocating weight of his body. Not for another instant.

She thrashed beneath him, kicking, bucking. "Let me up. *Let me up!*"

"For Christ's sake, you'll awaken the house again."

He clapped his hand over her mouth and lifted himself from her. Yanking Emma to her feet, he marched her down the shadowy passageway. She was forced to half run to keep pace with his long strides. The pressure of his palm muffled her cries of protest.

At the end of the corridor, he opened a door and shoved her inside. She lurched forward, gulping in air, and found herself in a large, dim-lit bedroom. A banked fire glowed on the marble hearth, and a four-poster bed with bronze velvet hangings dominated the room.

This must be her husband's bedchamber.

Spurred by terror, she whirled to face him. She swallowed convulsively before she could speak. ''Just what do you intend to do to me?''

Lucas closed the door with an ominous click. He sent her a black look, barely visible in the shadows. ''Exactly what you deserve.''

Striding across the room, he crouched down to light a candle at the hearth.

Emma slowly backed up against a tall desk, moving as far from the bed as possible. She glanced frantically at the sterling letter opener, the sharp pens. With her hands bound, she had only her wits to use as a weapon.

''Where is your valet?'' she asked.

Lucas walked toward her, and the flickering flame of the candle cast harsh shadows over his face. ''Gone for the evening. We're quite alone.''

''I—I feel rather faint. If you would be so kind as to ring for a maid—''

''No. But I'll be so kind as to offer you a seat.'' He hauled out the desk chair and shoved it against her calves. She plopped down, her bottom smacking the leather cushion with stinging abruptness.

He set the candlestick on a wooden chest at the foot of the bed. His mouth pressed into a grim line, he towered over her like Lucifer come to fetch her to Hell. ''Explain yourself.''

She moistened her dry lips. A simple request. An impossible dilemma. How could she reveal that her grandfather had stolen the mask? That she was merely returning it? Lucas would laugh in her face.

And if, on the off chance he *did* believe her, Clive Youngblood would arrest Lord Briggs as the Bond Street Burglar.

Feeling cornered, Emma assumed the pose of a helpless female. Men always fell for damsels in distress. Tilting her head back, she worked her expression into one of pleading repentance. "I'll be happy to tell you everything, Lucas. But won't you please untie my hands first?"

"No."

"Why not? Are you afraid of me?"

He arched a contemptuous eyebrow. "You break into my house in the middle of the night, attempt to steal my valuables, and then you expect mercy. Try again, darling wife."

No compassion softened his stern features. From his obsidian eyes down to his polished black boots, he was all cruel, unforgiving male. It took little effort to make her lower lip tremble. "I know how displeased you must be—"

"Displeased is not the word."

"Angry, then. Furious." She let her lashes flutter downward. "But I can assure you, my being here isn't so terrible as it would seem. You must understand, I am desperately in need of money—"

"Are you this Bond Street Burglar?" he cut in.

Her gaze flew to his. "Me?"

"Yes, you."

A sinking dread weighed on her confidence. "You cannot be serious," she said, feigning an airy laugh. "A lady making a habit of clambering on rooftops and picking locks? Why, it's beyond belief."

"On the contrary. You'll do anything to get what you want."

"I—" The denial stuck in her throat. She fancied his sharp eyes piercing her defenses, reading her darkest secrets, seeing the scar left by her brush with death.

He took a menacing step closer. She found herself recoiling, her spine bumping the back of the chair.

"The truth, Emma," he said. "*If* you know the meaning of the word."

His low opinion hurt more than she cared to admit, and she lashed back at him. "All right, then. Perhaps I *am* the Burglar."

His eyebrows rose a fraction. For a moment, there was only the muffled sound of a clock somewhere, ticking away the minutes of her doom. She had not meant to give him another weapon to use against her, yet he drove her to indiscretion.

Coming up behind her, Lucas lifted the unbound hair from her shoulder and let the silky blond strands sift through his fingers. "First a whore and now a thief. How do you manage to appear so angelic, Lady Wortham?"

Emma flinched. The brush of his warm hand against her neck jolted her as much as his condemnation. She struggled to keep from showing her fear. "I am not the villainess you think I am."

"No doubt you're worse." He braced his hands on the back of the chair and put his face close to hers. "Tell me, what other crimes have you committed? Forgery? Swindling? Murder, perhaps?"

"Confound you, I'm innocent."

Releasing a brusque laugh, he walked in front of her, his fists clenched at his sides. "Innocent? A strange description for you, dear wife."

Emma opened her mouth, then closed it. She must guard her temper. She would not gain her release by antagonizing him.

Swallowing the bitterness of pride, she dipped her chin in a pose of contrition. "I had no choice but to resort to stealing. Without an allowance from you, I was forced into thievery in order to feed my family."

"And what of Lord Briggs? Is the old goat still alive? Surely he can provide for you."

"Grandpapa is deeply in debt. I will not sit by and watch my daughter starve."

At the mention of Jenny, Lucas's countenance darkened. His hand slashed downward, causing Emma to jump. "Spare me your pretty tale of woe. I've heard enough of your excuses to last a lifetime."

"I'm not making excuses." She lowered her voice to a

sultry murmur. "Please let me go. You have the mask back. There's no harm done."

"No harm. I suppose you'd have me believe you crept into my house in the middle of the night merely to admire the tiger mask."

Frustrated by her inability to soften him, she threw back her head and glowered at him. "Have it your way, then. I wanted more jewels, more riches to satisfy my greed. So I decided to take what I'm entitled to."

"Then perhaps I should take what I'm entitled to, as well."

He loomed over her. His hand stroked downward over her black shirt and cupped her breast. The heat of him invaded her, crawling like spiders across her skin, descending deep inside her belly. The alien sensation made her flushed and dizzy. She was conscious of the shadow of whiskers on the lean line of his jaw, the blatant hostility on his face. He was her husband. He claimed the right to touch her. In the eyes of the law, he owned her.

Teetering on the verge of panic, she kicked him hard in the shins and stubbed her toes in the process. "Beast! You'll take nothing from me."

"Only because I want nothing." He stepped back, and his abrasive gaze scoured her mannish attire. "I can find a more honorable woman on any street corner in Whitechapel."

His fingers closed on her arm again, biting like a manacle as he jerked her off the chair. He pushed her ahead of him and thrust her into the shadows of the dressing room. Emma stumbled forward, bumping the hard edge of a clothes press. With her hands tied, she was unable to catch herself, and she fell to her knees.

The hulking black form of her husband filled the doorway. "I'll be back," he said. "With the authorities."

The door slammed shut and the key grated in the lock. The heavy tread of his footsteps faded away.

Emma crouched in the gloom, her head and shoulders bowed as the coldness of reality set in. An uncontrollable shuddering seized her. Dear God. She would be clapped in irons and thrown into a dank cell, there to molder until she was hauled before a judge. Based on her husband's testimony, she would be convicted and transported. Or worse, she might swing from the gibbet at Tyburn.

Lucas despised her that much.

I can find a more honorable woman on any street corner in Whitechapel.

She should be thankful he did not want her, that he had not forced himself on her. The wildness in him frightened her. He was too big, too powerful, too overwhelmingly male. Even now, the scent of him pervaded the dressing room: musky, faintly feral. She could feel a searing sensation where he had touched her breast. As if he had put his brand on her, the mark of the damned.

In defiance of logic, a lump of regret settled in her stomach. She had wrought the change in Lucas. She had turned him from a sensitive youth who'd adored her into a callous, uncaring brute who saw the worst in her. He believed her to be a wicked, amoral creature, beneath his contempt.

Perhaps he was right. Perhaps, deep down, she was no seeker of justice. She was a petty thief who made excuses for her reprehensible behavior.

Emma did not know how many hours she slumped there, riddled by self-doubt and robbed of strength. Although her eyes felt hot, she could not weep. She never wept. Maturity had made her realize the uselessness of tears. Rather than waste her energy, she always strove to make the best of circumstances.

Now was no different.

By degrees, Emma straightened her spine. All was not lost. If she escaped, she and Jenny could flee the country. She would find a post as a seamstress or a maid. She would do any honest labor if it enabled her and her daughter to stay together.

But first, she must get her hands untied. And quickly. She had squandered enough time already.

Struggling to her feet, Emma made her way through the darkened dressing room. She nearly tripped over a stool. Her legs prickled from kneeling so long, and her arms felt numb. Finally she found what she sought—a washstand in the shadowy corner. On a silver tray lay her husband's shaving implements—soap, brush, cup. And a long razor that glowed in the soft gray light from a small, high window.

It must be near dawn, she realized on a surge of alarm.

Turning around, she managed to pick up the blade in her fingertips. The task was difficult with her hands tied behind her back. The metal felt cold and slick to her clammy skin. Kneeling again, she gingerly maneuvered the razor until she could wedge it between her heels. Then she murmured a prayer and worked her wrists downward onto the sharp edge, sawing carefully through the silk cord.

The binding broke abruptly. Too abruptly. Before she could pull back, the razor sliced into the heel of her left hand.

Warm blood dripped down her wrist. The pain intensified as feeling returned to her deadened arms. She groped inside the washstand, found a white linen towel, and wrapped the wound, using her teeth to pull one end of the knot. Despite the throbbing discomfort, she was free. Free!

Almost.

Hugging her injured hand to her breast, she rummaged around in a drawer and came up with a gold stickpin. Emma smiled, her dismal mood lifting. As the rosy light of dawn tinted the room, she crouched by the door and went to work on the lock.

Lucas awakened to a throbbing in his temples. Stiff and cold, he lifted his head from the desk and found himself sitting in the library at Wortham House. The pearly light of early morning shone through the tall leaded windows, and the air reeked of brandy. An overturned glass had puddled its contents over the polished mahogany surface.

For a moment he could not remember why he had fallen asleep at his desk or, for that matter, why he was back in England. His thoughts flowed as thick as treacle. He'd been dreaming about a frenzied chase through a crowded bazaar. He could still feel his frustration at being mired in a mob of people, his fury at seeing the tiger leap to freedom over the colorful awnings.

The tiger mask.

The burglar.

Emma.

Stabbed by memory, Lucas sat up straight in his chair. Christ. Last night, he had surprised his wife in the act of thievery. He had left her tied up in his dressing room while he'd come down here to secure the mask in a safe place. Then, instead of sending a footman to fetch the magistrate, he had proceeded to get stone drunk.

Plunging his fingers into his hair, Lucas groaned. He'd spent the dark, predawn hours brooding about Emma. He still wrestled with disbelief that his wife was a robber, that she would break into his house and help herself to his priceless treasures. Yet why should he be surprised? She had already demonstrated her utter lack of principles.

Against his will, he recalled the soft feminine curves of her body lying beneath his. The memory alone was enough to ignite the fuse of his lust. Last night, he'd been sorely tempted to toss his wife onto the bed and claim the debt she owed to him. It had taken every scrap of his willpower to keep himself from ravishing the bitch.

Now, he came to a galling realization. Deep down, he had hoped the past seven years had changed Emma for the better. He'd wanted her to atone for the terrible wrong she'd done to him. He'd wanted her to ache with regret, to agonize over losing him, to burn with need for her husband.

Instead, she'd recoiled from him in disgust.

The damnable irony was, he had not conquered his youthful infatuation, after all. He would never find peace until he possessed her.

The cold light of morning had not cooled the blaze of his fury. To hell with the law. He would lock his wife in a prison of his own making. He would exact the perfect revenge.

The dark fire of anticipation scorched him. He couldn't wait to see the outrage on her lovely face when she learned of his plan.

The chair legs scraped the floor as Lucas shot to his feet. Ignoring the pounding in his temples, he strode out of the library and down the corridor to the entrance hall. His boot heels clicked on the marble floor, attracting the attention of a maidservant who polished the brass fittings of the balustrade and the footman who stood guard by the front door.

Affording them a nod, Lucas mounted the grand staircase. He needed to settle the matter before his family awakened and plagued him with questions about the Bond Street Burglar.

A ruthless rush of heat invigorated him as he reached the door to his bedchamber. Emma should be in a more agreeable mood after spending several hours tied up in his dressing room. If she had the sense to obey him, in a matter of moments, he would have her lying naked in his bed, her slim legs locked around his waist. . . .

As he thrust open the door and stalked into his bedroom, he nearly stumbled over his manservant, Hajib.

Clad in a gray robe and white cap, Hajib squatted in front of the entryway with a bowl of pinkish liquid beside him. Upon seeing Lucas, he waved a wet rag at several dark spots on the carpet. "Master, you must let Hajib shave you, always. I am your slave. I am here to serve you—"

"Later." Distractedly, Lucas stepped past the servant and stopped short. The fervor inside him chilled to ice.

The dressing room door stood open.

He wheeled around. "Where is she?"

"She? You bring Shalimar here, then?" Hajib's swarthy brow was smooth, inscrutable. "Or have you found an English rose to replace the lovely Lotus of Kashmir?"

Ignoring him, Lucas dashed into the dim-lit dressing room. It was deserted. In the middle of the floor lay the shreds of gold cord that had bound Emma's wrists. Bending, he picked up the long razor.

Damn her.

And damn himself for underestimating her.

Hajib padded barefoot into the dressing room and sank down with his water bowl to scrub at a cluster of dirty spots on the carpet. "Where have you cut yourself, master?" he asked querulously. "Beneath your neckcloth?"

Preoccupied, Lucas touched the crumpled linen at his throat. "Cut—?"

Then the servant's meaning clicked into place. Lucas stood very still, his fury fading as he stared down at the dark trail spattered across the carpet. It was blood.

Emma's blood.

"Where is that blasted George?" Clad in his crumpled night-shirt, Lord Briggs appeared in the doorway of Emma's bed-room. His nightcap sat askew, revealing wild wisps of white hair.

Emma stood by her bed, cramming a spare gown into her valise. "Grandpapa!" she gasped. "You're supposed to be dressed by now. George should be back with the hackney at any moment."

"So that's where the laggard's gone. Off running his own errands instead of fetching my shaving water."

Emma's heart sank as she recognized the confused look in his blue eyes. Of all times for him to suffer one of his infrequent spells of forgetfulness. Crossing the room, she took gentle hold of his arm. "Never mind shaving today. You must dress in your warmest clothes and hurry. We're very late."

"Late? Your grandmama didn't tell me we were going anywhere."

"Grandmama isn't here anymore, remember?" She tugged him down the passageway and into his own spartan chamber, where she snatched breeches, coat, and shirt from the clothes press. "We're going on a long trip, you and I and Jenny. We must make haste to reach Dover."

His expression cleared. He looked sadly sheepish a moment; then he shook his fist. "It's all the fault of that rascal husband of yours. Calling down the law on his own wife! He deserves to be jailed for neglecting you."

"Never mind," she said soothingly. "It isn't important now."

Leaving her grandfather grumbling, Emma rushed back to her own packing, her gray traveling dress swishing around her sturdy cotton stockings. Her nerves thrummed with tension. She hadn't ceased hurrying since she'd dashed pell-mell through the streets of London after the harrowing escape from Lucas's house. In the half an hour since she'd returned home, she'd rallied the household, changed from the Burglar's black garb, and packed the flotsam of her life into one valise. The wound on her hand trickled blood, but she ignored it. There would be time later to tend the cut.

She prayed that when Lucas discovered her missing, he would go first to the house she'd been living in as his betrothed. But she and her grandfather and Jenny had changed residences twice since then, each time moving to a house that charged cheaper rent. With any luck, it would take Lucas—and the law—several hours to track her down.

Precious hours in which she planned to be well on her way to the coast.

There was one last item to pack. Opening a dresser drawer, she drew forth a box hidden behind her unmentionables. The small case was covered in blue velvet, worn smooth near the clasp. Her fingers trembled as she opened the box and touched the string of milky gems inside. Her mother's pearls.

In Emma's last hazy memory of her parents, Lady Caroline had been wearing this very strand around her swanlike throat when she'd bent to kiss Emma good-bye. In a waft of violet perfume, she and Papa had gone off, never to return, for that night, they'd been overcome by smoke when a fire swept through a crowded opera house.

Emma hugged the necklace to her breast. She had kept the pearls even when selling them would have enabled her to put beef on the table and coal on the grates. They were meant to be her legacy to Jenny. But now the pearls must pay for passage to the Continent.

With the heaviness of regret, Emma tucked the necklace deep inside her valise. She took one last look around at the rosewood furnishings that had been hers since childhood, the bed with its lace canopy where she slept alone, the little desk with its collection of dog-eared books, the wooden chest where she kept a few foolish mementos of her wedding. Sadness pressed upon her, but she had no leisure to indulge in sentimentality.

As she hastened downstairs, she met Maggie in the corridor leading to the kitchen. The small, lively servant had carrot-red hair and a dusting of freckles that gave her a merry appearance. But today she looked as grim as the girl Emma had rescued from the gutter.

Maggie lugged a large wicker basket which she dropped with a thump. "Here's the provisions, m'leddy."

The rattle of carriage wheels stopped outside. "There's George now with the hackney," Emma said. "Where's Jenny?"

"In the kitchen, saying good-bye to them stray puppies George found. The little dodger tried to sneak one into the basket when I weren't looking." Stepping forward, Maggie clutched at her apron. "M'leddy, you dursn't leave. I'll hide you in the rookeries where the Runners don't go. And especially not that high an' mighty husband of yours."

Touched by Maggie's willingness to endanger herself, Emma grasped her hand. "Thank you, but I cannot risk Jenny's future. And you've done enough for me already by keeping silent about my burglaries."

"Can't never do enough. Bless you for saving me when me dad would've sold me for a doxy."

Emma squeezed her work-roughened hand. "How I'll miss you and George—"

A pounding shook the door. She started, her heart racing. It couldn't be Lucas. Not so quickly. But when she looked at Maggie, she saw alarm widen her eyes, too.

"Lud, mum. George don't knock."

Heedless of the stabbing pain in her hand, Emma snatched up the heavy basket and valise. "I'll hide in the kitchen. If it's Lord Wortham, tell him I'm gone already."

Maggie squared her shoulders. "I'll get rid of the bloody bugger, don't you fear."

"Pray God Grandpapa stays in his room." Emma glanced

up the narrow staircase, then turned to flee down the passageway.

She hadn't gone more than two steps when the door crashed open. His black cloak swirling, his face as wild-eyed as the devil himself, her husband charged into the foyer.

❦ Chapter 6 ❧

With a leaden sense of inevitability, Emma dropped the basket and valise. Her instincts screamed at her to run. To dash out the back way while Maggie used her street skills to stop Lucas.

But Emma could not—would not—leave without Jenny.

His footsteps rang out on the bare wood floor as he stalked straight toward her. Maggie glared daggers at him as he passed her by without a glance. Standing her ground, Emma could only be thankful that no magistrate followed him.

His dark hair disheveled, he stopped in front of her. "What the devil have you done to yourself?" he demanded.

Emma looked down at her gray gown in confusion. "Done?"

"You bled all over my floor." He reached for her hand, the one wrapped in his red-stained towel. Loosening the knot, he unwound the wrapping.

She pulled back, hissing through her teeth as the cloth stuck to the dried blood. "Let me go."

"Be still. From now on, we're doing things my way." In contrast to his harsh tone, his grip was amazingly gentle, his fingers strong and supportive as he examined the ugly gash across her palm. Blood oozed from the long cut. "You there," he said over his shoulder to Maggie, "go fetch a bowl of water and a proper bandage."

"Nay." The servant shook her head, her carroty curls

bouncing around her face. "I dursn't leave the likes of you alone with m'leddy."

"Go. Or I'll lash the backside of *you*."

Emma intervened. "Just do as he says, Maggie."

Nose in the air, the servant stomped down the passageway toward the kitchen. Lucas thrust the stained linen towel at her as she passed him.

He applied pressure to Emma's lower back, urged her into the tiny morning room, and bade her sit on a frayed yellow chair by the window. He unfastened his cloak and tossed it onto a footstool.

Suspicious of his motives, she kept her spine rigid. "I don't need your doctoring."

He crouched on one knee beside the chair, whipped out a crisply folded handkerchief, and pressed it to her injured palm. "Someone has to tend to you."

"Leave it to my jailer, then. Or are you feeling guilty for sending your own wife to prison?"

He gave her a hard stare. "On the contrary. I have good reason to require you to be in excellent health."

His voice held an ominous undercurrent. The rugged angles of his face cut starker than ever, and he reeked of brandy. Sunshine glossed the bronze highlights in his dark hair, hair that was wild and windblown. She had the peculiar urge to comb her fingers through the mussed strands. The lack of sleep must have brought on this giddy strangeness in her.

Maggie delivered the bandages and water, and Lucas sent her out the door again. Frowning with concentration, he set to work dabbing the blood from Emma's palm. Gritting her teeth against the stinging pain, she wondered how he could appear so concerned.

"I see a few calluses here," he said.

"Pardon me for lacking the soft hands of a lady. I'm a working woman now."

His expression remained unreadable. "Am I hurting you?"

"No." She held her breath until a horrid burning sensation

passed. "But if you wish to help me, then leave my house and never return."

"I will. And when I go, you're coming with me."

Her ribs seemed to crowd inward, squeezing her lungs. Her pride dwindled beneath the onset of alarm. Without thinking, she grasped his wrist with her uninjured hand, and felt the warm skin beneath his cuff. "Lucas, please. Don't take me to the Bow Street Station, I beg you. I've no one to care for my child."

"There's your grandfather."

"He's too old, too unreliable. Please, if you have a scrap of compassion left in you, let me go. I'll leave the country, and you'll never hear from me again, I swear it."

He picked up a fresh strip of linen and deftly wrapped her wound. Then he looked up, a cryptic intensity in his gaze. "Nothing would give me greater pleasure than to let you go. Once you've given birth to my son."

"Your . . . son?"

"I find myself in need of an heir. And you, dear wife, are sorely in need of salvation." .

His eyes were flat and frigid, hard as coal. A cold prickling spread over her skin, and she let go of his wrist. He meant it. He meant for her to submit to him. Was he addled from lack of sleep?

She shook her head in shock. "But I thought . . . your cousin . . ."

"On reflection, I've decided I prefer to have a son of my own blood." A small, insincere smile hinted at the dimples on either side of his mouth. "You will live in my house, so I can be certain the child is mine. Once you've done your duty by me, you shall relinquish the boy into my care. And you will be free to go on your merry way."

Frozen, she stared at him. "You wish me to give up my own son?"

"Or go to prison. The choice is yours."

Her pulse drummed in her ears, echoing the throbbing in her hand. His proposal was impossible, unthinkable, inhuman. He expected her to allow him to slake his lust in her.

If that was not a vile enough prospect, she must carry his baby for nine months and then give the child away like a bit of rubbish. How could Lucas ask her to make such a devil's bargain?

Yet the alternative was to leave Jenny without a mother.

"This is your notion of revenge, isn't it?" she whispered bitterly. "To force me into your bed and then rob me of my own child."

"It seems a fair exchange. And a far more lenient punishment than you deserve."

"What if I conceive a daughter?"

"Then we'll try again until I have my heir." He rose, looking down at her, his face impassive. "Understand that the courts will award me custody of any children born of our union. You will not be permitted any contact with them. Though you'll receive a handsome annuity, of course."

Heedless of the pain in her palm, Emma squeezed the coarse cotton of her skirt. "I don't want your money."

"It's yours—from your marriage portion. I would advise you to take it. I can see you're accustomed to living beyond your means." His lips thinned, he looked around the morning room in its pitiful state of disrepair. "And by the way, your daughter shall remain here."

"Jenny? No!"

"Yes. Briggs will look after her. You'll be permitted to visit her from time to time. Under supervision, of course."

Emma stared, speechless with horror. She felt as if a boulder crushed her breast. Lucas didn't seem to comprehend the sacrifice he asked of her. Live apart from Jenny? Bear children only to give them up? Surely he could know nothing of a mother's love.

Or perhaps he did. Dear God. Perhaps he did.

"What have you done to my mama?"

Emma looked up in astonishment to see a blur of amber shoot across the room. Jenny launched herself at Lucas, pounding her small fists against his dove-gray waistcoat and kicking at him with her slippered feet. He frowned down at her in bemusement as if she were a pesky gnat.

Emma sprang up, took firm hold of Jenny's shoulders, and pulled her back. The girl continued to fight and wriggle. "Jennifer Frances Coulter," Emma said in her sternest voice. "Stop it, this instant."

Jenny quieted, though she thrust out her lower lip. "I hate him. Maggie says he's come to cart you off to jail. He's going to lock you up and throw away the key."

Emma bent down and embraced her daughter. "Oh, darling, that isn't true. No one shall take me away from you. No one."

Lucas's throat went dry as the little girl buried her face against her mother's bosom. They might have been a portrait depicting maternal devotion, one blond head and one chestnut-brown. So this was Lady Jenny, by law his daughter.

As cold and clear as a shard of ice, bitterness pierced him. This was the child for whom Emma had deceived him. The child she had carried inside her on their wedding day. Emma had cheated him out of the chance to have children of his own. He knew then why he had stayed away from England for so long. It had been easier to ignore the girl's existence than to face the living proof of Emma's treachery.

I haven't the least notion who fathered my Jenny. He could have been any one of a dozen men.

Who was Jenny's father? A married gentleman? A charming rake? A handsome servant who had been seduced by Emma?

Lucas scrutinized Jenny for a clue to her paternity. She was a dainty bit of a thing, six going on seven. Clad in a too-short amber gown that showed her scuffed leather boots, she had inherited her mother's spirit along with Emma's delicate features. The only significant difference was her eyes; they were more green than blue.

Jenny turned from her mother. Her pixie face glowered at him, displaying a missing front tooth. "Why did you come back? We don't need you. You're not my real papa."

"Jenny!" Emma exclaimed. "That is quite enough."

Discomfited by the girl's resentment, Lucas shifted his feet. "I can see she gets her manners from you."

"Her manners are perfectly fine," Emma said.

She sent a warning look at Jenny, who sketched a curtsy. "Beg pardon," she mumbled with obvious reluctance.

"Apology accepted," Lucas said. And then, because he felt awkward and ill at ease beneath her suspicious stare, he held out his hand to her and spoke slowly. "I'm pleased to make your acquaintance, Lady Jenny."

She scowled another moment, then placed her small hand in his and gravely shook it. "Have you come to live with us?"

"No. Quite the contrary—"

"You and I are going to live at his lordship's house for a time," Emma broke in. "Both of us will be moving our things there today."

She gave him a challenging stare as if she expected him to dispute her statement. His triumph over trapping her was soured by the prospect of taking her love child into his home. He couldn't do it. His mother and sisters would have fits. Worse, society would view it as his acceptance of Jenny.

"But I want to go to France," Jenny objected. "You said we'd go boating on the Seine." An unholy gleam entered her eyes. "And we'd see the place where the king got his head chopped off."

"Shh," Emma said, stroking Jenny's hair. "We'll have to postpone our trip. We'll go later, just the two of us. Run upstairs now and finish packing."

"But I don't want to." She stamped her little foot. "I won't live with him."

Lucas knew he should follow his own edict. He should not permit this child to live under his roof. Yet when he looked at Jenny's pink cheeks and obstinate mouth, he found himself saying, "You'll obey your mother. You're coming to live at my house. And no more arguing."

Emma glanced at him, her eyes wide with a gratitude that gave Lucas an uncomfortable twinge of guilt. He quickly discounted it. Although she appeared to be a decent mother, he could not allow her to have any part in raising *his* child.

Emma was a liar and a thief, and she had brought her troubles onto herself.

"Who have we here?" A snappish voice broke the silence. "Zounds, if it ain't my long-lost grandson-in-law."

Lucas tensed as Lord Briggs strolled into the morning room. The old man was dressed entirely in black. Wisps of white hair stuck out from beneath his ebony cap, and his eyes were a startling blue against his soot-streaked face.

Lucas gave a curt nod. "Briggs."

"Great-grandpapa, why are you dressed so funny?" Jenny asked with a giggle.

Grinning, he polished his knuckles against his black lapel. "Because I'm the Bond Street Burglar, that's why."

Her eyes rounded like saucers. "Truly? Is that like Robin Hood?"

"Indeed so, my little imp—"

"For heaven's sake!" Clutching at her skirt, Emma wheeled toward her daughter. "He's only playacting, darling. Now go upstairs as I asked."

"But I want Great-grandpapa to tell me a story about the Burglar."

"Later," she said, herding Jenny out of the room. "Off with you now."

When the little girl trudged into the passageway, Emma closed the door. She leaned against it, the full appeal of her blue eyes turned on Lucas. "Don't listen to him, please. He isn't the Burglar. I am."

"Ha." Lord Briggs stabbed his index finger at his chest. "I'm your culprit. I stole jewels worth thousands from the finest homes in London. I'll be happy to make a full confession to the magistrate."

He was lying for Emma's sake; Lucas didn't doubt that for an instant. How did she inspire such loyalty? "You forget," Lucas said in a steely tone. "I caught her myself, breaking into my strongbox last night."

"Because *I* stole the tiger mask, and she was returning it. Just ask her. Ask her if she stole the blasted piece from you."

"I've no interest in playing games with you, Briggs."

"Games! That's what started this havey-cavey muddle."
The old man took off his cap and hung his head as if in
shame. "Every time I had a run of bad luck at the cards, I
robbed those who'd bilked me at the gaming table."

"I never bilked you," Lucas said in disgust.

"No, you only bilked my granddaughter."

Emma uttered a low, strangled sound of distress. She
walked swiftly to Lucas, stopping so close he caught a whiff
of her womanly scent, sending a rush of heat to his loins.
"Grandpapa is only trying to protect me," she said. "You
mustn't believe he's the Burglar."

A little devil made Lucas say, "And if I did? You'd be
free to go, then."

Her cheeks paled. "At his expense," she whispered. "And
anyway, you haven't a shred of proof."

"He has my word of honor as a gentleman," said her
grandfather. "Good God, put a mask on me, and Lord Jasper
Putney would swear I was the burglar he shot."

"Shot?" Lucas said numbly.

"I'll show you," Emma said. "Maybe then you'll believe
me."

In one swift move, she lowered her gown over her shoulder, holding the bodice over her breasts while revealing an
expanse of milky skin and the edge of the plain, bleached-
linen chemise that covered her bosom. Lucas felt a lightning
bolt of desire. The glimpse of Emma's bare shoulder left him
as hot and breathless as an adolescent gawking at his first
naked woman.

"See? This is where the bullet struck me." With her bandaged hand, she pointed at the white, upraised scar just below her left shoulder.

Shock reverberated through Lucas. The size of a farthing,
the knot of healed tissue was undoubtedly caused by a bullet.
Was Emma so greedy for wealth she would risk her own
life? Did she, too, have gaming debts to pay off? "What
happened?" he asked.

"Last April, while I was rifling through his jewel box, I

was surprised by Lord Jasper Putney. Before I could flee, he seized his pistol and fired—''

"Stuff and nonsense," Lord Briggs interrupted. "You won't be exposing yourself to the magistrate, so it's your word against mine. Now cover yourself, girl. Unless you want to give your laggard of a husband ideas."

A pink flush tinged her cheeks, and she spun around to repair her clothing. Lucas hated himself for the lust burning in him. He could scarcely wait until they could be alone. . . .

"And you," Briggs said, advancing on Lucas, "you should be ashamed of how badly you've treated my granddaughter. All these years you've neglected her. You let her and little Jenny live in poverty without so much as a penny of support. And you call yourself a gentleman."

With each accusation, Briggs marched closer until Lucas found himself backed against the wall. The slur on his honor rankled. How dare this man question his character.

He kept his fingers clenched at his sides. "Be careful, old man. Lest you find yourself choosing swords or pistols."

"Think you can best me on the dueling field, eh?" Briggs shook his fist at Lucas. "We'll see about that—"

"Enough," Emma said, stepping between them. "There will be no fighting. Grandfather, the past is best forgotten."

"The man has an obligation to you—"

"Which he intends to fulfill. You see, my husband has promised to take care of Jenny and me from now on. Haven't you, Lucas?"

Slipping her arm through his, she turned those guileless blue eyes up at him. The exclamation of disbelief from Briggs was mere noise in the background as Lucas again found himself entranced by Emma. How innocent she appeared. How adept she was at twisting the truth to suit her purposes.

But it was his turn to have the upper hand. His turn to have revenge. An undeniable surge of exultation poured through him.

Tonight she would finally be his.

❧ Chapter 7 ❧

As Emma descended the grand staircase at Wortham House, she heeded the urge to dawdle. It was strange to take her rightful place in this grand residence after seven years of ostracism. She felt like an impostor rather than the Marchioness of Wortham.

Her husband's ancestors glared down at her from the walls as if to accuse her of ruining his life. She glared back. Although it was true, she had wronged Lucas—wronged him most foully—she was here to make amends. And to do so, she had to sleep with him.

The oppressive darkness of memory threatened. She pushed it away. He had given Jenny the protection of his name. In return, he deserved a child of his own, a son or a daughter or both.

She knew that. Yet fear and loathing gnawed at her.

A casement clock ticked in the deserted foyer, marking the minutes until bedtime. Shivering, she paused on the stairway. The chill originated in a place hidden deep within herself. The sting of her bandaged wound served as a reminder that she was a prisoner, not the lady of the house.

The last of her bravado trickled away. The hum of voices drifted from the drawing room, where the household had gathered at the sound of the dinner gong. Lucas's two sisters were visiting from the country to celebrate the return of their prodigal brother. Emma dreaded facing his family. They thought her a harlot, a shameless hussy.

She alone knew the truth. For an instant, fantasy tempted Emma. She could march in there and tell them. She could relish the horror on their faces as she recounted that abominable event. . . .

But Jenny—sweet Jenny—might find out then. She never wanted Jenny to learn that her father was no knight in shining armor. That she had been conceived not in love but in violence.

Emma reached the bottom of the staircase and leaned against the newel post. Misgivings battered her breast. Had she been right to bring Jenny here?

In the nursery, Jenny had been delighted to discover she had five younger cousins to mother. Immediately she'd made funny faces to cheer up a crying girl, and then helped a little boy unbuckle his shoes. She had scarcely noticed Emma's departure.

But what if the family snubbed Jenny? What if, when they found out she was staying in the nursery, they forbade their children to play with her? And what of Lucas? Jenny was here against his express wishes. Emma didn't want to believe he had become so callous he would insult her child. Yet she no longer knew him; she could no longer predict his behavior.

She hadn't felt so dizzy with anxiety since she'd been a bride with a dark secret. Then, as now, she'd had no choice. Against her will, Emma tumbled back into the past, reliving that fateful day. . . .

Though she'd been unable to keep down any food on the morning of her wedding, far more than physical illness had plagued her. She'd felt trapped and terrified, ashamed to confide in anyone, least of all her betrothed.

I have no choice, she'd thought as she'd stood lifeless as a French fashion doll, while her grandmama fussed over the blue bridal gown and offered advice about the physical needs of one's husband.

Emma had blocked her mind to the wedding night. She

dared not consider that intimate act, when she must use all her wiles to charm Lucas.

No choice. No choice. No choice. The rattle of the carriage wheels repeated the refrain as she and her grandparents traveled to St. George's Church in Hanover Square. There, the murmuring of the guests and the swell of organ music nearly snapped the thread of her composure. The church seemed to tilt, and she clung to her grandfather's wiry arm.

"Chin up, girl," Lord Briggs whispered in her ear. "Wortham's a decent chap. Even if he can't abide gambling."

His affectionate wink only made her feel worse.

As he escorted her up the aisle, faces beamed at her in admiration. She forced a brilliant smile, letting everyone think she reveled in securing an advantageous marriage in her very first Season. She was the envy of every husband-hunting debutante, every social-climbing mama. At one time she would have savored the attention, yet on her wedding day she felt nothing inside. It was as if a glass dome insulated her from the world.

No choice. No choice. No choice.

At the altar, she swayed when her grandfather released his hold on her. For one horrid moment Emma feared she would collapse, and everyone would guess the scandalous truth. Then she felt the firm support of a man's hand.

Lucas Coulter, Lord Wortham. With adoration shining in his brown eyes and a lock of dark hair dipping onto his brow, he seemed more a bashful boy than a virile man. Though he was twenty and she but eighteen, she felt much older than he. Eons older.

His hesitant smile was strangely comforting. Lucas would never hurt her. He provided a safe harbor from the storm of her past, from the anguish of her future. Tonight he would learn the truth. And she would convince him to take care of her. It was the perfect solution to her desperate dilemma.

The bishop droned from his black prayerbook. Lucas spoke his vows with only a trace of his habitual stuttering. Then the clergyman turned his stern face toward her. " 'Emma Callandra, wilt thou have this man to be thy wedded husband, to live together after God's ordinance in the holy estate of matrimony? Wilt thou obey him and serve him, love, honour and keep him, in sickness and in health, and forsaking all others, keep thee only unto him, as long as ye both shall live?' ''

Her mouth went as dry as dust. Someone in the congregation coughed discreetly. She sensed everyone in the church staring at her, waiting, watching. Her heart thundered, and the air around the altar seemed to pulsate and shimmer. Madness crept from the edge of her consciousness. How could she make such a vow to any man? How could she let him do with her whatever he willed?

No choice. No choice. No choice.

The weight of Lucas's fingers on her arm gave her courage. She wanted to banish the darkness, to feel clean and good again, deserving of his love. She would make it up to him. "Yes," she whispered. "I will."

The remainder of the ceremony passed in a blur. Then he placed the dainty gold wedding ring upon her finger and bent down to brush his warm lips over hers. A shudder started at the core of her, but Emma controlled it with frantic effort. She was the Marchioness of Wortham now. Her exalted position would save her unborn child from disgrace. . . .

The yapping of a dog shattered the memory. Emma returned to the present with a jolt. From across the foyer, a bundle of white fur streaked toward her, claws clicking and paws skidding on the marble floor.

"Toby," she said in delight. "Have you come for your treat?"

The old terrier danced on his hind legs. Her spirits lifting, Emma fed him a bit of peppermint she had snitched from a jar in the nursery. Then she sank down and hugged his small, warm body. Wriggling with ecstasy, he licked her chin. She drew an absurd amount of comfort from the little dog.

"Toby!" spoke a regal voice. "Come."

Lucas's mother stood in the doorway to the drawing room. She looked thin and pale in a rust-colored gown with a feathered turban that hid her silver hair. No hint of welcome softened her face as she glanced at her daughter-in-law.

The dog cast a longing look at Emma, then trudged back to the dowager, his head hung low and his tail tucked down.

Emma hid her resentment behind a polite smile. "Madam. How good to see you."

The elder Lady Wortham arched an eyebrow. "Emma. I understand you've bedazzled my son again."

As much as Emma had prepared herself, she was taken aback by the dowager's open dislike. "I should think you'd be pleased for him, that we've reconciled our differences. Though I wouldn't precisely describe him as bedazzled—"

"I would," said Lucas.

Darkly handsome in a steel-gray coat and charcoal breeches, her husband emerged from the drawing room. He pressed his hand to the back of Emma's waist and smiled down at her, the dimples showing attractively in his tanned cheeks. "My wife is being modest. The truth is, she swept me off my feet. For the second time."

His suave tone stunned her into silence. Mockery glinted in his eyes. He stood close—too close—and she held herself rigid to keep from recoiling.

With a careless refinement he had never displayed as a youth, he escorted her past his mother and into the drawing room. Several branches of candles spread a golden glow over the group. Emma cast a wary smile at his sisters. They didn't smile back.

"Congratulate us, everyone," Lucas said, his words crisp and deliberate. "Emma and I are happy to be together again. We want all of you to share in our joy."

Despite a lackluster response from the family, he lifted her uninjured hand to his lips. The brush of his warm mouth against the back of her hand sent a flurry of shivers over her skin. She resisted the urge to yank her hand away. So he intended to hide his wicked plan behind a mask of civility, did he?

Two could play at that game.

"My dearest," she murmured silkily, forcing herself to run her fingertips over the strong line of his jaw. "I know you've missed me as much as I missed you. What God has joined together, let no man put asunder.''

''Or no woman,'' he said under his breath. Then, with a firm grip on her arm, he whisked her toward his sisters, who sat conversing on a blue-striped couch.

Olivia reclined against the cushions, her hands folded atop her gently rounded belly. A cascade of reddish curls draped the shoulder of her dark green gown. She worked her lips into a chilly smile. ''Emma. I never thought to see you again.''

''None of us did,'' blurted Phoebe. A rather plump lady in a high-waisted gown of clarence-blue silk, she vigorously fanned herself despite the evening chill. ''Oh, dear, this is all so sudden.''

Leaning toward her brother, Olivia said in an undertone, ''Mother is quite perturbed with you, Lucas. Considering her weak heart, you ought to have had the courtesy to give her some warning.''

''And especially so after that horrifying event last night.'' Phoebe turned to Emma. ''Did Lucas tell you?''

Paralysis gripped Emma's throat, and every muscle in her body went stiff. She glanced at her husband to find him watching her, a smirk on his face. The devil. He was enjoying her discomfort. ''He didn't say a word. What happened?''

''A robber broke into this house and nearly murdered us in our beds,'' Olivia said with a shiver. ''Lucas brought down the knave in the passageway right outside my bedchamber.''

''You don't say!'' Emma exclaimed, rounding her eyes first at Olivia, then at her husband. ''How brave of you, Lucas, to chase after so dangerous a criminal.''

''Indeed,'' Phoebe said, leaning forward, ''he might have been killed.''

''We've no wish to see our brother harmed in any way,'' Olivia put in primly. ''Now that he's finally come back to us.''

The pointed stares from both women pricked Emma. She

cursed the warmth that crept up her throat and into her cheeks. Resentful as she was, she understood their protectiveness. She felt the same fiery sense of guardianship toward Jenny.

"Come now, Livvie, you're being sensational," Lucas drawled. "The intruder was a petty thief of no consequence."

Olivia swung her gaze toward him. "Ha. Mama says he was the Bond Street Burglar. And I agree."

"Who?" Emma asked with wide-eyed innocence.

"Surely you've heard of so famous a villain," Phoebe said.

"The Burglar has been terrorizing London for the past few years," Olivia explained. "Stealing from decent, law-abiding people."

"Oh, I remember now," Emma said. "Like Robin Hood, he robs only the very rich. Men who have supplemented their wealth through gambling."

Olivia harumphed. Phoebe frowned over her fan.

Lucas cast a withering glance at Emma. "The Burglar uses that excuse as a license to steal."

"Or perhaps as a means to exact justice," she returned, batting her lashes in girlish naïveté. "The Runners must have been terribly impressed when you brought him in. Did they give you a reward?"

A warning flashed into those tarnished-gold eyes. For a moment she feared she had pushed him too far. Then he touched her hand, lightly massaging her bandage. "Reward? Hardly. Our thief managed to escape when I left him alone for a moment. If you ladies will excuse me." Releasing her, he walked to the sideboard and reached for a crystal decanter of brandy.

Emma was left standing before her two sisters-in-law. Aware of their barely veiled hostility, she took her time situating herself on a gilt chair. Long ago, she had been particular friends with Olivia, who had a generous heart and a fun-loving nature.

None of those qualities showed now. Livvie sat in frosty silence as if to punish Emma for her sins.

Emma was done being ashamed. She would meet their sourness with sweetness. "Where are your husbands? I had so hoped to meet them."

"Hugh and Ralph are at their club," Olivia said archly. "Lucas had intended to accompany them, but . . ." She compressed her lips.

In the awkward silence, Phoebe fidgeted with the ivory ribs of her fan. "Well. It has been quite a long while since we've seen you at *ton* events, Emma."

"Seven years," Olivia stated. "Surely you miss being the center of attention."

"On the contrary," Emma said, "I don't miss it a whit. I lead a much more useful life now." She stole a sidelong glance at Lucas. He stood alone, watching her, drinking his glass of brandy. Curse him for deserting her.

"Oh?" Olivia said, her chin held high. "And don't you care that you no longer set the fashion?"

Emma resisted the impulse to smooth her outdated pink gown. "We've all changed," she said softly. "I understand both of you have children now. They seemed a happy crowd up in the nursery."

Phoebe took the bait. "I have three," she said, clasping her folded fan to her pillowy breast. "Jane, Lydia, and baby Ralph. I must say, Longden strutted like a cock when I presented him with his heir last March."

"And the handsome, fair-haired boy guarding his regiment of tin soldiers, is he yours, then?" Emma asked Olivia.

"He's my eldest. We named him Andrew." Olivia's face softened ever so slightly, taking on a glow of maternal pride, before her mouth pinched tightly again. "Remember my brother Andrew? He died in the Portuguese War. We were in deep mourning for him when you lured Lucas into a hasty marriage."

Watching from across the room, Lucas saw Emma stiffen. She sat with elegant composure, as fragile as a porcelain doll, listening gravely as his sisters prattled on. He wondered how she managed to appear so cursed beautiful when her soul was so black. Her upswept hair glinted like gold in the candlelight. The bandage wrapped around her palm enhanced her vulnerable look. Her hands rested on the arms of her chair, and he fancied those delicate knuckles showed a hint of whiteness.

What were his sisters saying?

He felt an unexpected jab of pity for her. Livvie and Phoebe would be making sharp comments in the interest of defending their brother. They meant well. But he was a man now, and he did not need mothering.

He needed his wife. Naked in bed.

Uptilting his glass, he let the brandy slide down his throat, sweet and searing like the lust inside him. He had never felt this darkly haunting passion for any other woman, not even Shalimar.

Guilt twisted his gut. He'd called on his mistress that afternoon, told her of his intent to sire an heir, and renewed his vow to find her son. But his scruples would not allow him to visit her for now, not while he lived with his wife. Shalimar had reacted with inscrutable calm and quiet dignity. She was like a cool oasis in a burning desert, and Lucas hated himself for wanting to be scorched by the sun.

Tonight he would give himself up to the heat. He would go to Emma. She would be waiting in a temptingly sheer nightdress, and he would take his time kissing her, loosening the ribbons of her bodice, reaching inside to caress her silky skin. Emma hid a wild spirit behind her façade of frail femininity, a wildness he intended to unleash and then control with the whip of desire. He knew a hundred ways to arouse a woman, exotic techniques even a woman of her experience could not know. Tonight he would make her his willing slave; he would reduce her to a state where she begged for his touch. And never again would she scorn him. . . .

"M'lord?"

He realized that Stafford stood beside him, a silver salver in his white-gloved hands. The servant said in an undertone,

"Lady Wortham has a visitor. I—ahem—thought you might wish to know."

Setting down his glass, Lucas plucked the calling card from the tray, and his eyes narrowed on the printed name. The heat within him burned to cinders. An icy surge of anger immobilized him.

His mother motioned from the chaise where she sat with Toby in her lap. "Who is it?" she inquired. "Who would be so uncivil as to call upon us at dinnertime without invitation?"

"His name is of no importance," Lucas said, his voice low and curt. "If you'll excuse me a few moments—"

"*His* name?" His mother cast a scandalized glance across the room at Emma. "A *man* has come to see your wife? Kindly pass me that card."

"No. I'll handle the matter."

Emma rose from her chair and came toward them. "Did I hear you say I have a visitor?" She took the card from Lucas, made a little gasp, and murmured breathily, "Sir Woodrow!"

His mother's silvery brows rose in surprise. "Sir Woodrow Hickey? Good gracious! Stafford, send him in at once. And set another place at the table."

"Yes, m'lady." The servant marched out of the drawing room.

From across the room, his sisters watched with interest, murmuring to each other. At least, Lucas thought dourly, his family was spared the knowledge that Emma wished to divorce him and marry Hickey.

"Sir Woodrow came to see *me*," Emma objected. "About a business matter. I will speak to him in private."

She flounced away and Lucas stalked after her, seizing her by the arm just inside the doorway. Bending close to her ear, he whispered, "Let there be no mistake as to whom you belong."

Blue fire flashed in her eyes. "I belong to no man."

"You belong to the devil. And you're going nowhere without me."

"So you are the devil?" she said in a grating murmur.

"I'm your jailer. It's either this gilded cage . . . or Newgate."

Lucas watched in cynical amusement as Emma compressed her lips, the color bleaching from her face. So much for her stealing a moment alone with her lover.

Her bosom swelled as she drew in a deep breath to speak. His gaze flicked to her breasts, and she lifted her hand to her décolletage as if to hide herself. Her poisonous retort remained unspoken, for Sir Woodrow Hickey marched into the drawing room.

His receding, wheat-brown hair had a mussed appearance, though otherwise he was impeccably dressed in a dark green coat over tan breeches. The grim set of his mouth looked faintly ludicrous on his mild-mannered face.

He rushed straight to Emma. He stretched out his hands as if to take hers, then let them drop to his sides. "My dear Emma," he said in a low-pitched voice fraught with emotion. "I just heard the news from Briggs, that you'd taken up residence here. You and Jenny."

"We decided only today—"

"Good God," he exclaimed. "What have you done to your hand?" This time he ignored Lucas's glare, grasped Emma gently by the wrist, and clucked over her bandage. "Why, you poor darling, you've been bleeding."

"It's merely a scratch," she lied, drawing her hand back. "An accident with a knife, I'm embarrassed to admit."

"You should not work in the kitchen," he muttered. "Such labor is unsuited to a lady of your delicacy."

"Bless you for your concern. And I'm sorry I didn't have time to warn you about the change in my situation. Truly sorry."

They whispered to each other like two cooing doves. Hickey, apparently, was taken in by Emma's pretense of helpless female. She very nearly had the lack-witted fool groveling at her feet.

This was the man Emma wanted to marry. This uninspiring, weak-chinned milksop.

Lucas gritted his teeth. Damn her, she ought to be currying *his* favor instead. *He* should be the recipient of her desperate yearning, her heartfelt gaze, her loving pretense.

Lucas moved closer, molding her softness to his side and reviving his awareness of her treacherous charms. "I'll see to my wife's comfort," he said. "Henceforth, I would thank you to keep your hands to yourself."

"Wortham." Stepping back from Emma, the baronet acknowledged his host with a belated nod. "What a surprise that you've finally returned from your trip abroad."

"I couldn't stay away. You see, England holds a certain undeniable attraction for me."

Lucas caressed Emma's waist in a proprietary gesture. Her breathing caught, and when she flinched, she reminded him of a cornered doe.

But Emma was no fey woodland creature facing the hunter's gun.

"What is the meaning of all this secretiveness?" the dowager called across the room. "Sir Woodrow, have you no greeting for the rest of us?"

"Forgive me, ladies." Like a gallant courtier, Hickey bowed to each of the women in turn, ending with Lucas's mother. He stepped toward her and took her proffered hand. "The years have been kind to you. May I say, you are as lovely as ever."

"Why, thank you. You were always such a polite, well-mannered boy." Smiling, the dowager stroked the terrier in her lap. "I insist that you join us for dinner."

"Oh, yes, do!" added Livvie and Phoebe in unison.

Casting a troubled glance at Emma, he said, "I'd be honored to sup at your table."

"Excellent," the dowager said. Then sadness shadowed her gaunt features. "It's a pity we lost touch after my son's untimely death. But now we have the chance to share stories of happier times. I should like to hear all about your school days with Andrew."

The baronet took a seat beside her on the chaise. "Oh-ho, I don't know if my tales would be suited for the ears of ladies. He and I had a few exploits that would curl your hair.''

"He was ever the darling scamp," Livvie said wistfully. "I hope my own little Andrew takes after him."

A flash of bittersweet nostalgia penetrated Lucas's ill humor. He couldn't help smiling at his sister. "I can't believe what I'm hearing," he teased. "Have you forgotten the time Andrew snitched your diary and read it aloud to a roomful of your suitors?"

Livvie giggled. "Oooh, I was furious, but I had my revenge when Papa made him renounce his sins in front of the entire congregation at St. George's."

"I say, why don't we record our anecdotes in a memorial book?" suggested Phoebe. "So our children can know their uncle, too."

"How positively famous," Livvie said, clapping her hands. "Over dinner, Sir Woodrow can tell us stories about their stint together in the cavalry."

From the doorway, the butler intoned, "Dinner, my lord and ladies."

Chattering happily, Lucas's sisters rose from the chaise while Hickey offered his arm to the dowager.

Emma stepped away from Lucas. As the others started out the door, she gazed after Hickey, her expression stricken. Her fingers were clenched together, and the naked anguish on her face infuriated Lucas.

He came up beside her and dipped his head down to hers. Her warm, womanly essence swirled around him. "Mourning the loss of your lover?" he murmured.

She blinked, and he had the strangest feeling she wasn't even seeing him. The bruised darkness beneath her eyes accentuated her fragility. Of course, playing the Burglar, she hadn't slept last night.

Nor would she would sleep tonight.

Elation flamed inside Lucas. At last, he would possess her, bend her to his will. He would take his pleasure and purge himself of his obsession for her. He would prove she was only a comely body, a woman unworthy of his attentions.

"Have you nothing to say, my darling wife?" he taunted. "No recriminations for me now that everyone is gone?"

Her lashes fluttered as her gaze wavered on him. She swayed on her feet. Then, before he could catch her, she breathed a little sigh and crumpled to the floor.

∾ Chapter 8 ∾

$\mathcal{A}$ sharp odor stung her nostrils.

Moaning, Emma jerked her head away. She wanted to drift in a warm cloud of nothingness. To sleep in a soft nest of oblivion. But no matter how she shifted position, the acrid stench followed her. It drove her out of the protective cocoon, and she opened her eyes to glaring reality.

She was at Wortham House. In the candlelit drawing room. Gazing up at her husband's grim, unforgiving face.

He crouched beside the chaise and held a small brown bottle to her nose. Foul fumes emanated from the vessel.

She coughed, batted away his hand, and struggled to sit up. "What . . . happened?"

He pressed her back down. "You swooned."

"I never swoon."

"You did just now," he said flatly.

Several other faces swam into view. "It's the loss of blood from the wound on her hand," Sir Woodrow pronounced with a worried frown. "Emma is wont to neglect her own health for the sake of others."

"Will she be all right?" the dowager asked with surprising anxiety. Toby squirmed in her arms, his liquid brown eyes fixed on Emma.

"When was the last time she ate?" Olivia asked, absently touching her pregnant belly. "I get light-headed when I miss a meal."

"She looks positively exhausted," Phoebe observed, turning her fan on Emma and creating a gentle breeze. "Oh, dear. It's our fault for being so unwelcoming."

They cared about her? A bittersweet gladness flowed into Emma. Yet she also wanted to snap at them in frustration. If only they knew. If only she could tell them the real reason she had fainted.

Wracked by memory, she closed her eyes again. No, she couldn't bear their kindness. It kept her from shouting out the truth. The truth that had stained her soul for the past seven years. How had she thought she could live in this house?

Two strong arms slid between her and the chaise, one beneath her knees and the other supporting her neck. She opened her eyes just as Lucas swung her up against him.

He clasped her to his granite-hard chest. "Hold on to my neck," he said.

"No."

"Yes. I'm taking you to bed."

Her heartbeat surged so fast she swayed from another wave of dizziness. She grabbed at him and clung for dear life. Her cheek met the hard pillow of his shoulder. The lingering ammonia sting of the hartshorn was replaced by the clean scent of starched linen. And the musk of man.

"I'll send my maid to attend her," the dowager said.

"I'll fetch a physician," Sir Woodrow added. "She needs proper medical attention."

"Go on into dinner, all of you," Lucas said. "I'll take care of my wife."

A lightning bolt of fear struck Emma. His ominous words rumbled through her like the thunder presaging a storm. She was conscious of his physical strength as he carried her up the grand staircase and along a dim passageway. She could hear the thud of his footsteps, the harshness of his breaths. He stared straight ahead, his jaw set in stony determination.

I'm taking you to bed.

Sweet Jesus, save her. Lucas meant to assert his husbandly

rights. Now. While the rest of the family sat down to their dinner.

Emma resisted the dark force of panic. If she let herself sink into a black pit of despair, she might never climb out again. She must perform the duties of a wife, that was all. It was better to allow Lucas to have his way with her than to be tossed in jail. Or to risk being transported in a prison hulk halfway around the world to a penal colony—leaving Jenny alone.

I can find a more honorable woman on any street corner in Whitechapel.

She took a perverse comfort from his brusque words. Lucas wanted a child from her, an heir. He felt no driving, overpowering lust for her. He wouldn't grab her unawares, cast her to the ground, and yank up her skirts—

She shut out the memory. Yet a cold clamminess crept over her skin.

He shouldered open a door and conveyed her to the bed, depositing her on the counterpane as if she were an unwelcome burden. Emma's heightened senses registered the coolness of the sheets and a faint sunshine scent. At any other time, she would have found the bedchamber inviting. A cheery blaze on the hearth illuminated a room decorated in hues of peaches and cream accented by gold. The chairs were plump with cushions, the gilt desk dainty and feminine. Even the bed felt fluffy and comfortable with feather pillows and fresh linens.

Yet the walls seemed to press in on her as if she were locked in a cell.

No choice. No choice. No choice. . . .

Lucas towered beside the bed, his hands on his hips and his gaze sweeping over her revealing pink gown. Her flesh prickled from the heat of his stare. He must be anticipating stripping her naked, exposing her to his aggression. Would he snuff out the candles first? Would he press his hand to her mouth to keep her from crying out? Would he hurt her?

Slowly, unwilling to antagonize him, she pushed herself

into a sitting position against the pillows. And waited for him to ravish her.

"When did you last have your menses?" he snapped.

She blinked in bewilderment, feeling a flush crawl upward from her neck. "My . . . ?" She couldn't bring herself to say the word.

"Answer the question."

"F-four days ago."

"Are you lying to me?"

"N-no!" Moistening her dry lips, she realized she was stammering, just as he had once done. "Why would I?"

He flattened his palms on the mattress and thrust his face close to hers. "I should think it's obvious. You swooned. That can be a sign of impending motherhood."

His meaning struck her like a slap. She stiffened from the pain of it. He suspected her of tricking him. Again.

Emma drew up her knees to her chin, hugging them to her aching breast. The ticking of a clock vied with the fussing of the fire. Lucas stood watching her, his gaze dark with suspicion. She had the sudden, dismal view of herself through his eyes: the conniving wife who had vowed faithfully to honor him. When all the while she had been pregnant with another man's child.

"I fainted from exhaustion, that's all," she murmured. "I assure you, I'm not with child."

"You and Hickey have been lovers—"

"No! Never." She shook her head for emphasis.

One brown eyebrow arched in disbelief. "You are not to consort with him or any other man. Not until after you've given birth to my son. Is that clear?"

His autocratic command set her teeth on edge. For seven long years, she had answered to no one but herself. "Woodrow and I are friends. He's been like a father to Jenny. I'll see him if it suits me."

"You'll see the magistrate, then, too."

Emma clenched the bedlinens and tried to be reasonable. "You can hardly bar Woodrow from your house. You'd have to explain the reason to your mother. And her health is precarious.''

Lucas leaned closer, and she could feel the warmth of his breath. ''Heed me well,'' he said. ''Don't ever use my mother—or anyone else in my family—as a bargaining chip.''

She stared back, refusing to let him see her fear. ''You cannot dictate who my friends are.''

''I set the rules here,'' he said in a cold, hateful voice. ''And rule number one is, you'll give up your lover.''

''Only if *you* stop seeing your mistress.''

She froze, wanting to call back her feckless words. What madness had gotten hold of her? Let Lucas visit his foreign woman as much as he liked. He would have less time to debauch his wife.

A beastly brilliance burned in his eyes. He slid his knuckles down her cheek in an eerily erotic caress. ''There's one way to stop me from straying, dear wife. Keep me satisfied. Well satisfied.''

And then he pounced. His long, muscular form imprisoned her on the mattress. She lay numb with shock as a barrage of impressions assaulted her senses. The heavy weight of his body. The brandy-male scent of him. The firmness of his fingers tilting her face up to his.

Emma drew in a breath to protest, but his mouth swooped down to silence her. His tongue glided across her parted lips and delved inside, tasting, coaxing, invading. The velvety heat of him took her by surprise. Instead of using force, he sampled her as he might sip the finest of wines. His fingers slid into her hair and massaged in a mesmerizing pattern. Streamers of warmth swirled downward, penetrating even the part of her that was cold to the core. Something wondrous and terrifying loomed on the horizon of her awareness. The inexplicable allure of his kiss startled her.

Her hands rested on his shoulders, and the throbbing of her injured palm seemed to descend to her belly. Rather than thrust him away, she found a peculiar pleasure in the hardness of his muscles. He did not use his strength against her.

The tip of his finger traced her ear with a lightness that wrested a moan from deep in her throat. He touched her reverently as he might touch a goddess. As if he thought she might shatter. Perhaps this wouldn't be so bad, after all.

And then he moved his hand lower.

Her pulse surged as he feathered his fingers downward, tracing the shape of her chin, her neck, her bodice. He fondled the curve of her breast and, to her dazed astonishment, the tip contracted into a taut, aching pearl. He was far from done. Even as she shivered from the strange sensations, he boldly explored the contours of her body. His palm smoothed over her ribs, her waist. And lower. Between her legs. The shock of it turned her to ice. Panic clawed at her control. Any pleasure she'd felt vanished as she stiffened, resisting the memory that crowded her consciousness.

"I want you," he muttered against her mouth. "God help me, I want you."

That voice. It was the cultured voice of a gentleman, the dark voice of a demon. *His* voice.

God help me . . . don't fight . . .

She felt herself hurtling backward in time, into the spinning blackness of a nightmare.

. . . he pinned her to the ground . . . his guttural breaths raked her face . . . bile seared her throat and gagged her screams . . . he pushed up her skirt . . . pain lanced into her like a sword thrust . . .

"No," she cried. *"No!"*

Lucas froze. Her frantic voice penetrated the hot beating of his blood. Her hands shoved at him. He found himself holding a madwoman.

A moment ago, Emma had lain quietly beneath him. She had made no protest when he kissed her, had even enjoyed it. But now, she thrashed beneath him, wildly hitting him with her fists.

Her eyes were glassy, her face as pale as parchment. Wave upon wave of tremors shook her small frame. In India, he had seen fakirs in a trance who were not half so convincing.

Her frenzy astounded him, and he reacted without thinking. He caught her flailing arms and pinned them to the mattress. His thumbs moved assessingly over the rigid tendons of her wrists. "Shh. Lie still."

"Get off me. *Get off.*"

At her keening note of hysteria, he released her. Emma curled herself into a ball, drawing her knees up to her chin. He wondered what the devil had come over her. She reminded him of a hedgehog protecting its vulnerable belly, displaying its sharp quills to the world.

Except Emma had no bristles. Not now. She looked petrified. Cringing, as if she expected him to abuse her.

Baffled and angry, Lucas frowned. It was the second time this evening she had fallen to pieces. Her fearful reaction made no sense.

Or perhaps it did. Perhaps this was her way of gulling him again. The thought enraged him.

Regarding her closely, he sat up on the bed. "My, you'd make an excellent actress. Have you ever considered auditioning for the stage?"

For a moment he thought she hadn't heard. Then she shook her head, only a portion of her stricken profile visible to him. "I just don't want you to hurt me."

He took hold of her chin and made her look at him. "So help me God, don't play me for a fool, Emma. This fear of yours—it's all pretense. You'd do anything to escape our bargain."

She jerked out of his grasp and scooted herself backward, sitting up against the headboard. Wisps of fair hair framed the haunted desperation on her face. "You don't understand!"

"Yes I do. You think I'm a convenient dupe. Like all your other men."

Emma shook her head, more violently this time. "It isn't true. A man forced me to . . . he forced me. . . ." She squeezed her eyes shut and turned her face away.

Lucas felt as if someone had driven an iron fist into his stomach. Forced? Emma had been *raped*?

He remembered the way she froze whenever he touched

her. The alarm in her eyes whenever he came near. Her violent reaction to his kiss.

No. This was another ploy for sympathy. Women like her had a thousand tricks to get what they wanted. She wanted him to let her alone, to leave their marriage unconsummated. To free her to go on her thieving, merry way.

"When?" he taunted. "When did this terrible attack happen?"

"Why should you care? You abandoned me."

"Like hell. You drove me away with your deceit."

Her distraught gaze lifted to his. "I know," she said in a small voice. "And I'm sorry."

He brought his fist down hard on the mattress. "To hell with sorry." Seeing her flinch, he threw himself from the bed and began to pace, breathing deeply to dam a rush of rage. She was a flirt. A tease. A liar. He spun toward her. "You robbed me of a happy marriage. A family. The least you can do now is to be honest with me."

"I *am* being honest," she flared. "But go ahead. Believe what you will. I can't force you to listen to me."

"All right, then I'll play along. A man used his superior strength on you. He compelled you to engage in sexual relations against your will."

"Yes. That's why I had to marry you."

He froze. "You're saying this scoundrel . . . fathered Jenny?"

Those impossibly blue eyes focused on him. "Yes."

Resistance crowded his mind. This was all part of her game. It had to be. "How certain you sound," he mocked. "You yourself said she could have been sired by any one of a dozen men."

"I spoke in anger. To see if you would believe something so utterly ridiculous." Her teeth sank into her lower lip. "And you did."

She sat with her shoulders hunched and her knees pulled up beneath her pink gown. Surely no woman could fake that pale complexion. Or the melancholy that radiated from her in waves.

God. God! He couldn't believe she'd been raped. It was impossible.

Lucas braced his hand on the bedpost. The beliefs that had hardened him for seven years threatened to shift, and with iron effort, he resisted the earthquake. He didn't want to imagine Emma as a desperate girl, driven to marry lest her baby be born a bastard. He didn't want to think of her raising a child alone, enduring the snubs of society. He didn't want to feel this treacherous softening. Or the attendant guilt.

He searched for another way to prove her wrong. "Yet you've had other lovers."

"There's been no one."

He gave a snort of disbelief. "Not even Woodrow Hickey?"

"No! I told you that already."

"Then answer me this," he ground out. "Who did this to you? Who forced you?"

She lowered her gaze. "His name isn't important."

"The hell it isn't." He strode forward, jerking her chin up. "Tell me his name so I can verify your story."

"No."

Her eyes were big with fright, yet she stared obstinately. Seething with fury at his inability to trust her, he began to pace again. "Then that settles it. You must be lying."

She let out an exclamation of disgust. "You wouldn't believe me if I told you the night was dark. You'd have to go to the window to check."

"With you, yes." He paused. "And if a man truly dishonored you, then you should want him to pay for his crime."

"Stop badgering me." Her fingers dug into the counterpane. "You wouldn't find him, anyway. He's left London forever."

Why would she hide the identity of her attacker? Lucas stepped closer to the bed. "Then you should have no qualms about revealing his identity."

Her gaze wavered, then clung to his. "I do, indeed. It's

over with and done. I won't stir up the past and risk Jenny hearing hurtful gossip.''

Emma's voice was sharp, indomitable. The protective mother tigress. By the stubborn set of her jaw, Lucas knew he would not wrest the name from her.

The thought infuriated him. Fool that he was, he found himself half believing her. And it was easier to vent his rage on her assailant than to face his own guilt for leaving her.

But he hadn't abandoned her, not really. She had driven him away. And even if what she claimed were true, it didn't change their present situation. Emma had tricked him in the worst possible way. And now she wanted to deprive him of an heir.

She sat hunched on the bed, her knees hugged to her chin. Tendrils of blond hair drifted around her shoulders. The violet-gray shadows beneath her eyes enhanced her fragile appearance. Against his will, he felt a damnable rush of desire, the undeniable ache to hold her in his arms and hear her whisper words of wanting. For him alone.

"You claim to detest a man's touch," he said coldly. "Yet you asked me for a divorce so you could marry Woodrow Hickey."

"He promised . . . we would have a chaste marriage."

Lucas loosed an incredulous laugh. "I wonder how long that promise would have lasted."

"For as long as I wished it! Woodrow is the perfect gentleman." She looked Lucas up and down, and her lips compressed briefly as if she found him lacking. "*He* loves Jenny and me. We plan to be a family."

A hot, visceral reaction struck Lucas's gut. It was only natural to feel resentment, he told himself. Any man would want to kill the interloper who claimed the affections of his wife. "Hickey must be clay in your pretty hands. I've no doubt he would make the ideal husband for you."

Her eyes widened to a deep, drowning blue. "You'll let me go, then? You'll grant me a divorce?"

The hope brightening her face galled Lucas. Why couldn't she gaze at him with such yearning? He knew the answer.

Emma looked deceptively dainty, but when she wanted her own way, she had a backbone of steel. He would do well to remember that.

He strolled to her side and slid his fingertips down the silk of her cheek. ''In due time, dear wife,'' he murmured. ''For now, I'm afraid our bargain still holds.''

⤬ Chapter 9 ⤬

"Ah, Regent Street at last," Olivia said, peering out the window of the carriage. "I thought we would never arrive."

"Now, Livvie," Phoebe said with a nervous fluttering of her fan. "It's only been fifteen minutes since we left Wortham House."

"I suppose I'm anxious to reach our destination." Lips pursed, Olivia stared across the dim interior at Emma. "To help our dear sister select the new wardrobe our dear brother has been generous enough to provide."

"He wants only the best for you," Phoebe told Emma. "Madame Lascaux is the premier dressmaker in London." Eyes widening, she touched the fan to her plump cheek. "Forgive us. We don't mean to criticize how you're dressed now."

"Of course not," Olivia added politely. "You look quite fetching in gray."

Smoothing the drab gown beneath her ancient pelisse, Emma forced an ironic smile. "Thank you. Though I fear you're being too kind. As always."

The carriage rolled to a stop, and a white-wigged footman swung open the door. As Olivia stepped out, Emma breathed a sigh of relief. Her sisters-in-law had been ill at ease during the short ride, and Emma was more than happy to let them think she might swoon at the least provocation. At least it kept them from going too far with their insults.

She'd been pleased when Phoebe had invited her to go on a shopping expedition, even though Olivia had said with a sniff that Emma must spare Lucas the embarrassment of an ill-clad wife. She'd been tempted to thumb her nose at the lot of them. But the prospect of new clothes proved the greater temptation.

Vanity. She'd thought she'd matured beyond that. Yet a part of her yearned to look pretty again, to sweep back into society and outshine the gossips who'd shunned her. Beauty could be a formidable weapon, and she'd be a fool not to use it.

There was another reason, too, she forced herself to admit. She wanted Lucas to admire her again, instead of viewing her as stained by the past. Sickness churned in her stomach. Why, oh why, had she blurted out the truth to him? He hadn't believed her, anyway.

Accepting the footman's gloved hand, Emma stepped down to the pavement and lifted her face to the afternoon sunshine. She craved its warmth as if the healing rays could burn away the darkness in her soul. For a moment she felt bright and clean again, worthy of a man's love. Then she remembered.

Our bargain still holds.

She mustn't think of that now. She mustn't wonder if Lucas would come to her bed tonight. If he meant to force himself on her, surely he would have done so last night. Instead, he'd uttered his ominous statement, then had turned around and strode out of her bedroom.

As she trailed Olivia and Phoebe toward the dressmaker's shop, Emma happened to glance down the street. A man was hopping down from a public cab. He flipped a coin to the driver and then peered directly at her.

She came to an abrupt halt. Even from a distance, she recognized his drooping eyelid and the sallow cast of his face beneath the battered top hat.

"Come along," called Olivia from the doorway of the modiste's shop. "We've no time for dawdling. I promised my children I would take tea with them."

Emma longed to spend time with Jenny, too. Yet her blood ran cold with urgency. She had to get rid of Clive Youngblood. Before he said something damning in front of her sisters-in-law.

Her palms damp beneath her kid gloves, she lingered by the bowfront window. "You two go on. I—I need to stop at the stationer's next door. I won't be but a moment."

Phoebe ambled inside. Frowning, Olivia primly folded her hands on the gentle mound of her belly. Did she think Emma so brazen as to steal away on a secret liaison? Drat her for being right.

At last, Olivia nodded and disappeared into the shop.

Moistening her dry lips, Emma strolled to the adjacent building and pretended an interest in the stationery supplies displayed in the front window. During the spring Season, throngs of pedestrians crowded Regent Street, carriages were parked two deep along the curbstone, and footmen loitered outside the fashionable shops awaiting their master or mistress. On this late September day, though, few people browsed the elegant storefronts.

Gossip would spread like wildfire if the notorious Lady Wortham were spied conversing with a man of low character. She had to take the risk, but at least she could do so in an inconspicuous place. Casting a quick glance around, Emma slipped down the side alley and girded herself for the inevitable confrontation.

"Ah, m'Lady Wortham. Out spendin' yer 'usband's blunt, I see."

The Bow Street Runner strutted toward her. His chest was puffed out beneath his shabby brown suit as if he fancied himself a gentleman on a stroll.

"Mr. Youngblood," she said with a chilly nod. "Have you lost your way? I'm sure one of the shopkeepers can direct you to your part of town."

He clicked his tongue. "H'ain't you ashamed, insultin' an emissary of the law? You bein' a lady and all."

"State your business and be gone."

"Be pleased to oblige." Regarding her slyly, he rocked

on his heels. "Rumor 'as it, the Bond Street Burglar struck Wortham 'Ouse night before last. Tried to steal a fancy tiger mask, 'e did. But the robber got caught by yer long-lost 'usband."

Emma fixed Clive Youngblood with a frigid stare. "And—?"

"And alas, even though 'e was trussed up like a Christmas goose, our Burglar got clean away. Now 'ow do you s'pose 'e made 'is escape?"

"It is *your* job to find out, Mr. Youngblood."

He hung his head in phony abashment. "Beg pardon. I was only bein'—what do you top-drawers say?—rhetorical."

"Then kindly voice your rambling speculations to someone else."

She started past him, but he stepped out to block her path. The stink of rubbish in the alley was a fitting perfume for him. "I h'ain't done yet," he chided. "Your 'usband gave me only a vague description of the man. I wonder why."

"I suggest you take that up with him."

"Another peculiarity's got me stumped. The robbery 'appened only a day after yer grandsire lost a monkey at that gaming hell in the Strand. Five 'undred pounds, you toffs say. A chap like me could live fer years on such riches." Youngblood snapped his fingers. "And 'twas gone in one night on a roll of the dice."

"If you are quite done—"

"Ah, but I h'ain't come to me point yet. I 'ear tell Lord Briggs don't 'ave the blunt to pay back the gennleman."

This was her chance to find out. "And just who might he be?"

The Runner preened with self-importance. " 'E might be Lord Gerald Mannering."

In the sunless alley, the air took on an arctic chill. Lord Gerald Mannering, Emma thought with a mixture of hot anger and cold elation. So *he* was the young buck who had cleaned out Grandpapa.

She forced herself to gaze straight into the Runner's

heavy-lidded eyes. "Step aside, sir. Else you shall answer to the Marquess of Wortham."

Grinning, Youngblood held his ground. "Speakin' of such, will Wortham pay off yer grandpa's bad debt, eh? Wouldn't fancy seein' the old bloke climbin' over rooftops again. Or you, m'fine lady." He doffed his dented top hat, then sauntered away, whistling.

Emma stood in the alley and rubbed her shoulder, where the old wound ached. Dear God. At least Clive Youngblood wasn't certain which of them was the Burglar. Yet she couldn't have him harassing her grandfather.

She shook off a sense of impending doom. She had the upper hand now. Because now she knew the name of the rogue who held Grandpapa's markers.

For the second time in as many days, Lucas walked into the library and surprised an intruder.

He almost didn't notice her at first. With her back turned to the door, she stood on a crate and poked her small hand inside the opened safe. In her plain brown dress, she blended with the rows of leather-bound books. The afternoon sunlight glistened on the reddish strands in her chestnut braids.

For a moment, Lucas was caught in a maelstrom of fury and denial. To his chagrin, he felt the craven urge to tiptoe from the room before she spied him. Devil take his hesitance. The pint-sized trespasser was rifling through his treasures with the blithe disregard of a six-year-old.

He stepped briskly forward. "Lady Jenny."

She spun around and gasped, her blue-green eyes as round as saucers. Her rosebud mouth formed an O of guilt. Clasping a jade artifact to her flat chest, she hopped off the crate and bobbed a curtsy.

"Well," he said, gesturing at the opened safe. "What is the meaning of this?"

Jenny's gaze shifted downward as if she could find the answer written upon his waistcoat. Very carefully, she placed the statue on the desk. "I'm sorry for touching your things, m'lord. Please don't tell Mama."

Her meek voice and appealing gaze threw him off kilter. "She deserves to know when you've gotten into mischief. Just how the dev—" He paused and amended sternly, "How did you manage to get my safe open?"

"With the key. I heard Mama tell Great-grandpapa it was in the desk drawer."

Like mother, like daughter. No doubt Emma had bragged to her family about her exploits as the Bond Street Burglar.

Or was Lucas mistaken? Had she been driven to thievery out of desperation? Reluctantly he remembered the rundown state of her house, the shabbiness of her clothing, the calluses on her hands. In seven years, she had taken no allowance from him, although she might have done so. The oily Bow Street Runner who'd come nosing about this morning had seemed convinced the robberies were connected to Briggs's gaming debts. Lucas resolved to look into *that*.

He saw Jenny edging toward the door and stepped into her path. "You should not have come in here," he said. "It's wrong to poke about in someone else's things without permission."

The girl pushed out her lower lip. "I only wanted to find what belongs to my mama."

"There's nothing in here of your mother's." Lucas picked up the priceless jade statue of Buddha and placed it inside the repository, closing the door and locking it. He tucked the key into his inner pocket. Then he sat down on the edge of the desk and regarded Jenny. "I think you had better tell me the truth, young lady."

"I am! I was looking for the tiger. It belongs to my mama."

The mask.

Jolted, Lucas leaned forward. "It most certainly does not."

Jenny leaned forward, too, her hands perched on her skinny hips. "It does so! Great-grandpapa said as much. Where have you put our pretty tiger?"

She was a miniature version of Emma, and curiously, the observation took the edge off his anger. "It's in a secret hiding place now. And your great-grandpapa is mistaken. The tiger mask was a gift to me from the maharajah of Jaipur.''

She regarded him suspiciously. "What's a maharajah?"

"A very rich prince from a faraway land called India."

Jenny screwed up her face in doubt. "I don't believe you."

"It's true. He lives in a palace made of ivory and precious stones, and he eats off plates of gold. And he has a real tiger for a pet who wears a jeweled collar." Lucas stopped, surprised at his loquaciousness.

A look of wonder smoothed out Jenny's frown. She took a step closer. "And . . . is the tiger mask really magic like Great-grandpapa says?"

"Some believe so, yes." With a wry grimace, Lucas thought of Shalimar's fantastical prophesy of fertility. The mask had already brought him one child—this unwanted, inquisitive girl.

By law, his daughter.

"Are you going to thrash me?" Jenny asked.

Lucas realized he had balled his fingers into fists, which Jenny eyed with trepidation. She held her chin high like her mother, but he could detect a slight trembling in her shoulders. Good God. He'd never meant to scare the child. "Does your mother spank you when you get into trouble?"

Jenny shook her head, the braids swirling. "Oh, no! She makes me sit in the corner and think about what I did."

"Go back upstairs to the nursery, then, and sit in the corner. Shouldn't you be napping with the other children, anyway?"

"I'm not a baby. I'm nearly six and a half. I'll be seven years old on April the second." She held up seven fingers.

A ruthless ache seized his throat. So Emma had given birth in the spring. He'd always wondered about the exact date. She'd had no husband present to share in her joy. Or to comfort her in her suffering.

A man forced me.

Could he have been wrong about Emma? Her agonized

confession haunted Lucas, had kept him awake half the night, staring into the dark and wondering. If it was true, who was the scoundrel who'd impregnated her?

Lucas scrutinized Jenny for a clue to her father's identity. But he could see only Emma in those pixie features. He couldn't imagine how any man could abandon his own child, even at the risk of scandal.

"Six and a half is a very great age, indeed," he said. "No doubt you are old enough to know right from wrong." He had the strangest urge to talk further with her. But if his mother were to walk in and see this child who had caused so much strife in the family, she would have a relapse. "Now go on with you. Find a quiet spot in the nursery and reflect upon your misdeed."

"Yes, m'lord." Jenny started to trudge away, then swung back, opening her mouth and pointing to a gap in her top front teeth. "I have a loose tooth. See?"

Before he could respond, she skipped out of the library, her heels kicking up the hem of her too-short brown dress.

An unexpected pang of longing tightened Lucas's chest. How darling she was, how uncannily like the daughters he'd once hoped to have.

Glowering at the empty doorway, he disciplined the tender ache within himself. Lady Jenny Coulter meant nothing to him. She was Emma's child, Emma's responsibility, Emma's to love. Eventually, the two of them would leave this house forever.

No, if he felt any yearning, it was only because he wanted children of his own. *His own.*

And the sooner, the better.

Huddled in her voluminous nightgown, Emma sat at the gilt writing desk in her bedroom and thumbed through a stack of invitations. Apparently the news of her reconciliation with Wortham had spread faster than a brushfire. It seemed every noble family who had not left town for the country now planned a rout or a dance party or a musicale.

Unfortunately, Lord Gerald Mannering was not among them.

Emma ruffled the invitations as if they were a hateful deck of cards. She had hoped to gain entry to Mannering's house in a legitimate fashion, and to execute a daring theft in the midst of his party. Now she might have to resort to her usual modus operandi. And the mere thought of clambering on rooftops in the disguise of the Burglar gave her the shivers.

Closing her eyes, she placed her head in her hands. It was true; she had lost her nerve. Not only was she afraid of being shot, she feared Clive Youngblood. One wrong move and he would be waiting to arrest her. To separate her from Jenny forever.

Somehow, Emma had to obtain the funds to pay off Grandpapa's debt. Quietly and quickly. She would not take jewels from anyone but the man who had bilked him; that was the only way she maintained her self-respect. Nor could she bring herself to beg the money from Lucas. This dilemma was not of his making—

"Pining for your husband, I trust," spoke a deep, mocking voice.

She whirled around, almost oversetting the dainty chair. Like a demon materialized from the underworld, Lucas stood behind her. He had discarded the hunter's-green coat and waistcoat he had worn to dinner with the family. Clad in breeches and shirt, he had removed his stiff white cravat as well, and his shirt was unbuttoned to reveal a wedge of bronzed chest.

Emma swallowed, her heart thudding in her throat. She wore a new nightrail she had obtained from the dressmaker today; the other articles of clothing would be delivered later in the week. Though the white gown covered her from high neck down to bare toes, she was acutely conscious of her nakedness beneath.

"I was just—" Flustered, she paused. "I was looking at some invitations, my lord. Perhaps you would care to see them."

He watched her as a cat might watch a mouse. "Accept

whichever ones you like. It matters little to me.''

"You surely must have some opinion.''

"Only on more important matters.'' He walked to the bed-side table and placed something there. It was a small earthenware jar she had not noticed him carrying. Then he returned to her side and held out his hand. "Come.''

Her pulse increased its tempo. She stared numbly at his outstretched palm. His skin was the shade of teakwood, his fingers long and blunt-tipped.

Sweet Jesus. A man's hand. Capable of violence.

"Don't panic,'' he said calmly. "I shan't ravish you.''

Disbelieving, she lifted her gaze to his. With the candle-light carving shadows beneath his aristocratic cheekbones, he looked fearfully handsome. "Won't you?''

"Not without invitation.''

Reaching out, he took her by the hand and drew her to her feet. He stood there a moment, lightly running his finger over the clean linen bandage wrapping her palm. "The mark of courage, I wonder?'' he murmured. "Or of a coward fleeing her just reward?''

"I'm not a coward,'' she snapped.

"I'm pleased to hear that.'' His grasp was warm and firm, inspiring a tenuous trust. Emma found herself following him to the large, four-poster bed. There, to her alarm, he began to undo the small pearl buttons down the back of her nightgown.

She twisted around to face him. "You promised you wouldn't ravish me.''

"True. Yet I made no promise about not touching you.'' His expression was hard, intense. "And you *will* want that, Emma.''

"But—''

He put his finger over her lips, lightly yet insistently. "I make the rules. And I pledge not to consummate the act until you're ready.''

She quivered. "Then it won't happen. Not ever.''

A small smile revealed the dimples in his cheeks. "We shall see. Now lie down. On your stomach.''

The secret knowledge in his golden-brown eyes frightened her. What did he mean to do to her? And how could she refuse him?

No choice. No choice. No choice. . . .

Clasping the nightgown tightly against her breasts, Emma crawled onto the bed and lay herself down. The linens smelled like starch and sunshine. As she buried her face in the pillow, she was keenly aware of the opened buttons at her back. She felt as helpless as a sacrificial lamb.

No. She would not let him intimidate her. She would endure his vile touch with dignity. She would prove her mettle.

The mattress dipped to one side under his weight. His fingers brushed her vulnerable neck as he parted the back of her nightgown. Cool air whispered over her exposed skin, and she shivered in spite of her resolve to be brave.

Leaving her laid bare to the waist, he rose from the bed, and she heard him kick off his shoes. There was a small clinking noise, followed by the unexpected sound of him rubbing his hands together. Dear God, what torture was he planning?

She turned her head to peek just as Lucas got back onto the bed. This time, instead of perching on the edge, he straddled her, his powerful legs pinning her in place. He did not put his full weight on her, yet his groin nestled in the cradle where her buttocks and thighs met.

She clenched her teeth to contain a craven whimper. "Don't forget your promise."

"I never forget a promise," he said with a trace of irony.

Her nightgown had ridden up to her knees, and she could feel the fine cloth of his breeches. At least he wasn't naked.

His hands descended to her upper back, and she flinched. He slowly traced the knobs of her spine, his palms slick with an oily substance. She could smell the fragrance of it, potent and exotic. To her startlement, he began to knead the tight muscles of her shoulders and back.

His touch felt surprisingly good. The warmth of his body flowed into her, and the pressure he exerted was more pleasant than offensive. The ever-present fear drifted away like so much smoke. After all, hadn't he vowed not to force her into a carnal act?

Against her better judgment, she could feel herself relaxing, sinking deeper into the bed, her limbs melting like butter. Her eyelids drifted shut. Oddly, the heat of his massage burrowed deep within herself, as if a ray of sunshine glowed in the pit of her belly, and she found herself basking in the pleasure of it.

She lost track of time. After a while, he shifted position to stroke his hands over her feet, her calves, her thighs. Just as he neared her privates and she began to tense again, he moved to her fingers, her arms, and then her neck. He rubbed soothingly, compellingly, up and down her sides, and a curious thrill unfurled in Emma. She no longer minded his hands being inside her nightdress. It was almost as if Lucas were embracing her, caressing her, loving her. She craved the gentleness of his touch, oh yes, she did. Never had she dreamed she could so trust a man. . . .

His fingers brushed the sides of her bare breasts. Though she lay on her stomach, he delved deeper beneath her, moving slowly, until he cupped her in his warm palms. Still caught by languor, Emma floated in a strange aura of wonder. Then he lazily stroked his thumbs over the sensitive tips.

She could feel his swollen hardness against her bottom. She gasped as a jolt of physical sensation slapped her to an awareness of his sexual intent. A surge of panic rose to glut her throat. Trapped by his body, she half twisted herself to glare at him.

"Stop it! You've no right to touch me so."

"Don't I." It was not a question.

He removed his hands and sat back, a large and menacing presence in the candlelight. Fire gleamed in his tiger's eyes, and through his opened shirt, his chest was muscled and bronzed against the white linen.

Her flesh still burned where he'd touched her. Panic hovered at the edge of her consciousness. She'd been a fool to lower her guard with him, a man she no longer knew. He could do with her whatever he willed. And he did have the right. She had given it to him when she'd uttered her vows of holy wedlock.

Quite unexpectedly, he lifted himself from her and leapt nimbly to the floor. He went to the bedside table, picked up the small jar, and held it out to her.

"What's that?" she asked, cautiously sitting up.

"Scented oil."

Ignoring the jar, she hitched the bodice of her nightgown higher over her aching breasts. "I've had quite enough for one night. Or are you going to force me to accept your touch?"

"No." His mouth crooked into a half-smile, a devilish smile, and he began to unfasten his shirt. "Now it's your turn to touch me."

☙ Chapter 10 ☜

*H*e was a glutton for punishment, Lucas decided.

Wearing only his breeches, he lay prone on the bed, his cheek pressed to the pillow that bore the haunting fragrance of Emma. Beside him his wife perched like a nymph about to take flight. The feel of her hands on him was exquisite torture. He wanted to draw her down beneath him, to make violent love to her until he sated this damnable craving.

But she had been misused once, and she feared intimacy. His mission was to awaken his wife to the joys of physical love. Only then could he achieve his objective—to impregnate Emma.

Small fingers stroked tentatively over his back. The occasional brush of the linen bandage only heightened his awareness of her. She hadn't quite mastered the technique of applying pressure, of kneading his muscles, but he didn't care. She was touching him. That in itself was a miracle.

The massage coiled the tension inside him. Every inch of his back felt scorched. So did a certain other place she didn't touch.

She *would* caress him there—eventually. He had only to exercise the patience of a saint.

But God, she was killing him softly. The memory of the lush warmth of her breasts tormented him. He could feel himself sweating. He was alone in the bedroom with his own wife, and he couldn't have her. Not yet.

Lucas closed his eyes and concentrated on his breathing, making it slow and even. In and out. In and out. In and out. Instead of distracting him, the rhythm inspired another torturous fantasy.

He forced his thoughts to his estate in Northumbria. He would go there soon, ride over the rugged countryside. He would take Emma with him. She would be wild for him as he laid her down beneath an oak tree and stripped the clothes from her. . . .

Hell. This time, he tried turning his mind to Shalimar, and guilt sobered him. So far, the search for her kidnapped son had yielded only a cold trail. He'd spent the day tracking down yet another false clue. Tomorrow he would enlist Hajib to help trace that devil O'Hara.

It was the least Lucas could do. His mistress was patient and serene, everything he wanted in a woman. Their separation was only temporary. He would devote himself to her again. After he had planted a child in his wife.

How quickly would Emma conceive once he seduced her? He might have to make love to her for many nights before his seed took root. For many long and languid nights he could indulge the throbbing of his blood, the primitive instinct to mate with his woman. . . .

He was throbbing now. It took all his willpower not to turn over, to reach for Emma and end his torment by sinking into her. She would be hot and slick, a tight silken glove. The thought was maddeningly erotic. He would make their pleasure last, build sensation to the very peak of arousal. Then he would bring both of them to sweet, shuddering climax.

The stroking of her hands came to a gradual stop. She drew away quietly, and the bedropes didn't creak, so slowly did she leave his side.

Lucas lifted his head to see Emma tiptoeing toward the dressing room. "Where the devil are you going?" he growled.

She spun around with a gasp. "Lucas! I—I thought you were asleep."

"Asleep." He couldn't help a disgruntled grin. "Hardly."

She clasped her hands in front of her, an unlikely angel in her pure white nightgown, wisps of fair hair tumbling around her shoulders. "I'm terribly weary," she said in a small, meek voice. "Please don't take offense, but I must ask you to leave now."

Like hell you're tired. Seeing the wary desperation in her eyes, he bit back the retort. It was best not to push her. Best to keep chipping away at her defenses bit by bit. Best to ignore the hot pressure inside his breeches.

He rose from the bed and walked to Emma. Taking her chin between his fingers, he tilted up her face. Silvery-blond tendrils framed her perfect features, a breathtaking testimonial to a benevolent Creator.

She was his. His alone.

Cupping her face in his hands, Lucas kissed her slowly and deeply, letting his lips convey a promise of provocative pleasures to come. He felt the resistance in her, the alarm that stiffened her muscles. He thought he sensed also the agitation in her as the natural desires of her body waged war with her fears.

When he lifted his head, he was gratified that Emma no longer flinched from him. Her eyes were huge and blue, her mouth reddened from his kiss. He glided his fingertip down the charming slope of her nose. He knew now that her skin was even more creamy-soft elsewhere on her body, and the prospect of further exploration tantalized him.

It was too soon, though. Regrettably, he must resist her for now.

Bending close to her ear, he murmured, "Until next time."

Until next time.

Emma could still hear the echo of Lucas's parting words the following afternoon as she strolled with Sir Woodrow along the Serpentine in Hyde Park. Jenny skipped ahead on the earthen path, scuffing through fallen leaves in her eagerness to feed a family of swans gliding near the shoreline of the water.

It was annoying to think of her husband instead of the early autumn splendor of the park, Emma reflected. Wasn't it enough that he had spoiled her evening? Long after he had disappeared through the connecting door to his own suite, she had lain awake in the darkness, remembering how sleek and hard his back muscles had felt, how broad and imposing his shoulders were, how firm and narrow his waist. If she closed her eyes, she could smell the aroma of exotic oil blended with the musky scent of male.

An uneasy warmth lurked in the pit of her stomach. Never had she imagined herself touching a man so intimately. And of her own free will.

No, not free. Lucas had given her an impossible choice: prison . . . or procreation. She subdued an ironic chuckle. What a comedic farce she was playing! A marionette show—and Lucas was the puppet master.

"My dear, you are frowning quite fiercely," Sir Woodrow said. "Are you certain it's wise for us to walk together? If Wortham were to find out . . ."

She looked up into his steadfast gray eyes. "My husband does not govern my actions. Nor does he choose my companions."

"Yet I worry he might mistreat you. I fail to understand why he insists upon you and Jenny living there with him."

She took a deep breath. Woodrow deserved to know the truth. "That's what I needed to talk to you about today. You see . . ." A flush heated her cheeks, but she forced out the words. "He wants me to bear him an heir."

Woodrow stopped dead. His cheeks paled to ghostly gray. "What? That's outrageous! He abandoned you for seven years. He cannot demand your affections now."

"He doesn't care about my affections," Emma admitted. "He merely wants a son. As soon as I give him one, he's promised to seek a divorce."

Woodrow drew her beneath the spreading limbs of a chest-nut tree, out of Jenny's earshot. "And what if you bear him a girl?'' he asked. ''You might have a dozen daughters.''

The possibility worried Emma. How could she stay with Lucas for years? And how could she leave her children behind when she left?

Desolation washed over her, and she blinked to clear the hot dryness that stung her eyes. She mustn't think of that wrenching moment now, lest she go mad. ''Yes, I might have to bear him more than one child. And so . . .'' She paused, swallowing hard. ''So I wanted to offer you the chance to end our association. I cannot ask you to wait years for me.''

''You most certainly can,'' Woodrow asserted. He pressed her gloved hands chastely. ''Don't you know? I would wait forever for you, my dear.''

''But you deserve a wife, children of your own.''

''No other lady will do. Nor any other child but Jenny.'' Glancing at the girl, who stood among the reeds, tossing breadcrusts to the swans, Woodrow scowled. ''Blast Wortham! It's barbaric of him to demand you bear his son. Let the cad divorce you now, and *he* can marry someone else.''

Emma shook her head. ''He won't. He claims to love only his mistress. A foreign woman he met in his travels.'' To counter the rise of resentment, she strove for a droll tone. ''At least *I* come from excellent breeding stock.''

Woodrow shook his fist with rare vehemence. ''Breeding stock, bah. You're a lady who deserves to be honored.''

His unflinching support gratified her. Yet Emma couldn't bring herself to tell him that Lucas held the threat of jail like a guillotine blade over her neck. Woodrow didn't know about her masquerade as the Burglar.

''Lucas wants his own son to carry on the family name,'' she said resolutely. ''And I owe him a debt beyond measure. Without him, Jenny would have been born a bastard.''

''Yet considering the way Wortham has ignored her, the dear child might as well have been born out of wedlock.''

An agonizing remorse pierced Emma. ''Do you think I did wrong by her? At the time, I had no other recourse.''

Woodrow's frown lessened. ''Oh, my dear, I've upset you

now. Please forgive me. I'm angry at Wortham, not you. And of course you did right. It's only—''

"Only?"

"Had I only known sooner, had I already resigned my commission, *I* would have been proud to marry you. And even prouder to be a father to Jenny." He shifted his moody gaze toward the girl.

An aching love filled Emma as she watched Jenny, so intent on her mission to divide the crumbs equally among the birds. Never, not for all the jewels in the world, would she let her daughter come to harm.

She turned back to Woodrow. "We *can* marry . . . afterward. He'll set me free, then. He's given me his word."

"His word. Will you trust a man who knows so little of gentlemanlike behavior?"

"I have to," Emma said in a low voice. "It's the only way to win my liberty."

Woodrow grasped her hands with sudden fierceness. "If you wish to defy him, Emma, you'll have my staunch support. We can depart England together—live on the Continent. I'll take care of you and Jenny. And treat the two of you with all due respect."

His fervent offer took Emma aback. She withdrew her hands. "No. I—I couldn't do that. As I said, I feel an obligation to Lucas."

"So to suit his selfish purposes, he'll keep me from you and Jenny." The bitterness of pain etching his face, Woodrow gazed at the girl, who had doled out her supply of breadcrusts and now collected leaves on the pathway.

The soughing of the wind through the willows sounded sad and lonely to Emma. How frustrated Woodrow must be, for he had waited patiently to marry her, only to have his hopes dashed. Seven years ago, he had returned from the battlefields of Portugal to find her pregnant and alone, abandoned by her bridegroom, and under the dubious guardianship of her prodigal grandfather. Woodrow had lent a sympathetic ear during the difficult weeks of late pregnancy and then had helped her through the trials of motherhood, treating little Jenny as if she were his own daughter. Never had he chastised Emma for conceiving a child out of wedlock, nor had he probed for the name of Jenny's father. Yet Emma sometimes wondered why he didn't. . . .

A gust of wind snatched off Jenny's bonnet and sent it tumbling down the path. Laughing, she chased after it, and Woodrow dashed in pursuit. He caught the bonnet and held it aloft like a prize of war. The two of them fought a mock battle. Then he placed the bonnet over her chestnut braids and bent down to tie the green ribbons beneath her chin.

Watching them, Emma bit down hard on her lip. She felt safe with him, protected from harm. On more than one occasion, when a gentleman had attempted to procure her services as whore, Woodrow had defended her honor. Never had he treated her as less than a lady. And never had he pressed his physical attentions upon her. He was content with a fond peck on her cheek.

Unlike Lucas.

Emma shivered from more than the cold wind. With Lucas, she had the disquieting sense of being stalked by a tiger. It was in his eyes, the hunger, the relentlessness, the pitiless pursuit of the predator. He would come to her night after night until he had claimed what he wanted: her body, his for the taking. Her stomach fluttered with a troubling mixture of dread and anticipation. She despised his manhandling of her. That must be why she could not banish the memory of his heated hands on her breasts.

Until next time.

"A rather paltry gathering, to be sure," Olivia commented, scanning the half-empty ballroom, where a group of musicians tuned their instruments in an alcove. "Those people with sense enjoy the autumn months at their estates in the country."

"And here, there are only those too dissipated to stay away from the gaming tables of the city," Emma whispered back. "And those too dull to know the difference."

Olivia's mouth twitched. Her eyes took on a merry sparkle. ''And I wonder where that leaves us—'' Abruptly, she clamped her lips into a tight line and swung her attention back toward the dance floor.

Unwilling to let her disappointment show, Emma restrained a sigh. Perhaps Olivia would never let down her guard. It shouldn't matter, since Emma had no intention of remaining a part of Lucas's family.

Yet it did matter. To be here at a ball with Olivia reminded Emma of happier times. No, not happier, for now she had Jenny and a deeper, richer meaning to her life. So what was the right word to describe herself at eighteen? Carefree . . . whimsical . . . naïve. It was a time when she had been innocent of the realities of life.

The light from hundreds of candles in the crystal chandeliers cast a golden glow over the glittering scene. Emma controlled her queasiness about this, her first evening back in society. She and Olivia had walked on ahead of Lucas and Olivia's husband, Hugh. Phoebe had stayed home since one of her children was ill, and Lucas's mother had also pleaded an indisposition. Aware of an awkward silence now, Emma was about to suggest to Olivia that they take a stroll around the room when their host and hostess swooped down on them like twin birds of prey.

Emma's skin crawled. She was not unnerved by an encounter with the snooty Lady Jasper. It was her stout husband who caused the tension in Emma. She had last seen Lord Jasper Putney over the smoking barrel of his pistol.

''Ah, my dear Olivia,'' Lady Jasper Putney said, blinking her brown bug-eyes. ''So pleased you could attend, considering your happy circumstances.'' She glanced at Olivia's gently rounded belly.

''I'm pleased to be here, though I believe I will sit out the dancing,'' Olivia said with a smile. ''Wortham has returned, you will have heard. Otherwise, Hugh and I would be rusticating in the country.''

''Then we have his long-absent lordship to thank. And this must be Lady Wortham.'' One large eye magnified further by her quizzing glass, Lady Jasper subjected Emma to a keen scrutiny as if she were a specimen in a museum. A rather nasty specimen. "I recollect your wedding, madam. You were rather pale that day. Too pale even for a bride."

The innuendo hurt even though Emma had braced herself for sly comments. "How kind of you to remember me," she said with studied cheer. "I've kept my dancing shoes polished, ready for another foray into your house."

"But I don't believe you've been here before." Lady Jasper shook her wispy brown ringlets. "In truth, since we only just let the place two years ago, I'm certain you haven't."

Not to your knowledge at least, Emma thought with silent mirth. Smiling was so much easier when she was privy to a private joke.

Olivia briefly slipped her arm through Emma's. "My sister is looking the very height of fashion. Do you not think she is as pretty as ever?"

"Well, I . . ." Lady Jasper sputtered.

"I most certainly do," rumbled Lord Jasper.

Baffled by Olivia's defense of her, Emma reluctantly turned her gaze to her host. He was the picture of dissipation. His protruding belly strained the gold buttons of his maroon waistcoat. Spidery red veins webbed his cheeks and nose. He clutched a nearly empty glass in his beefy hand.

He thrust the glass at a passing servant. Then he bowed over Emma's hand, and she controlled a shudder, glad for the shield of her long white gloves. Even so, she felt a bubble of laughter rise to her throat. By his idiot grin, he clearly had no clue as to her secret identity.

She couldn't resist asking, "Are you not the hero who shot the infamous Bond Street Burglar?"

"'Deed so. He was a fierce villain, the stuff of nightmares. But I kept a clear head. I got out my pistol, took steady aim"—Putney sighted down the barrel of an imaginary gun—"and *pow*! Winged the fearsome blackguard."

Emma resisted the urge to rub her shoulder. "What a pity he got away, then."

"Luck of the devil," Putney grumbled.

"Unfortunately for us," Olivia said darkly. "He stole into

my brother's house a few nights ago. Dressed all in black like a demon. He frightened us out of our wits.''

"Boo," said Lucas, coming up from behind them.

Emma jumped as her husband's warm and heavy hand settled at the back of her waist. His presence coincided with a sudden weakness in her knees. She had the irritating impulse to lean against him for support. Instead, she stood ramrod straight, looking anywhere but at him.

Olivia's husband chuckled. Slender and even-featured, Hugh gazed fondly at his wife. "If you'd awakened me, I would have been glad to defend you," he said. "However, all's well that ends well."

"But the cunning criminal is still at large," Lady Jasper said with a refined shiver. "One cannot feel safe these days, not even in one's own home. Where will the Burglar strike next?"

While their hostess spoke, Lucas slid his hand up Emma's spine to her shoulderblades. Starbursts of sensation marked the path of his touch. She felt her limbs dissolving as they had the night before. The cad. With the large potted plant behind them, she was certain no one could see him kneading the place where the bullet had exited.

"I'd venture to guess the Burglar has lost his nerve," he told their hostess. "Getting caught in his last two robberies has surely taken a toll on his confidence."

"And I helped put him out of commission," boasted Lord Jasper. "Come along, Wortham, Hugh. We'll have us a round or two of cards in the drawing room."

"As you like. Unless my wife desires me"—Lucas paused a bare instant—"to dance."

Emma looked sharply up at him, and her heart stumbled over a beat. Those golden eyes gleamed a dark promise in the candlelight. How dare he tease her in public—and question her confidence as the Burglar.

Playing the demure miss, she curtsied. "Do not let me keep you from your amusements, my lord."

He lightly tapped the end of her nose. "Save a waltz for me."

Lucas strolled away with the other two men as they headed into the drawing room. Emma's skin burned where he had touched her. She didn't like the sensation. No, she did not.

Lady Jasper and Olivia stood together, trading stories about the Burglar, but Emma had lost her taste for baiting them. It was just as well Lucas had left her. She had a mission tonight, a reason for coming here that no one else must guess. This was precisely the sort of event Lord Gerald Mannering might attend.

She excused herself from the ladies and struck off on her own. As she made her way through the throng of guests, she ignored the shocked glances, the whispers behind fluttering fans. Emma knew she looked stunning in her gown of clarence-blue silk with scalloped embroidery along the hem and sleeves, and her mother's pearls gleaming at her throat. She had dressed soberly for so long, she had nearly forgotten how a fine appearance could lend power to a woman. She needed the extra edge. Suffering the arch looks of the ladies and the lusty leers of the gentlemen, she smiled coolly, nodding like a queen to those subjects she recognized.

It had been important to her at one time to have men fawning over her like so many butterflies around a bloom. But no more. Now she must concentrate on keeping Grandpapa out of debtor's prison.

Where *was* Lord Gerald Mannering? Perhaps he had left town in the few days since milking her grandfather of five hundred pounds.

Emma tempered that hope with reason. Surely he would not depart without collecting on his markers. And if she remembered him well enough, he wouldn't miss a soiree like this one.

There was only one place left to look, the most logical place—and the most dangerous one. Keeping a smile firmly fixed on her face, she strolled through the crowded foyer and peeked into the drawing room.

The long chamber was elegantly appointed in mint-green with gilt cherubs grinning down from the ceiling. A number of guests, men and ladies alike, sat at the small tables that had been set up for card playing. As she looked for Lord Gerald's distinctive copper curls, she spied the dark hair of her husband instead. Her heart lurched. He sat with Hugh and Lord Jasper. At the moment Lucas was studying his cards, and she prayed he wouldn't look up and wonder at her purpose.

"It must be my lucky night," drawled a male voice in her ear. "To see my dearest Emma again."

She whirled around and blinked at the object of her search. While she stood stupefied, Lord Gerald Mannering reached for her hand and brought it to his lips. In full view of the assembly of guests, he planted a lingering kiss in her gloved palm. His action jolted Emma to her senses.

She quickly drew him to the side of the doorway. Smiling brilliantly, she said, "I am Lady Wortham now."

"To the wounded hearts of a score of gentlemen. I myself have been pining these past seven years." He paused, a lusty slyness brightening his brown eyes. "Would you care for a stroll in the garden? The moon is lovely tonight."

With an arrogance he wouldn't have displayed before her fall from grace, he hauled Emma by the arm down the corridor leading toward the back of the house. Alarmed and incensed, she stopped by a large brass urn on a pedestal. They were still within sight of the other guests, and Lord Gerald scowled, apparently reluctant to drag her and cause a scene.

She mustered a flirtatious smile. "Oh, la, my lord. My husband is present. Pray keep in mind he is a very jealous man."

"And your grandfather is a very indebted man," Lord Gerald countered, while ogling her breasts. "I merely thought to suggest there are ways other than money to repay a debt."

His blatant offer made Emma ill. She was tired of being presumed promiscuous, tired of feeling shame for the loss of her reputation. "What makes you think my husband will not repay the debt?"

"Because he told me so himself. Paid a call on me today at my club."

Lucas *knew*? And he had refused to save her grandfather from disgrace? Cold surprise shuddered through her. She ought to have expected as much from a man so changed. She ought to . . . and yet she hadn't.

Smirking, Lord Gerald leaned closer and grasped her hand. A diamond stickpin winked in his cravat like a third eye. "Briggs has only a fortnight to pay up. So, my lady, perhaps you'll think twice about my proposition. Answer quickly, for there's Wortham now."

Scanning the crowd, Lucas stood outside the drawing room. She knew the instant he spotted her. His gaze narrowed and his countenance seemed to darken. Then he strode toward them, his footsteps ringing like a death knell down the corridor.

Emma made a swift and rash decision. "Are you planning any parties at your house in the next fortnight?" she whispered to Lord Gerald.

"A ball next week. But that's hardly the time for you and I—"

"Invite me," she hissed. "And trust me, your debt shall be repaid in full." *With the money from your own fenced jewels,* she thought. *Perhaps even that lovely stickpin. . . .*

Not a moment later, Lucas's fingers closed around her arm. A dark thrill quivered through her, and she turned with a gay, determined smile. The effort was lost on him, for he was glowering at her companion. "Mannering," he said. "What an unpleasant surprise."

"Wortham." Lord Gerald bowed, the handsomeness of his face spoiled by his twisted smile. "I was just commenting on the danger of leaving such a lovely woman alone for so many years."

"It's nothing compared to the danger of touching my wife."

The two men shared a long, hard look. Then Lord Gerald chuckled, stepping back from Emma. "She's all yours, Wortham. Far be it from me to keep two cooing doves apart."

"Have a care," Lucas said. "Lest you find yourself challenged by a hawk, instead." With that, he propelled her away from the party, through a glass-paned door at the rear of the house, and out into the chilly night.

Their footsteps scraped on the flagstone path of the garden. An occasional lantern cast a circle of light through the gloom, and large black lumps of shrubbery gave the small area an ominous aura. The pungent odor of the mews came from beyond the brick fence.

A gust of cold wind made Emma shiver. So did a glance upward to the cramped ledge along the top floor of the row of town houses. It was there, nearly six months earlier, that she had made her way, dazed and bleeding, narrowly escaping disaster.

"Why did you drag me out of the house?" she asked. "It can't have been simply to ruin my evening."

"I want some answers. Specifically, one answer."

He spoke harshly, furiously. Her irritation at his high-handedness faltered beneath her budding alarm. A frisson of unease coursed over her skin. Music lilted from the ballroom, but they were alone out here in this intimate, enclosed garden.

She stopped by a small fountain that gurgled water from the mouth of a satyr. "Well, *I* want my pelisse," she said, searching for an excuse to escape back indoors. "It's chilly out here."

"Take this, then." He shrugged out of his coat and draped it around her shoulders.

Automatically she burrowed into the big garment. His body warmth wrapped around her like an embrace. "There was no need for you to make a scene in there," she said. "I've done nothing wrong. Lord Gerald and I were merely renewing an old acquaintance."

"Ah, so I was right," Lucas said tersely. "You two have known each other for quite a long time."

He loomed over her, and shadows shrouded his expression. She could hear him breathing in the darkness, could feel the pounding of her heart. Warmth pulsed in the depths of her stomach. He knew of Grandpapa's debt. Yet surely he couldn't have guessed at her plan to play the Burglar again.

That left only one impossible, yet logical explanation for his abrupt behavior. He was jealous. Jealous that she had been speaking with an attractive rogue.

Flush with power, she couldn't resist needling him. "Lord Gerald once courted me, yes. Does that bother you?"

"It does," Lucas grated. "Is he the one?"

"What one?"

He caught her arms in the vises of his hands. "Christ, Emma, don't play games with me. I want the truth for once."

Bewildered, she blinked at his tall, dark shape in the gloom. "The truth about what?"

"Tell me," he said, his voice strained, as if pulled from a well of fury. "Did Mannering father Jenny?"

๑๑ Chapter 11 ๑๑

Lucas had not meant to fling the question so bluntly. He should have waited until later, when they were alone in her bedroom, when he could read Emma's expression in the candlelight. But he couldn't delay, not when he burned with the need to uncover the truth.

"No," she murmured. Then more vehemently, "No, confound you!"

Disdainful surprise lifted her voice. In spite of his rage, he found himself believing her. Lord Gerald Mannering was not her rapist.

Lucas experienced no surge of relief. Instead he felt cheated, deprived of the chance to strike out at that lecherous jackass. "Then who?" he demanded. "Tell me who fathered your child."

"Remove your hands, you brute."

He realized he held her arms in a bruising grip. "Forgive me," he grunted, letting loose of her. "Now answer my question."

She turned away and rubbed her arms beneath his coat. "You may be my husband in the eyes of the law, but I don't have to bare my soul to you."

He strode around in front of her, forcing her to look at him. "If you expect me to believe you, I deserve to know his name, by God. Were it not for his vicious act, you wouldn't have married me."

"Don't you think I know that?" she flung back. "Don't you think I would have acted more honorably had not the welfare of my child been at stake?"

Moonlight painted the purity of her skin and the agony in her eyes. He girded himself against a rush of tenderness. Her beauty was only a shell, he reminded himself. "No, I don't know what you think," he said. "I cannot trust you to be honest with me."

"I could say the same about you." She poked her finger at his chest. "Why didn't you tell me you knew about Grandpapa's debt to Lord Gerald?"

Lucas lifted his shoulders in an impatient shrug. "It's a man's business, that's why."

She stabbed him with her finger again. As if she thought she still had the ability to hurt him. "And you refused to repay his debt. You, who brought back riches beyond a nabob's dream."

Bitter accusation tainted her voice, and Lucas regretted he couldn't put his arms around her and hold her, just hold her close. Devil take it. Devil take *her*. That sort of affectionate intimacy belonged between two people who loved each other.

He paced back and forth along the flagstone path. "No, I won't save his skin. It's high time Briggs learned to pay the consequences of his actions. My rescuing him—*your* rescuing him—will only tempt him back to the gaming tables. He'll keep losing money until he beggars me."

"So to prove your point, you would throw an old man into Fleet Prison."

"He can't be jailed for a gaming debt. It isn't legal."

"But he *can* be jailed if he runs up other legitimate debts because all his assets are spent paying back Lord Gerald."

"It won't come to that. Briggs is resourceful. Give him the chance and he'll manage to come up with the blunt." Against the dank odor of humus, Emma smelled fresh and flowery. Her hair shone as pale as moonbeams. Through the shifting shadows, she looked small and fragile, incapable of deception. But Lucas knew better. "And you are not to play the Burglar again in this situation with Mannering. Is that clear?''

She stood very still. Too still. ''Why would you think I would?''

He controlled the urge to shake a truthful answer out of her. ''You were flirting with him. Since you profess to despise men, you must have had an ulterior motive.''

''I wasn't flirting, I was being polite,'' she said, huffing out an indignant breath. ''And if you must know, *he* approached *me*.''

Lucas clenched his fists. Unprepared for his resurgence of wrath, he took a step closer. ''If the knave made you an indecent proposal—''

Her trill of laughter warmed the cold night air. ''We exchanged a few pleasantries, nothing more. It's what we social butterflies do at parties.'' She strolled to the fountain and gracefully seated herself on the rim. Then she dipped her chin coyly and gazed up at him. ''You aren't jealous, are you?''

He gritted his teeth, glad the darkness hid his flush. Though his coat swallowed her shoulders, he could see the gleam of white flesh revealed by her bodice, and a damnable desire heated him. She was his, by God. All his. ''You mistake my purpose, madam. This time, I intend to make certain the child you bear is mine.''

She gave a little jump as if she'd sat upon a nettle. ''Why don't you keep me under lock and key?'' she snapped. ''Then you wouldn't have to follow me about, spying on whomever I happen to speak to.''

''Don't tempt me. Now, I would have the name of the man who attacked you.''

''No.''

Her stubbornness irritated him. Why did he have the peculiar feeling she was protecting her despoiler? ''If you don't tell me, I'll find out somehow. I swear it to you.''

Her sharp intake of air cut through the gloom. ''Don't you dare poke into my past. It's no concern of yours.''

''I beg to differ. There is a man somewhere who should

be held accountable for his crime. I will not rest until I've had my revenge on him.''

Emma lowered her head a moment, and the water played musically into the silence. When she spoke, he had to strain to hear her. ''Do you truly wish to defend my honor, then?'' she asked wistfully.

He didn't want to glimpse vulnerability in her. It shook the foundation of his resentment and made him question his cold-blooded plan. ''My reason, dear wife, has little to do with you. I wish to ruin the bastard's life. To repay him for ruining mine.''

''Why, you . . . you *oaf*!'' Her hands gripped the stone edge of the fountain as if it were his throat. ''You selfish, unfeeling *lout*. I'm willing to admit I did you a terrible wrong, but you can't see your way to forgiveness. All you can do is rant on and on about a past that can't be changed. I ought to have married Sir Woodrow. *He* never pesters me so. *He* respects my desire for privacy.''

''Then Hickey is a craven ass.''

''Hah. He's ten times the man *you* are.''

''Is he? I wonder.''

Provoked by her scorn, Lucas took two strides forward and hauled her up from the fountain, crushing her slender form against his. His coat slipped to the ground, leaving her shoulders bare. Never in his life had he been more aware of a woman, of hating her and craving her all at the same time.

Her eyes shone darkly in the moonlight. ''Don't—'' she moaned breathily in the instant before he kissed her.

The storm of frustration inside him loosed its fierceness on her soft lips. God, she was soft, a warm, curvaceous woman, though she held herself like a marble statue. Her lack of response taunted the angry, aching place inside him. He wanted to dominate her, to make her view him as more than the gullible, adoring boy who had once worshiped at her feet.

In some rational part of his mind, Lucas knew he should treat her gently, but he couldn't stop himself from conquering her mouth with hard, hungry force. When she tried to squirm away, he brought up his hand to hold her head firmly in place. His other hand cupped her rounded bottom and pressed her lower body to his.

The fury of feeling within him funneled into the single-minded need to coax a reaction from her. He wanted Emma, but more than that, he wanted *her* to want *him*. With his tongue, he caressed the vulnerable interior of her mouth. She tasted of wine and woman. Though she did not kiss him back, she did not pull away again, either. Ever so slowly she relaxed into him as if relinquishing herself into his keeping.

His chest ached with a peculiar breathlessness. He wanted to weep with need for her. His wife. *His wife.* How he had dreamed of holding her on all those long, lonely nights, thousands of miles from home. Seven years of hell had brought him to this heaven. He cupped her face in his hands, his fingers stroking the downy tendrils behind her ears. He could feel the swift beating of her heart against his chest, could sense the swirl of confusion in her. Tenderness and triumph swamped him, and he burned to introduce Emma to all the ways he could delight her, one by one.

Sounds intruded. The husky notes of a man's voice. The trill of a woman's laugh. The scrape of footsteps in another part of the garden.

With a groan of frustrated yearning, Lucas clutched Emma close. Here, anyone could trespass on their private pleasures.

Reluctantly he broke the kiss, picked up his coat, and slid his arm around her slim waist. She leaned against him as if her legs trembled. He was mortified to discover his did, too.

As he guided her along the shadowed pathway, the music of a waltz drifted from the ballroom. She glanced ahead at the town house, where the windows shone golden with candlelight against the dark brick.

"The party," she murmured, as if she'd just recalled where they were. "Yes, it's high time we return to the ball."

"No, it isn't. We'll say our good-byes, then go to my carriage."

"I beg your pardon?" Her voice quickened with tension.

"The dancing has only just begun. People will talk if we leave so early."

"Come now. Don't tell me you would cater to the good opinion of these small-minded snobs."

Her chin lifted. "I'm of a mood to waltz."

"And I'm of a mood to cause another scandal." Scorched by the prospect, Lucas smiled. He traced the edge of her bodice, his fingertip rising over warm flesh, descending into the vale, and then rising again. "Let them all say the Marquess of Wortham couldn't wait to get his wife home to bed."

Emma paced the length of her bedchamber and back again. She had done so half a hundred times since returning from the soiree at the house of Lord Jasper Putney.

The cheery yellow decor, the fire crackling merrily on the hearth, mocked the dark chaos within her. Lucas would be coming to her at any moment. Bold as brass, he had escorted her out of the party, disregarding the snide queries of their host and hostess. He had wanted to accompany Emma straight to bed, but she had begged a few minutes alone to tend to private needs.

It was a lie, but Emma didn't care. She was desperate. Desperate to regain her composure. Desperate to shed the feeling that she was trapped in a runaway coach, careening into the darkness.

The nightgown swished around her icy, bare feet. She had undressed without ringing for a maid. She wanted no one chattering at her, no one asking why she looked so pale, no one offering to fetch a tonic from the kitchen. Medicine couldn't cure the illness biting at her stomach. The turmoil was caused by Lucas.

When he had kissed her in the moonlight, a peculiar fervor had melted her misgivings. It was the same feeling that had come over her when he had rubbed her back and touched her breasts—a deep heating inside herself and a yearning for . . . something more.

The sense of losing control of her own body appalled

Emma. Somehow, Lucas could mold her reactions as if she were clay in his competent hands. He had kissed her again in the carriage on the way home, and she had put up no resistance. She had wanted to go on kissing him, even though she knew it would lead to that painful, disgusting act. She had wanted to snuggle against his muscled body, even though she knew his tenderness was merely a ruse. She had even been tempted to reveal the truth about Jenny's father. And *that* would be the ultimate folly.

She wasn't safe with Lucas. Her husband had become a hard, cruel man, and he was holding the threat of prison over her in order to get himself an heir.

A son whom he would wrench from her arms.

Emma walked to the bed, leaned her brow against the post, and closed her eyes. She could never give away her own child. Never. Somehow, she would have to find a way to change his mind. The trouble was, she did not know how.

A faint tapping on the door broke her concentration. The doorknob rattled slightly, and cool air eddied over her.

She tensed, clutching the bedpost. He was here.

She could sense him behind her, as if his powerful presence displaced the pleasant aura of the room. In the garden, he had induced her to lower her guard. Now, no doubt, he would move in for the kill.

He approached with the hushed footfalls of a tiger. God help her if he turned violent. When it came to fornication, even a genteel and amusing man could show a vicious, animalistic side.

With sick dread, she waited for Lucas to speak, to order her to the bed. Instead, she felt the faintest tickling sensation along the nape of her neck.

A tingling chill spread down her spine and around to her breasts. She flinched in surprise and spun around to face him.

A secretive half-smile lent a sinister handsomeness to Lucas. He wore a shirt and breeches, thank heavens, though his throat and feet were bare. His state of partial undress would have been perfectly normal for a real husband in the privacy of the bedchamber. But, given the circumstances, Emma felt disturbed in a strange, inexplicable way.

She didn't like the feeling. Not one bit.

Frowning, she fixed her gaze on the long feather he had used to brush her neck. At the tip, the green fronds formed a circle with an eye in the center.

"The plumage of the male peacock," Lucas said, twirling it in his long, brown fingers. "Rather extravagant next to that of the drab peahen. The male bird spreads out a fan of these feathers to attract the female."

"How appropriate," Emma muttered. "Men behave like strutting cocks, too."

He chuckled, a diabolic sound that prickled the fine hairs on her skin. "In the human courting ritual, women preen as well as any man."

"I beg your pardon," she said coldly. "We're not courting, you and I."

"I never said we were. So we needn't bother with outer trappings." He let the tip of the feather drift down her cheek. "Remove your nightdress."

She pressed back against the bedpost and stared at his great, hulking shape in the shadows. "No!"

"Yes. Do so in your dressing room if you must. Then come straight back here." He nodded toward the huge four-poster, where a candle flickered on the bedside table and created a deceptively romantic bower.

"I won't," she said.

"You will."

His voice was as dark and dangerous as his gaze. Her heart beating in her throat, Emma clutched the high neckline of her gown. She acknowledged bitterly that he had the right to direct her as he pleased. He was her husband.

Her gaoler.

On wooden legs, she walked past him and into the dressing room. Just as on the night of her wedding, the oval pier glass reflected her image, the upswept blond hair, the pale skin and dainty figure. She had been afraid then, too, cold and shaking and desolate.

Yet wisdom and experience had firmed her girlish weak-nesses. The years had made her stronger, braver. She had endured worse hardships than a man's sweaty body pumping into her. At least that nightmare would last for only a few minutes.

Turning her back to the mirror, Emma stripped off the nightgown and let it drop into a heap on the rug. The chill in the air raised goosebumps on her bare skin. She snatched a dressing gown from a hook on the wall and thrust her arms into the garment, the silk folds settling over her nakedness. With a firm yank, she secured the sash at her waist.

There. Let Lucas be angry. She wouldn't prance past him in all her exposed glory.

But when she ventured back out into the bedroom, he merely looked amused at her small defiance. Strolling to her side, he plucked the pins from her hair until it fell in a rip-pling veil down to her waist. He seemed pleased by the effect and combed his fingers through the silvery-blond strands. For some odd reason, she felt as revealed as if she wore no dress-ing gown. He was the first man to see her with her hair unbound.

"Lie down now," he said. "On your back."

Taking her time about it, she climbed onto the high bed and arranged the robe to cover herself. It was a futile gesture, Emma knew. Yet it enabled her to retain a semblance of dignity. She lay stiffly with her arms at her sides, her head resting on a pillow, as she stared straight up at the yellow brocade canopy with its festoons of blue ribbon.

She heard her husband walk to the side of the bed, but she refused to acknowledge him with even a glance. Her pulse pounded so fiercely she felt dizzy. What did he intend? Another prolonged session of stroking—of her front side this time? Would he expect her to reciprocate? Or would he get straight to the business of copulating?

Then his hands were at her waist, untying her robe, draw-ing back the edges and exposing her breasts, her legs, her privates. Mortified, she flushed hotly. In an agony of suspense, she squeezed her eyes shut and waited for him to pry her legs apart. To violate her.

He would have to use force. She would not—could not—open herself to his male invasion.

The mattress dipped beneath his weight. She could smell him, the deep alien scent of male. Her muscles clenched so tightly they trembled. Dear God, he must be gawking at her nudity. And refining his plan of attack.

His touch came at a surprising place, along the sensitive arch of her foot. It felt like the brush of a demon's wing. Tendrils of sensation unfurled up her legs and made her shiver.

Startled into opening her eyes, she saw Lucas plying the peacock feather along her ankles and calves. A spontaneous warmth snaked upward into her most secret place. To her consternation, she could feel her body weakening, softening, heating.

She hated it. She hated *him*.

Emma jerked over onto her side and covered herself. "Stop it," she hissed through gritted teeth. "*Stop.*"

"Don't tell me you're afraid of a feather."

"I am when it's in *your* hands."

One corner of his mouth quirked upward in a shameless grin. "I'm merely touching you. That's part of our bargain."

"I should have known better than to bargain with the devil."

He laughed with black amusement. "You should have known better than to marry him, too. Now turn back. Lest I be forced to tie you to the bedposts."

She had the sudden, horrific image of herself, lying naked and spread-eagled, with her wrists and ankles secured to the four corners of the bed.

He wouldn't.

He would.

She couldn't be sure.

He sat patiently watching, waiting. She didn't dare put herself at the mercy of the husband she no longer knew.

Emma slowly rolled onto her back. Lucas leaned over her

and, with the delicacy of a master thief, parted the flaps of her robe again. She braced herself for his triumph, but his expression was inscrutable, unsmiling. His dark eyes burned with the reflection of the candle flame on the bedside table.

"Why?" she managed, her voice strained. "Why don't you just take me and be done with it? Why are you torturing me like this?"

He brushed the feather across her midsection, and her abdomen contracted involuntarily. "Just wait, dear wife. It's the most enjoyable sort of torture."

She didn't understand. She would never understand. Who in her right mind would relish being so debased?

Slowly he traced the slimness of her waist. The silky fronds set off ripples of response that eddied over her skin. Her woman's place constricted and released in a tiny pulse of sensation that verged on pleasure. To her dismay and humiliation, she wanted to experience it again.

He seemed to know exactly what she wanted—and then denied it of her. Lazily, he plied the feather over her abdomen, inching closer and closer to her breasts. The tips drew taut and she closed her eyes, her entire being focusing on his progress until she wanted to scream at him to hurry. When at last the feather caressed her bosom, she bit her lip to keep from sobbing with blessed relief.

Her satisfaction was short-lived. As the feather gravitated lower again, a bewildering tapestry of responses unraveled inside Emma. She felt the restless urge to squirm on the bed, to move her body, especially her hips. Not away from Lucas, but toward him in invitation. Most shockingly of all, she wanted to unlock her legs so he would tickle her . . . *there*.

She dug her fingers into the bedclothes in an effort to hold herself still. Every part of her skin felt fevered. Her breath came faster, snagging in her throat. It was the utter embarrassment of her predicament, she told herself. No woman could enjoy having her body manipulated by a man. No decent woman at least—

The feather alighted on her knees and slowly flirted its way up her thighs. Higher . . . higher . . . higher. A heated moisture dampened her inner folds of flesh. Emma was surprised by how soft and languid she felt, yet how charged with energy. She ached with a desperate intensity, though she could not say for what. *Sweet Jesus, save her.* She heard a whimper and realized it came from herself. Unable to look at her tormenter, she turned her head on the pillow and bit her lip. She wanted . . . she wanted . . . she wanted. . . .

As if swept up in a darkly sensual dream, she found herself raising her knees slightly, parting them in order to grant the feather deeper access. Anticipating the sweep of its downy fronds, she felt something foreign touch her instead. Something warm and firm that insinuated itself into her throbbing depths. Something *male*.

Terror flashed from the dungeon of her memory. *His hands, tearing at her underclothes. His legs, pressing down on her. His member, impaling her like a sword.*

Seized by a frenzy of fear, she lunged out from under him. Her fingers scrabbled on the bedside table and closed around a cold metal shape. The candlestick.

Heedless of the dripping wax, she swung wildly at her assailant. "Never again! I'll kill you first. I'll kill you!"

Jolted from a reverie of lust, Lucas swore viciously. He yanked up his forearm to deflect the blow. He was fast, but not fast enough. The candlestick struck his right arm with numbing force. Hot wax splattered his shirt and seared his chest.

Pain shot up and down his arm, emptying his lungs in a roar. "Bloody *hell*!"

But there was no time to indulge his rage. The candle flew out of its holder and landed on the counterpane. Quick as a blink, the lace caught fire. He snatched up a pillow and beat out the flames. Satisfied that the smoking black spot would not ignite again, he hurled away the pillow and spun toward Emma.

"You little fool!" he shouted. "Isn't it enough that you've blighted my life? Must you burn down my house, too?"

Emma crouched against the headboard, the dressing robe clutched around her quaking body. She said nothing, though the wild fear in her eyes spoke volumes. He had pushed her over the edge. He had overwhelmed her with his aggressive desire. In his arrogant hunger to possess her, he had demanded too much, too quickly.

His arm throbbed as a punishing reminder of his folly. A livid, purplish bruise was already forming from his wrist to his elbow. Cursing his stupidity, he flexed his fingers. No broken bones.

He should have been content with plying the feather and stirring her slumbering passion. Considering her traumatic experience, he should have exercised restraint. He shouldn't have succumbed to the maddening urge to touch her.

Sentimental nonsense. She was his wife, for God's sake. He had every right to hold her to their bargain. And her desire had not been a product of his imagination. Whether or not her mind accepted it, her body was primed for mating.

As primed as his.

She huddled in a ball, watching him as if he were a savage beast about to rip her apart. His fit of temper eased into a gnawing frustration. Who had done this to her? Who had made her fear the pleasures of her own body? Dammit, who? And what would it take to rebuild her trust?

Ah, Emma.

The need to comfort her overshadowed the pain in his arm. Ignoring his better judgment, he clambered across the patch of stinking soot and gathered Emma into his embrace. She didn't draw away, didn't move, didn't acknowledge his presence in any way. He resisted the growing tenderness inside him, yet it was there in every beat of his heart.

He passed his hand over her silky hair. It sifted like spun moonlight through his fingers. "Emma," he said, groping for the right words, "forgive me. You needn't be afraid of me. I shan't force myself on you. Not ever."

She sat stiff and silent. No tears, no hysterics. It was as if he held a beautiful porcelain doll.

His throat tightened. He had driven Emma to this state. By the selfish indulgence of his own desire.

"I want us to share pleasure," he went on gruffly, "and

I'm willing to wait until you're ready. Until you want it as much as I do.''

She raised her head slightly. "Liar," she whispered. "I won't *ever* want something so disgusting. Since you've only one use for me, you may as well take what you want and get it over with.''

She spoke with the conviction of the doomed. It made Lucas burn all the more to banish her fears, to woo her and win her trust. Perhaps by confining his efforts to the bedroom, he had approached her seduction all wrong.

You've only one use for me.

An implausible solution struck him. Unfortunately, it would require offering *his* trust first.

Logic struck back. The last thing in the world he wanted was to involve Emma any further in his life.

Yet if his plan worked, the reward would be well worth the price.

Hoping he didn't regret his rash decision, he tapped her beneath the chin to make her look up at him. "Meet me in the library tomorrow morning," he said. "Nine o'clock.''

"Why?''

"You'll see." In the firelight, her eyes were fathomless pools of vulnerability. He rose from the bed, ruthlessly denying the insidious softness inside himself. "It seems I may have found another use for you, after all.''

◈ Chapter 12 ◈

When Emma slipped into the library the next morning, Lucas was absorbed in writing at his desk. Even from the other end of the long chamber, she could tell he favored his right arm because he stopped a moment and flexed his fingers as if they pained him. Ashamed, she leaned against the doorframe. Had she really struck him with such savagery?

Idiot. Why had she antagonized the man who could have her tossed into Newgate at a snap of his aristocratic fingers?

The memory of her outburst made Emma cringe. Yet Lucas had provoked her. He had humiliated her, tricked her into lowering her guard yet again. What was worse, afterward, he had held her close as a friend might do. He had shown her consideration.

I want us to share pleasure. And I'm willing to wait until you're ready. Until you want it as much as I do.

Was it true? Could a woman enjoy the act? Certainly she had luxuriated in his touch. She had felt an undeniable delight until the shocking moment when she had mistaken his finger for a different intrusion, a violation that opened the floodgates of the past.

Isn't it enough that you've blighted my life?

He had spoken in anger, whipping her with words. But for her, he would never have left England for seven years. He might have married an honorable lady, a sweet-tempered woman who would have given birth to his children. He would have settled into the comfortable life of a gentleman, surrounded by his family. Instead of being saddled with a wife he despised.

He looked lonely, sitting behind the desk and making notations in a journal, his brown-black hair gleaming in the watery sunlight. His coat was draped over the back of the chair, and he worked in his shirtsleeves. Had Lucas finally realized that she could never submit to him willingly? Did he mean to release her from their bargain? Perhaps there was still a chance he would grant her a divorce. She had spent the night fretting over the possibility and wondering why she didn't feel more thrilled.

Emma cleared her throat. "Good morning."

He looked up, his mouth tightening. "You're early," he said, his deep voice echoing down the long room. He replaced the quill in its silver holder. "It's only half past eight."

An unfamiliar shyness descended over her. She, who could charm any gentleman, hardly knew what to say to her own husband. "I'm accustomed to rising at dawn."

"Oh? And here I thought burglars kept late hours."

Was he teasing? Emma wasn't certain. She was never sure of anything with Lucas, not since he'd returned from his travels a cynical, brooding stranger. "Well," she said brightly, "I haven't been burgling lately."

He made no reply. A closed expression on his face, he leaned back in his chair and watched her walk toward him. A strangely sensual feeling stole over her. She was aware of the coffee-brown silk dress caressing her curves. She felt the softness of her chemise, the pressure of her garters, the firmness of her corset embracing her breasts. The last time he had seen her, she had been naked. Well, nearly so. It was an erotic secret shared by only the two of them. Was he remembering, too?

She stopped before the desk. "If I've come too early to suit you, I would be happy to read until nine."

He smiled blandly, displaying the dimples in his tanned

cheeks. "Emma, believe me, you could never come too early."

His smirk held a covert quality as if he were privy to a jest beyond her comprehension. As he looked her over, his smoldering gaze sparked shivers up and down her back. "Tell me why you asked me here," she said. "I confess you've aroused my curiosity."

"Curiosity," he said dryly. "At least that's something."

He motioned her over to the pile of crates. Lifting the lid off the topmost one, he dug into the packing straw and drew forth a silver cylinder elaborately inscribed with gold.

She ventured closer, close enough to detect his scent, the hint of darkness and desire. She wrenched her attention to the object he held by its long handle. "How beautiful," she said. "What is it?"

"A prayer wheel from a monastery high in the Himalayan mountains. It spins like so"—a twist of his wrist started the cylinder twirling—"and sends prayers wafting up to heaven."

He handed the artifact to her, and she ran her fingers over the cool, smooth surface, then the gold inscription. "Do you know what this says?"

He leaned closer and glanced at the lettering. " '*Om Mani Padme Hoom.* O Jewel of the Lotus.' It's a Buddhist mantra—a sacred chant. Legend has it that Buddha was born in a lotus flower."

A thrill sped through Emma, and she wasn't sure if it came from holding the prayer wheel or from her husband's nearness. "This was used by holy men thousands of miles away," she said musingly. "I should like to learn more about their customs."

"Your wish is my command," Lucas said, a gleam in his eyes. "Since you've little to occupy yourself during the day, you may catalog the artifacts in these crates. My notes on each piece are scattered throughout the journals on my desk. You'll need to make up a master notebook and also label the contents of each box."

"Me?" Emma said in astonishment. "Why me?"

"As I recall, you've a lady's skill for sketching. Each entry in the journal requires a drawing of the relic along with a written description."

"But . . ." Feeling overwhelmed, she looked around at the piles of crates. "Lucas, I can't possibly do this."

He took hold of her hand and lightly rubbed his thumb over the small calluses on her palm, then her healing scar. "Don't plead helplessness, Emma. By your own admission, you're no idler."

A shock tingled up her arm and turned her knees to jelly. She snatched back her fingers. "Running a household doesn't qualify me for this task. You need a scholar, a historian."

"I need someone who is a quick study. Someone who is intimately acquainted with precious gems."

She felt staggered by his confidence in her. In truth, the notion of examining the boxes gave her an exhilarating lift, as if it were Christmas and these were her gifts. Yet she peered suspiciously at him. This had to be a trick. "You can't have forgotten the tiger mask. Why would you trust me with your treasures?"

Shrugging, he caressed her cheek. "It's a way of keeping you out of trouble. I'm too much the gentleman to lock you up, and too busy to watch over you every minute." He glanced at the clock on the mantelpiece. "In fact, the sooner I depart, the better. I'll return later in the afternoon to check on your progress."

Emma watched, stunned, as he walked away from her. Where did he disappear to every day? Did he meet his mistress? He had found no satisfaction in his wife's bed.

Emma's heart gave a curious little twist. Was his foreign woman beautiful, a perfect match for his tall, handsome form? Or perhaps her beauty was of the soul, for he professed to love her dearly. She was the reason he did not wish to marry another English lady.

So let him go, Emma told herself as he neared the door. She didn't care. Let him slake his lust in some other female.

Let him ply her with peacock feathers and rub her with scented oil. . . .

"Wait!" she called.

In the doorway, he turned on his heel, his head cocked inquisitively. The lock of hair that had tumbled onto his brow gave him a dashing air. "Yes?"

"Where—" Her courage fled, and she waved her hand at the crates. "What are you planning to do with all these things?"

"To open a new exhibit at the Montague House Museum. A tribute to Asian antiquities, by the patronage of Lord and Lady Wortham." With a small smile and a click of his heels, he strode out of the library.

He would commemorate *her*? No, surely he must mean his mother.

Yet an odd little hope warmed her well into the morning. Emma found herself humming as she dug through the crates and carefully placed a variety of artifacts on the desk. The straw tickled her nose and made her sneeze. An apron would have protected her gown from dust streaks. But she was too fascinated by her gargantuan task to leave the library.

What had Lucas done during those seven lost years? Each new discovery revealed a bit more about his travels and fed her hungry curiosity.

She lifted out a sandstone carving of a fierce goddess with many arms, and imagined Lucas exploring a ruined stone temple. She opened a mother-of-pearl box filled with gold and copper coins, and fancied him bargaining with a merchant in a bazaar. She uncovered a bronze ewer inlaid with silver and sapphires, and saw him accepting it from a turbaned prince in an ivory palace.

But when she came upon a statue of a bare-breasted maiden holding a peacock fan, Emma's daydreams took a decidedly different turn.

Clutching the figurine, she sank cross-legged to the floor and relived the memory of her encounter with Lucas the previous night. How delicately he had stroked the feather over her skin, how extraordinary the sensations he had wrought in her. It was almost as if she were awakening from a long, deep slumber. Even now, the secret glow of pleasure warmed her innermost place—

"Mama! Mama, look what I've found."

Emma's eyes snapped open as fantasy faded to reality. Jenny trotted toward her, weaving through the litter of straw and boxes and chairs. A bundle of white fur filled her small arms. Toby.

The little dog wagged his tail and licked Jenny's face joyfully.

Concealing a stirring of disquiet, Emma smiled and set aside the statue. She rose to her feet, kissed her daughter on the top of her sweet-scented head, and then scratched Toby behind the ears. "Good morning, you two. I didn't know you knew each other."

"We met on the stairway just now." Jenny giggled in delight as the dog licked her nose. "Oh, Mama, I do think he wants to be my friend."

"It certainly would seem so."

Her blue-green eyes sparkled. "Do you suppose I could take him up to the nursery and introduce him to my cousins?"

Thinking of the crotchety dowager, Emma hesitated. Instinct warned her to keep Jenny ensconced in the nursery. "Lambkin, I'm afraid Toby already has an owner who loves him very much. She might worry about him if you took him away, even for a short while."

"But Mama—"

"I'll take him back while you run along to your lessons." Detesting the necessity of hiding Jenny away, Emma guided the girl toward the door of the library. "And you know what I told you about wandering through the house. You must be careful not to disturb anyone—"

Emma stopped abruptly as the elder Lady Wortham walked into the library. Regally imposing in a gown of violet poplin, she took the careful steps of an invalid and clutched a lace handkerchief in one hand.

Her heart pounding, Emma stepped in front of Jenny.

"Good morning, madam. Should you be out of bed?"

"I am in the pink of health. Besides, it is well past noon, and you missed luncheon." Her mother-in-law's expression lightened as she asked, "Now where is Toby? I heard him barking and then a little child's laughter. Which of my naughty grandchildren has escaped the nursery?"

"None of them," Emma said quickly.

"But I was certain—I recognized that laugh. Who is that behind you?"

"Only my daughter, I'm afraid. She came to visit me for a few minutes."

The dowager's mouth pinched tightly. All semblance of polite good humor vanished as she drew herself up with hauteur. "Your daughter."

"Yes." Resenting the woman's demeanor, while anxious to defuse a volatile situation, Emma turned to fetch Toby.

But Jenny popped into view with the dog in her arms. Her lips parted in awe as she gazed up at the dowager. She smiled with the trust of the innocent. "I have him, ma'am. He only wanted to play."

Lady Wortham stared at the girl. A look of utter confusion arched her silver brows and eased the tension from her mouth. Very slowly, she braced her hand on the back of a chair and knelt before Jenny. With a hand that visibly trembled, Lady Wortham reached out and touched the crown of Jenny's hair. "My child," she whispered in wonder.

Her voice broke the spell of agonized suspense that gripped Emma. She swiftly moved to her daughter. "Give me Toby, darling. You mustn't bother her ladyship any longer."

"Nonsense. She isn't bothering me." Amazingly—alarmingly—a smile gentled the dowager's face as her keen gaze studied Jenny. "You run along, dear. Bring Toby back in half an hour, mind, and we'll have a little visit."

"Thank you." Jenny bobbed a curtsy and then darted out of the room.

The dowager stood up by degrees, a strange warmth on her fine-lined face. Her gaze was piercing, assessing, questioning. "Well, Emma, you have some explaining to do. Why have you kept my granddaughter from me all these years?"

A chilling frost swept through Emma. It could not be. She could not have been found out.

She turned away and blindly touched the books on a shelf. "I—I don't understand. Jenny is not Lucas's daughter. For that very reason, you banished me from this house the day after the wedding."

Silk rustled as the dowager came closer. Her quivering, birdlike hand alighted on Emma's shoulder. "My dear, if only you had confided in me, I would have helped you smooth things over with Lucas. The very moment I saw the girl I knew." Anguish roughened the older woman's voice. "Jenny is the daughter of my son Andrew."

"You need only to identify him and leave the rest to me," Lucas said, holding Shalimar's cool hands. "Are you certain you're ready?"

A white veil draping her dark hair, his mistress sat beside him in the Wortham coach. She kept her head bowed. "Yes, my lord. I am not afraid."

Yet a tremor ran through her, and Lucas knew she feared not her former lover, but the fate of her only child, Sanjeev. Many months had passed since her son had been kidnapped by his ne'er-do-well sire. Today, they were investigating another actor who fit O'Hara's description.

"Hajib, you'll stay with Shalimar," Lucas said. "Behind me."

The servant's chocolate eyes gleamed in woeful sympathy at her. "As you wish, master. It is an honor to escort the lovely Lotus of Kashmir."

Lucas unlatched the door of the coach and stepped out into the bright sunshine. Drays and wagons rattled down the narrow street in the Covent Garden district. The sour smell of the gutters melded with the pungent odor of horse droppings. On the corner, a pieman shouted out his wares to the common folk passing by. A little boy dodged in and out of the pedestrians, chasing after a squawking rooster. Across the street, on a seedy brick theater, the marquee announced a revival of the popular old play *The Way of the World*.

Spotting a break in the traffic, Lucas struck out for the playhouse, Hajib and Shalimar at his heels. The pair in their foreign robes garnered a few stares from the passersby. To Lucas's relief, one of the front doors was unlocked, and he led the way into the dimness of the deserted lobby.

The hollow sound of upraised voices echoed from the amphitheater. As Lucas motioned to his companions to be silent, the soreness in his arm made him grimace. He'd never have thought dainty little Emma capable of delivering such a blow. But then, he had underestimated her before.

Was she still in the library, classifying his artifacts? He gritted his teeth, thinking of her having free access to his priceless antiquities. What madness had seized hold of him?

He was a bloody fool to let the vixen into the proverbial chicken coop. Right now, she might be falsifying his records and pocketing a valuable relic. Not since he'd succumbed to her pretty pleading and married her posthaste had he made a decision with his loins rather than his logic. If Emma took it into her mind to have revenge on him, she could vandalize his life's work.

But he had to trust her. Or at least pretend to do so. Because then, she might be inspired to trust *him*. In bed.

God, yes. In bed.

"Pssst, master," Hajib whispered. "Look."

With no memory of having entered the amphitheater, Lucas realized they stood in the shadows at the back of the immense room. Rows of seats formed a half-circle around the stage. Above the common area, the more expensive, gilt-painted boxes were dark, empty of patrons. The curtains were lifted to reveal the wooden stage, where the drop scene showed the interior of a house. Lamps flickered over a small group of actors rehearsing their lines.

Bloody damn. Lucas frowned. He didn't know which one of them might be O'Hara. The actors wore elaborate costumes, with the painted faces and white wigs of the previous century.

" 'Gad, my head begins to whim it about—why dost thou not speak?' " one man boomed. " 'Thou art both as drunk and as mute as a fish.' "

Another actor staggered out of the wings and swayed in front of an actress in a massive hooped gown. " 'Look you, Mrs. Millamant—if you can love me, dear nymph—say it . . .' "

The new actor gave a passable performance of an inebriated sot. Big and burly, he wore a powdered bagwig and old-fashioned breeches of shiny violet satin. A black patch dotted his cheek.

Shalimar made a sound of distress. Her anguished eyes were luminous in the gloom. Struck by concern, Lucas touched her smooth hand. The veil stirred around her dark features as she gave a jerky nod.

He felt a jolt of success, tempered by the grimness of anger. The bastard in the purple pants was O'Hara.

"Stay here," Lucas muttered. "Both of you."

Without a backward glance, he stalked along the perimeter of the theater until he came to a door in the shadows beside the stage. The actors were quarreling now in raised voices, and no one noticed him slip backstage. He threaded his way past piles of props, ropes for the curtains, and canvas backdrops. Musty smells hung in the air: sweat and cosmetics and smoke from the lamps. In the wings, he found a vantage point near a rickety screen that formed a dressing area. Costumes were flung over trunks and stools.

O'Hara minced around the stage in his role as a foppish drunk. Lucas knew better than to mistake the Irishman for a weakling. The villain had torn a son from his mother.

You intend to do the same to Emma, his conscience jeered.

Lucas clenched his jaw. The circumstances were different for him. Worlds different. Emma knew—and agreed even before conception—that she would give up their son to him. So what if he'd coerced her into the bargain? She'd done her share of coercing *him.*

Yet guilt fueled the violent rage within him.

On stage, O'Hara intoned, " 'Go flea dogs, and read romances! I'll go to bed my maid.' " He hiccuped loudly and then reeled off into the wings.

Lucas stepped out of the shadows. "Patrick O'Hara."

The actor's demeanor sobered as he shed his onstage persona. He arched one bushy, white-powdered eyebrow. "That I am," he said gruffly, looking Lucas up and down. "And just who might be askin'?"

"Your nemesis."

Seizing the brawny man by his purple lapels, Lucas shoved him up against the back wall. His wig tumbled off and bits of broken plaster rained down on his short, carroty hair. "Here now!" O'Hara blustered. "If you've come to collect on a bill, you've only to ask—"

"Where is Sanjeev?"

O'Hara's brown eyes narrowed warily. "Sanjeev?"

Lucas shook him. "Don't play the dolt. He's your son."

"What's he done now? I'll have you know, I'm not liable for the brat anymore. Not since he run off."

"Ran off. Where? When?"

" 'Twas nigh on a month ago," the actor whined. "Devil if I know where."

"And you haven't tried to find him? Bastard! You should never have taken him from Shalimar."

O'Hara stared. "So you've been to India and met the harlot. Faith, a more tender piece of ass never warmed me bed— *ooph!*"

Lucas hurled him away. Arms wheeling, O'Hara staggered sideways into a dressing table and fell to the floor. Jars of cosmetics clattered and shattered. A snowstorm of spilled powder filtered down on his sprawled form. Gasps came from the other thespians who had gathered to watch.

For a moment O'Hara lay like a grotesque marionette with his arms and legs flung wide. Then, with a mighty bellow, he leapt to his feet.

Lucas met O'Hara with a fist to his belly. Pain blazed up Lucas's bruised arm, but he scarcely noticed. He could think only of punishing the man who had abandoned his own child, of silencing his own conscience. Props and people scattered until Lucas's arm went numb and he found himself pinned to the wall by fifteen stone of angry Irishman.

" 'Tis surprised I am that a fine gent like yourself would defend a strumpet," O'Hara said between bursts of ale-stinking breath. "If you pay me well, I might just remember where you can find her brat."

Lucas answered by bringing up his left fist from outside and jabbing O'Hara in the ear. The actor loosened his stranglehold for an instant. It was long enough for Lucas to throw him off balance and wrest him to the floor.

"If you value your life," Lucas said, "you'll tell me for free."

"Yes, *sahib*," said Hajib. "Or my blade will pierce your black heart."

In a flutter of gray robes, the valet appeared out of nowhere to press a wickedly curved knife to O'Hara's chest. A collective gasp eddied from the onlookers.

O'Hara went still, though he glowered at Hajib. "Who is this cheeky Hindoo?"

"I am no Hindu, but a follower of Mohammad. And you will meet your infidel God this day if you fail to tell the truth about Sanjeev."

Several wheezing breaths came from O'Hara. "Faith, 'tis caught in a farce, I am, and a badly written one at that," the actor grumbled. "The lad boasted of earning his passage back to that godfersaken hellhole he came from. After all the opportunity I gave him, bringing him to Mother England!"

"You let him look for work at the docks?" Lucas said.

"Aye. Though don't blame me if the ungrateful wretch has taken ship already. Now get away from me, both you scurvy gents."

Lucas sprang to his feet and stalked away. The group of actors parted to give them wide berth, especially when Hajib brandished his curving knife.

Shalimar stood waiting in the shadows outside the stage door. Her palms pressed together, she asked, "My son?"

Lucas gently took her by the arm and steered her up the aisle. "He's gone to find work at the docks. So that he might return home to you."

Her steps faltered. "My poor Sanjeev!"

"We'll find him," Lucas said gruffly. "I promise you that."

"I will help," Hajib said, sheathing his knife beneath his robe. "Even if the boy has stowed away aboard a ship, I will follow him to the ends of the world. For you, O Lotus of Kashmir."

Lucas vowed to leave no stone unturned until Shalimar held her son in her arms again. He owed her that much and more. She had brought him out of the darkness of despair. She had taught a callow boy how a man pleases a woman. She had given him serenity. So why did he long for Emma?

As he crossed the busy street to his carriage, he felt no peace. Since the day Emma had sauntered back into his life with yet another scheme to manipulate him, he had been caught up in turmoil again—in an exhilarating tumult of passion and anger and yearning. Even now, he burned with impatience to return home and match wits with her.

Bloody hell. He wanted a son, not a wife. He wouldn't let Emma distract him. Except at night.

Ah, yes. At night.

❧ **Chapter 13** ❧

Aghast, Emma stared at her mother-in-law. A clock ticked on the mantelpiece. In the corridor outside the library, a servant walked by with a swift tapping of footsteps. Emma wanted to bolt out the door, but her legs wouldn't move. They were as paralyzed as her tongue.

The dowager knew. She *knew*.

Her blue eyes brimming with tears, the elder Lady Wortham groped for Emma's hands. "Do not deny it," she said in a pleading tone. "Have pity on an old mother. Tell me that little Jenny is really my Andrew's daughter."

The quivering of those gaunt fingers dissolved the wall around Emma's emotions. In that moment she understood how deeply the dowager had loved her youngest son, how much she longed to know that a part of him lived on in Jenny. And Emma knew it was too late to withhold the truth.

She trudged to the door and closed it. Then she turned to the dowager. "Yes, it's true," she said in an anguished whisper. "How did you guess?"

"It was her laugh . . . I heard it from the corridor. I thought . . . I thought for a moment it was twenty years ago, and my sweet boy had come back to me. And then when I saw his blue-green eyes twinkling up at me . . . but it was Jenny."

The dowager swayed alarmingly, and Emma hastened to help her across the library to the chaise. She was thin as a cadaver, flesh on bones. "Madam, remember your health. I'll ring for a tisane."

"Never mind the tonics. This news is the best remedy for what ails me. Sit, my dear." She patted the cushion beside her. "We have so very much to discuss."

Weighted by a sense of doom, Emma sank to the chaise. Her heart thudded in painful strokes, and her eyes burned. She had imagined this moment a thousand times, when she could shout out the truth and vindicate herself to the Coulters. But oh, sweet Jesus. How could she shatter a mother's cherished memories of her son? How could she accuse a war hero of so despicable an act? "There's little to tell," she said tonelessly. "Please, try to understand. It's difficult for me to speak of . . . what happened."

"Of course I understand. And I respect your privacy." Haloed by the golden light that streamed through the window, the dowager smiled like a radiant madonna. "No lady would wish to make known a love affair that went on before she was married."

Love affair?

A furious denial choked Emma's throat. *No*, she wanted to scream. *No, you're wrong, horribly wrong! I could never love such a monster.*

Then it struck Emma that the dowager's assumption gave her the perfect explanation. She had but to remain silent, to contradict nothing.

"It must have happened months before your betrothal to Lucas," the older woman went on, a faraway look in her eyes. "It was the height of the Season. Andrew's regiment was about to be deployed to that horrid war in Portugal. Lucas used his influence to obtain a few days' leave for Andrew to visit us here in London." She clasped her milk-white hands to her bosom. "Ah, how dashing and handsome he looked in his uniform. You must have seen him at one of our parties and fallen instantly in love. So many of the young ladies did, you know."

Emma kept her eyes downcast. Yes, it had been a party.

A large, boisterous group at Vauxhall Gardens, and she had come upon him in the dark. . . .

"Oh, my dear, you look deathly pale," exclaimed Lady Wortham. "Forgive me for asking so many painful questions, but I must know. Why did Andrew not offer for you? I can't imagine my son dishonoring a lady and then not doing right by her."

Emma plucked a bit of straw off her skirt and gave it a hard twist between her fingers. Clearly Andrew had hidden his true nature from his family. "I have no idea. We had . . . been together only once, the night before he left to rejoin his regiment. A month later, he died at Talavera. Before he knew about my delicate condition."

"And you must have been terribly distraught. You married Lucas so that Andrew's child would be raised a Coulter." The dowager closed her eyes, her shoulders slumping. Faint blue veins showed on her lids, and a tear traced a path down her cheek. "To think I forced you to leave here. How cruel I've been. Can you ever forgive me?"

Emma told herself to feel a triumphant sense of vindication. Yet she merely felt drained and aching. "You didn't know. You thought I'd brought shame on your family—on Lucas. And I was confused and frightened. I found . . . I couldn't reveal the truth. Not to anyone."

Her mother-in-law slowly straightened. An indomitable will shone in her eyes as she looked at Emma again. "You did right, my dear. This must remain our little secret. No scandal must tarnish Andrew's memory."

With a snap, the straw broke in Emma's fingers. It galled her to think she was protecting that brute. In one act of violence, he had ruined her life.

Yet she couldn't allow him to ruin Jenny's life, too.

As if she'd read Emma's mind, the dowager went on, "If word slips out, we will lose all hope of society ever receiving Lady Jenny. You must be accepted, too. Lady Jenny's background must be unblemished."

"I fear it's already too late," Emma said. "It was too late seven years ago when I left here in disgrace. At Lord Jasper

Putney's party, many people avoided me, even though Lucas was there with me." Regret wrenched her insides. "Everyone knows Jenny isn't his."

"Bah," said the dowager, with a wave of her hand. "They know only rumors. My daughters and I were never so vulgar as to confirm the vicious tale-telling. Now, we shall convince the *ton* that you and Wortham had a falling-out over some inconsequential matter. The two of you have repaired your differences and are back together for good."

Caught in a tangled web of deception, Emma stared at the array of exotic artifacts on the desk without really seeing them. Securing Jenny's future was the answer to her prayers. Yet she couldn't stay married to Lucas, not forever. They had made a bargain, and he expected her to leave after giving birth to his son. She would seek a bill of divorcement and marry Sir Woodrow. It was what she wanted. Wasn't it?

"When *I* accompany you out into society," the dowager added in a steely tone, "everyone will know you have my seal of approval. No one will dare to suggest Lady Jenny is not Wortham's true daughter."

Athough gratified by her ladyship's offer of sponsorship, Emma foresaw a catastrophe. "What will Lucas say to that?"

"I'll tell him we must be a family again, all of us. And Jenny must call me 'Grandmama.' " The dowager nodded decisively. "Yes, that will do. It is past time there was harmony in this house."

Uneasiness nipped at Emma's stomach. "Surely you won't expect Jenny to address him as Papa," she said. "Lucas will never agree. And if you insist, he'll wonder why. He might guess she's his own niece."

"The resemblance between Andrew and Jenny is something only a mother would notice. Wortham wouldn't dream of looking for his brother's features in her, I am certain of it." The dowager smiled wryly. "Nevertheless, I take your point. My son has become a masterful man. Just as his dear father once was."

Emma pressed her lips together. *Masterful?* Autocratic

was a more fitting description. Arrogant. Dictatorial.
Seductive. Persuasive. *Dangerous*.

The dowager clung tightly to Emma's arm. Those blue
eyes burned into hers. "Heed me well. Wortham must never,
ever know you had an affair with his brother. He would hate
Andrew. That is the way men are, jealous and possessive of
their women. If Wortham were to learn the truth, it would
destroy him. And this family."

She only confirmed what Emma already knew. That was
why she had never been able to bring herself to hurl the ugly
truth in his face.

She could have married any one of a score of ardent gentlemen. By choosing Lucas, she had planned to have her
revenge on Andrew. She had intended to tell the Coulters
that he was a beast, not a hero—and then force them to
accept her child. But when the moment had come, when she
had faced Lucas on their wedding night and realized how
she had devastated his heart, the words of retribution had
withered in her throat.

The memory stirred queasiness in her stomach. Now, more
than ever, she must guard the secret of her attacker's identity.
Because Lucas knew what his mother did not. He knew that
Emma's innocence had been taken by force.

Everyone found a woman with a shady past fascinating, Lucas thought cynically.

In a foul mood, he stood in Lord Gerald Mannering's town
house and watched Emma waltz with yet another besotted
gentleman. He fancied he could hear her throaty laughter
over the lively tune played by the orchestra and the tapping
of a hundred dancing feet. His wife was enjoying a popular-
ity unparalleled even by her first Season. Mannering, in particular, was salivating over her. Already their host had
danced twice with her.

Lucas wanted to land his fist into the lecher's face.

By circling around Emma, these vultures hoped to feed off
the carcass of scandal. He himself had had to direct his most

freezing glare at several guests who had asked too many probing questions about his long absence.

When his mother had announced her decision to see Emma accepted by society, he had been unable to deny her. She had suffered enough for one lifetime. Now, enthroned in a gilt chair at the end of the long room, she reigned over a court of matrons who sat out the dancing. Campaigning for peace in the family had brought the bloom of improved health to her cheeks. And when Emma left him for good, his mother would adjust to the shock of the divorce. She would have an infant grandson to fuss over.

Her abrupt turnabout still troubled him, though. She, who had held Emma in contempt, now treated her like a beloved daughter. Adroitly, his mother had proclaimed that since his marchioness was living with him, she could hardly remain a pariah. Yet he sensed there was something more, else why would she permit Jenny to address her as "Grandmama"?

The very notion set his teeth on edge. It was like announcing to the world that *he* was Jenny's father.

Not that he despised the child. The animosity he had harbored toward Jenny had lessened upon meeting her. He remembered how fearlessly the little girl had faced him after he'd caught her rifling through his safe, how endearing was her gap-toothed smile. Yet he couldn't—he wouldn't—lay claim to her. She belonged to Emma, not to him. Never to him.

Lucas took a glass of champagne from the tray of a passing servant. Brandy was what he really craved. A decanter of the finest French reserve to drown the frustration gnawing at him. But he needed a clear head tonight. He needed to watch Emma. He didn't believe for a minute that she'd given up on robbing Mannering in order to repay her grandfather's debt.

Moodily, Lucas observed her from behind the screen of a potted fern. She was light on her feet, nimble and lovely as the saucy chit who had taken his youthful heart by storm. The misty blue skirt swirled around her, and he imagined those slim, white legs against a tangle of bedsheets.

It had taken him several nights of concentrated wooing to convince her to let him touch her again. Since he spent his days on the search for Sanjeev, he had not been able to devote much time to working with Emma in the library. But at night . . . ah, at night. Slowly he was stripping away her defenses and revealing her sensual nature. Soon she would lie naked with him, her moonbeam hair drifting over the pillow. He would take her with infinite patience, like a bridegroom loving his bride for the first time.

And like as not, she would clobber him with another candlestick.

Lucas balled his fingers into a fist. Damn the rogue who had despoiled her. Was he here tonight? Did he dare to mingle in decent company?

Lucas caught himself gazing into the face of every gentleman present, and forced himself to relax. It was ridiculous to torture himself. He had better things to do than to chase the demon of revenge.

The music ceased. On the other side of the assembly room, Emma took leave of her partner. She glided through the crush of attendees, pausing now and then to speak to someone. She made her way straight to Sir Woodrow Hickey, who stood talking with her grandfather. Emma looped her arm through Briggs's and directed a warm smile at Hickey.

Lucas set down his empty glass before he could succumb to the urge to smash it. Damn it, he wanted her to come to *him*. She was his wife. They were supposed to be happily reconciled. Perhaps she needed to be reminded of that.

He had started across the crowded floor when a smiling, dark-haired lady stepped into his path. "Ah, Lord Wortham. What could there be to scowl about in such amiable company?"

She had a gypsy beauty, her black hair piled high and her wine-colored bodice cut low to show an expanse of dusky skin. She was exactly the sort of predatory female who would have launched him into a fit of the stutters as a youth. "Have we met?" he said with cold precision.

She sank into a graceful curtsy. "I am Mrs. Boswell, my

lord. There, the proprieties have been observed." She stepped closer, giving him a whiff of her musky scent and a peek at her magnificent bosom. "I'm being terribly forward, I confess. But only because I'm curious. You've just returned from India, have you not?"

"Yes."

"By odd coincidence, so have I. My husband owns a fleet of merchant ships, and I've traveled to many strange and wonderful ports of call."

"Indeed. And where is your husband tonight?"

"Oh, la. He is already gone off to sea again." Her lower lip thrust out in a pout, and she looked up at him from beneath the veil of her lashes. "Leaving me all alone."

"Ah." It was almost amusing to watch her flirt. And gratifying. At present his wife was absorbed in conversation with Hickey, her hand on his arm and her adoring smile focused on him. "Would you care to dance, Mrs. Boswell?" Lucas said abruptly. "I should like to hear more about your strange and wonderful experiences."

Emma burned.

Discipline kept the smile on her face as she listened to Sir Woodrow and her grandfather trade stories about their trouble in getting a proper fitting from their favorite tailor. Across the assembly room, Lucas waltzed with a gorgeous, black-haired woman. He had not danced so closely with *her*, Emma fumed.

Was it her imagination, or did his hand slip tighter around his partner's trim waist as he dipped his head to speak to her? Emma knew the feel of that hand, big and warm, a hand capable of both protecting and arousing. Perhaps he preferred women of dark beauty.

Like his mistress, the love of his life.

Emma's rancor seared deeper. She resented another woman touching her husband. It was only that he was making a mockery of their marriage, flaunting the freedom of a gentleman to have assignations. While his wife must behave with perfect decorum.

"Hssst," said her grandfather. "Methinks I spy the lady of my dreams."

Emma turned to see his nimble form flit over to a gathering near the orchestra. "The lady of his dreams?" she repeated in bafflement. "What is he talking about?"

Sir Woodrow leaned closer to her ear. "Briggs has fixed upon the idea of marrying an heiress," he said in an undertone.

"Grandpapa?" Emma could not get over her amazement. This must be his way of heeding Lucas's advice and taking responsibility for his debts. She had no more time to ponder the matter, for Lord Briggs was guiding a young—a very young—woman toward them.

She had a long, narrow face and a whippet-thin body. Wearing a high-waisted green gown of the latest fashion, she topped Lord Briggs by a good four inches, not including the dyed ostrich plume bobbing above her tight, Grecian curls. Gaudy emeralds glinted at her throat and ears. Clutching his arm, she simpered at him, looking ridiculously juvenile.

"I've brought someone to meet you," he announced. "May I present my granddaughter, Lady Wortham, and Sir Woodrow Hickey. This is Miss Minnie Pomfret."

The girl looked struck dumb as Woodrow made his bow to her. Gaping at Emma, she opened her mouth and closed it. A ruddy hue stained her cheeks. "Lady . . . *Wortham,* did you say?"

"Yes," Emma said with a smile. "I'm pleased to meet you."

She held out her gloved hand, and Miss Minnie Pomfret stared at it as if it were a snake. "Oh, my stars! Mama says I am not to associate with women of your character," she blurted out. "Forgive me, Lord Briggs, I didn't realize . . ." Turning, she took herself off at an unladylike trot, the plume bouncing above her head.

Emma felt herself blanch. The opinion of a callow girl didn't matter. Yet she couldn't deny an ache deep within herself. Despite the dowager's concerted efforts, there were still people who believed the old gossip.

"Cheeky little baggage," Lord Briggs grumbled. "Ought to go after the chit and tan her hide."

Emma placed her hand on his arm. "No, Grandpapa. Let Miss Pomfret be."

"How exceedingly ill-bred of her," Sir Woodrow said, his lip curled. "I'm sorry you were so insulted, Emma. Would you care to sit down?"

"No, thank you."

"The music is lovely, is it not? Perhaps we should dance, after all."

He was trying to distract her, and his solicitousness suddenly annoyed her. "If you could fetch me a lemonade?"

"At once." He went off to join the throng around the refreshment table.

"I've ruined your courtship, I'm afraid," Emma murmured to her grandfather. "Though she was a bit young, don't you think?"

"Her papa made a fortune in coal. Money can make up for many a flaw." His eyes danced with merriment. "But if truth's to be told, with that long face, Miss Minnie reminds me of an old hound of mine." He threw back his head and howled like a dog.

"Grandpapa, hush!" Emma exclaimed, as several guests turned to stare. "You should be ashamed."

He sobered. "I am. I'm ashamed Mannering holds my markers, after I promised not to gamble anymore. But never fear. I'll find another heiress to charm." Grinning, he rocked back and forth on his heels. "There's plenty as wants a title who'll take a creaky old codger like me."

Emma bit her lip. No matter what Lucas said, she could not stand idle while her grandfather shackled himself to a featherbrained debutante fifty years his junior.

She glanced around the crowded ballroom. Another set was about to begin, and she recalled promising this dance to a sallow-faced viscount. Lucas and his gypsy were nowhere to be seen.

Wait. There he was. She caught a glimpse of his arrestingly handsome profile and longish dark hair as he headed out the terrace door. With that woman.

Emma stiffened. They'd gone out to the garden. Would he kiss her in the moonlight, too?

Resentment ravaged Emma's heart; then she told herself to be glad he was gone. All evening, he'd been watching her like a hungry tiger. Now she could slip away, and quickly, before her next partner claimed his dance. And before her host came in search of her, seeking to cancel Grandpapa's debt.

A shudder gripped Emma. Weaving her way through the throng, she kept a watch for Lord Gerald Mannering. Upon seeing him leading a large-bosomed beauty onto the dance floor, Emma breathed a silent sigh of relief.

Now was her chance to play the Bond Street Burglar.

On the terrace outside the ballroom, Lucas brushed the twigs off his brown brocaded coat. He stank of Mrs. Boswell's perfume.

Fool. What had he hoped to accomplish by taking her outside? The very instant they'd stepped into the shadows, she had thrown herself at him in a brazen kiss, and he'd had to wrestle himself free. They'd ended up tumbling ignominiously into the shrubbery. When he made clear his lack of desire for her, she had called him a few choice names and stalked back into the house. In search of more docile prey, no doubt.

She was merely a distraction, he acknowledged with a grimace. A way to forget Emma.

He stepped into the ballroom and surveyed the swirling hordes of guests. Briggs chatted with a plain-faced miss. Hickey stood near the refreshment table, engaged in conversation with a curly-haired dandy. But Emma was nowhere to be seen. Nor was Mannering.

Damn. *Bloody damn.* He shouldn't have taken his eyes off her, not even for an instant.

Prodded by suspicion, Lucas swiftly made his way to the door. Guests strolled through the foyer, heading toward the card room or the dining chamber. Black-coated footmen bearing trays of food hastened up and down the passageway to the kitchen, in preparation for the midnight supper.

And then he saw her. A flick of blue skirt and a flash of fair hair.

He went after her, nearly knocking down an under-butler toting a tray of wine bottles. Catching up to her by the ornate newel post, Lucas closed his fingers around her warm, bare shoulder and murmured in her ear, "Where are you going?"

She spun around, her eyes big and blue in the faceted light of a crystal chandelier. "Lucas!" Her gloved hand flew to her throat and toyed with the pearls there. "You nearly frightened me out of my skin."

He drew her into an alcove beneath the stairs. "Where are you going?" he repeated.

"Why, to fetch a glass of rum punch from the supper room." She dipped her head so that he could not help but admire the fine curve of her neck. "They're serving only lemonade and champagne in the ballroom, and I confess, I wanted something a little less . . . tedious."

"I'm surprised you didn't ask one of your spaniels to fetch for you. Hickey, for one. Or have I caught you in another lie?"

Her mouth pursed in pretty annoyance. "Who are you to question me? *You* disappeared with that gypsy woman." With a disdainful sniff, she added, "You reek of her."

Something sparked in her eyes, something he couldn't quite credit. Something that gave him great satisfaction. He ran his finger down the satiny smoothness of her cheek. "Jealous?"

She stood there a moment, her pink lips parted and her eyes rounded, focused on him. "I could ask the same of you. But I shan't." With unexpected wifely care, she stretched up on tiptoe and plucked a leaf out of his hair, crumbling it between her gloved fingers. "In truth, I'm too parched to quarrel. And my feet ache from dancing. If I sit right here, will you be so kind as to fetch my drink?"

She settled herself on a gilt chair and gazed up sweetly at

him. His suspicions melted like wax to a candle flame. With her hands clasped in her lap, Emma looked like an angel. An angel who made him suffer the fiery torment of the damned.

"Wait here," he said gruffly, and stalked away.

The moment her husband vanished into the assemblage of people, Emma sprang up and slipped out of the alcove. She hastened down the passageway that led to the kitchen. She had intended to go up the grand staircase, but she dared not risk him turning back and seeing her.

Finding a door cleverly disguised in the paneling, she took a swift glance around, then entered the servants' staircase. It was dim and dingy, a narrow shaft designed for utilitarian purposes. At least she could be reasonably certain of encountering no one since all the servants would be engaged in catering to the guests. Her skirts rustling, she ascended the steep wooden steps, opened another door, and peeked out.

The corridor was empty. She could hear muffled voices coming from one of the bedrooms that had been set aside for the ladies' convenience. Emma's slippers made no sound on the thick carpet runner. Judging by her knowledge of similar town houses, the master's bedchamber would be at the end of this passage. Emma planned to make short work of pilfering Lord Gerald's jewel case.

What a shame she had not been accepted by society these past few years. Really, this sort of burgling was so much easier than creeping along a narrow ledge three floors above the ground.

Emma was almost to Lord Gerald's bedroom when a hand clamped down on her shoulder. For the second time that evening, she jumped in surprise and whirled around. Instead of her husband, she saw the sly face and lush copper curls of Lord Gerald Mannering himself.

His brown eyes undressed her. "Emma, fancy meeting you up here. Were you looking for me?"

Of all the ill luck. She steeled herself against a shudder

and worked her dry lips into a flirtatious smile. "Oh, you startled me. Where did you come from?"

"Your erotic dreams," he said, reaching for her. "It's time for our tryst, darling. Time to settle your grandpapa's debt."

"No, no, no," she said, shaking her finger at him teasingly while backing away. "We agreed on half past midnight, remember? By then, supper will be over and my husband will be engaged in cards. And I'll be free for you."

"We're alone now." Lord Gerald uttered a playful growl. "Come, my pet, give me a bite of those luscious breasts."

"Not now," Emma said, when his fingers brushed her bosom. To soften her sharp response, she ducked her head shyly. "I'm embarrassed to admit, you caught me on my way to the necessary room. I'm afraid my need is rather pressing."

He let his hands fall to his sides. "I'll wait here for you, then."

"I fear to enrage his lordship. He has a horrid temper." She tapped her finger on her lips. "But perhaps I can persuade him to engage in card playing sooner. I'll rendezvous with you in an hour."

"As you say, then," Lord Gerald muttered. "We'll meet here at eleven and don't be late."

"I won't be," she promised, her fingers crossed behind her back. "And please bring along a glass of champagne, will you? I'm ever so thirsty."

Grumbling, he started for the grand staircase. When he turned back to look, she blew him a shaky kiss. He pretended to catch it, pressing his fingers to his own lips. Then he disappeared down the stairs.

She hastened to Lord Gerald's bedchamber and went inside, closing the door behind her. There, she leaned back against the white-painted panel and hissed out a breath of relief. Her heart pounded so hard she felt dizzy. Dear God. That was close. Too close for comfort.

Then she couldn't help but grin, imagining three men wandering around the house, carrying drinks and searching for her. Really, men were so easily gulled.

The twin flames of a bronze torchiere on the bedside table flickered over a room of gaudy decor. Pea-green walls set off the red brocaded draperies. The bedposts were topped by gilt sphynx heads, and the Egyptian motif continued in the red chaise longue and the ornate cabinetry. A shiny ebony screen in a corner bore paintings of nude dancing women. The very thought of being alone here with Lord Gerald sickened her.

But Lucas? What if she shared that massive bed with her husband?

Warmth glowed deep inside her, and she wondered when she had ceased to fear his touch. She almost looked forward to their time together each night, when he would hold her and kiss her, never pushing her farther than she was willing to go, yet coaxing her to the limits of her desire.

A clock chimed softly on a table, snapping her back to the present. She had justice to mete out. Of course, Lucas would challenge her on *that*. He would accuse her of being a petty thief.

She squared her drooping shoulders. Fie on him. He didn't understand her need to protect Grandpapa. Now, where did Lord Gerald Mannering keep his precious gems?

She tiptoed into the dressing room and glanced around. The place was tidy, the mark of a diligent valet. No jewel case had been left conveniently on the dressing table or chest of drawers or clothes press. She squandered five minutes on an efficient search of the usual hiding places, but came up empty-handed. There wasn't so much as a ha'penny to steal.

Drat. Every moment she tarried here increased the risk of discovery. The thought raised a prickling of fear, a fear she hadn't known in previous burglaries. It wasn't that she expected Lord Gerald to appear with a pistol. She was on edge because Lucas would be looking for her.

But she had time yet. A thin margin of time before he made his way through the crush of people, fetched her that punch, and then guessed where she'd disappeared to. She intended to be long gone from here by then, and back downstairs at the party.

Emma forced her mind back to the burglary. Gentlemen most often kept their jewels in a repository in their dressing room. But Lord Gerald might have a safe in his bedchamber.

She hastened out and peeked behind the gilt-framed paintings, wrinkling her nose at one of a naked entwined couple. How tasteless. It was worse than the lewd screen in the corner. Thinking of which, she started across the crimson rug to check behind the screen.

The quiet click of the doorlatch sounded like thunder. She spun around, caught in the center of the room. The gilded white door framed the tall, dark shape of a man. A man whose chilly gaze froze the breath in her lungs.

"My dear wife," Lucas said, raising a glass to her, "would you care for a drink?"

ᥱ **Chapter 14** ᥲ

Lucas had the grim satisfaction of seeing Emma turn pale. The loss of color in her cheeks heightened the illusion of an alabaster statue. But no stone goddess had ever had such luxuriant silvery-blond hair or a heaving bosom designed to catch a man's eye. No stone goddess had Emma's talent for making a fool of him, either.

Leashing his wrath, he strolled toward her. "I'd a suspicion I might find you here," he said. "Next time you want to get rid of me, try a better excuse than sending me for a glass of rum punch."

Pink color rushed back into her face. She thrust out her lower lip in a sulky pout. "Next time, try staying out of my affairs."

"Affairs?" He gave a contemptuous laugh. "I suppose you're going to pretend you're here because you've an assignation with Mannering."

"And if I do?"

"I'd say you were lying again. And then I'd order you to get into that bed so I could lay claim to you first." He burned to do just that, to lift her skirts and teach her to cease tormenting him. He mockingly indicated the drink in his hand. "I believe this is yours, madam."

"Thank you, my lord." She took the glass from him. And promptly dashed the contents in his face.

He leapt back. Too late. The sticky liquid dripped down

his cheeks and nose and drenched his clothing, soaking through his coat and shirt and cravat. He blinked his stinging eyes. ''What the devil—''

He whipped out his handkerchief and mopped the mess from his face. His angry gaze flicked to Emma. She held the empty glass in one hand and covered her mouth with the other. Impishness danced in her blue eyes.

She was laughing. The shameless chit was *laughing*.

''I'm so sorry,'' she said demurely. ''I simply don't know what came over me.''

''You . . . don't . . . know.'' Lucas was so furious he nearly stumbled over his words. He wanted to turn her over his knee, civilized behavior be damned. Then, in the midst of his rage, a germ of humor infected him. How ridiculous of them to be quarreling instead of kissing.

He took a step toward her. ''I know what came over you. The desire to distract me.''

She took a step backward. ''Distract you? What rubbish.''

''You don't want me to guess you're here to rob Mannering.''

''I beg your pardon? I threw the drink because you spoke crudely to me.''

''No.'' He advanced slowly, forcing her to retreat. ''There's more to it than that.''

''Of course there is. I also wished to cover the stench of that woman's perfume.''

''Don't bring her into this. You threw the drink because there's a passionate woman hiding inside you. A woman who wants to learn how to make love as well as she can plot a burglary.''

Emma bumped into an elephant's foot stool, then regained her balance. ''Ha! I wanted to teach *you* not to treat me like your possession.''

''On the contrary, I've yet to possess you.'' He backed her into an ebony screen exhibiting a parade of naked Egyptian dancers. He had no interest in the vulgar display, not when he could plant his hands on Emma's bare shoulders and draw her against him. "It's past time to rectify that over-sight, hmm?" he said silkily.

She tipped back her head. Wariness glinted in her eyes, yet there was a trace of seductiveness, too, in the way she lowered her lashes a bit. She had the look of a woman who wanted to be kissed.

Emma desired him. But she was afraid to admit it.

He told himself to feel triumph, but tenderness stole over him instead. She had haunted his heart for so long, and now he was haunting hers. He was shaken by the fierce longing to make her love him.

Fool. He could never trust her. She was a liar, a thief. She cared nothing for him. She wanted to divorce him so she could marry someone else.

Yet none of that seemed important now. They were husband and wife, bound by sacred vows and by a devil's bargain. He bent his head to her, and her lips parted. A breath away, he paused to savor the moment of her surrender. He fancied he could hear their hearts beating in unison.

In the next instant, he realized it was the tapping of footsteps. A woman's throaty laugh sounded out in the corridor, followed by a man's deep voice.

Acting on instinct, he thrust Emma behind the screen and then followed her, urging her to her knees so she could not be seen. He dropped down behind her, hugging her close in the tight corner space. And not an instant too soon.

On a rattling of the latch, the door opened, then shut. The scuffling of feet indicated that more than one person had entered. There came the unmistakable smacking of lips and a woman's murmur of pleasure.

"Mmmm. Delicious. I do so love the taste of a man."

Her partner loosed a growl. "What luscious breasts you have, my pet. Give me a bite."

"You're an impatient one, my lord," she said on a breathy laugh. "I don't believe I've ever made love to a man no more than five minutes after our first meeting."

"I wish to give you another strange and wonderful experience to add to your collection."

Clothing rustled, interspersed with giggles and more noisy kisses.

Lucas clenched his teeth. Hell. *Bloody hell.* He recognized those voices. They belonged to Mrs. Boswell and Lord Gerald Mannering.

Lucas crouched behind Emma, holding her wedged between his thighs. His arm beneath her breasts, he felt the drumming of her heart. He detested being a voyeur, and he knew Emma must be mortified. Yet his body responded to her nearness with throbbing intensity.

They could yet make their presence known, claim to have borrowed the bedroom for their own tryst, and apologize for the intrusion. But then Mannering might guess the truth—that Emma had come to steal from him.

Had she already done so? Did his wife have five hundred pounds' worth of jewels secreted in a hidden pocket?

Lucas smoothed his hands down the back of her gown, along the slim curve of her waist, and over the flare of her hips. She shuddered out a breath and turned her head back to look up at him with wide, inquiring eyes. A pretty flush tinted her cheeks.

He lifted his finger to his lips to indicate the need to remain quiet. She bit her lip and nodded. At least she had the sense to realize the danger of her situation. And it only went to prove her guilt, Lucas sternly reminded himself. Damn her willfulness to perdition.

If Emma were caught with Mannering's jewels in her possession, Lucas would be forced to buy Mannering's silence. But what if the devil took it into his mind to win acclaim for capturing the Bond Street Burglar? What if Mannering had Emma arrested? Lucas dared not take the chance.

He could hear Emma's soft breathing over the grunts and giggles coming from beyond the screen. Very slowly, she placed the empty glass on the floor, beside a ball of dust where the upstairs maid had skimped on her cleaning. The smell of rum punch pervaded the air, but Lucas hoped Mannering was too preoccupied to notice.

The bedropes groaned—followed by a human groan. "So you like to be on top, do you, minx?"

"Yes, and I see you've risen to the occasion quite admirably," Mrs. Boswell said. "Perhaps a rubdown is in order. To prepare my stallion for mounting."

The bed squeaked again, then Mannering cried out, "Oh, yes, my pet. Yes!"

The sounds of their lovemaking touched only the edge of Lucas's attention. He was keenly aware of Emma, kneeling in front of him with her fists resting on her thighs and her head bowed. He wondered what she was thinking as she listened to the pantings and moans of the bedroom's other occupants.

His own thoughts were decidedly carnal. The blue silk of her gown enhanced the beauty of her womanly form. He was tempted to continue his search, to seek out jewels more precious than stolen booty. And why shouldn't he? She was his wife.

With a few flicks of his fingers, he undid the buttons at the back of her dress. He pushed down the short, puffy sleeves along with her bodice. She gave a little gasp and flinched. Yet she made no move to stop him as he loosened her corset and then slid his hands inside, finding the sweet, silken roundness of her bosom.

Her back arched against his chest, offering him two lush handfuls. He stroked the pearly tips with his thumbs. Instead of resisting him, she turned her head to the side, her cheek nuzzling against his dampened shirt like a kitten begging to be petted. God. God! Still cradling her warm flesh, Lucas bent down and captured her lips, taking possession of her mouth in a long, deep kiss.

The blood burned through his veins. He could not remember when his urge to mount a woman had been stronger. He wanted to strip off Emma's clothing, to arouse her to mindless yearning, to become one with her at last. But not now. Not here.

Reluctantly he broke the kiss, letting his hands rest lightly around her breasts as he struggled to master himself. What a damnable fix. Even if Emma were willing, he could not risk their being overheard. They must wait out the conclusion of this awkward predicament.

A rhythmic squeaking came from the bed. "Faster, my prize mare, faster," Mannering gasped out.

"Slower," Mrs. Boswell panted. "Let us not gallop to the finish—let us savor the ride."

"A canter, then. Tallyho!"

Emma made an almost inaudible sound, and Lucas looked down to see her face still turned toward him. Her blush had deepened to a rosy hue, and she pressed her fist to her mouth. Her gaze touched his, skittered away, then returned. In the dimness behind the screen, her eyes sparkled. To his amazement, he felt her body shake with near-hysterical mirth. The absurdity of the situation struck him, too, and he was tempted to throw back his head and howl with laughter.

Lucas could think of only one distraction before they gave away their presence. He kissed her again.

The moment his mouth touched hers, the world fell away. It was only the two of them, bound together in tender torment. Her hand stole up to stroke his jaw, and that gentle touch added fuel to the furnace inside him. He should not want Emma with such keen desperation. But he did. God, he did.

Her warm bottom was snuggled into his groin. The flimsy layers of gown and petticoat could not prevent him from appreciating her softness. Despite the risks, he had to touch her.

He tugged at her skirt, and she shifted slightly so the silk garment lifted. Reaching beneath her hem, he settled his hand on her slim, warm thigh, over the garter that secured her silk stocking. Her body went taut, and he brushed his lips and tongue across hers, blatantly using his expertise to keep her from crying out in fear.

He slid his hand higher . . . and higher. And this time, he wasn't looking for a hidden stash of pilfered stones. When at last he touched her intimately, her muscles quivered as if

she were on the verge of panic. Into her ear, he breathed,
"Look at me."

Her eyes opened and she gazed warily up at him. He
willed Emma to see that he was not the villain who had
attacked her, that he was the man who would awaken her
sensuality. A sensuality far deeper than the sexual lust being
shared beyond the screen, where stirring moans and blissful
sighs indicated the rise toward climax.

"Trust me," he whispered.

Holding her gaze, Lucas found the parting in her under-
drawers. So soft she was there. A lush tangle of curls. A
moist feminine mystery. She clutched at him, and he kissed
her again, to halt her descent into the terrors of memory.
Ever so slowly she leaned her head back into the crook of
his neck. With a sigh, she adjusted her position, allowing
him deeper access.

A fierce exultation seized Lucas. At last . . . at last he
could touch the heat of her. Nestled within her dewy folds
lay her pearl, and when he caressed it, she squirmed against
him in glorious abandon, the friction torturing the swollen
rod inside his breeches.

But he cared not for his own gratification. His physical
need was drowned by his turbulent desire to satisfy Emma.
He craved nothing less than her full surrender.

Half turning to hide her face in his throat, she clung to his
neck, clung with dainty fingers and sharp nails, heedless of
his rum-dampened shirt. She pressed shamelessly into his
hand, and he could feel her warm, panting breaths. At last a
long, low sob escaped her, and a shudder coursed through
her slim body. She convulsed around his fingers once . . .
then again . . . and yet again before falling limp in his arms,
her bare bosom rising and falling.

Lucas drew his hand from beneath her skirts. A foolish
grin on his face, he tipped his head back. The black expanse
of the screen stretched above him. He shouldn't feel so
damned good. His legs were numb and tingly from crouching
so long, and Emma had consigned him to the fires of unre-
quited passion.

Only then did he notice the silence in the room.

"What the devil was that?" Mannering said.

"Mmmm?"

"A moan—or a sob. I say, there's someone in here, spying on us."

Lucas's arms tensed around Emma. She drew her head up sharply as if coming back to an awareness of their surroundings. Christ. If they were caught hiding . . .

The bedlinens rustled. " 'Twas a reveler out in the corridor," Mrs. Boswell said. "Now lie back, my horny beast. We've time for another tumble."

There came a long stretch of noisy kissing. Then Mannering exclaimed, "Good God! It's nearly eleven. We daren't linger a moment longer." Bare feet smacked the floor. Clothing slithered as he began to dress. "Come, up with you."

"Why the haste?" Mrs. Boswell's voice rose shrilly. "Why, you've another assignation planned. Don't you?"

"Now, now, my pet. Leave off the fussing, and there'll be a present for you on the morrow. From the jeweler."

"Why, my lord," she purred. "You're endowed with generosity—as well as other, naughtier assets."

Amid the sound of more kisses and clothes rustling, Lucas stayed very still. Emma huddled against him, barely breathing, her head lowered. At last the amorous couple tripped out of the bedchamber, leaving behind a heavy silence. And a great lifting of relief in Lucas.

With fingers that trembled visibly, Emma drew up her bodice. He fastened the back of her gown, entranced by the vulnerable curve of her nape. A deep tenderness suffused him. Now that she'd had a taste of the ultimate pleasure, she would welcome him into her bed. They would be a true married couple, if only for a short time. He found he wanted that very much—to see her smile at him over the breakfast table, to talk to her of inconsequential matters, to feel his baby kick inside her womb. . . .

She stood up, wobbling on her feet and bracing her hand on the wall. He rose, too, holding her arm to steady her. His legs tingled as the blood rushed back into them. Still, she kept her face averted. She was feeling awkward, no doubt, shy in light of her surrender to passion.

"Emma," he said, touching her silken cheek. He couldn't trust himself to say more. His throat was strangely taut.

She brushed past him and went around the screen. Resisting the urge to strut, he followed her out into the bedroom. The faint smell of sex mingled with the muskiness of Mrs. Boswell's perfume.

He saw Emma glance toward the bed with its tangled sheets; then she turned away. She shook out her skirt, but it was crumpled hopelessly. "I wish to go home," she said in a subdued voice. "Immediately."

"Of course. We make a disgraceful pair, don't we? You in your wrinkled gown and I in my rum-soaked shirt. We'll have to steal out the back door so we won't shock the *ton*." Lucas walked to her, slid his arm around the hourglass curve of her waist, and nuzzled her ear. "Then we can go home . . . to bed."

She wrenched herself from him. "Stay away from me."

"Emma?" he said in confusion. "What's wrong?"

"That was *her*, wasn't it?"

"Who?"

"Your gypsy. I can smell her perfume." Screwing up her nose, Emma paced in agitation. "That's the sort of woman you prefer. A strumpet who will engage in lewd acts. And you're trying to turn me into a slut like her."

Her behavior made sudden, chilling sense. "Emma, I'm not after some sort of twisted revenge. I don't want to change you into a whore. I want to give you pleasure, that's all."

Avoiding his gaze, she hugged herself. "I don't know what you did to me just now. I don't know how you made me feel so . . . so shattered. But I shan't be so humiliated ever again."

"There is nothing humiliating about physical passion. It's a natural part of marital intimacy."

"Then I wish I'd married Woodrow," Emma said in a rush. "*He* would never have taken advantage of me. He would have behaved like a gentleman and kept his hands to himself.''

Her words struck a clean blow straight into Lucas's unguarded heart. She cared nothing for him. She never would. He was a fool to hope for more. Twice a fool.

He retreated into the cold shell of indifference that hid his pain from the world. Striding to her side, he took firm hold of her chin, forcing her to look at him. Even now, her big blue eyes had the power to weaken his knees.

''I will not apologize for taking what you offered to me,'' he stated icily. ''Nor will I cease to seduce you. By God, Emma, you'll give me a son. Whether you're willing or not.''

The next morning Emma emerged from her bedchamber, dressed in a warm walking dress and pelisse, only to spy several footmen carrying trunks and boxes out of the room occupied by Olivia and her husband. They were leaving today, Emma remembered. As anxious as she was to escape Wortham House, she would have to stop and say her farewells.

She knocked on the door. A maid allowed her inside. Olivia stood looking out the window, the misty morning light silhouetting her maternal form clad in a plum-colored traveling dress. She pressed one hand to her lower back.

''Are you having pains?'' Emma asked, hurrying toward her sister-in-law. ''Perhaps you should sit down.''

Olivia smiled fleetingly. ''No, it's only the weight of the baby. I've another six weeks until my confinement.''

''Are you sure you oughtn't to stay here?''

Olivia shook her head. ''Hugh and I wish our child to be born at our country estate. It's a tradition in his family.'' Closing her eyes, she smoothed her hands over the ripe curve of her belly.

Emma felt like an intruder on a private moment. Though Olivia had grown friendlier, there was still an invisible barrier between them—the wrong Emma had done to Lucas by foisting another man's child on him. Olivia couldn't know Jenny was her niece.

A deep longing tugged at Emma as she recalled her own pregnancy, the bittersweet joy of knowing new life grew within her. How she wanted to experience that again. And she could, if she let down her defenses and allowed Lucas to consummate their marriage.

I will not apologize for taking what you offered to me. Nor will I cease to seduce you. . . .

Remembering the shocking pleasure he had aroused in her the previous night, she felt flushed and weak. She had lain awake half the night, waiting for him, yet despite his threat, he had not come to her. And she didn't know whether to be gladdened or saddened. . . .

"Oh!" Her sister-in-law's eyes flashed open. A beautiful smile softened her mouth. "He moved. The baby moved."

"Or perhaps *she*." Impelled by yearning, Emma asked, "May I feel?"

Olivia hesitated, then gave a nod. Emma came forward and placed her hand atop the curve of Olivia's belly.

"Not there," Olivia said. "Here."

She took Emma's hand and moved it lower. Immediately, Emma felt something jab her palm. She laughed in delight and Olivia did, too. Her hand remained over Emma's and, as they looked at each other, warmth flowed between them, the nostalgic warmth of friendship.

"I shall miss you," Emma said softly. "I've never thanked you for standing up for me at Lord Jasper's soiree."

"I couldn't bear for Lady Jasper to make nasty innuendos." Olivia's smile turned wry. "I daresay I thought that was *my* prerogative."

"You were right to hate what I did," Emma said, drawing back her hand. "I only hope you can find room in your heart to forgive me someday."

Olivia tilted her head to the side, her reddish hair glinting in the light. A gentle wisdom entered her gaze. "I believe I already have."

She opened her arms and, with a glad cry, Emma hugged her sister-in-law. Their embrace brought a buoyant relief to Emma, at least until Olivia spoke.

"I cannot hold a grudge," she said, "because I know you truly love Lucas. I've seen it in your eyes."

Startled, Emma drew back. "You have?"

"Yes. Every time you look at him, your whole face lights up." She smiled. "It's the way I feel about my Hugh."

She was mistaken. *Mistaken.* Somehow Emma managed to say her good-byes without drowning in a tide of agitation. She hastened down the stairway, avoiding the library for fear she might encounter Lucas.

Yet perversely, she yearned to see him.

Emma nodded to the footman who held open the door for her. Though a chill breeze blew, her face felt hot as she walked along the street. Olivia was wrong—she had to be. Emma loved Woodrow, a kind, considerate gentleman who had proven himself a staunch ally to both her and Jenny. She couldn't possibly love a domineering rogue who demanded she submit to him, create a new life, and then relinquish her son forever.

Yet Lucas exerted a dark power over her. Last night had proven as much. She'd been utterly mortified while listening to the erotic antics of Lord Gerald and his bedmate, but she had been swept away by a scandalous temptation, too. She had wanted Lucas to touch her. She had reveled in his caresses. She had lost all shame and behaved like a wanton. The intense pleasure of it had shattered her, body and soul.

That's the sort of woman you prefer. A strumpet who will engage in lewd acts. And you're trying to turn me into a slut like her.

She cringed to remember her vicious words. She had meant them at the time. She had wanted to run and hide, to deny that she'd succumbed to him. She had wanted to punish him for tempting her into abandonment, when she had vowed never to be at the mercy of a man, ever again.

But did Lucas deserve all the blame?

No. He had given her ample opportunity to refuse him. If anything, she'd been titillated by the risk of discovery. The extent of her loss of control frightened Emma. Lucas had transported her beyond the hellish experience with Andrew and into a sensual heaven. How could he evoke such glorious feelings in her? She wouldn't dream of letting Woodrow touch her so.

Emma jumped back from the curbstone as a carriage careened past. A few passersby, mostly servants or tradesmen, gawked at the sight of a lady alone and on foot. No doubt she would be chastised by the dowager for venturing forth without a coach or a retinue of servants. But Emma needed time to think, to sort through her scattered emotions. She needed to reassure herself that last night hadn't changed anything.

And in the interest of peace, she owed Lucas an apology. But she wasn't ready to face him yet. She was fleeing like a coward to the man who made her feel safe. And God help her if Lucas discovered her destination.

∽ **Chapter 15** ∽

"Do you know where my mama went?" Jenny asked.

Disconcerted, Lucas turned from the mirror in his dressing room where he had been tying his cravat, and frowned down at his visitor. Emma's daughter was scrubbed and dressed in a white pinafore over a green gown. Two neat white bows tied the ends of her braids. He glanced beyond her, into his deserted bedroom.

"Who let you in here?" he asked sternly.

"I let myself in, m'lord," Jenny said, sketching a curtsy. "I tapped on the door, but no one answered."

Of course not. Hajib had already left for the docks. And Lucas had been absorbed in a dark fantasy about the object of Jenny's search. "I haven't the least notion of your mother's whereabouts," he said dismissingly. "I'd suggest trying the library."

Jenny shook her head, her braids flying. "Mama isn't there. And she isn't in her room. The footman saw her go out for a walk."

"I see." But Lucas didn't see. Where would Emma have gone on foot? For a stroll around the square?

The little fool never obeyed propriety. He'd like to teach her a lesson or two in private. Foremost of which would be gratitude toward the first man to bring her to ecstasy.

A tug on his sleeve distracted him. "Please, sir," Jenny said. "Will you draw my tooth?"

"Your tooth."

"It's ready to come out. And I'm afraid to eat 'cause I might swallow it."

She pointed to her top front tooth, the one beside the gap. He very nearly crouched down to examine it, then caught himself. She seemed to take it for granted he would perform the duty of a parent. "Isn't there a nanny or nursemaid who can help you?"

Jenny shook her head. "All the nursemaids are in a dither, what with the packing. The other children are leaving today." Her lower lip quivered. "Anyway, my mama is more gentler. But I don't know where to find her."

Her woebegone expression did him in. "Come along, then," he said in resignation.

Turning on his heel, he stalked out to the bank of windows in the bedroom, where a watery sunshine cast sufficient light for the task. Jenny tagged along after him. When he placed his hand beneath her small chin and tilted her head up, she obligingly opened her mouth for his inspection. The loose tooth hung askew.

"A string," he pronounced. "Tied to the doorknob. That is how my governess pulled teeth."

Eyes rounding, Jenny clapped her hand to her mouth. "No!" she said, her voice muffled by her fingers. "Mama uses her handkerchief."

"Her handkerchief."

"Uh-huh. She wraps it around the tooth and pulls."

"That sounds simple enough," Lucas muttered.

He fetched a clean handkerchief from the dressing room. Then he nudged up Jenny's chin again. She stared up at him, and her blue-green eyes shone with the purity of trust. A trust that made him feel unequal to the task.

Nonsense. It was only that he hated to cause the child pain.

"Let's get on with it," he said crisply.

His palms felt damp as he looked inside her mouth. Carefully he approached the tooth with the starched linen.

"Thtop!" Jenny lisped.

He snatched back his hand. "Did I hurt you?"

"No. But don't forget to say the magic words."

"The magic words."

"You know. The ones Mama always says. To scare the hurt away."

"What words are those?"

"I don't know. Mama says they're a secret between her and the tooth fairy."

Jenny looked up at him so earnestly he didn't have the heart to scoff at magic spells and fairies. Nor could he bring himself to tell her that words had no power over pain. That left him with only one alternative. To fib.

"All right, then," he said. "But as it's a secret, I shall say the spell to myself."

He reached into her mouth again. He could feel the wobbly tooth. If he hurt her, she would think ill of him. He didn't know why that disturbed him, except Jenny seemed to have complete faith in him, and he hated to fall short of her expectations. How the devil did Emma extract a tooth painlessly? A tug downward? A twist? Did she do it fast? Or little by little?

Bloody hell. It was only a tooth.

He took firm hold of it and moved his lips soundlessly as if uttering an incantation. Before he could even wrench downward, the tooth came free into his handkerchief. An absurd sense of victory suffused him——as if he had negotiated the purchase of a rare artifact. He held out the baby tooth for Jenny's inspection. A droplet of blood reddened the end.

She took the tooth and examined it, then stuck it into the pocket of her pinafore. With the tip of her tongue, she probed the gap in her front teeth. "You *did* thay the thpell," she said, her eyes rounded. "I thought you might be jutht pretending."

He bent down to meet her at eye level. "Now where would you get a silly idea like that?"

She retracted her tongue and gravely regarded him. "Because Mama says you're not my real father. But I think . . . I think I will call you Papa, anyway."

Her announcement knotted Lucas's throat. He could only gape at the little girl, who beamed as if he had just passed a test and received his reward. Before he could fashion a reply from the blankness of his brain, she added generously, "You may go out tomorrow with Mama and me to celebrate my half-birthday."

"Half-birthday?"

"I am exactly six and a half tomorrow. Mama always lets me celebrate twice a year. Because, you see, I'm her only child." Like a miniature governess, she shook her finger at him. "Mind, you must be ready at ten o'clock. Mama doesn't like tardiness."

Quite unexpectedly, she threw her arms around his middle and hugged him. He could think of nothing else to do but hug her back. How small she was, how defenseless. "Good-bye, Papa," she said, and skipped out of the bedroom.

Papa.

Lucas gripped the handkerchief in his fist. His throat felt unnaturally taut, as if his neckcloth were suffocating him. Uttering a low curse, he stalked into the dressing room to retie his cravat.

This incident should not have happened. Emma should not have gone off without a word to anyone. Then he would not have been thrust into the role of tending to her child. He had more important business awaiting him at the docks.

So where the devil was his wife?

Emma sat on a gold-striped chair in the drawing room of Sir Woodrow Hickey's town house and looked about her with interest. Because of his high regard for propriety, she had never been here before. It was more tastefully decorated than she had expected of a bachelor's dwelling. The soothing yellow walls complemented the parquet floor and gold-sprigged white draperies. Glass-paned doors were opened to a small conservatory, where roses bloomed and ivy climbed.

Setting down his teacup, Sir Woodrow sat bolt upright on the chaise across from her. "Are you quite certain it's wise for you to come here?'' he asked for what seemed like the tenth time.

Emma hid her annoyance. "I hardly know what is wise anymore," she said. "Nor do I care."

"But I don't understand why you couldn't simply have sent me a message. Do you have reason to believe that you may already be"—he paused to clear his throat—"carrying Wortham's child?"

"No." *Because I've been too afraid. Afraid of intimacy. Afraid of my own passion.*

"Ah." Relief flitted across Sir Woodrow's face, and he leaned forward, his fair eyebrows drawn together. "Then you can still reconsider the cruel bargain he forced upon you. It is unthinkable that you should tie yourself to Wortham for months, perhaps years. You scarcely know the man. It isn't too late to change your mind."

"I cannot renege on my promise to him. Once I give Lucas a son, I'll be free."

Scowling, Sir Woodrow jumped to his feet and began to pace before the white marble fireplace. "And meanwhile, when am I to see you and Jenny? Only when you can creep out of his house unnoticed. That is no way for us to live. The three of us used to go on outings, share our meals, sit together in the evenings. And now I must allow you and Jenny to live with him."

They *had* been like a family, Emma reflected, caught in a mixture of nostalgia and guilt. She had never, ever meant to hurt Woodrow. "You haven't lost us," she said gently. "Jenny regards *you* as her father. Not Lucas."

Woodrow clenched his fists. "How is he treating Jenny? I cannot imagine so proud a man welcoming her into his house."

"They never see one another," Emma assured him. "Jenny stays in the nursery or with me, in my room." Except for the time when Jenny had been playing with Toby in the library and had encountered the dowager.

Emma took a sip of tea without tasting it. She dared tell no one about her mother-in-law guessing the identity of

Jenny's sire. Not Woodrow. And especially not Lucas.

"And so the dear girl must suffer the lack of a father."
Woodrow brought his fist down onto the mantelpiece, rattling
a pair of small porcelain spaniels. "This situation is intol-
erable. I wish to heaven Wortham had granted you a divorce.
And Briggs hadn't stolen that blasted tiger mask."

Emma's fingers tensed around the delicate handle of her
teacup. She stared up at Woodrow, startled as much by his
vehemence as his words. He was usually so mild mannered.
"What do you know about the mask?"

"Forgive me," he said stiffly. "I wasn't supposed to mention what your grandfather told me. But I can no longer hold
my tongue when your honor is at stake. I know he took the
piece to compensate for all Wortham owes to you. And when
you returned it, Wortham unjustly accused *you* of stealing
the mask."

"Yes," she murmured, gazing down into her empty cup
and turning it in her hands. "I've had a time convincing him
to trust me. But I think . . . I hope he is beginning to do so.
He's even asked me to help him catalog the rare artifacts he
brought back from the East."

Yet seldom did Lucas work with her on the fascinating
project. Where did he spend his days? With his mistress?
The questions burned like poison in Emma. And if he *was*
developing faith in her, had she destroyed it when he'd
caught her prowling in Lord Gerald Mannering's bedchamber?

What was worse, she would have to play the Burglar
again, and soon. She didn't know any other way to repay
Grandpapa's gaming debt.

To her utter surprise, Sir Woodrow dropped to one knee
in front of her. "My dear Emma, you fret overly much about
gaining a place in Wortham's good graces. I confess to fear-
ing you will forsake me."

In his charcoal breeches and silver-gray coat, he reminded
her of a knight kneeling before his lady fair. How stalwart
and honorable Sir Woodrow was, how loyal and devoted.
Yet why did he never seize her in his arms and kiss her

passionately? Why did he not sweep her off her feet and carry her to bed? Her wayward fantasies turned to Lucas holding her in the darkness, Lucas kissing her deeply and intimately, Lucas stroking the places that ached for him alone. . . .

Flushed, she realized Sir Woodrow was gazing at her, awaiting an answer. ''I shan't forsake you.'' The words sounded so hollow, she added on impulse, ''In fact, perhaps you'll join Jenny and me tomorrow. We're taking a picnic luncheon to Hyde Park to celebrate her half-birthday.''

He acquiesced with such eagerness that she felt a renewed surge of dismay. When he kissed the back of her gloved hand, she experienced no tingling sensation, no thrill of excitement as she did whenever Lucas touched her. Lucas had only to look at her, and she melted with longing.

Did that mean she loved Lucas? Or were desire and love two separate forces?

Emma had not arrived at an answer by the time she descended the grand staircase the next morning. For all that she told herself to be glad Lucas had not come to her bed the previous evening, she felt an undeniable disappointment. It was the second night since their encounter in Mannering's bedroom that her husband had stayed away. She was uncomfortably aware he was angry at her.

That's the sort of woman you prefer. A strumpet who will engage in lewd acts. And you're trying to turn me into a slut like her.

Emma winced again to remember the words she had flung at him out of the desperate need to deny her own passion. The knowledge of her cruelty weighed upon her conscience. She would seek him out tonight and tell him so. The decision lightened her mood so she could again look forward to spending the day with Jenny.

But when she reached the foyer, Jenny wasn't there. She hadn't been in the nursery, either. According to the kindly old nursemaid, Jenny had gone downstairs to wait a quarter of an hour ago. Worry crept over Emma. Surely Jenny wouldn't have ventured outside alone. Would she?

Emma hastened across the foyer, her shoes tapping on the cream-colored marble tiles. As she neared the white-wigged footman, he swung open the door before she could question him.

"M'lady," he said, bowing. "His lordship and Lady Jenny await you in the carriage."

His lordship? Her heart leaping to her throat, Emma halted in the doorway. There, in a high-perch green phaeton at the curbstone, sat Lucas with her daughter on his lap. It appeared he was instructing Jenny on how to hold the ribbons.

Stunned, Emma stood with her gloved hand pressed to her aching bosom. What an endearing picture they made, the loving father teaching his little girl. It was a glimpse into the joyous family they could never be.

Jenny spied her and waved. "Mama, look at me! I'm driving the carriage."

A picnic basket was lashed to the back of the phaeton, and a groom held the single black horse. The sight gave Emma an unpleasant jolt. *Lucas* was going along on their outing? He couldn't. She'd told Sir Woodrow to meet them at Hyde Park.

"Don't look so frightened," Lucas called. "The seat isn't so high as it appears."

He smiled at her, and she felt herself tremble as she walked forward to take his outstretched hand. How handsome he looked when he smiled. What had put him in such a good humor this morning?

His fingers closed around hers, warm and firm, causing a flutter of anticipation inside her. She grasped the hand rail, placed her foot on an iron rung, and allowed him to swing her up into the open carriage.

She settled herself beside him on the leather seat, and his smoldering appraisal of her seemed to heat the cool October morning. She was glad she had chosen a flattering gown from her new wardrobe. The gold and green satin spencer showed off a skirt of moss silk trimmed with pale green ribbons. A matching bonnet covered her upswept hair.

Their legs were pressed together, and his enigmatic stare held hers for what seemed an eternity. Was he still furious about her unfair accusations? Or was he remembering their erotic encounter behind the screen, when dark desires had overwhelmed her, when he had plumbed her deepest yearnings and transported her to heaven?

"Mama?"

Emma felt a tug on her skirt. She pulled her gaze from her husband and looked down at Jenny, perched on his lap. "Yes, darling?"

"Papa says I may help him to drive."

Emma was reaching out to tuck a stray curl into Jenny's pert crimson bonnet. Only then did her words register. *Papa?*

Appalled, Emma flashed a glance at Lucas, but he was giving instructions to the groom. And then she noticed just how dizzyingly far down the cobbled street lay. She clapped one hand on Jenny's shoulder and the other on the flimsy side rail. "I don't know if this is wise—or safe. Perhaps we should take the coach—"

"Nonsense," Lucas said crisply, his gaze boring into hers. "Have a little faith in me."

"In *us*," Jenny piped up. "I'm driving, too."

Lucas flashed a grin at her. "Indeed you are, sweet pea. So long as you allow me room to see our way." He shifted her on his lap and wedged her between his thighs.

Emma had only a moment to wonder at his easy acceptance of Jenny. Then the groom mounted the rear pageboard and the phaeton set off with a jolt, the black horse prancing, harness jingling. The cool wind rushed at Emma, and she was torn between clinging to her bonnet or her daughter or the hand rail. Dear God. What was she doing? She was heading into disaster.

Oh, why hadn't she made up an excuse about forgetting her handkerchief? She could have dashed back into the house and penned a note to Sir Woodrow. The footman might have delivered it in time. But one look at Lucas had addled her brain.

Jenny giggled in delight. "We're having an adventure. Aren't we, Mama?"

Emma caught the flash of deviltry in Lucas's eyes as he glanced at her, and suddenly all her worries blew away with the wind. The high spirits she had repressed for too long came forth in an overwrought laugh. "Yes, it's an adventure. A wonderful adventure."

Deftly guiding the phaeton through the crowded streets, Lucas had the carefree look of a young buck. The wind whipped his dark hair into dashing disarray. The white cravat and buff-colored coat emphasized his bronzed skin, his well-muscled physique. She wanted to be here with him; she wanted it with all her heart and soul.

Was this love?

Instead of holding on to the rail, she slipped her hand beneath his arm and leaned against him. She had never before felt so . . . alive. The pressure of his thigh against hers spread warmth throughout her body. What would it be like to let him consummate their union and join their bodies? The prospect held a shining allure. She would go wherever Lucas wished to take her. . . .

And then she realized they were heading northward rather than to Hyde Park. "Where are we going?"

"Out of town," he said with a keen glance. "To Hampstead Heath. Do you mind?"

"No. No, of course not."

It was the answer to her prayers. Sir Woodrow would be perturbed when she and Jenny failed to appear in Hyde Park at the appointed time. But better that than a confrontation. She was in no mood for quarrels today. She would send Woodrow a mollifying note on the morrow.

Within the hour, they left the hubbub of the city and drove through a rolling countryside dotted with ponds and striped by forest and pastureland. There were stone farmhouses and stubbled fields, shorn of their summer crops. An occasional manor house perched grandly on a hill.

Jenny kept up an incessant chatter. When she asked for the twentieth time, "When are we going to be there?" Lucas chuckled, answering, "Now, sweet pea. Right ahead." He pointed with his whip to a sunny meadow.

They found the perfect spot for a picnic near a stand of tall beeches. A stream trickled merrily over the rocks. As Emma prepared to unpack their picnic luncheon, Lucas caught her arm. "Not yet," he said. "I've a surprise first. For the half-birthday girl."

The groom brought over a large, flat package that had been lashed to the back of the phaeton. Jenny tore off the brown wrapping, and a fantastically decorated object fashioned of red paper emerged into the sunlight.

"What is it?" Jenny asked. "There's a strange creature on it."

"It's a dragon kite I brought all the way from China." As Lucas picked it up, the paper rustled in the wind. "Would you care to fly it?"

The girl's eyes and mouth rounded in awe. "May I, truly?"

"Of course. Come, I'll help you launch it." He looked at Emma. "With your mother's permission."

Emma could only nod. She couldn't trust herself to speak, so touched was she by his gift to Jenny. What had wrought this change in him?

Baffled yet happy, she followed them into the meadow, heedless of the heath grasses and bracken that brushed at her hem. Lucas tramped ahead with the kite, Jenny skipping at his side. Then Emma sat down on a large flat rock while he explained the principles of flight.

"First, we'll set the kite on the ground here, and I'll get it airborne for you. Then you can take hold of the ball of string and fly the kite. But you must hang on very tightly, lest the wind snatch it from you. Ready?"

Jenny nodded, her worshipful eyes fastened on him.

Lucas peeled off his coat and gloves and handed them to Emma. She clutched them in her lap, inhaling the scent of him. Trailing twine behind him, Lucas took off at a run into the meadow. The kite caught the wind and lifted, then wobbled and dipped. Even as Jenny and Emma cried out in dismay, another gust carried it aloft, a red dragon with a long golden tail that flashed against the blue sky. Jenny went running after Lucas, who had slowed to a walk, his head tilted back to watch the bobbing kite ascend higher and higher. He handed the ball of string to Jenny and bent down to speak to her.

Something very sweet tightened inside Emma. The sensation stung her eyes. She blinked, shaken by the blur of tears. She had not wept since that long-ago night of her wedding, when Lucas had spurned her because she had been pregnant with another man's child. The very child he now taught to fly a kite. His brother's child.

If only she could tell him. Would it be so dreadful for Lucas to know the truth, to shed herself of this terrible secret?

He stood watching Jenny fly the kite. Her laughter trilled on the wind. After a moment, he came striding toward Emma, his hair tousled and his bootheels crunching over pebbles and dry grass. The crease of dimples in his cheeks softened his harshly handsome features.

He seated himself beside her on the broad rock. His scent came to her, deep and male, stirring heat inside her. "This brings back old times," he said, watching the kite. "My brother and I used to fashion kites out of newspaper and scraps of cloth. It seems a lifetime ago."

Emma tensed. It was almost as if he'd read her mind. Now was her chance to tell Lucas the truth about Andrew. A heaven-sent opportunity. Or was it a temptation from hell?

She couldn't imagine Andrew as a young, innocent boy who flew kites. She wanted to think he'd been a brute who'd tortured cats and plucked the wings off butterflies. "You and Andrew," she said, her mouth dry, "were you good friends?"

"The best—and the worst." A half-smile on his face, Lucas hooked his arms around his knees. "We were only two years apart in age, you see. And since he was the youngest, my mother spoiled him outrageously. I'm ashamed to admit to taking great delight in teasing him about being a baby. We had many a fistfight over the topic.''

''You did?''

''Unfortunately, yes. But we had our share of fun, too—fishing, catching tadpoles, climbing trees.'' A suspicious brightness entered his eyes, and his voice grew raw. ''Andrew was keen on joining the cavalry the moment he reached eighteen—I suppose to prove to me he was an adult at last. Somehow he persuaded me to buy him a commission. Ever since, I've regretted it, bitterly regretted not refusing him. His death . . . came as a tremendous shock to all of us.''

If Wortham were to learn the truth, it would destroy him. . . . He would hate Andrew.

The confession lodged like a festering thorn in her breast. Lucas had loved his brother dearly. And seven years ago, while the family was in deep mourning, she had taken advantage of Lucas's grief by pretending to love him, by trapping him into marriage. She couldn't break his heart again.

''I'm sorry,'' she murmured hoarsely. ''So terribly sorry—for all that's happened.''

He nodded, his eyes on the kite. ''Let's not spoil this day. Ah, it's been so long since I've sat idle.''

The question popped out before she could stop it. ''Where do you go each day?''

Lucas slanted an oblique glance at her. ''Lately, the docks.''

''The docks?'' That was the last answer she had expected. Yet she knew so little about his life. ''Have you a business concern there?''

''Quite an important concern, yes.'' He seemed to weigh his words with great care.

''But not today?''

He smiled secretively, his gaze turning back to the high-flying kite. ''Let's just say I found something yesterday. Something vital that had been lost. Something that belonged to someone dear to me.''

Dear? Surely he didn't mean . . . his mistress.

Resentment flashed in Emma, but she swiftly subdued it.

It was ridiculous to assume that foreign woman occupied every moment he spent away from Wortham House. Besides, Emma could think of nothing significant the woman could have lost at the docks, other than a piece of jewelry, which would be long gone by now. "What did you find?"

"Never mind. It has nothing to do with you."

He looked so smugly pleased that it piqued her curiosity all the more. "It's certainly put you in high spirits."

"Yes. It enabled me to fulfill a personal quest. A quest that brought me halfway around the world."

"What sort of quest—?"

His finger came over her lips and lightly rested there. "Enough."

A slow pulsing started deep in her belly. She was aware of the masculine feel of his fingers, warm and firm against her mouth. Without thinking, she nudged her tongue between her lips and tasted his skin.

His eyes darkened. His hands moved to cup her jaw, and he leaned closer to her. But he didn't reward her with the kiss she craved.

He reached down and cradled her breast instead. "Don't play games with me, Emma. Lest you find yourself being used like a strumpet."

A tingling awareness sizzled through her. All lightness had fled his expression. But she felt no fear, only a rush of passion. She wanted the dark side of him, too, the harsh, tight-lipped stranger and the clever, merciless seducer. They were all part of Lucas. *Her husband.*

She placed her hand on his cheek, and the faint bristles prickled her palm. "I'm sorry I accused you of treating me like a strumpet the other night," she whispered. "I lashed out at you because I was confused . . . and shaken."

He stared coldly, giving her no encouragement. She was aware of his hand, still heating her breast. Jenny's gleeful cries sounded faint in the distance. They were alone, the two of them. And Emma ached to explain feelings she couldn't quite fathom herself.

"It wasn't fair of me to blame you, Lucas. I *wanted* you

to touch me—I wanted every glorious moment of it. I never dreamed such rapture existed—I was frightened by it. But ever since, I've dreamed of . . ." Her voice faltered to a stop as she recalled the pain, the degradation, in her past. She couldn't take the final leap of faith. But she wanted to do so. Oh, yes, she did.

He tipped up her chin. "Dreamed of what?"

His gaze was steady, relentless, daring her onward. "I've dreamed of you . . . in my bed . . . making love to me. Will you?"

The tic of a muscle in his jaw was his only sign of emotion. "Only if you grant me your full surrender."

"I will."

"I intend to consummate our marriage, Emma. Fully and completely. Make no mistake about that."

"Yes."

His eyes held hers. She had the heady sense that this was the true moment of her yielding—here in the sunlit meadow with the cool breeze tugging at her bonnet and the heath grasses whispering in the wind. The enormity of her consent shot a quiver through her that was part excitement, part apprehension. She held her head high, determined to look forward, not back into the past.

His lashes lowered slightly into an expression of sinful promise. The pad of his thumb brushed lightly over her lips. "Tonight, then."

"Tonight," Emma echoed, wondering how she could wait so many hours and at the same time wishing the day could last forever.

"Papa, Mama, help!"

They sprang apart. Lucas surged to his feet, Emma at his side. She couldn't see Jenny or the kite. A variety of horrid and bloody possibilities raced through her mind. "Where is she?"

He shaded his eyes with his hand and peered across the meadow. "Ah," he said. "The little scamp has gotten her string tangled in a tree."

He loped off toward a distant clump of oaks, where Emma

spied a splotch of red kite against the golden autumn leaves. She headed after him, proceeding more slowly, for the brambles threatened to snag her silk skirt. "If only women could wear Hessians," she grumbled to herself.

By the time she reached the small party, Lucas was high in the tree, unraveling the last of the string while Jenny stood below, watching in awe. She clapped her hands when he shinnied down like a conquering hero, holding the kite.

She seemed to regard Lucas as her own brave cavalier. And Emma found out why when, over a luncheon of cold chicken and cheese, Lucas teased Jenny about the gap in her smile from the tooth he'd drawn. They engaged in a lively debate over which tooth would fall out next. Afterward, they shared a pink-frosted plum cake in honor of Jenny's half-birthday.

Replete with food and laughter, they wandered down to the stream so Jenny could try her hand at fishing. Emma thought wistfully of giving her daughter a carefree childhood in the country. She wondered when Lucas intended to visit his estate in the wild fells of Northumbria. Would he take her and Jenny with him? Emma fervently hoped so. For a little while at least, they could be a family.

Until she bore him a son.

She wouldn't let herself think about that now. She wanted to savor the joy of the moment, the golden hours of the afternoon.

The sun rode low in the western sky as they drove back into the city. Jenny lolled sleepily in Emma's lap, her grimy hands clutching the red kite. Emma relaxed against Lucas in contentment. Every now and then he glanced down at her, and his lazy half-smile stirred a tingling heat inside her. She knew what he was thinking—the same thoughts that hovered at the edge of her consciousness.

Tonight he would come to her. Tonight she would cleave to her husband in the manner sanctified by their marriage vows. Tonight she would become his true wife. The prospect made her tremble inwardly, as if she were about to step off a precipice without knowing if she would plunge into the darkness or soar to the heavens.

Yet she wanted to take that daring step. She was ready for it. She could face the pain for his sake . . . and her own.

Dusk had fallen by the time they arrived home. The cheery yellow glow in the windows of Wortham House welcomed them. Lucas handed a yawning Jenny down to her waiting nursemaid, an apple-cheeked older woman who clucked over her charge and hastened her off to bed. Lucas jumped down from the phaeton and then turned to help Emma, clasping his hands around her waist—and luckily so, for her legs felt as weak as water. Clinging to his arm, she walked up the steps and into the house.

Stafford, the footman, hastened across the foyer. "M'lady," he said, his lip curled in distaste, "there's a man asking to see you. I bade him wait in the kitchen—"

"Aye, and I've been coolin' me 'eels fer 'alf the day. As if I h'ain't nothin' better to do." The speaker marched into the foyer.

Emma's heart jolted. An arctic blast of alarm blew away the warmth in her as the sallow-faced man with the drooping eyelid stalked toward her.

It was Clive Youngblood.

✺ Chapter 16 ✺

Lucas could have cheerfully strangled Youngblood.

He glanced down at Emma. The brim of her bonnet framed a face of breathtaking beauty. But the glow had gone out of her cheeks, and her lips had lost their joyous luster. He could feel the tension in her fingers as she gripped his arm. No longer was she the warm, laughing wife who had cheered her daughter's kite-flying and shared a picnic luncheon with her husband—as if they were a real family.

God knew, *that* had been an illusion. A dream that had died an instant ago.

The Runner from the Bow Street Station had the audacity to sweep off his battered top hat and bow, revealing a bald spot in the middle of his dark, greasy hair. "If I could beg a few minutes of yer time, m'lord and m'lady."

Lucas placed his hand over Emma's. The fragility of her fingers enhanced his need to protect her. "Go upstairs," he murmured. "I'll handle this matter."

"Wid all due respect, m'lord, allow me to finish. 'Twere after midnight last night when a Miss Pomfret of Portland Place was woken up by the Burglar." Youngblood shook his fist. "He clutched her emerald necklace in his thievin' 'and."

"Miss Pomfret?" Emma said, staring at him. "Miss Minnie Pomfret?"

"Ah-hah," he said, pointing a finger at Emma, "so you're friendly wid 'er, too. You and yer grandsire, both."

"We're acquainted, but hardly friends." With a show of polite disdain, Emma removed her bonnet and settled herself on a chair by the fire. The golden light from a nearby candelabra gilded her hair. She gave a ladylike shudder. "I must say, though, I'm appalled to hear of her misfortune. How frightened she must have been."

Emma knew something, Lucas could tell by her too-innocent expression. Suspicion slithered into his mind. He'd foiled her attempt to steal from Lord Gerald Mannering. And last night she had been alone. All alone during the dark hours until dawn.

He turned his attention to Youngblood. "Get to the point."

"Aye, m'lord. You're the only one 'oo's caught the Burglar. If you and Miss Pomfret was to compare hobservations—"

"Tell me what she saw."

The Runner noisily cleared his throat. "She says the robber were a small bloke, maybe a few inches shorter than 'er. 'E wore a 'alf-mask and black clothes. When she attacked 'im wid her pillow and knocked 'is cap askew, she saw a glimpse of pale 'air."

Moonbeam hair. "The man I apprehended had dark hair," Lucas lied. "So that settles it. Miss Pomfret surprised a common robber."

"But he nicked only one necklace and left a pile of other jewels. That's the way of the Burglar." Youngblood rocked back and forth on his heels. "Odd thing is, Miss Pomfret says the necklace is worth five 'undred pounds. H'ain't that 'ow much your grandsire owes, m'lady?"

For once, Emma offered no tart answer. She sat in somber dignity, her gaze fixed on the Runner. Her knuckles shone pale as pearls against the moss-green of her gown. Lucas remembered how she had looked riding beside him in the phaeton—her eyes alight with enjoyment, her soft mouth curved into a laugh. All day he had ached to kiss her.

Now he itched to blister her hide . . . and then kiss her.

Lucas glowered at Youngblood. "I've heard quite enough of your insinuations. Get out."

"But m'lord, I h'ain't done—"

"Now. Before I throw you out."

"Wait." Emma jumped to her feet, her hands extended to stop the Runner from backing out of the library. "I must know. Did you arrest the Burglar?"

"Nay, m'lady. But I will soon. What I were tryin' to tell m'lord is that the Burglar dropped this." Digging in the voluminous pocket of his coat, Youngblood pulled forth a black glove and gloatingly displayed it.

Emma's gaze focused on the glove. If anything, she grew paler, a goddess turned to stone.

Lucas strode to Youngblood and snatched up the evidence. It was a man's glove made of thin, expensive kid leather. And small enough to fit Emma's dainty hand. "This glove has no distinguishing marks," he said flatly. "I fail to see how it will help you catch your thief."

" 'Twas made fer a gent of the Quality," Youngblood said, retrieving the glove. "I'll be showin' it around to the fancy glovers 'ereabouts. Some shopkeeper might remember who bought such a pair." With a sly smile, he added, "You look awfully interested, m'lady. Care to try it on?"

"Me?" Her voice rose in breathy surprise. "What exactly are you implying?"

A bolt of fury struck Lucas. He controlled himself with effort. "We've no time for your games," he said coldly. "Now, go on with you."

Beneath his glare, Youngblood wilted like a weed nipped by a frost. He inched toward the door. "Y-yes, m'lord, if you'll forgive me one last question. Just where was Lady Wortham last night?"

"With me, you dolt. She was with me."

Striding forward, Lucas grabbed the man by the scruff of his neck. He marched Youngblood out of the library, down the corridor, and into the entryway, where a goggle-eyed Stafford whisked open the front door.

Lucas dumped the Runner in a heap on the porch. The

dented top hat went rolling down the marble steps, and Youngblood scrambled to catch it. Only strict discipline kept Lucas from using his fists on the wretch. Nothing short of murder would be adequate penalty for badgering Emma. Nothing short of drawing and quartering for laying ruin to their plans for the evening.

By the iron gate, Youngblood jammed the hat onto his head and turned to flash a dark look at Lucas. Then he went scuttling off like a rat into the night.

Lucas stalked back into the house to find his wife standing with one hand on the newel post. Her pensive gaze was focused on the high ceiling of the foyer. She might have been an angel looking wistfully toward heaven. A fallen angel.

I've dreamed of you . . . in my bed . . . making love to me.

Like a spinning prayer wheel, her confession played through his mind. But there was nothing holy about the effect it had on him. He burned with fury and frustration. Even now, lust knotted his loins. The swanlike curve of her throat begged to be kissed—yet he couldn't banish the image of a rope circling her neck, bruising that smooth, white skin.

His bootheels rang out on the marble tiles. She blinked at him, and he had the impression her thoughts roamed miles away. Likely she was debating where to fence Miss Pomfret's emerald necklace.

He marched Emma into the drawing room and closed the doors. Seizing her by the shoulders, he snarled, ''Don't you *ever* do that again.''

''Do what? Speak my mind?'' she said, wrinkling her nose in a frown. ''I had a right to face Mr. Youngblood, too.''

''Spare me the naïveté. I'm no longer the fool you married.'' His mouth felt dry with horror. He gave her a hard shake. ''If you're caught in a criminal act, Emma, being the wife of a peer won't save you. People will be out for your blood, blue or not. You'll end up with a rope around your neck. And I won't . . . won't be able to do a damned thing to . . . to stop it.'' Breathing harshly, he fought off a wave of helplessness. He would not shame himself by lapsing into incoherent stuttering.

"Dear God," Emma said in a faint voice. "You think *I* robbed Miss Pomfret."

"I don't think, I *know*. The facts prove your guilt."

"Yet you told Mr. Youngblood we were together last night. You lied to protect me."

Amazingly, a smile flitted across her face. Its softness hit him harder than a fist. "Of course I lied," he retorted bitterly. "Our sleeping arrangements are none of his bloody business." His fingers flexed around her delicate shoulders. "Hear me now, Emma. I shall not allow you to dishonor me, ever again."

Scowling, she lowered her face for a moment. When she looked at him again, her expression was sober. She lifted her hand to his cheek. "Lucas, I never left my room last night. I swear it to you."

The caress of her fingertips drained him of breath. Her eyes were so big and blue he wanted to drown in them. Though he fought against it, a treacherous doubt crept into his mind. "Then explain how Miss Pomfret came to be robbed by a dainty thief clad in black clothing." None too gently, he threaded his fingers into her silken curls. "A thief with hair as pale as yours."

She grasped his wrists and stayed his hands. "Pale can mean anything from golden to gray. Youngblood was making wild accusations because he hasn't a scrap of proof beyond a glove that could have been purchased by anyone."

"I see," he said, imbuing his voice with sarcasm. "Someone was impersonating the Bond Street Burglar."

"Precisely."

Her small white teeth worried her lower lip. Lips that might have been moving over his naked flesh right now if not for Emma's penchant for trouble. Perhaps it wasn't too late to salvage the night. They were alone, behind closed doors. And she had promised him the privileges of a husband.

I've dreamed of you . . . in my bed . . . making love to me.

Hot blood pumped through his veins. To hell with quarreling. He had only to settle her against him, lean down, and take what he wanted.

He did just that. He trapped Emma's slim body in the circle of his arms and tilted her chin up. Her moist lips parted. Her eyes widened. His warm breath mingled with hers—

"Stop." Emma pressed her hands to his chest and pushed him back. She looked annoyed, not enamored. "This is important. Aren't you listening to me?"

"This is important, too." He placed his hands on her soft, round bottom and rubbed his hips against hers. The keen pleasure of it throbbed through him. "And this, at least, is the truth—this passion we both feel."

She caught her breath and closed her eyes for a fleeting moment, then squirmed free. "Lucas, please. Someone *is* playing the Burglar. And I know who."

An hour later, the Wortham coach rolled to a halt in a dilapidated neighborhood near Cheapside. Stepping down to the broken pavement, Emma waited for Lucas to emerge. In the more affluent areas of town, gas lamps shone like hazy beacons, but not here. Here, the night was dark and deep. Fog had crept in on ghostly feet, and the air had a cold, clammy quality that made her shiver despite the warmth of her cloak.

Then Lucas stood beside her, a tall and domineering presence. Still smarting from his lack of faith in her, she reluctantly took the arm he offered. She told herself not to be so irritated that he had leapt to a conclusion. After all, she had lied to him often enough.

Yet it hurt to remember the carefree day they'd spent together, and her hope that he was softening toward her and Jenny. Lucas could never love her. He had defended her only to stop another scandal. He wanted a son from her, that was all.

Straining to see into the gloom, she turned her attention to the house where she and Jenny had lived only a fortnight ago. Odd, she didn't consider it home anymore. The entry-

way was dark, the outside lamps unlit. Emma wondered uneasily if her grandfather was even here. He might be
gambling again—or worse, endangering his life.

In response to Lucas's knock, the door opened a crack and
a woman held up a candle that illuminated her carrot-red
hair. Her freckled face brightened with a smile, and she flung
the door wide.

"M'leddy! You've come home!"

Emma caught the small, spry servant into a tight embrace.
The familiar scents of coarse soap and lemon wax wafted
over her. "Oh, Maggie, how wonderful to see you again.
How is Grandpapa?"

Maggie motioned them inside and closed the door. "Shh.
He's in the morning room. That scoundrel Runner was here
this morning, plaguing the poor man—until I ran him off
with my broom. His lordship hasn't come out since."

Lucas handed her his cape. "Then you can't be certain
he's still in there."

"You dursn't call me a fool, m'lord," the servant retorted.
"I took him in his supper but fifteen minutes ago."

"We aren't here to question you, Maggie," Emma said
hastily.

"On the contrary," Lucas stated, "I should like to know
if Briggs went out last evening. Around midnight."

Maggie's defiant look dwindled as she lowered her jutting
chin. She glanced at Emma.

"It's all right," Emma assured her. "You can tell Lord
Wortham."

"Humph. 'Bout ten o'clock last night, George drove your
grandpa to a party, then waited down the street with the other
coachmen. Didn't see hide nor hair of his lordship again till
the clock struck two." Maggie's work-worn fingers clutched
at Emma's. "I'm sorry, m'leddy, truly I am. George and me,
we tried to keep your grandpa out of trouble. I swear it on
me own dear mother's grave."

Emma squeezed the maid's hands. "I know. It isn't your
fault."

It's my fault.

With a heavy heart, she walked over the bare wood floor and knocked on the door of the morning room. A muffled curse emanated from inside. Lucas's hand settled on her shoulder in a brief, reassuring grip. Then she opened the door.

Her grandfather sat hunched before the old secrétaire. A single candle dripped wax onto its tin holder, shedding meager light over the sheaf of papers on the opened desk. On a nearby table sat his untouched supper tray with brown gravy congealing atop a mound of roast beef and potatoes. He was scribbling furiously, and the pen sounded like the mad scratching of a mouse.

"Grandpapa?" she said, venturing into the dim room.

He gave a start of surprise. The quill pen flew into the air and then twirled downward. He leapt up so fast the rickety chair crashed to the floor. As he spun around, the monocle fell from his eye and swung crazily from the leather ribbon attached to his lapel. "Confound it, girl! Must you send me into a heart seizure?"

"I knocked." Too curious to be contrite, Emma walked closer. "What are you writing? It can't be letters. You despise correspondence."

"Hah. 'Tis never too late to teach an old dog new tricks." He shoveled the papers inside and slammed the lid shut before she could catch more than a glimpse of his flamboyant, ink-blotted handwriting. "Now, why the deuce are you here? You striplings ought to be out dancing at a party somewhere. *I* would've been at your age."

"Speaking of parties," Lucas said from behind her, "we're here in regard to the party you never attended last night."

Lifting the monocle to his eye, her grandfather peered closely from Emma to Lucas. "Oh-ho. I see Youngblood's been pestering you, too. Well, devil take that sly fox. And that tale-telling Miss Pomfret. Time was, a homely gel like her would have been glad to have me in her bedroom."

"Grandpapa!" Emma's breast ached as she closed the distance between them. He stood only an inch taller than she, and she looked him straight in the eyes. "How could you rob an innocent lady? It's Lord Gerald Mannering who won our money, not Miss Pomfret."

" 'Tis tit for tat. Don't forget what she stole from you." He wagged an ink-stained finger at Emma.

"From me?" she asked in confusion.

"Aye, the little chippy insulted you. 'Tis her and other gossipmongers who filched your good name."

"Insulted?" Lucas stepped into the small circle of candlelight. His sun-burnished features were drawn into a scowl. "Just what did this woman say to you?"

"It was nothing—" Emma began.

" 'Twas at Mannering's ball," her grandfather put in. "The hound-faced chit thought herself too good to speak to my granddaughter. So I decided Miss Nose-in-the-air deserved a good fright in return. I sneaked into her house, found the necklace, and shook the blasted thing in her face whilst she was sleeping." Slapping his knee-breeches, he let out a cackle of laughter. "She jumped nigh to the ceiling. And tried to hit me with her pillow."

Emma subdued the urge to giggle hysterically. "That isn't amusing. Grandpapa, you left your glove behind. What if Youngblood traces it back to you?"

"So what if he does? I'll swear I was there at her invitation. And let her rich, title-hunting parents prove otherwise."

"You'd ruin her—if you haven't already," Lucas said thoughtfully. He pulled up a chair and straddled it, resting his arms on the ladderback. "Of course, she deserves just that."

He and Lord Briggs shared a long look. Glancing from one man to the other, Emma felt a prickling of alarm. "What are you two thinking?" she asked. "Surely you wouldn't plot the ruin of a silly young girl."

"No," Lucas said. "I suggest we turn our attention elsewhere. Livvie told me about Lady Jasper Putney's ill-mannered remark to you. About how unnaturally pale you looked on our wedding day."

His hard brown eyes held a hint of fury. Was he truly angry at Lady Jasper? Or, Emma wondered, had the old, hurtful memories surfaced again?

"What can we do to hoist the old witch by her own petard?" Lord Briggs snapped his fingers. "I have it. At the next party, I shall invite her outside, then tear open my cravat and my shirt so that everyone thinks she attacked me."

"No one would believe it—she has ice in her veins," Lucas said. "I should engage her husband in cards and then accuse him of cheating. The *ton* will shun him—and her."

"Don't you dare." Emma whirled on him in horror. "He'd challenge you."

Lucas smiled wolfishly. "Let him. I hear he's a poor shot."

Her grandfather chuckled. "Couldn't even bring down the Burglar at ten paces."

"How can you two jest about this?" She paced in front of his chair. "I won't have you dueling, Lucas. It's madness!"

"Would you care if I died?"

He spoke in a negligent tone, though he watched her with that taunting half-smile. She wanted to slap the smirk off his sinfully handsome face—and fall to her knees and confess her love for him, too. "Dueling is not only against the law, it's barbaric," she said evenly. "I forbid you to fight on my behalf." She swung toward Lord Briggs, who observed their bickering with keen interest. "Nor will I allow *you*, Grandpapa, to sneak into ladies' bedrooms and steal from them."

"I didn't steal," he said, folding his arms.

"Call it whatever you like, but give the necklace to me." She held out her hand. "I'll make sure it's discreetly returned."

"Don't have it—I tossed it 'neath her bed. The minx will find it soon enough."

Emma lowered her arm. "You didn't take it?"

"Of course not. As I said, I meant only to scare her." An unholy gleam shone in her grandfather's blue eyes. He leaned against the closed secrétaire. "I've a better plan for repaying Mannering. It's quite clever, if I may say so myself.''

''What plan?''

''Can't tell now. 'Tis a secret.''

She noted the glee on his weathered features. ''Is it legal?''

''Utterly.''

''If this has anything to do with gaming—''

''No. I give you my solemn promise.'' He clapped his hand to his chest.

Emma hoped she could believe him this time. She didn't have the heart to remind him he'd already broken his vow not to gamble. He'd be wounded by her lack of faith in him. And she knew how badly mistrust could hurt.

Lucas rose from the chair and slid his arm around her. ''Now that we've solved our little mystery, my wife and I can turn our attention to other matters.'' His fingers stroked the curve of her waist, his warmth penetrating her body. ''Do join us for dinner one night this week, will you, Briggs?''

''I'm rather busy, but I'll make the time.'' Her grandfather grinned. ''The real question is, will *you* two have the time?''

Even as she puzzled over his conspiratorial wink at Lucas, Emma found herself being whisked out of the house and into the coach. She was frustrated by her inability to read the communication between the two men. Why wouldn't Lucas have time to dine with guests?

Determined to find out, she turned toward him in the darkened coach. And found her breasts crushed against his solid chest. His warm breath plumed over her mouth, weaving a thrill through her raveled senses. ''At last,'' he murmured, ''we can tend to those other matters.''

And then his hard and hungry lips came down on hers.

Chapter 17

Among the few kisses Emma had known, this one far outranked all others. It was both harsh and tender, terrifyingly intense and unbearably exquisite. He kissed her until she felt weak from wanting and dizzy with pleasure. When at last he dragged in a long breath and rubbed his stubble-rough cheek against hers, she clung to him, gasping for air in a sea of sensation.

His heart beat fiercely against her breasts. His eyes glittered through the darkness. "You're mine, Emma," he said. "I shan't wait any longer. Tonight is the night."

"Yes," she murmured. "Yes."

She told herself to resist, for he meant to claim her firstborn son. If she'd thought him a poor prospect for a father, she might have found the strength to refuse. But she remembered the kite he had given to Jenny today, his acceptance of the little girl whom he might have scorned.

Nothing else seemed to matter when she could feel the tenderness of his touch. A gas lamp on the street cast shuddering shadows inside the dim coach, echoing the dark thrill that spun through her. Pondering the mystery of her surrender, she shaped her hand around the side of his neck and felt the throb of his lifeblood. Lucas. Her husband. Who would have thought she would come to care for him so deeply?

She wanted to be his wife in truth. Her decision had been made that very afternoon in the sunlit meadow. She wanted his hands on her body, fondling her as he had done behind the screen. But at the same time she dreaded what would follow. How could she not, when the violence of that long-ago night lurked at the edge of her consciousness? Her belly tensed at the thought of him overpowering her, sweating and grunting and pumping, revoking ecstasy for something sordid and painful.

"You're shivering," he said.

"Am I? I—I can't imagine why."

"Can't you?" Sounding amused, he trailed his lips over her cheek, soothing the skin that tingled from the raspy growth of his whiskers. "It's called desire, Emma. For better or for worse, our bodies respond to each other. There'll be no more teasing, no more courting, no more games."

His deep voice unsettled her, and she tucked her face into the crook of his shoulder. The alien musk of man scented his skin. The rhythmic clatter of wheels and hooves marked each passing moment. It brought her and Lucas closer and closer to home . . . to their marriage bed.

Seeking respite from her inner turmoil, she blurted, "Why did Grandpapa say you won't have much spare time next week? You told me you were finished with your work at the docks."

"Perhaps he suspected you and I"—Lucas bent to nuzzle the hollow of her throat—"had finally"—his mouth drifted lower—"reconciled"—he moved her cloak and kissed the scar on her bare shoulder—"our differences."

The black shadow of his head loomed above her breasts. She could scarcely think for the warmth pulsing through her. But she wanted to think—to hope. "Do you . . . do you still despise me for tricking you into marriage?"

His lips paused just above her bosom. His torrid breath bathed her tender skin. "Forget the past. It doesn't matter tonight."

How deftly he sidestepped her question. Perhaps the barriers between them would never be scaled, for she could not tell him her greatest secret: that the man who had dishonored her was his own brother.

Even as bitterness tightened like tentacles around her emotions, Lucas distracted her. He loosened the buttons down her back, gave a pull and the layers of silk fell away, exposing her ghostly-white chemise in the darkness. To her amazement, she felt a moist tugging sensation on her breast. She gasped, flooded by a deep melting warmth. He was kissing her through the chemise, suckling her like a babe. Without thinking, she slid her fingers through the coarse silk of his hair.

"Oh, Lucas," she breathed. "Lucas."

"So," he said on a hiss of satisfaction, "you like that."

He exposed her breasts and kissed them again, this time using his teeth and tongue, alternately nipping and then soothing her. The exquisite sensation lured a moan from her throat. Passion leapt inside her, creating a hunger inspired by his feast.

Abruptly, the coach turned a sharp corner and she collapsed against him. He held her close as the vehicle slowed to a stop. Peeking past the tasseled curtain, Emma spied the torchlit entrance to Wortham House. And here she sat like a hussy, the cool night air wafting against her bare, dampened breasts.

She yanked at her gown but the layers of silk caught beneath her legs. "Do up my buttons. Quickly. We'll create a scandal."

"We always do," Lucas said dryly. "But never mind, the cloak will cover you."

He wrapped the garment around her, tying it at her throat. His movements were easy and matter-of-fact, as if saving a lady from disgrace were nothing new to him.

Emma clutched at her bodice just as the coach door swung open and she was forced to step out into view of the footman. Beneath the enveloping cloak, her unfastened gown slipped lower and lower. She clamped her arms across her bosom to catch the slippery fabric before it puddled around her feet.

"Allow me," Lucas murmured.

His lips quirked into a smile that was half amusement, half impatience. He looped his muscled arm around her waist and urged her up the steps to the porch, where a liveried footman opened the front door. Lucas's heavy tread harmonized with the light tapping of her own slippers as he guided her inexorably across the marble floor and up the grand staircase.

A sense of inevitability inundated Emma. It was going to happen now. Lucas intended to bed her. There would be no more reprieves. Her insides churned with a mixture of dread and delight. She felt as if she were astride a stallion, galloping headlong into a dense mist, never knowing if the ride would end in death . . . or new life.

A tomblike silence permeated the upstairs. They passed no one in the shadowy corridor. Somehow she'd known they wouldn't. The time had come to fulfill her promise to Lucas. To open herself to him. To take his seed into her womb. Her legs wobbled and she would have fallen had he not gripped her arm so firmly.

Upon reaching her bedchamber, he escorted her inside and dismissed her wide-eyed maid. He kicked the door shut, unfastened Emma's cloak, and pressed her against the wall with his chest and thighs. His face was stark with passion. "So," he said in a gruff voice. "We'll finally have the night we should have had seven years ago."

The chilly purpose she sensed in him belied the heat of his body. His mouth came down on hers again, and he tugged at her dress until only her shift and his breeches separated their lower bodies. His ardor alarmed her, even as his kiss fed the fire of longing in her, the yearning to relinquish herself into his keeping. He caressed her breasts again, his thumbs rubbing the tips, until rapturous sensation crowded out coherent thought. She arched against him, savoring the pressure of firm muscles and hot skin.

His hands roamed downward, measuring her waist and hips and bottom, exploring her curves until she wanted to cry out in frustration. If only he would lift her chemise and touch her. If only he would stroke her to wanton ecstasy. If only he would show her joy first, she could endure the pain later. Instead, he grasped her wrist and dragged her hand down to the front of his breeches and held it there.

Through the superfine cloth, her fingers absorbed the un-mistakable shape of him. He was stiff. Thick. Long. A sword of steel burning for her tender sheath.

He pushed himself against her hand. "God help me," he muttered, his voice so like his brother's it sent an eerie prick-ling over her skin. What had seemed so marvelous in a sunlit meadow took on a sinister aspect in this shadowy bedroom.

His feral groan sent her spinning down, down, down into the dark well of memory. *"God help me"* . . . *and he thrust hard . . . again and again . . . ripping into her . . . grunting like a beast . . .*

Panic shattered her passion. "Stop it!" she cried. *"Stop!"*

She pushed Lucas away, and he staggered backward into a table. A black basaltware vase tipped over, flinging hot-house roses and water onto the carpet.

His breath came harsh and fast. A muscle worked in his jaw. "What the hell—? We have a bargain."

"I know. But I'm not ready. I—" Emma could say no more. She trembled uncontrollably. Her teeth chattered, and she clasped her hands over her bosom, hugging herself.

Lucas straightened to his full height, his cheekbones taut and hard. As if struggling against himself, he gripped his hands into fists. Where desire had warmed his eyes, a curious blankness now shuttered his thoughts. "Have it your way, then. Come to me when you're ready."

Leaning weakly against the back of a chair, Emma watched him walk away. Her fingers tingled; she could still feel his male part as if he had branded her. He was so large. Too large for a small woman like herself.

Yet despite her revulsion, she ached to call him back. What had she done?

He wrenched open the connecting door and entered his bedchamber. The click of the latch resounded through the room. She was left with only the drip-drip of water from the spilled vase.

Lucas strode across his bedroom, flinging off his coat, then his waistcoat, dropping the garments in a trail across the floor. His nerves smoldered on the verge of an explosion. Damn. Damn. Damn! How could he be so lack-witted? He had overwhelmed Emma. He had completely disregarded her need for gentleness and patience. He had been so caught up in his own hard, driving lust that he had ignored her fears.

Curse the scoundrel who had raped her. If it took a lifetime, he'd find the craven wretch and make him pay!

Lucas yanked off his cravat and hurled it away. And damn himself, too. He had never lacked control. The greater the discipline, the higher the ecstasy. But with Emma, he had lost mastery over himself. He had destroyed the patient seduction of nearly a fortnight.

Self-loathing lay like a stone inside him. There was something else, too, a truth he couldn't deny. Deep down, he *wanted* to remain aloof. He wanted to know he had the power to hurt Emma. Because then she could not hurt him.

"Hell-bent fool!" Blindly he lashed out with his fist and struck the bedpost. The wood groaned as if to mock him. White-hot pain speared through his knuckles and up his arm. The bronze-colored bedhangings swayed madly.

Hajib appeared in the doorway of the dressing room. "Master," he said, hurrying forward. "Have you hurt yourself?"

Feeling like a chastised boy, Lucas tucked his smarting hand behind his back. "No."

"Praise be to Allah." Hajib bowed low. "How may I serve you?"

"By leaving me alone."

Oblivious to his black mood, the servant knelt before him. "Permit me to assist you."

Lucas grudgingly let the valet tug off his knee-high boots and stockings. Then he stalked barefoot to a decanter of brandy on the fireside table. "That's all. I shan't require anything more tonight."

Hajib rose lithely, his gray robe whispering as he moved around the room, picking up the clothing Lucas had discarded. "Your English wife displeases you. Will you soon return to Shalimar's bed?"

"It's none of your concern," Lucas snarled. The notion of seeking relief with his mistress left him cold. Glass in hand, he scowled at the servant, who stood with his palms pressed together and his gaze faintly accusatory. Lucas drew a ragged breath. He *had* been neglecting Shalimar. "She's happy with Sanjeev back, isn't she? Has she given you cause to think otherwise?"

"Her happiness is not for me to judge."

"For God's sake, don't be coy. Is she anxious to return to Kashmir?"

"My lord, she is pleased to do whatsoever you wish. You have her undying gratitude for the return of her son yesterday."

He sounded too much like Shalimar, humble and submissive. At one time, Lucas would have accepted the difference in cultures, even appreciated it, but now he experienced a flash of intense irritation. How much more satisfying was a battle of equals. How much more stimulating the company of a bold, outspoken Englishwoman.

He gulped down the brandy, and his guilt seared deeper. "I want you to go to Shalimar. Make certain her needs are fulfilled. Furnish her household with trinkets from Kashmir. The expense is of no consequence."

Hajib's eyes were dark and inscrutable. "And the tiger's head? Might I take her that, then?"

"The mask?" Lucas started in surprise. "No, the mask is too costly to serve as decoration for someone's home. It shall be part of a museum exhibit as soon as the new wing is built."

Hajib lowered his gaze. "Yes, master."

"Tell Shalimar that I'll take her and Sanjeev back to India eventually, but not yet. Not for a year at least." Lucas glowered at the remaining amber liquor in his glass. "My business here may take longer than I expected."

"It shall be as you wish." The turbaned servant bowed and left the room.

Lucas stared at the closed door with its gilt trim gleaming dully against the white paint. Business. He had business, all right. He intended to remain in England long enough to bed Emma and to see her give birth. He needed—he wanted—a son. By God, he *deserved* a son.

He wanted what Emma had already—a child to brighten the darkness of his life. A son or a daughter like Jenny. Emma had robbed him of a normal family, and now he would demand his due. It was as simple as that.

Or was it? Aware of a rigidity in his muscles, he very carefully set down his empty glass. The truth was, he wanted Emma to desire him. He craved her surrender on a deeper level than physical passion. He wanted to own her soul. As she had owned his for far too many years.

His hands shook with unmanly emotion. He braced them against the mantelpiece. It might take weeks of seduction to coax her into trusting him again. Weeks of denial before he finally sated the raging hunger inside himself. But he would woo her gently if it killed him. He would have her willing— or not at all.

The faint rattling of the doorknob broke the silence. Cool air whisked against him. In no mood for company, especially not Hajib again, Lucas wheeled around. "I thought I told you—"

He froze. In the connecting doorway stood his wife.

His mouth went dry. His palms dampened with sweat. His inner turmoil exploded into renewed desire.

Emma's unbound hair shimmered like a mass of moonbeams around her shoulders and down to her waist. The sheer fabric of her nightgown embraced her breasts, then cascaded to the floor. Beneath the scalloped hem, her feet were small and bare.

Her gaze skittered to the huge bedstead; then those big, blue eyes focused on him. "I'm sorry for panicking, Lucas. It was just . . . an unexpected memory. I—I hope you can forgive me."

Words failed him. His groin tightened unbearably, swelling against his breeches. He could think only that she was naked beneath the gown. The shadow of her sex showed faintly against the virginal white cloth. Why did she continue to torture him?

She ventured a few steps into the room. Her fingers pleated the sides of her nightdress. "You told me to come to you when I was ready," she went on. "Well, I am ready. I made you a promise, and I fully intend to keep it. Tonight."

"I won't force an unwilling woman." Each word felt dragged from him.

"I know that now." She held out her hand. "That's why I want to be your wife. Will you show me how to please you?"

Lucas could scarcely believe she was giving him a second chance. A chance to rectify his clumsy mistakes. A chance to show her she had nothing to fear from him. And a chance to prove to himself he had nothing to fear from her, either.

He took her hand. It felt as sweet and dainty as a bride's. "It would please me to bring you joy. A man likes to know he's given as well as received."

"Not all men."

Her eyes went cloudy with memories. Interwined with his fury at her attacker was a thread of powerful tenderness. He settled her against him, one hand at the base of her spine, the other tipping her chin up, forcing her to look at him. "I'm not like that bastard. Just remember that."

"Of course," she said, too quickly.

"I mean it, Emma. If you tell me to stop, I will." He twisted his mouth into a wry grimace. "No matter how difficult it is."

"I know. You've proven that to me."

"And I can promise you pleasure. The same pleasure you felt a few nights ago. You only have to trust me."

She bit her lip and nodded slowly. "I do."

"Good."

Scorched by the heat of his stare, Emma felt a thrill of trepidation. Lucas looked so fierce, so wild. He had stripped down to a white shirt opened to the waist and the dark breeches he had worn on their picnic. His chest was a beautiful burnished tan, and now the black thatch of hair pressed against her breasts. There was nothing between them but a few scraps of cloth. She was aware of his body heat, his male scent. And the deep, disturbing pulse that throbbed within her.

He wanted to kiss her; she could see it in his eyes. The knowledge made her glow. Unwilling to lose the feeling, Emma urged him toward the bed. "Come, Lucas," she said in a husky murmur. "Come with me."

He smiled then, a secretive smile that deepened the dimples in his cheeks and made him look extraordinarily handsome. "Ladies first."

She sensed a hidden meaning to his words, but before she could puzzle it out, his arms caught her up and she found herself sprawled atop him on the bed. The heavy bronze silk hangings enclosed them in shadow. Lucas reclined beneath her, large and dark against the snowy linens. Her heartbeat surged into a maddened rhythm. She lay very still, absorbing the strangeness of his hard, masculine body under hers.

"Shouldn't we . . . switch positions?" she asked.

"You said you wanted to pleasure me." He glided the flats of his palms down the back of her nightdress. "And I like it this way."

"I just thought . . . this doesn't seem . . ."

"Proper?" His big hands cupped the curve of her bottom. "There can be nothing improper between a husband and wife, Emma. Surely you know that by now."

He was referring to their other intimate encounters—when he had massaged her, when he had plied her with the peacock feather, when he had transported her to heaven with his clever fingers. And then she realized what was different this time. She was no longer under his subjugation. He was giving control over to her. "But what shall I do?" she whispered.

"Whatever feels good."

He lay back, waiting, a devilish smile on his lips. Lucas wanted her to take the lead. He wanted *her* to seduce *him*. This was not how she had envisioned the consummation of their marriage.

The rise and fall of his chest tickled her breasts. The night-gown had ridden up past her knees and their legs were tangled together. His hands felt warm and possessive, his thumbs rubbing lazily against the fabric covering her bottom. She knew a flash of frustration, the shocking desire to feel his touch on her naked flesh.

Without daring to think, Emma sat up, lifted the night-gown over her head, and flung the garment to the floor. Stark naked, she scrambled back into place over Lucas. His hands spanned her slender waist. The texture of his shirt and breeches rasped delightfully against her skin. Only then did she risk looking at his face.

The smile was gone. His eyes burned with intensity again, an intensity that sent a compelling quiver down to her secret core, where she could feel herself growing damp and soft and ardent. His lips were parted invitingly. Dear heaven. *Dear sweet heaven.*

Feeling decidedly wicked, she scooted herself closer to those lips and rested her hands on his strong shoulders. How heady was the power he had given to her. It banished the fear that had long ruled her. "Lucas," she whispered, wishing she could put into words the tumultuous feelings tumbling inside herself. "May I kiss you?"

"You don't need my permission."

Their warm breath intermingled. His eyelids were lowered halfway as he waited patiently. She touched her lips to his and savored the surprising suppleness of him. She tasted brandy on him, licked the essence and followed the flavor into his mouth. Like a delicious elixir, it spread through her body, warming and strengthening, stoking the blaze within her.

Lucas returned the kiss with equal fervor. His hands found her breasts and adorned them with lavish caresses. Somehow he seemed to know exactly what she wanted. And yet there were other wants inside her, enticements she did not wholly understand.

Whatever feels good.

She could not keep herself still, especially her lower body.

She gave in to the urge to rub herself against him, and the pleasure of it quaked through her. Lucas's chest expanded with a harsh breath. His fingers convulsed around her arms, but he made no move to overpower her. Emboldened, she pressed herself to him again, and yet again. Each time felt more compelling than the last. Each time multiplied her aching need for relief. Each time satisfied her less.

She reached down blindly between them, fumbling with the buttons on either side of his breeches. His hand circled her wrist. "Emma?"

She couldn't bear to stop and think. She trusted him, and that was enough. "Please," she begged.

His fingers tightened a moment; then he brushed her hand aside and unfastened the front placket. With a sigh, she closed her eyes and lowered herself against him, though not inviting him inside yet. He was thick and hard, a potent contrast to her feminine softness. Giddiness swept over her, a harbinger of panic. What was she doing?

Whatever feels good.

Obeying instinct, she slid herself along the length of his shaft. Lucas groaned. His mouth was hot against her breasts, his breath shuddering in and out, in and out. Yet still he did not wrest control from her. She gave herself up to the sweet friction that tantalized her with the glimpse of paradise. If only she could reach the shattering glory first, perhaps it would ease the agony of his entry. If only . . .

Grasping her hips, he muttered something she didn't quite catch . . . and then his lower body gave a sudden upward thrust, filling her with a pressure so extraordinary she tensed and went still.

He held her close and rubbed his cheek against her hair. "Emma. Sweet Emma. Forgive me—" He exhaled in a strange sort of groaning laugh. "Hell, don't forgive me. Just let me stay."

She heard him through a haze of amazement. "We're joined."

"Yes." He took her face in his palms and rained kisses over her. "And for God's sake . . . don't tell me to stop."

"Why would I? Oh, Lucas. This feels so . . ." Words failed her. She felt no pain, no revulsion, only a boundless pleasure that expanded far beyond the physical. She laid her cheek against his sweat-slickened chest and heard the strong beating of his heart. The musky perfume of passion enveloped her. She cherished their unique closeness, the precious delight that pulsed through her as she rocked her hips experimentally, accepting him deeper into herself.

"Oh, my. *Oh, my.*" It was the most awesome feeling to be one with him. As if she had stepped off a ledge and found herself soaring instead of falling. She kissed his corded throat, taut with the strain of holding himself back. "Lucas . . . my husband . . . I'm yours now. Your bride. Your lover."

"Yes," he grated. *"Yes."*

Never taking his dark gaze from hers, he rolled Emma onto her back, laced his fingers through hers, and pressed their entwined arms onto the pillows. He almost withdrew, then moved slowly into her again, initiating a rhythm somehow recognized by her untutored body. The absence of fear created an infinite capacity for joy, for the splendor of rising with him, faster and higher, their hearts beating as one, their bodies bonded in perfect rapport, their souls ascending to the summit of ecstasy and then floating in the sweet aftermath of release.

⸛ **Chapter 18** ⸛

"*P*ardon me, m'lady," Stafford said. "There is a visitor to see you."

Standing in a pool of late morning light that poured through the library windows, Emma looked up from the small elephant-god statue in her hands. She resisted the urge to grin foolishly at the footman. He couldn't know her mind had been occupied by far more earthly thoughts than Hindu deities. She had been remembering the rapture of the previous night.

All those years of fear and loathing had been cast aside. Today, a languid peace flowed through her body, and yet at the same time she felt revitalized, tingling with the marvels of life. In one tumultuous encounter, she had risen from the darkness of hell into the brilliance of heaven. Even more wondrous, Lucas had clasped her close as if he too could not bear for the night to end. He had said little, and she had been happy to set aside their differences for the moment. Later, they had made love again, and afterward, drowsy and replete, she had fallen asleep in his arms.

The sun was shining when she had awakened alone to see the swarthy, smiling face of his manservant, Hajib. She blushed to recall his glee at finding the marchioness tangled in the sheets of the master's bed. Lord Wortham had left in his carriage some time ago, he said, but to a destination his humble valet knew not. And Emma had spent the morning in a state of restless anticipation, wondering when Lucas would return and imagining how he would sweep her into his arms—

"The gentleman's card, m'lady." Stafford's voice startled her. The bewigged footman pointedly held forth a silver tray in his white-gloved hands.

"Thank you," Emma said, amused at her own wool-gathering. This sudden propensity for daydreaming had her behaving like a starry-eyed miss when in fact she felt as if she'd just been initiated into a secret sorority of womanhood.

Setting down the little elephant god, she picked up the card. The name printed on the white pasteboard jolted her like a thunderclap. Dear God, how could she have forgotten—? Composing herself with a deep breath, she said, "Send him in at once, please."

"Yes, madam." The footman bowed and left.

With trembling hands, Emma smoothed her peach gown and then hastened to the wall mirror to tidy her hair. She paused, struck by the change in herself. Her skin had a rosy tint from Lucas rubbing his cheek against hers. There was a softness about her that had been absent a day ago. A sweet, heavy ache warmed her womb.

Her hands strayed to her midsection. Perhaps she had already conceived. The thought filled her with dread—and an undeniable yearning. God forgive her, she wanted to bear Lucas's child. She wanted it with all her heart. She wouldn't let herself think beyond that.

If only she and Lucas could shut out the rest of the world. If only they could make up for all those lost years. She wanted Lucas, holding her. Lucas, kissing her. Lucas, moving inside her. . . .

The tread of footsteps sounded in the corridor. Sir Woodrow Hickey came through the doorway and walked toward her, his shoulders held in a stiff military bearing. He was dressed with customary elegance, his cravat perfectly tied, his buff breeches and blue coat tastefully matched, his shoes shined to a glossy sheen.

He bowed over her hand. "Madam."

"Sir Woodrow." One breath of his familiar sandalwood scent banished her sense of well-being. "Please accept my apologies," she said quickly. "I promised to bring Jenny to Hyde Park yesterday morning, but I was unavoidably detained. I hope you didn't wait long."

"Three hours, but that is of little consequence," he said, his lips unnaturally taut.

Guilt wrenched her stomach. Words seemed inadequate, but she said them anyway. "I'm terribly sorry. Truly, I am."

He walked back and forth in front of her. "My dear Emma, what matters is that I was concerned about you. I was afraid you and Jenny might have been found out and forbidden to contact me." He lowered his voice and sent her a piercing look. "Forbidden by your husband."

"Lucas?" She could feel herself blushing as his name evoked thoughts of dark delights. "No. No, he did nothing of the sort."

"Perhaps you should enlighten me, then."

Emma swallowed to ease the dryness in her throat. How could she admit why she'd been so preoccupied? She and Lucas and Jenny had spent a wonderful day at Hampstead Heath; they had laughed and played as a family. Then later—much later—Lucas had swept her away on a private journey of joy beyond her wildest dreams.

Sir Woodrow lifted his sandy eyebrows. "Well? Your husband's disapproval is the only reason I can think of to explain why you never sent me a note. It isn't like you to be so thoughtless."

And it wasn't like Woodrow to express his annoyance so plainly. He was a mild-mannered gentleman who seldom spoke a sharp word. When other men had regarded her as a fallen woman, he had treated her with unfailing kindness and respect.

"I . . . was gone all day," she said. "Lucas required Jenny and me to accompany him out of the city."

Woodrow's eyes widened. "Jenny, too? What would he want with her?"

"He thought we needed an outing, that's all. In the rush

to depart, I forgot to send word to you.'' She bit back another apology. She refused to grovel.

"I see."

Could he? Could Woodrow perceive the shattering emotions she was only just realizing, that she loved no man but Lucas?

She turned, walking swiftly to one of the leaded windows that overlooked the small garden, golden with autumn leaves. The warmth of the sun could not match the radiance inside her. She had been resisting the truth for days, ever since Olivia had pointed it out. *Every time you look at him, your whole face lights up.*

The insight threw her long-held plans into chaos. She knew with searing certainty that she wanted to stay with Lucas, to win back his love. No longer did she desire a divorce—and marriage to Woodrow. And therein lay her dilemma. She dreaded the thought of hurting the man who had stood so loyally by her through scarcity and scandal.

Woodrow's gloved hand came to rest on her shoulder. "My dear, don't take my chastisement to heart. It is only that I care very much for you and Jenny."

"It isn't that," she whispered. "I deserved your reprimand."

"Then tell me what has put the frown on your pretty face. If Wortham has been mistreating you—"

"No!" She whirled to face him. His sober gray eyes shone with loving concern. Why had she never desired Woodrow? Why did he not rouse the fire of yearning in her?

Considering the upheaval in her emotions, she couldn't—she mustn't—let him go on hoping. "I don't quite know how to say this. I'm not sure anymore that you should wait for me. What I mean is, I cannot hold you bound to a promise of marriage. Heaven knows when—or if—my husband will ever agree to a divorce."

Sir Woodrow stood stock-still. His ruddy cheeks turned ashen. "You're casting me off? After all our years of friendship?"

"We can remain friends," Emma hastened to assure him.

"I treasure your company and so does Jenny. Our relationship need not change so very much."

"Not change," he repeated woodenly. "This changes everything. Everything!" Abruptly he grasped her hands, his expression almost panicked. "Emma, please reconsider. You cannot throw away our seven fine years together for a man with whom you've lived for less than a fortnight. He could discard you both at any moment, and you'd have no one. Jenny has come to think of me as a father. I am more than happy to wait for you, however long it takes. If my hasty words have given you cause to think otherwise . . ."

She shook her head with aching regret. "Dear Woodrow. There are so many other ladies who could give you the love and honor you deserve."

"Pray, do not diminish my heart by implying it is so shallow. You are the lady of my choice. You and no other."

The anguish in his eyes touched her deeply. Was it possible he loved her desperately and she had never known? "I'm sorry," she whispered. "I don't mean to hurt you. I only wish to honor my vows to Lucas. Our marriage has never had the chance to thrive. But now . . . perhaps . . ."

His nostrils flared. His eyes became cold storm clouds. "So. Wortham has finally enticed you to his bed."

She gazed mutely at Woodrow, unable to deny it and unwilling to speak of something so precious and intimate.

"Be forewarned," he said, clutching at her hands when she would have pulled free, "men like him make promises in the dark they never intend to keep. He wants only a son from you. Then he will cast you and Jenny out on the street."

Was it true? Could Lucas be so heartless? He could, for that was the bargain they had struck. He had left her this morning without a word of farewell. And he had made her no promises last night. It was she who had changed, she who had discovered a dazzling new world that roused a high hope for the future. And now, Woodrow's warning wormed into her heart. Had Lucas experienced the same soul-deep connection? Or had their lovemaking been a mere physical interlude for him, a passing pleasure?

The door slammed. "Take your hands off my wife."

Lucas stalked toward them. He looked heartbreakingly handsome in the stark refinement of a charcoal suit and casually tied neckcloth. A lock of windblown hair lay upon his brow, the only softness about his thunderous expression. In the crook of his arm, he carried the tiger mask. Its stripes of brown jasper and yellow diamonds glinted in the sunlight.

Woodrow released Emma's hands and stepped back. "Wortham."

"Hickey. I trust you were saying good-bye." Lucas strolled to Emma and kissed her on the cheek. "Sleep well, darling?"

Emma nodded as her heart swelled with gladness. Colors suddenly seemed brighter, sounds more resonant, smells richer. Then doubts struck. Did he truly mean the display of husbandly affection? Or was he merely staking his claim for the sake of her visitor?

Woodrow made no move to depart. The two men regarded each other like a pair of snarling dogs.

Irked by her inability to read her husband's heart, Emma stepped between them. "Lucas, how charmingly you welcome our guest." Before he could do more than raise an eyebrow, she spun toward the other man. "Sir Woodrow, would you care for some refreshment? I'll be happy to ring for tea."

"Perhaps it would be best if we spoke another time." He bowed jerkily to her. "If it wouldn't be too much to ask, madam, may I stop and visit Jenny on my way out?"

"Yes—"

"No," Lucas stated pleasantly. He placed the tiger mask on the desk, then settled himself on the mahogany edge, his long legs stretched out and crossed at the ankles. "Lady Jenny is in the company of my mother—her grandmother, in the eyes of the world. So shut the door on the way out, if it isn't too much to ask."

Sir Woodrow clenched his jaw and glowered.

"Another time," Emma murmured to him.

He cast a guarded look at her, then nodded crisply and left the library.

The moment the door clicked shut, Emma wheeled on Lucas. "Must you be so rude?" she chided. "He has every right to visit my daughter."

"And I have every right to monitor the company my wife keeps."

"When pigs fly, *darling*."

"You seem a trifle peevish this morning." A small smile flirted with the corners of his mouth. Cocking his head to the side, he lazily looked her up and down. "M'lady must not have gotten sufficient sleep last night, after all."

She blushed. The scorching heat rushed up her throat and into her cheeks. Her lips parted, but nothing came out. Really, it was ridiculous to let him disconcert her. She, who had once ruled society with her wit and beauty.

"I'm perfectly rested, thank you." With studied sophistication, she walked around the desk, intending to pick up pen and paper, anything to give her fingers something to do. The tiger's head caught her attention. "By the way, where did you go with the mask—oh!"

She found herself caught by Lucas, his hands firm around her waist and her bosom crushed to his waistcoat. Nestled between his legs, she could feel a distinct swelling in his breeches. Her own legs had all the substance of jelly, and Emma was certain if he weren't holding her, she would melt in an inglorious puddle of longing.

"I had a meeting this morning at Montague House," he said in a husky tone. "There's to be a new wing constructed to display the objects I've collected." His finger lightly followed the line of her jaw. "Funded by Lord Wortham . . . and his lady."

"By me?" To her chagrin, her voice sounded breathy and girlish. "I haven't the means to build a doghouse."

"Then let's pretend that whatever is mine is also yours." His hands cupped her bottom and snuggled her closer to him. "To do with whatever you like."

There was no mistaking the twinkle in those dark eyes. Or

the keen ache where their bodies touched. Deliberately mis-understanding him, she walked her fingers up the front of his starched linen shirt. ''And if I were to ask you for a thousand pounds?''

''You won't.''

''Hah. How can you be so sure?''

''Because''—he leaned closer—''at the moment''—his hot breath gusted against her ear—''you're not thinking about money.''

Something light and damp traced the whorls of her ear. A shivery warmth waltzed downward, dancing to the drumbeat in her belly. She closed her eyes and savored the sweetness of passion. She and Lucas were perfect partners. Her body responded to his, only his. Surely it was only a matter of time before he realized that, too.

He kissed a path over her cheek and his mouth met hers, softly at first, then with deepening arousal. She opened herself to him, giving back as much as she received, letting instinct be her guide as Lucas had taught her.

She felt herself melting, melting in his arms until her back met a hard bed and she realized he had lowered her to the desk. He tugged at her skirt. ''Lift up,'' he said hoarsely.

''Here?''

''Now.''

''The door—''

''Is closed. The servants have strict orders not to disturb us.''

''You told them—?'' The half-formed thought slipped away as he worked the skirt to her waist and then caressed her masterfully, first with his hand and then with his mouth. Emma groaned in shocked denial as his tongue sought her most sensitive secrets. Then the searing pleasure of it over-came her scruples, and she gave herself up to the alluring sensations. Within moments he lifted himself over her and made them one, taking her on a swift ascent to the sun and the radiance of release.

As the sounds of their pleasure subsided, Emma basked in

an incomparable awe. "I didn't know it could happen so . . . *fast*."

"Tallyho," he said.

She laughed—she couldn't help it—even though shyness swept over her. The desk pressed against her back, and sunlight spilled its golden glory onto them. Above her, Lucas braced himself on his arms, taking most of his weight and making her more aware of the one place they were joined. His eyes were a deep, dense brown, shaded by thick dark lashes. Though he wasn't smiling, she could see the indentations in his cheeks. From the depths of her heart surged a rushing river of love, a tender tide of hope. She swallowed against the thickening in her throat. "We'd better get up," she whispered.

"Perhaps so." The dimples deepened with the curving of his mouth. "But I can't think of anywhere else I'd rather be right now."

Did he care for her, just a little? Or was his lovemaking only a means to an end? "I expect you say that to all your women."

His smile waned. "I've had only two women in my life, Emma."

Two women. Herself. And his foreign mistress. A strange, sharp emotion cut into Emma's breast. Until now he had been faithful to his concubine, as faithful as a husband. How many years had they taken their pleasure together? How many times had he visited her here in London?

Strangled by resentment, she turned her head to the side. And found herself staring into the glowing, emerald-rimmed eyes of a tiger. "Oh!"

"It seems alive, doesn't it?" Lucas murmured. "It's reputed to have magical powers."

An eerie energy emanated from the mask, as if it were possessed of a seductive sorcery. Resisting a shiver, Emma looked curiously at Lucas, aware of how many things she didn't know about him, how many things she wanted to learn. "Are you superstitious, then? You'd trust an object to bring you good luck?"

"Luck? No." He smiled wolfishly. "The tiger is a fertility god. I have it on the best authority. The mask bestows great potency on its owner."

His cocky conceit took a moment to register. Then the source of it hit her with an unwelcome jolt. *Fertility.*

Her hands thrust hard against his chest. "Get away from me. You and your plaguey mask." Sitting up, she grabbed the heavy tiger's head, preparing to hurl it at him.

"Have a care," he said, taking it from her and placing it back down. "It's a priceless objet d'art."

"And you brought it into the library on purpose." She stabbed her finger at him. "You *planned* this little tête-à-tête."

He elevated an eyebrow. "I'd have to believe in magic, then."

"Are you saying you don't?"

"Are you saying you do?"

"No!" She didn't quite understand why she felt so distraught. "I'm merely pointing out that you deliberately put your *fertility* charm beside us. To help you conceive a child."

He made an exaggerated grimace. "You wound me. Surely my own virility suffices to the task."

"Don't laugh at me!"

"I wouldn't dream of it."

She almost asked him what he *did* dream of, but caught herself in time. He regarded her with insufferable interest as she struggled to adjust the gown twisted around her waist. He produced a folded handkerchief and made a move toward her.

She snatched it from him. "I can manage."

Presenting her back to Lucas, she tidied herself with shaking fingers, though the silk skirt was hopelessly wrinkled. The knot in her throat returned with a vengeance. She was scandalized at how easily she'd lost control. Anyone might have walked in—a servant . . . the dowager . . . Jenny.

Out of the periphery of her vision, Emma saw Lucas straighten his own clothing. How could he be so casual about making love to her on a desk in the middle of the day? Because for him, the experience was only a pleasurable means to an end. He wanted to get his heir and then divorce her. And return to his precious mistress.

With the suddenness of a thunderclap, Emma realized she was foolish enough to hope for more. Foolish enough to dream of love. Foolish enough to want to stay with him forever.

His hand brushed over her back. "Emma. Don't be angry."

His voice held a trace of tenderness, and she immediately took offense. "I'll be angry if I like," she said, spinning around to face him. She slapped the handkerchief into the palm of his hand. "You cannot dictate my feelings."

He stood gazing at her strangely, moodily, his earlier mirth vanished. "I fail to see what's put you in an ill humor," he said. "Conceiving a child is what we agreed upon."

And then you'll take our son away. She hugged her arms to her aching bosom. "It's a cold-blooded plan, that's what. And I don't care to have your tiger mask here to remind me of it."

Compressing his lips, Lucas stared at her consideringly. "The truth is, I showed the mask to the director of the museum. Then I brought it here so you might catalog it in your journal. The rest . . . simply happened."

It wasn't much of an apology. Yet she was mollified to know he had been overcome by passion for her rather than merely pursuing his heartless scheme. A fierce resolve took shape in Emma. If he did not see a place for her in his future, then she would have to create one. Smiling determinedly, she moved into his arms and curled her hands around his neck. "Then I do hope *the rest* happens again soon, my lord."

He lifted his eyebrows quizzically. "You aren't angry anymore?"

She shook her head, arched up on tiptoe, and touched her lips to his. After a moment's hesitation, he tightened his grip and returned the kiss, a light and playful action that held the affection she craved. At least the wall of hatred and mistrust was gone, and that left the way open for love.

"Women," he growled. "I'll never understand you."

"There's something I don't understand," she said, drawing him over to the desk. "Perhaps you can answer my questions about this strange elephant creature."

Obligingly, he took the piece in his hands. "Ah, Ganesh. He's a lovable fellow with the face of an elephant and the spirit of a child. He's from a district in India called Gujarat." Lucas ran his finger down the stone trunk. "Every Gujrati home has a shrine to Ganesh. The natives burn incense to him in order to invoke his good will."

Emma listened, fascinated by his tale as much as the tender care with which he turned the statue in his big, competent hands. The same tender care with which he had delivered her out of the darkness of fear and into the light of hope. For better or for worse, she loved Lucas Coulter, this man who had once loved her, too. She had wed him for revenge, to take his name in exchange for nurturing his brother's seed. And now she didn't regret any of it, not even the rape, for it had brought her Jenny . . . and Lucas.

Little did he know, she considered their bargain nullified. She had no intention of handing over the child they would conceive and then meekly walking away. Nor would she allow Lucas to seek out any other woman.

She meant to fight for her husband's love.

❦ Chapter 19 ❦

Memoirs of a Burglar
Installment, the First

Upon a moon-dark night, along the steep rooftops of London, walks the Seeker of Justice. Fleet of foot and noble of purpose, he is garbed in black, a shadow darting from chimney to chimney, nimbly balancing on the narrowest of ledges and bravely risking the maws of Death in his quest to aid those poor souls who have suffered at the whims of Evil Gamesters.

By night he journeys along the upper stories of the city; by day he promenades with the upper reaches of Society. Be not alarmed by this stealthy visitor, ye who live a life of Goodness. Do not hide your jewels or secure your valuables—there is no need. Only those Amoral Others, those who think naught of beggaring a decent man at the toss of the dice or a turn of the cards, have reason to fear, for the Burglar walks among you.

And I am he.

Lord Anon, known as the Bond Street Burglar

At the breakfast table, Lucas dropped the newspaper he'd been reading aloud and looked at Emma. She sat to his right, close enough for him to smell her feminine fragrance, not close enough to satisfy him. Her cheeks were as pale as the cream she had been pouring into her tea. Her eyes were big and pansy-blue against a face of such exquisite beauty he felt thunderstruck anew each time he gazed at her.

Lately he had spent an inordinate amount of time in a state of dazzlement. And an equal amount of time resenting Emma's mastery over him.

She set down the cream pot with a distinct clink. "It's Grandpapa," she declared. "*That's* what he was writing last week when we went to see him about stealing from Miss Pomfret. He hid a stack of papers in his desk, remember?"

Lucas did, indeed. But his mind dwelt on what had happened later that night in the privacy of his bedchamber. And every night since, not to mention the trysts during daylight hours. He couldn't fathom his obsession with a woman who should mean less than nothing to him.

"You're right—this is Briggs's work." Lucas glanced down at the newspaper. "And apparently there's more to come. It says here that tomorrow we shall find out about Lord Anon's first escapade as a 'Seeker of Justice.' "

Making a small sound of distress, Emma lifted her gaze to the ceiling. "Grandpapa has gone too far this time. If the publisher of this scandal rag knows Lord Anon's real identity, then others can find out, too."

"I very much doubt Briggs would be so foolish as to tell anyone, let alone a stranger."

"I pray so." Heedless of crumb-laden dishes, she reached across the table and placed her hand in his. How soft was her skin, especially beneath her clothes, the breasts and hips, the velvety cleft between her thighs. "Oh, Lucas. If Clive Youngblood discovers the truth, he'll drag Grandpapa off to prison. These memoirs will be like a signed confession."

"Youngblood won't find out. I'll make certain of that." Lucas pushed aside the remains of his breakfast. "And in the meantime, I believe I shall pay a visit to your grandsire."

"Don't be angry at him. He did this for me." Her voice lowered to an anguished whisper. "Bless him, he wants to clear my name."

"And pay off Mannering," Lucas muttered, half to himself.

"But Grandpapa surely wasn't paid five hundred pounds for *this*." She tapped the newspaper.

Lucas shrugged noncommittally. He was sorry he'd reminded her of the gaming debt Briggs still owed. It was better that Emma didn't guess the suspicion that nagged at him.

"Dear heaven," she said.

Lithe and graceful, she rose to her feet and paced the dining room. Lucas was fascinated by her low-cut apricot dress, by the swish of the skirt around her legs. He knew precisely how those legs felt, slender and silken, wrapped around his waist—

"I see now," Emma said, with a snap of her fingers. "If Lord Anon were to threaten Gerald Mannering with being made a laughingstock in a future installment, then Mannering might be induced to pay out blackmail money. Which Grandpapa would turn around and use to reimburse Mannering."

Pushing back his chair, Lucas went to her, unable to stop himself from lightly touching her cheek with the backs of his fingers. "I fear that may indeed be his plan. But you needn't worry, I'll take care of the matter."

A smile blossomed on her face, and her eyes sparkled. "Worry? Why, I think it's exceedingly clever of Grandpapa."

Lucas dropped his hand to his side. "It's exceedingly foolish, you mean. Not to mention illegal."

"Oh, nonsense. It's far safer than scrambling around on rooftops and pilfering people's jewels." She absently rubbed her shoulder. "A person could get shot doing that."

"A person could also get hurt while attempting to dupe a scoundrel like Mannering." Lucas fisted his fingers in a vain attempt to erase the feel of her. "And that settles it. I'll pay off Mannering myself. If I hadn't been so thick-skulled, I would have done so at the start."

Emma stood very still. "You would discharge his gaming debt? You would do that for Grandpapa?"

''Not for him,'' Lucas said roughly. ''For you.''

The truth slipped out before he could stop it. Emma would be devastated if anything happened to the wily old man. And Lucas could not bear to cause her pain.

Her hands alighted on the lapels of his coat. She lifted herself on tiptoe and touched her lips to his in a butterfly kiss. ''Thank you,'' she murmured, and laid her cheek against his chest.

A treacherous softness unmanned him. He was conscious of her slim body, how well she fit his arms, how sweet and guileless and loving she was. His wife. *His wife.* There was nothing suggestive about her embrace, yet he craved her again, even though they had welcomed the dawn with a private celebration of pleasure.

He shouldn't be holding her like this. There was no point to affectionate hugs. He needed a child from her, that was all. Only a fool would want more from a woman who could not be trusted.

And if she did not become pregnant? In the two years he and Shalimar had been together, his mistress had not conceived. Perhaps the fault lay in him. Perhaps he wasn't so virile a man. Perhaps, deep down, he was still that green boy who had worshiped at the feet of a goddess. . . .

He subdued his doubts. So much the better if the task took months. Those were months in which he could purge himself of this white-hot passion for Emma. Even then, she might give birth to a daughter. And he would have to take Emma to his bed again . . . and again.

Each time he clasped her to him, it was more difficult to remember that he held an illusion. Each time, he reminded himself. She had beguiled him once into believing she loved him. She had lied to him, stolen his chance to have a family of his own. Because of her, he had spent seven years as an outcast, wandering the world, belonging nowhere.

Because she had been raped, his conscience argued. She'd been young and frightened and desperate.

She was also amoral. Prideful of the fact that she had

broken into the homes of the nobility and pilfered their jewels.

Because she'd had to pay off her grandfather's debts. And pride also had kept her from demanding the allowance due her as the Marchioness of Wortham.

She wanted an end to their marriage. She had made that clear from the start and had accepted his terms—their son in exchange for a bill of divorce. Already she had selected her next husband, a fact which infuriated Lucas.

So why, then, this past week, had Emma acted the devoted wife? Why did she tease Lucas with the finesse of a seductress? At first he'd thought it was her brand of revenge, her way of punishing him for his abandonment, for demanding she give him a child. But now he knew. Quite simply, Emma was mad about sex.

For most of her adult life, her natural sensuality had been locked within the walls of fear. Now, with her inhibitions shattered, she was like a child let loose in a confectioner's shop. And he was the lucky proprietor who fulfilled her every appetite.

Love had no place in their marriage. It never had. It never would.

"Mama, look!" Jenny skipped into the room, her braids flying. Against her green dress, she cuddled a squirmy ball of white fur.

Emma drew away from Lucas and knelt down to touch the ball. "Mercy! What do you have here?"

"It's Toby's great-granddaughter. And Grandmama says I may keep her." Jenny giggled as a tiny pink tongue licked her cheek. Beseechingly she looked at Emma. "But only if you and Papa say so."

"A puppy is a great obligation. You should have to feed her and care for her."

"I will! I'll save the very best morsels from my plate."

"She'll need to be walked outdoors, too."

"Nurse promises to take us to the park every day." Growling playfully, the puppy pounced at Jenny's braid.

"Please, Mama," Jenny begged. "I've already named her Sissy. Since I don't have a real sister."

Emma uttered a small sound of distressed sympathy. She glanced up at Lucas. "What do you think?"

He stared into her clear blue eyes, surprised she would consult him in a decision regarding her daughter. And confounded by how pleased he felt.

He crouched in front of Jenny. There was something inexplicably familiar about her eager blue-green eyes, something that caught at his heart. "There's one more important duty," he said. "You'll have to mop up any puddles she leaves indoors."

Jenny screwed up her nose. "I will, Papa. I promise. You won't be sorry. I'll be your best girl, forever and ever."

He felt the most curious twist of pain in his chest. Jenny didn't know she would one day leave here with her mother. She didn't know the danger of growing attached to him.

Yet it was impossible to resist her innocence when she looked at him so anxiously, her tongue worrying the gap in her front teeth. "That's quite a pledge," he said. "All right, then, you may keep her."

"Oh, thank you!" She launched herself at him, and for the second time that morning he found himself holding an armful of female—and this time a wriggling puppy as well. Over Jenny's head, he could see Emma watching, a soft wistfulness in the downward curve of her mouth. The look swiftly vanished, and she smiled again.

"Come," Jenny said, tugging at Emma's hand. "Let's go tell Grandmama."

"All right." Letting herself be dragged toward the door, Emma murmured to Lucas, "You'll visit Mannering today, then?"

Lucas nodded curtly. As she blew him a kiss and left in a flash of apricot skirts, an unwelcome thought struck him. If people believed the Burglar to be Lord Anon, then Emma was cleared of suspicion and Lucas had lost his leverage with her.

She could refuse to bear his child. She could leave his bed

forever. She could move out of Wortham House immediately and return to the estimable Sir Woodrow Hickey. *He* would not demand she relinquish her own son; in fact, he had promised her a chaste marriage.

A violent resentment choked Lucas. He assured himself it was concern for her well-being. Now that Emma knew the joys of intimacy, she wouldn't be happy with a cold fish like Hickey.

And it was up to Lucas to make her realize that.

That afternoon, in another part of the city, Clive Youngblood glowered at the master printer, a rawboned wretch without a brain inside his bald skull. The cluttered office stank of ink and cheap paper. Little sunlight penetrated the soot-grimed windows, rendering the place dim and cold. The clack of the handpress came from the other end of the long room, where a whey-faced apprentice was cranking out additional copies to meet the high demand for *Memoirs of a Burglar*. A burly laborer hefted armloads of the edition to the boys waiting outside to hawk them all over the city.

Clive rattled the news sheet at the man. ''What d'you mean, you hain't no idea 'oo wrote it?''

The printer splayed out his skinny, ink-stained fingers. '' 'Tis what I said, sir. The story came by post. There wasn't any return address.''

''You must've sent payment somewhere.''

''He gave it for free, I swear it. The Burglar's like Robin Hood. He steals from the rich and gives to poor, hard-working citizens like me.'' The stoop-shouldered man bowed to the Runner. ''If I might beg leave, sir, I have tomorrow's issue to set up.'' He scuttled off toward the trays of lead type stacked against the back wall.

Clive seethed. He wouldn't be outsmarted by toffs like Lady Wortham and Lord Briggs. They was no better than pickpockets from Petticoat Lane. Nobody made a fool of Mr. Clive Youngblood and got away with it.

Then a thought struck him. *Tomorrow's issue.*

The Bow Street Runner marched past the jumble of files

and papers and stopped behind the master printer. By the yellow light of an oil lamp, the man used wooden tweezers to transfer bits of type into a press tray. When he paused to squint at the manuscript beside him, Clive snatched up the top sheet.

"Lemme see this," he said, his eyes avid on the spidery handwriting. "Ah-hah. *'Installment, the Second. Whereby the earl of F—— lures several gentlemen into a game of Speculation and leads them to Ruin—'*"

The paper vanished from his hand, snatched back by the printer, who glared with surprising defiance. "Please, sir! You are not permitted to peruse this episode until the morrow. The Burglar was quite specific about releasing only one chapter a day."

"Too bad fer the Burglar, then. That there is evidence."

Clive started to reach for the manuscript, but the brawny laborer who'd been hauling newspapers appeared out of nowhere and stepped in front of him. His meaty face wore a sneer. "Come back wid a warrant, then, ya bleedin' worm."

Clive's palms broke out in a cold sweat. Not for the first time, his bravado failed him. He glanced from the brute to the glowering printer and decided to err on the side of caution.

"'Ave it yer way, then," he said. "I'll be tellin' the magistrate that yer aidin' and abettin' a criminal."

It was an empty threat. But they couldn't know that just this morning he'd been ordered off the case. Clive's stomach went queasy at the memory of the head magistrate's stern reprimand about harassing the nobility. Lord Wortham's doing, no doubt.

Clive adjusted his battered hat on his head. Ignoring the snickers of the apprentices, he made for the door.

At least he had a bit of new information. Judging by the handwriting, the Memoirs was writ by Briggs, he'd bet a crown on that. And somehow Clive Youngblood would find a net to catch the old codger.

And Lady Wortham, too.

❧ Chapter 20 ❧

Memoirs of a Burglar
Installment, the Twenty-second

Of all the feats of daring performed by the Bond Street Burglar, this one I shall relate today has naught to do with gambling. It is the sad story of a virginal lady who faced Ruin after being seduced by Lord Villain. This sweet gentlewoman loved the virtuous Lord W——, and thence married him in haste, lest her innocent babe suffer the slurs delivered by the ungenerous tongues of the Public. Thusly would Society's strict rules of propriety punish the Pure and reward the Debaucher.

Aye, this is a tale of woe and of wonder, of riches and of redemption. And of the Burglar's quest to save Lady W—— from destitution by delivering unto her a precious artifact from the East, the fabled tiger mask. . . .

Until now, Emma decided, she had not known the true meaning of happiness. On this blustery gray day, the first of November, she sat sipping tea in the drawing room while Lucas, the dowager, and Lord Briggs conversed around the fire. Jenny squealed with laughter at the antics of her puppy. It was a cozy scene of perfect domesticity.

The sound of her husband's voice made Emma soft and shivery inside. So did the secret she guarded deep within her womb.

She had not had her monthly flux since September. Last week had come and gone without a sign of it. And the past few mornings she'd awakened with a slight but telltale nausea that subsided upon eating a light breakfast. As with her first pregnancy, she felt languid and contented, prone to napping in the afternoons.

She hadn't told Lucas yet. Her heart took a momentary dive, for nothing between them had been resolved. Though she loved him more deeply with each passing day, he guarded his own emotions. He kept their relationship light and teasing, and seldom did he exhibit true affection. Always it was she, reaching out to him, embracing him, pursuing him. Except, of course, whenever they made love, which was often and exhilarating. There had been one particularly memorable night in the conservatory, the scent of hothouse roses all around, their bodies bathed in starlight as Lucas loved her with an earthy sweetness. . . .

"Mama, what's a masquerade?"

Emma blinked at Jenny, who sat on the hearth rug, sneaking morsels of cake to her puppy, Sissy. "A masquerade? It's a party where grown-ups dress up in costume and wear masks. Why do you ask?"

"Little ears," Lucas said, "overheard us discussing the Guy Fawkes masquerade on Thursday. Remember? Vauxhall Gardens is being opened out of season for the Pomfrets' party. But don't tell me our scintillating conversation bored you."

She blushed as everyone looked at her. "Don't tell me you want a truthful answer," she said archly. "I should claim to be contemplating my costume."

"There's no need for *me* to contemplate," Grandpapa said, winking at her. "*I* plan to garb myself as the Bond Street Burglar."

The fire crackled into the silence. Lucas frowned, but said nothing. Emma didn't know whether to protest the risk or applaud her grandfather's audacity. In the past weeks, *Memoirs of a Burglar* had become all the rage. Each new installment was snatched from the hands of hawkers almost before the ink was dry. Although "Lord Anon" only hinted at the names of notorious gamesters, talk buzzed at every social gathering, and the tide of opinion turned against those rakes who frequented the dice tables and profited from the misfortune of others.

And of course, the *ton* speculated wildly on the identity of "Lord Anon." The gentlemen wished to throttle him, while the ladies . . . Well, they claimed to disapprove of the Burglar's actions, but more than one had expressed a dark fascination for the mysterious antihero in their midst.

Emma was especially touched by her grandfather's eloquent defense of her in the latest episode. She only hoped that portraying her and Lucas as the virtuous victims of a mysterious Lord Villain wouldn't hint too strongly at the Burglar's connection to her. She didn't doubt Clive Youngblood would seize any chance to jail Briggs.

Apparently oblivious to the undercurrents, the dowager petted old Toby in her lap. "How typical of you, Briggs, to make a spectacle of yourself," she said, her smile taking the sting out of her words. "You almost tempt me to attend the party myself."

"Why don't you?" Briggs said. "We'd make a grand entrance, you on my arm as my accomplice in crime."

Her cheeks bloomed pink. "In my younger days, perhaps. Now I prefer a quiet evening at home. Just Toby and me."

"You'd favor a dog over the dashing Burglar? Why, you wound me to the quick."

Jenny clapped her hands. "May I go to the masquerade?"

"Absolutely not, young lady," Lucas said. "You'll be fast asleep in your bed."

Jenny stuck out her lower lip. "Then Sissy and I must see you and Mama in your costumes. What shall you be?"

"We haven't yet decided—" Emma began.

"But undoubtedly your mother will be a goddess," Lucas said with a rakish wink. "Nothing else would suit."

Her heart beat a little faster. She treasured his half-smile, the show of dimples in his cheeks. Over the past few weeks, he had come to enjoy her company, she was sure of that much. Their newfound ease with each other buoyed her hopes that his fondness for her might grow into love.

The footman came in, bearing a letter on a tray. "The late post, for you, m'lady."

With a smile of thanks, Emma picked up the letter. It was thick, with her name printed in an unfamiliar hand on the outside. "How singular," she murmured, noting the plain red seal. "I wonder who's written to me."

She excused herself and strolled away for a moment of privacy. A gust of wind rattled the panes of glass as she settled onto a window seat. The draft raised gooseflesh and she shivered, wishing for her shawl. Breaking the circle of wax, she unfolded the missive to find two sheets of cream vellum. Instead of a flowing script, both papers bore printing in block letters, much like the work of a schoolboy.

Mystified, she glanced down at the signature at the bottom of the first page. She blinked. Her heart lurched into an erratic rhythm. The room fell away, leaving nothing but herself . . . and the paper clutched in her hands.

With great effort, she dragged her gaze to the top, where the date was written: *27 July.*

Emma, the message began, *Pray, do not crumple this note when you see the identity of its author. I have attempted to write to you many times in the past month, but tore up each inadequate endeavor in despair. I beseech you now, heed my abject apology and know my abominable behavior that night has tormented me ever since. No lady—no woman—no human deserves such abasement, and as the perpetrator of your dishonor, I am damned to the fires of Hell. There is no excuse for my infamy, yet please know I was driven to madness over a happening I dare not explain to you.*

I humbly beg your forgiveness, not for my peace of mind, but for your own. God will punish me in His own way and time. I pray only that His justice comes soon. I remain
Your servant, Lord Andrew Coulter

*   *   *

That night, the wind blew in a bank of sullen clouds, and by morning the wind died and the clouds wept. The dreary drizzle lasted for four days. Four days of worry and fretting until Emma dared to delay no longer.

On the afternoon before the masquerade ball, she donned her warmest pelisse, descended the servants' staircase, and left the house by way of a little-used side door. Her nerves thrummed from the strain of keeping up the pretense of normalcy. Lucas planned to work in the library after luncheon, and she had laughingly begged leave so she might devise her costume. How ironic that she was compelled to lie in order to find out the truth.

The rain had stopped. A chilly mist hung in the smoke-laden air. She hurried along the wet pavement, only half noticing the festive preparations in the city. Everywhere, servants and tradesmen and urchins sought out dry kindling for bonfires along the curbstones. The notorious Guy Fawkes was hung in effigy, celebrating the foiling of his gunpowder plot to blow up Parliament back in the time of King James I.

Too preoccupied to summon any patriotic fervor, Emma rushed toward her destination. Her mind was focused on the letter, and the sickening sense of unreality that had struck her upon seeing the signature—and the date.

27 July. For one terrible instant she'd fancied the letter had been written only a few months previous, that Andrew had returned from the dead to haunt her. Then she'd realized the letter must have been composed seven years ago, on the eve of Talavera. The night before Andrew had been killed in battle.

Only then had she turned to the second sheet of paper. It had been written in the same juvenile hand: *I have come into possession of the actual letter written by Lord Andrew Coulter. It is yours to burn in exchange for the tiger mask. Bring the mask to Vauxhall on Thurs. night and leave it in the Temple of Daphne. Should you fail to comply, the letter will go to Wortham.*

There had been no signature.

It all made horrid sense now, Emma thought as she hastened along the back streets. Andrew's letter was a copy. The forger had obviously disguised his own penmanship.

She prayed she found the blackmailer before it was too late. Today, before she was forced to steal the mask and destroy Lucas's faith in her.

Who possessed the original letter? Apparently Andrew hadn't had time to post it before the battle that took his life. Over the years Lucas himself had kept Andrew's personal effects. Her stomach performed a sickening flip. That only went to prove how much Lucas treasured the memory of his brother—the hero of Talavera.

Tamping down her loathing, Emma forced herself to think. Could her mother-in-law have found the letter? The dowager would never have shown it to Lucas.

If Wortham were to learn the truth, it would destroy him.

Could the elder Lady Wortham, in some twisted, half-mad way, be plotting to push Emma out of the family? Perhaps the dowager planned to separate Jenny from her mother.

The damp weather had little to do with the chill that invaded Emma. Breathing deeply, she clung to common sense. If her ladyship had possessed the letter all along, she surely would have guessed from the start that Andrew had fathered Jenny. And she would have known Emma had been raped, not overcome by passion for the cavalry officer about to go off to war.

Who else, then? Someone in the Wortham household, a servant, perhaps, who coveted the tiger mask?

She could think of many people who had had an opportunity to find the letter, but had no reason to resent her. She could think of others who had reason, but no knowledge of Andrew's connection to her past. Clive Youngblood, for one. For months, he'd skulked around, seeking proof to toss her or her grandfather into prison. She didn't doubt he might maneuver her into stealing the mask—if it weren't absurd to think he could possess such a letter.

That left her most likely candidate. One whose guilt would hurt her grievously. Woodrow.

She hadn't wanted to consider him. But of all the suspects, he had the strongest reason to wish her marriage destroyed. And there was the damning fact that he and Andrew had been friends, comrades in the cavalry. What if Andrew had given Woodrow the letter for safekeeping?

She wrestled again with the disturbing questions the possibility raised. Why would Woodrow keep the letter all these years? Why had he even read so private a note? And upon reading it, why would he deny her the comfort of knowing that Andrew regretted his brutal act? It made no sense.

Her footsteps slowed as she reached Woodrow's lodging, a well-proportioned town house in a row of similar residences. The brick dwelling appeared rather forlorn today, the curtains closed and the windows dark. A thin curl of smoke wafted from one of a pair of chimneys.

The mist beaded on her lashes and she blinked hard. Hesitating on the pavement, she wanted to turn and run. She dreaded finding out that Woodrow was not the kind, considerate man who loved her and Jenny. She couldn't bear to see him as a cruel stranger.

But the alternative was far worse—to lose Lucas. He would never forgive her if she stole the mask. And she might never again soften his heart.

Beneath her pelisse, her hand smoothed over her flat belly. In eight months, if their child was a son, Lucas would seek a judgment in civil court proving her infidelity, and then submit a divorce petition to Parliament. The law would award him full custody of their baby.

No. *No!*

She mounted the narrow steps to the door flanked by Palladian half-columns. Her shoes felt sodden, her feet frozen. She lifted her gloved hand and rapped hard.

Water dripped from the small overhang of the porch. The cold moisture plopped onto her hood and rolled down her woolen pelisse. It seemed an eternity passed before she heard footsteps inside the house, and the door swung open.

A jowly, careworn housekeeper peered out from the darkened foyer. A ring of keys dangled from her broad waist. With curious brown eyes, she scanned Emma's fine garb and bobbed a curtsy. "Aye, mum?"

"I'm looking for Sir Woodrow Hickey."

"The master isn't here. Left nigh on three weeks ago."

"It's most important that I speak with him. Where has he gone?"

"Why, t' Gloucester, mum, takin' all the staff wid 'im but me. They won't be back till the springtime."

"Are you sure?"

"Aye, mum. If ye'd like t' send a message, why I'd be more'n happy t' give ye the address."

"No. No, that won't be necessary."

Her emotions in turmoil, Emma slowly descended the steps. Blast. *Blast!* She didn't know whether to be glad or sad to discover that Woodrow had departed London after their final, painful interview. And now she was more thoroughly confused than ever. If Woodrow was more than a day's journey away at his estate near Gloucester, then he could hardly be plotting to exchange the letter for the mask tonight.

And if it wasn't him, then who? *Who?*

The clopping of hooves and the rattling of wheels approached from behind her. Automatically she veered away from the street to avoid being splashed by one of the many puddles. The vehicle slowed and stopped. She turned her head in vague curiosity to see a footman leap down and open the door of an elegant black coach.

A gentleman sat in the dim interior. He snapped out a command to her. "Get in."

Her heart bumped into her rib cage. It was her husband.

✺ **Chapter 21** ✺

Lucas kept his face impassive as Emma stepped into the coach. Seating herself opposite him, she arranged her damp skirts. The coach started smoothly down the street.

When she lifted her gaze to him, her mouth was curved into an enchanting smile. "What a wonderful surprise, Lucas. You're a gift from heaven, I vow. When the rain stopped, I couldn't bear to stay cooped up in the house any longer. But I didn't take into account the effects of a stroll through so many puddles—"

"The truth, if you please," he broke in.

"It is. I went for a walk—"

"Emma, I know who lives in that house back there. So do you."

Her smile died a slow death. "Then perhaps you also know he's gone. Woodrow left town three weeks ago."

"Yes," Lucas said.

She sat back, her gaze direct and her lips curved into a kissable pout. At one time he would have fallen for her air of innocence. But not anymore. Emma had been on edge these past few days, her smiles too bright and her conversation too distracted. More than once, he'd caught her staring out the window as if in deep thought. It was a jolt to realize he'd grown accustomed to her staring at *him*. He was consumed by the dark dread that she'd lost interest in her husband. After all, it wasn't him she loved, but coupling.

He'd given her that. Plenty of that. Their encounters were hot and lusty and intensely satisfying. So why the devil would she seek out Woodrow Hickey? Unless for her, something was missing. Unless she longed for the man she loved.

"You won't get what you need from him," Lucas said without preamble.

Her tawny lashes fluttered. Her cheeks turned paler. Very cautiously she asked, "What . . . do I need?"

"Sexual intercourse."

The color rushed back into her cheeks. Her lips parted in surprise. "You think . . . I went to visit Woodrow for *sexual intercourse*?"

To his utter chagrin, she tilted her head back and laughed. Her hood fell back, revealing the shining abundance of her hair. The chime of her merriment rang through the confines of the coach.

"I don't mean you intended to leap into bed with him today," Lucas said irritably. "I meant later, when you marry him."

"Oh."

"He's incapable of fulfilling your needs, Emma."

Her mirth faded into puzzlement; then a soft, serene light came into her eyes. Rising, she crossed the swaying coach and sank down beside him, reaching for his gloved hand. "Oh, Lucas. There's no cause for you to feel jealous of Woodrow—"

"You mistake me. Woodrow Hickey wants a chaste marriage for one reason, and one reason alone." Distaste made his grip tighten on hers. There was no way to varnish the truth. "He's a sodomite."

"A . . . what?"

"He prefers men to women."

She gazed blankly at him. "Certainly he enjoys the company of men. He often goes to his club—"

"I mean in bed, Emma. He desires men."

Horrified comprehension darkened her eyes. She slowly shook her head in disbelief. "That's a lie. Such things are impossible."

"It's the truth." Then, to soften the shock, he *did* lie. "I'm sorry."

The distant noise of merrymaking came from outside as the coach passed a gathering of Guy Fawkes revelers. "Oh, mercy," Emma said in a throaty whisper. "It cannot be. How could I not have *known*?" She stared at him as if begging for an answer.

The craving for violence seized him. He could cheerfully strangle Hickey for deceiving Emma. Denied that chance, Lucas hauled her into his arms and held her tightly. "He hides his predilection well," he said into the cloud of her hair. "If the merest whisper of it became known, he would be shunned, reviled. And if it could be proven . . . Well, homosexuality is a capital offense."

"Dear God," she said in a faint voice. "If he feels no desire for women, whyever does he wish to marry me?"

"Respectability. With a wife and a stepdaughter, he would appear the decent, honorable gentleman. No one would suspect he led a secret life."

She pressed her fist to her mouth. Huddled against him, she felt small and vulnerable. He could feel her quiet breaths, warm against his skin. His compassion was entwined with the need to make love to her, to show her how very much she was desired.

The coach drew to a halt in front of Wortham House. His arm around her waist, Lucas helped her out. It was highly improper to hold a lady close in public, even when the woman was his wife, but he couldn't release her when she looked so dazed and forlorn.

And as they entered the house, he allowed himself a surge of pure masculine triumph. He had eliminated his rival. Granted, he regretted distressing Emma, but there had been no other way. He couldn't let her love any man but himself.

Love. Like a door opening to heaven, the thought dazzled him. No longer could he label his feelings for Emma as animal lust. As much as her body, he wanted her heart and soul. Forever.

The revelation staggered him. For better or for worse, he

loved Emma. He loved the woman who had once betrayed him. He was twice a fool, and he didn't give a bloody damn for the pain he undoubtedly would suffer in the future.

Emma pulled away from him. They were standing in her blue and yellow bedroom. And he had no notion of how they'd gotten here.

She removed her damp cloak and murmured something to her maid. The girl bobbed a curtsy, then scurried out the door. Seating herself on the stool at the dressing table, Emma removed the pins from her hair. The sobriety on her face pierced his heart. It was almost as if she'd forgotten his presence.

Lucas shrugged out of his greatcoat. He crossed the room and lifted the luxuriant fall of her hair into his hands. How thick and silky it was, damp from the mist. Bending, he kissed the tender nape of her neck. Then he picked up the silver brush and stroked it from the crown of her head down to her waist. The sheer sensual pleasure of it made him hard. No other man had seen her with her hair unbound. No man but her husband ever would.

No other man.

She took the brush from him and clutched it to her breast. Their gazes clashed in the mirror. "Why did you do it?" she whispered.

"Do what?"

"Why did you go poking into Woodrow's private life? Why couldn't you have let him be?"

She sounded almost angry. As if she resented him for pointing out Hickey's base secret. Lucas gritted his teeth and strove to be understanding. "I was loath to see you hurt. The paragon seemed too perfect, and so I asked some discreet questions."

"Of whom? Who would tell you . . . about *that*?"

He hesitated to describe the oily little pimp in the genteel bordello with its private back rooms. "There are places—private clubs—where a man can indulge his fantasies." She needn't know those fantasies often involved young boys, driven to prostitution in order to live. Hickey, at least, shunned that particular depravity. "According to my informant, Hickey is devoted to one man. They've been meeting regularly for five years."

"Dear God. Who?"

"A certain illustrious member of Parliament who shall go unnamed."

Sighing, she bowed her head and closed her eyes. The golden crescents of her lashes edged the delicacy of her eyelids. How pale was her skin, how vulnerable her fine-boned face.

Her melancholy rankled him. He felt the nagging urge to shake her, to make her notice him. "Of course, this revelation only confirms another important fact."

She opened her eyes, her gaze wary. "What's that?"

"He couldn't have fathered Jenny."

Emma stiffened. Jerkily she began rearranging the already tidy pots of cosmetics and flacons of perfume on the dressing table. "I see. You didn't believe my word. That's the real reason you investigated Woodrow."

"Maybe so." Catching gentle hold of her shoulders, Lucas swiveled her to face him. "You haven't been entirely truthful with me about your past, Emma. You're protecting the scoundrel who defiled you."

"I'm not." She lowered her gaze, her fingers slim and pale around a blue bottle of scent. "It's simply best left forgotten."

"Fine. Tell me his name, and then we'll forget about him."

"Stop badgering me, you . . . you . . ." With an exclamation of frustration, she flung the bottle at him. He caught it just as the stopper fell out and perfume spilled down his shirt and waistcoat.

"What the hell—" Whipping out his handkerchief, he scrubbed at the potent aroma of roses. "I can't stop badgering you," he snapped. "Any more than I can stop wishing you'd trust me instead of pushing me away."

Rising, she faced him. "All right, then, I'll entrust you with a secret. I broke off with Woodrow three weeks ago."

That stopped him. "You did?"

"Yes." She snatched the handkerchief from his motion-less fingers and busied herself with cleaning his coat, then blotting his soaked shirt. "So you see, my lord detective, your little investigation was quite unnecessary."

"Yet you went to see him today."

"Of course. I consider him a friend. So does Jenny. I merely thought to invite him to visit us."

Lucas tilted her chin up. He wanted to see Emma's eyes when she answered his next question. "And why did you break off with him?"

"Because I want . . ." She pursed her pretty lips, then hurled the handkerchief to the floor. "Oh, blast you. Don't you know? I want *you*, Lucas, and no other man. Only you."

He gazed down into her flushed face and knew she spoke from the heart. The violent joy he felt defied words. It was every bit as frightening as it was awesome. She gazed at him anxiously, as if expecting his scorn.

To hide his own emotion, he spoke lightly. "Even if I stink of ladies' perfume?"

"Even so," she said, relaxing into a wistful laugh. "As long as the perfume is my own—and easily disposed of."

She loosened the folds of his neckcloth and dropped it carelessly to the rug. Then she worked on the buttons of his waistcoat; it went the way of the neckcloth. Soon a pile of his clothing lay beside them, and she caressed his bare chest with her hands and mouth. Her pale hair rippled against his skin. With unsteady fingers, he unfastened her gown and let it fall. Willingly she lifted her arms as he removed her chemise. He kissed the upraised scar on her shoulder, her badge of dishonor, and the thought of losing Emma added urgency to his burgeoning desire.

Bringing her up against him, he held her silken body, the womanly curves he knew with intimate detail. She was his universe. The rest of the world faded away and there was only the two of them, needing each other, taking sustenance from the act of love.

"Emma," he murmured. "Emma."

She arched hungrily against him, her breasts brushing his chest, her lush curls teasing his loins. ''Oh, Lucas. Love me.''

''Yes.'' He couldn't say more. He couldn't voice the promises that knotted his throat. He was too afraid of losing her again. And so with wordless eloquence he showed Emma, carrying her to the bed and laying her down, where he could worship her with his body.

He loved her slowly, exquisitely, using rigorous restraint to prolong the building pleasure. And she loved him back with the tenderness of her touch and the softness of her cries. Letting his hands speak for his heart, he stroked her until she writhed and moaned on the verge of climax. Only then did he enter her, savoring the radiance in her beautiful eyes when their bodies became one.

No matter what mistakes had been made in the past, they belonged together. She was his woman, his wife, his long-lost mate. He moved inside her perfect passage, and the sweet agony of passion flared high and bright between them. It seemed he could never get enough of her; he could never get close enough. His blood pumped furiously with the effort. All at once, she cried out his name and her inner muscles spasmed around him, milking the seed of life from him, causing his body to convulse with the violent splendor of release.

They lay entwined in the timeless aftermath, with the fire whispering on the hearth and the afternoon slowly darkening to dusk. Lucas resisted thinking beyond the contentment of the moment. Doubts would come then, but for now, it was enough to hold Emma, to bask in a world alive with color and lit by his reckless love for her.

They shared a lingering kiss. She sighed and stretched, turning her head to rub her cheek to his chest—and recoiling with a cough. Wrinkling her nose, she waved her hand to clear the air. ''Phew! You still reek of perfume.''

He chuckled. ''Through no fault of my own. Pray I succeed in scrubbing the stuff off before the masquerade tonight.''

Something flashed through her eyes, like the brief shuttering of light. Then she smiled again, the smile that always enslaved him. "Lucas. May I beg a favor of you?"

"That depends upon what you'll give me in return." His hand roved down her side, dipping into the curve of her waist and rising to the smoothness of her hip. "I can think of a few favors I'd like to beg of *you*."

"Perhaps you'd better hear what it is first," she said. "It's in regard to my costume."

"Ah, the goddess. If you wish me to play your adoring mortal, I am honored to do so."

Her eyes sparkled up at him. "Don't be silly. This is a matter of grave importance."

"Then, pray, don't hold me in suspense."

"I've been pondering your idea of a goddess. And the problem is, I suspect half the ladies in attendance will dress as Diana or Aphrodite."

"Then you shall play Venus. Hair like moonbeams." He sifted the silken strands through his fingers. "A face to inspire a thousand sonnets to beauty." He lightly ran his knuckles down her cheek. "A body to drive a mortal man to madness." Feeling the rise of heat, he caressed her perfect breasts, watched the tips turn to rosy buds.

Laughingly, she caught his wrist. "Lucas, do let me finish. I should like to portray an exotic goddess from a faraway land. And therein lies the favor I must ask." Her smile lessened, and she regarded him attentively. "May I wear the tiger mask to Vauxhall tonight?"

The request surprised him. Especially considering her antipathy toward the mask that day in the library. Against his will, the old suspicions seeped into his mind, testing the resiliency of his faith in her.

"Thieves and cutthroats prowl any public place," he said. "I can't be by your side at every moment."

"This is a private party. And I'll be surrounded by the *ton*. I've no intention of wandering away."

"The gold will weigh heavy on your delicate head."

"I'll wear it for only a short time," she said. "Just a few dances. And your valet can wait in the carriage to guard the mask later. Please, Lucas, I would have the most brilliantly original costume. Only think how amazed everyone will be.''

"They'll appreciate your beauty more without a mask covering it.'' He could have sworn she had changed, that she no longer needed to attract hordes of admirers. Yet he was unable to resist her appealing look. "However, if it pleases you, then yes, you may wear it.''

Closing her eyes, she lifted his hand to her lips and kissed it ardently. "Thank you.''

He had the strange, fleeting impression of a desperate relief in her. He told himself he was mistaken. It was an unthinking suspicion brought on by too many years of cynicism. Why would she steal the mask, anyway? Her thieving days were over.

Caressing her hair, he pulled her closer to him, enjoying the softness of her breasts yielding to his chest. Yes, if he truly loved Emma, he had to learn to trust her.

Better he risk losing a priceless mask than her precious heart.

∞ Chapter 22 ∞

*Memoirs of a Burglar
Installment, the Last*

*. . . And so my friends, this final tale, like all the others,
proves that a man may call himself a gentleman while
lacking the honor of the lowliest groom in a stable.
Lord J—— P—— may boast of shooting the Bond
Street Burglar, but like all the Scoundrels of Society,
he plays deep and uses his superior skills to ruin eager
young blades and to gull amiable old men. Though his
crime was avenged when I relieved him of his ill-
gained bounty, he will forever bear the notoriety of
felling the Seeker of Justice.*

*Aye, one fateful bullet has ended the illustrious career
of the Burglar. I bid thee farewell, faithful Readers, and
beg only that you shun those Amoral Gamesters who
would dupe the Unwary. Beyond an occasional foray to
seek the comfort of a Lady, I hereby retire myself.*

Lord Anon, known as the Bond Street Burglar

"The tall one with the ginger hair must be the Burglar,"
declared a rather stout lady dressed in the flowing white
robes of Aphrodite. She nodded toward one of the many
black-clad revelers at Vauxhall Pleasure Gardens. "How

dashing he looks. Why, even his cravat is the color of midnight.''

"That is Lord Gerald Mannering, and he's far too thin and lofty,'' Miss Minnie Pomfret informed the group of awestruck ladies. "The Burglar is a smaller, stronger man. A most charming gentleman.'' She lowered her voice. "As you know, he makes forays to visit his chosen ladies.''

A collective sigh swept the gathering, followed by a delirious gasp from Miss Pomfret. Garbed like a gawky Roman statue, she clasped her hands to her flat bosom. "Oh, my stars, it's him. The masked man standing below the orchestra box.''

The stout lady raised her lorgnette. "But who is he? We simply must determine his real name.'' In a twitter of excitement, she and the other women rushed into the throng of dancers and revelers.

Emma lingered alone in the shadows of a giant beech tree. She held the tiger mask in the crook of her arm. Her costume was a deep golden brown, and a hood comprised of the same dark hue concealed her pale hair. Certain she could not be detected in the gloom, she dawdled, watching the festivities for a moment and wishing she could be so carefree.

The lights of a thousand colored lanterns twinkled down from the grandstand. The traditional Guy Fawkes bonfires burned at the perimeter of the dancing area and warmed the chilly air. At least half of the gentlemen present wore black in imitation of the Bond Street Burglar. It made for an amusing sight. There were stout Burglars and skinny ones, swaggering Burglars and bashful ones. Some wore masks of ebony silk; others a more elaborate hooded cape. She'd like to see how many of these pampered noblemen could manage a narrow ledge four stories above the ground. At midnight, no less, and hampered by rain or fog.

And then her merriment vanished as she wondered which—if any—of these aristocrats was the blackmailer.

In a moment, she would have to make the exchange and betray her husband. She had to go now, while Lucas led an elderly duchess in the steps of a country dance. He looked magnificent in the peacock-blue robe of a maharajah, a golden turban upon his dark hair. A demimask made of peacock feathers hid his handsome features. How she longed to be whirling in his arms, lighthearted and happy. . . .

"Plottin' yer next burglary, m'lady?"

The voice startled her. Jolted by dismay, she turned to find herself staring into the sly features of Clive Youngblood. The pigeon-breasted man wore his usual drab brown coat and battered top hat. He rocked back and forth on his heels as if he'd made a great discovery.

Little did he know.

With effort she composed herself. "Present your invitation, sir," she said icily. "This is a private party."

"Don't get 'igh and mighty wid me." The Runner stepped closer and whistled. " 'Hain't that the tiger mask yer 'oldin'? The one what's worth a king's ransom?" His drooping eyelid blinked in suspicion. "Does yer 'usband know you 'ave it?"

"Naturally. In case you failed to notice, everyone is wearing a mask." She waved a graceful hand at the crush of dancers, the many black-clad men squiring white-gowned goddesses. "By the by, this is your golden opportunity to find the Burglar. You've plenty to choose from."

Youngblood scowled, and she knew she'd struck a nerve. He hitched his thumbs in his lapels. "Well, now. I might be lookin' fer yer grandsire."

"Then do run along. Before my husband notices you're badgering me."

She thought his face paled in the gloom. Casting a wary glance at the dancers, he said, "I do got business t' tend to."

Her knees weak with relief, she watched him scuttle away, skirting the edge of the throng. He was heading away from Grandpapa, thank goodness.

Miss Pomfret and her court of ladies had reached their black-garbed quarry. Like a swarm of bees, they surrounded Lord Briggs. Even over the noise of the orchestra, Emma could hear his chortle of laughter. Dear Grandpapa. He did so enjoy the speculation, the notoriety, the queries about being the celebrated Burglar. These days, to keep the ladies guessing, he never so much as looked at a deck of cards. He'd been so lonely after Grandmama's death. What a boon the *Memoirs* had been to his spirits.

The music stopped. The dancers would be seeking their next partners. Unable to spy Lucas in the crowd, Emma wondered if he had noted her absence yet. Pray God she could make the exchange before he realized she was gone. Pray God he would believe her trumped-up story that the tiger mask had been stolen from her.

Resolutely, she turned and headed down one of the many walkways that wended through the trees. The weather had cleared and the moon shone against the starry sky, though the air was damp and chilly, rich with the scent of autumn leaves. Jewel-bright lanterns were strung from tree branches to illuminate the path. A layer of straw had been spread over the muddy earth to protect the ladies from soiling their slippers.

Emma kept her head down as she passed a few strolling couples who had wandered away from the main party to steal a moment alone. She had been one of them once. On that long-ago night seven years ago, she had gone off for a promenade with a laughing group of young gentlemen and ladies. She had been a foolish girl, eager to taste life, impatient with proprieties, and when one penniless swain enticed her into lagging behind, she had gone with him. She did not now even recall his name. She remembered only that he had kissed her, fallen to his knees and begged for her hand in marriage, and with a few arrogant words of refusal she'd sent him packing. Heedless and headstrong, she had stormed off the opposite way, down a darkened path. . . .

A wave of dizziness washed over Emma. It had happened here at Vauxhall on a warm summer night. Stupidly, she had struck off alone along a deserted track, much like the one she entered now.

There were no lanterns here, and gloom lay thick over the gardens. Clutching the tiger mask, Emma walked slowly, aware of the beating of her heart. Surely it was only her imagination that caused her eerie sense of foreboding. Scores of little pathways crisscrossed the gardens. This could not be the same one. The coincidence would be too hideous.

Her feet splashed through a puddle, soaking her slippers. She scarcely noticed the cold wetness. Ahead, something white glinted through the darkened trees. The same ghostly gleam she had glimpsed that other night. Then, as now, the merry splashing of a fountain masked the distant noise of the orchestra.

She forced herself to keep walking, though a pall of horror descended over her. As if it were yesterday, she remembered her delight at stumbling upon an airy little temple with stone pillars. The same temple that loomed before her now, with dark ivy climbing up the white marble and inside, the statue of a goddess.

The temple of Daphne.

Earlier, a bored attendant had pointed out the pathway to her. Emma had never dreamed it was the place of her nightmare. She had never known the name of it, one of many rustic shrines scattered throughout the gardens.

It was an appalling mischance. Her blackmailer could not have known the implications of the rendezvous he had chosen. Or could he?

Ice prickled down her spine. Had he been watching that night? Had he seen Lord Andrew violate her?

Her stomach crawled. Was he even now observing her from the nearby bushes? Or from the murky depths of the temple?

She could not go on. Her feet were rooted to the ground. Every instinct screamed at her to run. To run as far and as fast as she could. To flee the danger of the present as much as the demons of the past.

But to do so was to lose Lucas. Her love for him gave her strength. She had to fetch that letter and burn it.

Gripping the heavy tiger mask, she cautiously approached the temple. She glanced around, but saw only the darkness of the trees. Slowly she mounted the marble steps, half expecting to find a man slumped on the stone bench within, his head in his hands, the gold trim on his blue uniform glinting in the shadows. . . .

He was weeping. Deep, wrenching sobs of raw emotion. She paused, paralyzed by compassion and awkwardness. Never before had she witnessed such undisguised pain in a man. He thought he was alone, unobserved.

She backed away. He must have caught her movement, for his head shot up and he stared, his face wet with tears.

With a jolt, she recognized him. Lord Andrew Coulter. She had thought him a handsome and entertaining man, always smiling, ever ready with a witty remark. But not now. Now his expression showed a harsh, unsightly anguish.

He said nothing. The moment seemed to pulse with some unnamed intensity, something savage, beyond her ken.

She took a clumsy step backward, bumping into a column. "I—I—"

He lunged off the bench. Before she could even recoil in surprise, he seized her by the waist and propelled her down onto the stone floor, at the base of the statue. His body slammed onto hers. For an instant, she lay there, stunned. Then she panicked, lashing out with her fists, sucking in air for a scream.

His hand clamped over her mouth. "God help me," he said in a guttural tone. "Don't fight. . . ."

Breathing hard, he yanked up her skirts. The shock of it galvanized her. Shoving, kicking, biting, she battled his feral attack. His relentless fingers tore at her undergarments. Cool air slapped her naked flesh. Then a brutal thrust of his hips hurled her into a hell of fiery pain.

She thought he'd plunged a knife into her. Tears stung her eyes, tears of agony and hysteria. Her fists beat against his straining muscles, but he was oblivious to her blows. Grunting and muttering, he rammed into her, again and again and again.

"I want—I need—a woman—only this—nothing more— nothing—"

He jerked and cried out, panting harshly. Then he rolled off her and lay prone on the floor of the temple, his face

buried in his arms. While she huddled at the base of the
pedestal, shaking and burning. . . .

Emma trembled now, dizzy from the memory. She stood
inside the shadows of the temple, gazing at the very spot
where Andrew had raped her. The pale square of a folded
paper lay on the floor, beneath the statue of the beauteous
Daphne, begging her father to save her from Apollo's passion.

The old feeling of helplessness choked Emma, along with
a rising rage, a tempest of anger at the man who had ended
her innocence. He had not even seemed to notice her weeping that night as she'd dragged herself to her feet, clutched
the torn gown around her blood-smeared thighs, and stumbled away to her carriage.

My abominable behavior has tormented me ever since . . .
I am damned to the fires of Hell.

The words he had written fed her fury. He knew nothing
of torment. Nothing of suffering scorn, of facing pregnancy
alone and in disgrace, through no fault of her own. "Curse
him," she said aloud.

And now, just when she'd found happiness once more,
Andrew was reaching out from the grave to hurt her again.
Him, and whoever sought to use the ruinous apology he had
committed to paper. "Curse them both!"

Half-blinded by tears, she dropped the tiger mask and
snatched up the letter. She rushed out of the temple, down
the steps, and into the moonlight. She paused only long
enough to ascertain that she possessed the genuine letter.
Crushing it in her palm, she headed for the trees. Her only
thought was to find a lantern on a deserted path. She'd burn
the evidence. And Lucas would never know. He would
never, ever know.

Suddenly, as she ran headlong down the shadowed path,
she saw him.

Despite the gloom, there was no mistaking the peacock-
blue of his costume or his tall, princely form. He had discarded his mask. He surged toward her, the haste of his
strides betraying his concern.

It was too late to flee. But Emma didn't care. She wanted only to feel her husband's arms around her, safe and warm and strong.

He fulfilled her wish, enclosing her in his embrace. "Emma? You frightened me. Why were you running? What's wrong?"

"Oh, Lucas, I saw it," she whispered brokenly. "The place . . . where he forced me."

Like a protective band, his arm muscles stiffened around her. The breath came out of him in a harsh gust. He pressed her cheek to his chest, his fingers stroking back the hood and threading into her hair, tilting her face up for his healing kiss. "My God. What possessed you to go there?"

"I—I just went for a walk. . . ." She couldn't tell him what she had done. She could never tell him, though her shoulders drooped from the weight of her lies.

"Who was he?" Lucas said in a low, hard voice.

She shook her head in bitter despair. If only he knew, the truth was written on the ball of paper clutched in her hand. The terrible truth that would destroy him and his family. "Please, I beg of you. Don't ask me anymore."

A long moment passed. A lively tune played in the distance, where people laughed and danced and made merry. It seemed a world separate from this moonlit place in the trees. "I can't help myself," Lucas said gruffly, rubbing his cheek against the top of her head. "I wish to God I'd been there to protect you."

"Yet if you had been, I wouldn't have Jenny. She makes the memory bearable."

"And us, Emma. Don't forget that bastard's act of violence brought you and me together."

Radiance trickled into the darkness of her soul. Lucas spoke as if she mattered to him. Dare she hope he could forgive her? She lifted her head, searching out his dark gaze in the moonlight. "I owe so much to you," she whispered. "You taught me how wonderful a man's touch can be." Emma paused, her heart overflowing as she reached up to caress his hard jaw. "No, not any man. Only you. I love you, Lucas."

The tightening of his hands on her back acknowledged her avowal. Yet his eyes were strangely watchful. "Then tell me." The words sounded dragged from him. "What have you done with the tiger mask?"

The chill of reality invaded Emma. The burden of her secret weighed upon her conscience. She had intended to claim she'd been robbed and throw herself upon his mercy. But the lie died on her lips. She lowered her head in shameful despair, praying he would never find out, even if it meant him losing faith in her, never trusting her again.

He let go of her abruptly. As she looked up, he brushed past her and plunged down the path toward the distant temple. Her heart leapt into her throat. A pinprick of light moved in the gloom of the shrine.

The blackmailer.

"No." The wind caught her whispered moan as she ran after Lucas. A stone cut into her slipper. Heedless, she followed him, but it was too late. He pounded up the steps of the temple. A moment later, he hauled out a man clad all in black and holding a lantern in his gloved hand.

She knew him at once, though a dark cap covered his sandy hair. "Woodrow," she said in anguish.

He gazed at her across the small, moonlit clearing. The music of the fountain played into the quiet night air. His shoulders were bowed, his chin lowered. "Emma," he said, holding out his hand in supplication. "My dear Emma."

Sickened by his betrayal, she stood mute. He had put her through hell. Because he wanted to shatter her marriage.

Lucas gave him a hard shake. "Tell me what this is all about. Has my wife been passing stolen goods to you?"

"Good God! No!" Woodrow paused, his chest heaving. With slow, thoughtful movements, he set down the lantern on the marble step. "I—I wanted you to blame her. If you must know . . . I was blackmailing her."

"On what grounds?"

"I was in possession of a letter"—he paused as if the

admission pained him—"from the man who had dishonored her."

"No," Emma moaned. *"Please."* Willing him not to go on, she crushed the balled-up letter.

Neither man seemed to notice her distress. They faced each other like combatants on a battlefield.

"A letter," Lucas repeated in a strange, raw voice. "From whom? Damn it, man, *who*?"

Woodrow's expression took on a certain satisfaction. "I'm afraid . . . it was written by your brother. Lord Andrew."

Turning her head away, Emma squeezed her eyes shut. She could not bear to look at Lucas. To see the pain on his beloved face. She could sense his agony as if it were her own.

"You lie. *You lie.* I'll kill you for that." Then his harsh tone was directed at her. "Emma? Is this true?"

She opened her eyes. He stood in the moonlight, his features stark and noble, the man she had grown to love. The last time he'd been betrayed, he had fled England for seven years. And in a cruel flash of insight, she realized that without honesty she was unworthy of him.

Wordlessly, she held out the crumpled letter.

He took it from her, walked away, and propped his foot on the step, smoothing out the wrinkled paper against his thigh. By the light of the lantern, he read silently, shadows hollowing his cheekbones. It seemed an eternity passed before he lifted his head and turned his haunted eyes to her.

"My brother . . . did that to you . . . here." His voice sounded lost, bewildered, ashamed. "Why didn't you tell me?"

"I couldn't." The barrier of the past stood between them now. Gazing at him, she felt his torment along with her own helpless anger. Damn Woodrow. He had succeeded in his plot. How could he, when she had trusted him for so long?

Lucas looked at her as if seeing her for the first time. As if realizing all she had suffered. And then without touching her, he turned to Woodrow. "Why did you have this letter?"

"Andrew gave it to me. At Talavera. As he lay dying . . .

in my arms.'' His voice broke as if from the strain of emotion. ''I would have cut off my right arm to save him. He was my life . . . my love.''

Mired in disbelief, Emma stared at him.

He's a sodomite. He prefers men to women.

Lucas seized Woodrow by the black lapels of his coat. ''You bastard! What the hell are you saying?''

''I loved him. I loved your brother with all my heart and soul.''

''And with your body?''

''With all that I was.''

Lucas released him abruptly and stepped back. Pacing in agitation, he rubbed his brow. ''No. Surely I would have known.''

''Not about that.'' A trace of smugness on his face, Woodrow sat down on the step. ''It started when we became friends at Eton. One night, we had a bit much to drink . . . and it just happened. Neither of us planned to make love. Neither of us had any experience, either.'' He paused, his head in his hands. ''Forgive me, Emma. I shouldn't speak of such things with a lady present.''

His misery touched Emma in spite of her shock. But she resisted feeling sympathy for him. For all his pain, Woodrow had knowingly betrayed her. ''Never mind propriety,'' she said sharply. ''I would hear your explanation for Andrew's treatment of me.''

''It's my fault, I fear, though inadvertently so. You see, I fell deeply in love with him and wanted to continue the . . . the affair. But Andrew fought against his own nature. He feared his family discovering such a secret. Until that night here at Vauxhall.'' Woodrow's voice shook. ''Yes, we met that night. We had a brief encounter here . . . but the struggle within him was too great. He ordered me to leave him. And so I did.''

Emma tasted the saltiness of blood. She had bitten her lip. Numbness shrouded her body. In her mind's eye, she could see Andrew sitting on the bench, his face buried in his hands. She could hear his wrenching sobs. And this time, she could sense his despair, too. His hopelessness. He had been in the grips of a monstrous dilemma, torn by a love and longing that society considered to be evil, deviant, punishable by death.

Lucas's shoes crunched on the gravel around the fountain. "So," he said in an oppressive voice, "you let him rape an innocent girl."

"No." Woodrow sat up straight. Repugnance darkened his voice. "I didn't know what had happened until later, much later. We were due to depart for our regiment early the next morning. Andrew arrived drunk, scarcely able to walk, and in so desolate a temper I feared he would harm himself. And he did, in the end."

"What do you mean?" Emma whispered.

"He was withdrawn for the next month, in the blackest of moods. I blamed myself, of course. And I feared the worst when we met the French at Talavera. Andrew wanted to die. We were separated during the fighting, yet whenever I caught a glimpse of him, I saw him take chance after chance, riding into the thickest of the fighting, until at last he went down, felled by a French saber." Woodrow bowed his head a moment before continuing. "He confessed all to me as he lay dying. That he had forced himself on you. That he had been frantic to prove his virility with a woman. Any woman. And you had the misfortune to be there." Woodrow fell silent, weeping soundlessly, his face contorted.

Emma sank to her heels. Andrew's actions made a tragic sense now. And knowing the story brought a certain lifting of relief inside her. "You should have given me his letter. Why did you keep it from me?"

"It was wrong of me. I beg your forgiveness. You see, I couldn't bear to relinquish the last words he had written." Woodrow paused, wiping his eyes while gazing beseechingly at her. "When I found out you were carrying his child, I befriended you. At first, I wanted to assuage my own guilt over the terrible turn of events. But when Jenny was born, she brought light into my bereavement. Andrew lives on in her. Surely you can understand how precious she is to me."

"And so you threatened my wife," Lucas stated harshly. "You pretended to leave town, and then sent her a blackmail note—you would give me the letter if she did not steal the tiger mask. Either way she would be forced to betray me."

Woodrow gave a jerky nod. "When Emma said she wished to stay with you, I could not bear it. I had no choice but to win her back however I could. Otherwise, it meant losing Jenny. Perhaps forever."

"There is no 'perhaps' about it. You are never to come near my wife—or my child—again."

Desolation twisted Woodrow's face. He sprang up from the step, the starkness of horror in his wild eyes. "No. Please. You can't mean that—"

"I do, indeed."

Hearing the cold rage in his voice, Emma stood up. "Lucas, there's no need to be so severe. Jenny regards Woodrow as a father—"

"I am her father now. By the blood of my brother."

Emma hugged her arms to her breast. She had never heard him speak in so flat and icy a manner, not even on the night of their wedding. It was as if all warmth in him had died. There was no joy in his claim to Jenny. Nor had he mentioned he was also Jenny's father by virtue of his marriage.

He opened the glass door of the lantern and set the letter ablaze. The paper curled and darkened in his hand. He did not release it until the flame burnt down to his fingers and surely blistered him. Then he dropped the charred letter to the ground and crushed it beneath his heel.

He looked at Woodrow, who stood with his face in his hands. "The tiger mask. Where is it?"

Woodrow lifted his head slowly, his eyes dull. "I—I don't know."

"The devil you don't. Emma must have left it for you."

"It wasn't here." He spread his hands wide in obvious bewilderment. "I—I looked all over the temple, but someone else must have gotten to it first."

Lucas grabbed the lantern and stalked up the steps. Emma hastened after him. The shrine was small, the statue of

Daphne at one end and the bench at the other.

"I remember dropping the mask right there." Emma pointed to the base of the pedestal. The white marble glowed softly through the darkness.

"There's nothing back here but a few dead leaves." Lucas held up the lamp, lighting the gloom behind the statue. "Damn. He must be lying."

Emma tagged behind him onto the steps. Only to see Sir Woodrow trudging away, his shoulders slumped, his posture one of abject misery.

Lucas made a move to pursue him, but Emma stopped her husband with a hand on his rigid arm. "Let him go," she said. "Woodrow doesn't have the mask. Someone else must have taken it."

∽ Chapter 23 ∽

*H*e was aware of her following close behind him.

The patter of Emma's soft footfalls echoed his slow, heavier steps. Dry leaves crunched beneath his heels. The music in the distance had ended and an unearthly silence enveloped the wooded gardens, as if the very air braced itself for the noise of the fireworks display. Only an hour ago, Lucas had looked forward to watching Emma's joy as the dazzling show lit up the night sky.

He had no stomach for amusements now. He doubted she did, either. Their relationship had altered irrevocably.

He had condemned her as a coldhearted conniver. But their marriage was not her fault, not really. She had chosen him of all men to be her husband because, as head of the family, he was accountable for the actions of his brother. It was as simple as that.

Lucas couldn't blame her for fighting back the only way she knew how. She'd had an unborn child to protect. And he understood why she had withheld the truth. It had been an act of selfless mercy. She had wanted to spare him the pain that now corroded his soul.

God! Andrew had had her first. Witty, irreverent Andrew, always smiling, the youngest of the family, and the light of their mother's heart. The hero of Talavera was a villain and a coward. He had forced himself on Emma. He had hurt her, ruined her, then left her alone to raise his child.

Lucas blinked away a stinging heat. Jenny. Little Jenny was not the daughter of a stranger, but his niece. He should have recognized those distinctive blue-green eyes . . . Andrew's eyes.

But Lucas had been too caught up in his own selfish needs to notice. He had barred Jenny and Emma from his house for seven years. He had compelled them to live in poverty, the subject of scorn.

The dark knowledge assaulted him. Was he so much better than his brother? He too had run away. He had left Emma to fend for herself. He had abandoned her in her time of need, when she carried his brother's child in her womb. Not knowing didn't excuse his actions.

And upon his return to England, he had treated her with contempt. Granted, he hadn't used violence to force her into his bed, but he *had* coerced her. He had threatened to turn her over to the law if she did not bear him a son. A son whom he intended to wrench from her arms.

The cruelty of his terms shamed him. He could only imagine the suffering his arrogant demands had inflicted on her. Emma, who deserved so much more than a brutal, compassionless husband.

As they neared the edge of the gardens, he slowed his steps so she might catch up to him. It wouldn't do for anyone to spy him striding ahead of his wife, as if she were a servant trailing after her master. Yet even as he silently offered her his arm, and her small fingers curled around his sleeve, he sensed an insurmountable barrier between them. It seemed as if a thick glass wall separated them. And he was suffocating slowly, unable to seek the comfort of his wife. He needed Emma as much as he needed air to breathe.

A boom resounded through the gardens. Over the trees appeared a shower of twinkling, colored lights against the night sky. "The fireworks," Emma murmured.

She stood beside him, the brightness reflected on her wistful, uptilted face. Fierce regret seized him. She should still be innocent of the evil in life. She should never have known the dark side of human nature. But it was too late to erase the past.

They had reached the line of carriages. It was a cold night, and few guests had come by boat across the river. Here, the coachmen and footmen held their own celebration, singing boisterously around a huge bonfire. The ribald song ceased when someone spied the approach of Lord and Lady Wortham. Their burly coachman set down his mug of beer and hastened to their carriage.

"Where is Hajib?" Emma asked.

The coachman tipped his hat. "Don't know, m'lady. 'Em foreigners, they don't be interested in our English celebrations, I trow."

As they entered the dark confines of the coach, Emma said, "Lucas, wasn't Hajib to wait here for you to bring him the tiger mask? He must be around somewhere. Shouldn't we go and look for him?"

"He'll find his way home."

"And what of the mask? Perhaps we should tell Clive Youngblood—"

"To hell with the mask," Lucas said savagely.

She went quiet, and the directness of her gaze chastised him. Despite his remorse, a choking sense of unworthiness kept him from touching her. "Forgive me," he said, though words seemed inadequate to span the chasm between them. "I should not have snapped at you."

"You've every right to be angry," she said in a soft, sad voice. "Now that you know I married you for revenge."

"Andrew gave you no choice." To Lucas's chagrin, tears blurred his vision. He denied the weakness with a violent slash of his hand. "God damn him. *God damn him.*"

"He damned himself. Must you damn him, too?"

"Don't defend the bastard. He might have offered for you. He might have made reparations. He did nothing. Nothing to rectify the depravity of his actions toward you."

"I'm not defending him. But Andrew is dead. For me, that's retribution enough." She leaned forward, groping for his hands. "Let it be enough for you, too. Don't let his mistake ruin your life."

It was too late for forgiveness, too late to salvage any love for his brother. Lucas drew his hands out of hers. "I believed Andrew a man of valor. But he was a craven beast." With iron effort, Lucas kept his voice steady, though emotion seared his chest. "Were he alive today, I would call him out for what he did to you. I would kill him."

The chill fingers of horror crept down Emma's back. Lucas couldn't mean that. He couldn't. But the finality in his voice convinced her, as did the terrible expression on his face. Through the darkness, his features appeared hewn from stone, cold and dead and implacable. Then he turned his head toward the window and stared out into the night.

It was just as the dowager had predicted. *If Wortham were to learn the truth, it would destroy him.*

And his ability to love.

The sounds of revelry on the streets contrasted with the bleakness inside her. So her secret was out. How gladly she would resume the burden of it if only to bring back the teasing, carefree Lucas, the man who had learned to laugh again. But the damage had been done. And now a dark fear haunted her. Could he tolerate seeing her every day, being reminded that his brother had brutalized her? Could Lucas regard her with anything but pity and repugnance? Andrew's ghost would always stand between them. Andrew's child would always bring to mind the violence of her conception.

Dear God. Overwhelmed by pain, Lucas might seek refuge in the arms of his foreign mistress. The woman to whom he had run once before.

Emma's throat tightened with raw anguish. It hurt to think of him devoting himself to another woman. But if she truly loved him, she must let him go. He could never find peace of mind with the wife who embodied the tragic mistakes of the past.

Surreptitiously she pressed her hands to her belly. She and Lucas had created a precious new life through the beauty of their passion. This child, at least, was no mistake.

Tonight, she would tell Lucas about the baby. He needed to know the terms of their bargain had been met, that he was free to leave her bed. But she would not give up their son. She would raise him with love and teach him to be as fine a man as his father. And if she bore a daughter instead, she would treasure the little girl and tell her stories about her wonderful papa.

Unencumbered by the duties of a parent, Lucas could leave England with his mistress. He could escape the constant reminders of the past.

They arrived at Wortham House. Stepping out of the carriage, she looked up at the stately, torch-lit entrance with its tall columns and shiny brass door fittings. A sharp ache throbbed in her breast. Strange, how in the space of a few weeks she had begun to think of this house as her home. Perhaps, when he went away, Lucas would allow her to stay here. Yes. She would insist upon that. It was only fitting that Jenny and the baby took their rightful places as proud members of the Coulter family.

As she and Lucas entered the foyer, Stafford rushed forward in a state of unusual agitation. "M'lord," he said, wringing his white-gloved hands. "That plaguey Runner from Bow Street Station is here again. He's waiting in the library."

"Send him away."

"But m'lord, you don't understand. He's arrested your man, Hajib."

Emma's mind reeled in confusion. What absurdity did Clive Youngblood entertain this time? Lucas's valet had no knowledge of the Bond Street Burglar.

She hastened after Lucas, who was already halfway down the corridor, his bootheels ringing on the marble floor. Sweet heaven. She and Lucas needed no more complications in their lives. She wanted only to be alone with him, to spend one last night in the arms of her beloved husband.

The moment she entered the library, Emma faced the impossibility of that wish.

Brandishing a truncheon in his hand, Clive Youngblood stood before the hapless servant, whose hands were bound behind the straight-backed chair in which he sat. To one side of Hajib huddled a lovely, dark-skinned woman who hugged a half-grown boy.

Youngblood spun around and doffed his dented top hat. His thin lips were curved in oily triumph, the self-important smile making his drooping eyelid more prominent.

"Ah, m'lord and lady. I reckoned you'd like to meet the Burglar afore I took 'im off to the magistrate. It h'ain't Lord Briggs, after all. I caught this sneaky foreigner wid the goods meself."

"What goods?" Lucas demanded.

"Why, the tiger mask, o' course." With a flourish, Young-blood stepped back and pointed at the desk, where the mask glowed in savage glory. Backlit by a branch of candles, the emerald-rimmed eyes seemed eerily alive.

Gasping, Emma swung toward the valet. "It was you, then. You took the mask from the temple."

Hajib raised his turbaned head and turned his mournful gaze to her. "Yes, O Great Lady. I followed you through the gardens. You do not need the mask anymore. It has already worked its magic on you."

"What the devil are you saying?" Lucas snapped.

"She bears your child in her womb, master."

Emma stood paralyzed as Lucas wheeled toward her. "Is this true?" he said hoarsely.

She could only nod. How had Hajib guessed? Her throat was too choked for speech as she searched Lucas's face for a sign of gladness. But his expression was remote, unreadable.

"A toast to m'lord's prowess," declared Youngblood, raising his billy club in the air. "We both 'ave cause to celebrate, me fer following the Burglar to the 'ouse of his 'arlot, and you fer—"

"My mother is no harlot," the boy shouted. "You are a demon for saying so."

He rushed at Youngblood, all flailing arms and brown fists and kicking feet. With a cry of surprise, the Runner lurched backward, but the boy kept at him, landing blows to Young-blood's jaw and chest, and kneeing him in the groin. Yowling, the officer doubled over a moment before coming up with his wooden club raised.

"Sanjeev, get back!" Lucas bellowed. He leapt forward and caught the truncheon before it could crack open the boy's skull. And then he used the length of wood to pin the Runner by his throat to the wall.

Books tumbled from the shelf behind Youngblood. His face turned purple. He sputtered and gasped for air.

Emma hastened forward. "Lucas, no! You'll kill him."

"The weasel deserves to die."

She pulled at his steely arm, but couldn't budge him, couldn't stop him from committing murder. To her alarm, he was driven by a force greater than his fury at the Runner. All the pent-up emotion of the night incited him to violence.

"Please," she said over her shoulder at the foreign woman, who comforted her son. "Help me."

She came at once, a willowy beauty with sultry dark eyes. "My lord," she said, touching his straining arm. "Think of your child. You have been blessed by the gods. Just as I said you would be."

His strident breathing rent the air. Then he released Youngblood and hurled away the truncheon. The officer slid to the floor, where he lay panting and choking.

Emma watched in dawning shock as Lucas turned to speak to the woman, his voice too low to discern his words. Like a humble supplicant, she sank to her knees before him, a length of white silk draping her black hair. She was more than a friend to Hajib. This enchanting, graceful foreigner was Lucas's mistress. The woman he loved.

"Rise," Lucas said, before turning to Hajib. "So she begs for your worthless life. And you, a thief. How well you hid your greed."

"Shalimar has become beloved of me, and I wish to take her as my wife," Hajib said proudly. "The tiger mask will bring us many children, brothers and sisters for Sanjeev."

"Please, my lord, he meant no harm," Shalimar said in her smoky-soft voice. "We must take the mask back to our homeland. It is a treasure of my people. It was never meant to molder in an English museum.''

Lucas stood silent, his hands at his lean waist. A sharp ache assailed Emma. With his peacock robes and his sunburnished skin, he looked as if he belonged with them.

Not with her. Never with her.

"Untie him," he told Shalimar. "He's free to go."

She rushed to do his bidding. In a moment Hajib stood beside her, one arm protectively around her shoulders, the other holding Sanjeev close. The boy wore an expression of dazed wonder.

Clive Youngblood hauled himself to his feet. "You can't let the blighter go. 'E's the Burglar! Caught 'im red-handed wid the goods.''

"Ah, but you're mistaken," Lucas said. "Hajib didn't steal the mask. It belongs to him. And to Shalimar."

While Youngblood sputtered and Emma stared, Lucas walked to the desk, picked up the tiger mask, and delivered it to Hajib.

The valet gazed wide-eyed at the priceless golden mask he cradled against his gray robes. Then he fell to his knees before Lucas. "Master, a thousand blessings upon you. May you have twenty children to bring comfort to you in your old age.''

"God forbid—this place would be worse than Astley's Circus. Now get up. There'll be no more prostrating yourselves, either of you.''

Emma listened in stupefied amazement as he spoke of making arrangements for their passage back to Kashmir. He was letting Shalimar go. He was giving his mistress over to another man. Didn't Lucas care? Or had all emotion withered in him? She could read nothing but coldness in the stern angles of his face.

Certainly he had been kind to Hajib. She suspected he had another purpose. He hadn't bothered to point out to Clive Youngblood that almost all the robberies had occurred *before* Hajib had even set foot on English soil.

Now, with Hajib out of the country, Clive Youngblood

would believe the Burglar was gone for good. How clever of Lucas.

As the happy trio left the library, Lucas picked up the truncheon and tested the solid end of it against his palm. Still, he did not look at Emma. His eyes were hard and dark as he turned to the Bow Street Runner, who had untied his neckcloth to rub his bruised throat. "As to you, Mr. Young-blood, if ever I see your face again—anywhere, anytime—near any member of my family or my household, I'll finish you off. Have I made myself clear?"

"Q-quite, m-m-m'lord. N-never again." His hands visibly shaking, Youngblood snatched off his hat and bowed repeatedly as he backed toward the door. "N-never." The moment he was out of range of the truncheon, he turned and scuttled out, nearly knocking over a side table in his haste. The pounding of his shoes echoed down the passageway and then died into silence.

She was alone with Lucas.

He stood watching her, his face somber, his thoughts unfathomable. Against the quiet hissing of the fire, the mantelpiece clock chimed the hour of midnight. The witching hour, she reflected. The time when fairy tales ended.

Her heart ached so badly she wanted to run and hide, to find a private place to curl up and mourn. But with a greater fierceness, she wanted a new beginning. She would make it happen. No matter what the cost, whether she had to beg or bribe or seduce, she would not allow Lucas to walk out of her life,

The resolve steadied her. Going to him, she placed her hands over his on the hefty wooden club. How warm was his flesh in contrast to his cold manner. She forced a teasing tone. "You aren't thinking about beating me, are you?"

As she'd hoped, that grabbed his attention. His eyes narrowed and he scowled. "God, no. Why would you say that?"

"For not telling you about our baby. For withholding the truth from you again." She attempted a charming smile, but to her distress, a sob broke loose instead. Her eyes flooded with tears, clouding the image of him.

He tossed the truncheon onto a chair and folded her into his arms. ''Don't weep,'' he murmured, stroking her hair and holding her close. ''Please, don't weep.''

''I'm not weeping,'' she said, sniffling against his chest. ''I never weep.''

''Ah. I'd noticed that about you. You're a strong, courageous woman.''

''Lucas, believe me, I never meant for you to find out this way,'' she sobbed into his musk-scented robes. ''But I—I was afraid . . .''

''Afraid of what?''

''Afraid that once you knew about the baby, you'd consider your duty done. You'd stop holding me, kissing me, loving me.'' The notion brought a fresh spill of tears, and she fancied her heart was bleeding, a crystalline stream of pain.

From somewhere in his robes, he produced a handkerchief, which he used to blot her cheeks. ''So you think only duty enticed me to your bed.''

His voice held the faintest hint of teasing. It was enough to bring her head up and lock her gaze to his. Though his mouth was unsmiling, his eyes held a certain softness. ''Well, of course you took pleasure in what we did,'' she amended.

''I'm pleased you noticed.''

''But we did make a bargain.'' Mustering the shreds of her dignity, she lifted her chin higher. ''And I wished to speak to you about that.''

''I'm listening.''

She drew a shaky breath. ''I know the conditions we agreed upon. However, I shan't give this baby over to you. I cannot bear to be separated from my own child.''

''As you wish.''

He answered so quickly, she looked at him uncertainly. ''And that's not all,'' she ventured softly. ''I should also like for us to be a family—you and I, Jenny and the baby.''

He gently splayed his fingers over her abdomen. A look of torturous longing lit his face. Then he closed his eyes a moment. When he opened them, all tenderness had vanished. She might have been gazing into dark, desolate blankness. "No, Emma," he said in a fatalistic tone. "You ask the impossible."

He released her, walking away to flatten his palms on the desk. The bow of his broad back spoke poignantly of his deep despair, a despair echoed in her own heart. She would not let him go. She could not.

Heedlessly, she ran to him. "Why? Do you regret losing Shalimar so much?"

Frowning, he turned his head. "No. She filled a place in my life once, a much-needed place. But we spoke a mutual farewell weeks ago, shortly after you and I had sealed our bargain." He straightened, raking his fingers through his hair. "That cursed bargain. I was unspeakably cruel to you, Emma. When I think of how you must have suffered . . ."

A ray of hope shone into her heart. At least now she had an inkling of what tormented him. She wrapped her arms around his waist, loving him, willing him to love her back. "Oh, Lucas, if you refuse to live with me and our children, well, then, you'll make me suffer for the remainder of my life. *That* would be unspeakably cruel."

His hands tightened around her shoulders. His taut lips and lowered brow reflected his inner battle. "And you . . . do you regret losing Woodrow Hickey?"

She shook her head. "When I agreed to marry him, I was seeking a father for Jenny. For all his lies to me, he does love her. All along, he wanted Jenny, not me."

Andrew lives on in her. Surely you can understand how precious she is to me.

Woodrow's plea saddened Emma. She remembered the look of wild desolation on his face when Lucas had forbidden him to visit Jenny. Emma too was loath to let her child associate with the man who had tried to wreck her marriage. "Poor Woodrow," she said. "He has nothing left now. It pains me to admit it, but I didn't know him. I didn't know what he truly wanted.''

"Jenny," Lucas said in a strange, harsh whisper. "He wants Jenny."

Their gazes caught and held in a wordless exchange of dawning horror. The nape of her neck prickled. Emma began to shake. A terrible, fearful shaking.

She didn't know Woodrow.

Lucas snatched up the branch of candles. He and Emma raced out of the library to the nearest staircase, the one used by the servants. The pounding of their feet echoed in the dim tunnel of the stairwell. It seemed to take an eternity to reach the top floor. Emma felt sluggish and slow, trapped in a nightmare. They were mistaken, she told herself in a litany. *Mistaken.*

They burst into the nursery. The banked fire cast a faint orange glow over the schoolroom with its tidy cupboards, the sturdy chairs and tables, the globe atop the bookcase. Hastening through the gloom of an opened door, Emma stopped short. The candelabrum in Lucas's hand illuminated the cozy bedroom with its tasseled rose curtains, the miniature dressing table where Jenny liked to play grown-up, the four-poster bed trimmed in frilly lace.

And Emma's nightmare changed to hideous reality. The bed was empty, the covers thrown back. The pillow held a small indentation where the little girl had rested her head.

Jenny was gone.

∽ **Chapter 24** ∾

Staving off panic, Lucas strode into the next room and awakened the nurse. The apple-cheeked woman expressed bewilderment over the disappearance of her charge. She struggled into her wrapper and declared the wee girl must have wandered off on some innocent task, perhaps to fetch her dear puppy a midnight treat.

Lucas harbored no such hope. With the faith of the innocent, Jenny trusted Woodrow Hickey. The scoundrel could have concocted any lie to convince her to leave the house with him.

"Dear God," Emma whispered in the darkened schoolroom. "He can't stay in England. He'll spirit Jenny out of the country. I'll never see my little girl again." She seized hold of Lucas's arm, her nails pressing into his flesh. "We must leave for Dover immediately. He'll be at least an hour or more ahead of us. If they sail off to a foreign port on the morning tide, we'll never find them!"

"Shh." Subduing his own fears with difficulty, Lucas held her close and forced himself to think. A spark of hope burned in him. "Hickey would have acted on impulse," he said. "He was distraught because I forbade him to see Jenny. That means he isn't prepared to leave England."

"You're right," Emma said, her voice catching. "He'll need money, clothing, legal documents. He'll surely stop at his town house."

"Precisely. He won't expect anyone to notice Jenny's disappearance until morning."

Lucas swiftly guided Emma down the stairs. The urge to protect her drummed in his chest. Yet he knew it would do no good to command Emma to stay behind, to keep herself safe. She would follow in an instant, risking all to save her daughter.

Their daughter. He felt as if blinders had been removed from his eyes. Jenny was his now as much as Emma's. He would never forgive himself if anything happened to either of them. Never.

Assisted by a sleepy stable lad, Lucas had the curricle ready in record time. Dying bonfires illuminated the streets, a lucky happenstance as he sent horse and carriage careening through the night. Wrapped in a warm pelisse, Emma sat huddled against him. The cold wind slapped their faces, but Lucas dared not drive slower. Not when every moment counted.

He found himself praying for the first time in years. *Punish me if You will, Lord. But spare Emma the agony of losing a child. She's suffered too much already.*

At last they arrived at the quiet residential road where Woodrow lived. To avoid alerting their quarry, Lucas stopped the curricle halfway down the street. No lights glinted in the front windows of Woodrow's town house. No carriage waited out front for the flight to Dover.

They might have guessed wrong. The bastard might already be gone.

Lucas's heart sank, but he kept the doubts out of his voice. "We'll try around back."

Emma nodded. Her face shone a pale oval against the darkness. She trusted him to rescue their daughter. Lucas only hoped he would not betray that faith.

His hands spanning her slim waist, he swung her down from the high perch. Fleetingly he wondered how many weeks would pass before her belly began to swell to beautiful roundness, making room for their baby. With a fierceness that shook him, he wanted to be with Emma every step of the way, to share the joy of anticipation, to watch their child thrive and grow.

He locked away his longing. There was no time for self-indulgence. They hastened through the night and reached the darkened mews behind the row of residences.

"Stay close to me," he whispered.

He took her hand and quietly led the way through the narrow alley. A horse snorted in a stable nearby. The odors of manure and rubbish hung in the gloom. Emma's fingers felt small and delicate nestled inside his palm. Yet for all her daintiness, she had an inner strength that set her apart from other women. How he loved her. No other lady of his acquaintance would have the pluck to accompany him on such a dangerous mission.

He spied Hickey's town house, the third in the row. A fury of exultation jolted him as he saw an unattended horse, harnessed to a phaeton, outside the tiny stable. And just above the ground floor of the dwelling, a corner window glowed with a halo of light.

"They're here." Emma clutched his arm. "Oh, Lucas, Woodrow must be in his study. Jenny will be up there with him. Let's go fetch her."

As she started across the small yard, Lucas stopped her with a hand on her shoulder. "Wait. He's a desperate man. He may be dangerous."

"He won't hurt Jenny. I know he won't."

"But he could hurt you—shoot you," Lucas whispered grimly. "Don't forget, you stand in the way of what he wants. Now, you'll remain here—"

"No!"

"Yes. I can't protect both of you, and we daren't risk Jenny being harmed."

Through the fire of her fear, Emma acknowledged the logic of his words. Lucas stood before her, a big, black silhouette in the moonlight. They had not spared the time to change, and the garb of a maharajah only added to his aura of command. His hands were gentle yet firm on her shoulders. She had to trust him. She *did* trust him.

"I'll wait here," she said reluctantly.

"I'll bring Jenny to you," Lucas said. "That's a promise."

After brushing a swift kiss to her lips, he was gone, a shadow stealing across the yard and through the rear door. Ah, he would make a grand thief, Emma thought with pride. She looked up, wanting to be certain he hadn't been spotted. And she gasped.

The corner window was dark now. Woodrow and Jenny might be on their way downstairs. Tension gripped Emma. They might run straight into Lucas. . . .

Then to her relief she saw the light had moved higher. A glimmer appeared on the floor above, where the bedrooms were situated. Woodrow must be packing his valise. And Lucas wouldn't know where they'd gone.

Emma wasted no time. Rushing to the back door, she slipped into the house. Her eyes adjusted quickly to the gloom of a passageway. She knew the general layout of his house from her visit here, and with a burglar's instinct she felt her way through the darkness to the stairs. At this late hour, the housekeeper would be fast asleep—in an attic bedroom, perhaps. Emma doubted the woman would be of much help, anyway. She was far more likely to side with her master than come to the aid of a stranger.

Hitching up her costume with dampened palms, Emma quietly climbed the steps to the first floor, which held the dining room, morning room, and study. She hastened from room to room, peering desperately through the shadows, but saw only the black lumps of furniture. Where was Lucas? Had he spied Woodrow on his way upstairs? She thought she detected the murmur of voices overhead.

It maddened her to think of Jenny, scared and bewildered, on the floor above. Dread thickened Emma's throat. What if she were wrong about Woodrow? What if he abused her little girl?

She could not bear to wait. Finding the ornately carved newel post in the darkness, she gripped the balustrade and started to mount the steps.

* * *

Lucas crept along the upper passageway. Candlelight spilled from an opened door at the end of the corridor. He could hear the sound of voices. That deep, chiding tone belonged to Woodrow. Jenny's incoherent reply had the whining quality of an overtired child.

Hot anger spurred Lucas. He'd like to string up the craven bastard by his cock. He forced himself to cool down and think. Whatever the cost, he must avoid frightening Jenny. He would subdue Woodrow, then turn him over to the magistrate. He doubted Woodrow would spill out the truth about why he'd kidnapped Jenny. Not when the news of his secret predilection would put a noose around his cowardly neck.

His fingers curled into fists, Lucas reached the doorway. A bedroom lay within, lit by a pair of candles, one on the mantelpiece, the other on the dressing table. His back to the door, Woodrow rummaged in an opened wardrobe. Jenny sat yawning on the bed, Sissy in her lap. The puppy spotted Lucas and yapped, tail wagging.

Holding an armload of shirts, Woodrow turned, his gaze on Jenny. "You must keep Sissy quiet, remember? We mustn't wake Mrs. Quimby in the attic, though she's a sound sleeper."

But Jenny wasn't looking at him. A big smile brightened her sleepy face. "Papa!"

Scrambling off the bed, she flung herself at Lucas. He caught both her and Sissy up in his arms. His throat knotted. Nothing in the world could match the sweetness of hugging his own little daughter. Andrew's daughter, too. Without his seed, Jenny would not exist. That realization brought a searing ray of forgiveness into Lucas's heart. He could not hate his brother, only pity him for never knowing Jenny.

"Sissy and me were missing you and Mama," she chirped. "Are you going to the fireworks with me and Uncle Woodrow? He's promised me a grand view."

"We shall see." Lucas set her down and smoothed his hand over the crown of her soft chestnut hair. "You wait a moment in here, sweet pea. I need to have a private word with . . . Uncle Woodrow.''

As she trudged back toward the bed, Lucas turned his gaze to her kidnapper. Woodrow stood by his opened valise, his arms clenched around the shirts, his gray eyes wary and watchful.

Seized by the raw urge to kill, Lucas jerked his head toward the corridor. ''Step out here,'' he said quietly. ''Now.''

Woodrow bent with jerky movements to set down the shirts by the valise. Seething with frustrated fury, Lucas stood in the doorway and kept an eye on his quarry. Until he noticed the shrine on the bedside table. A candle shed light on a collection of military paraphernalia—a silver flask, a blue sash, a pair of white gloves. On the wall hung a small painting of Andrew, handsome and smiling in his cavalry uniform.

Lucas's temples pounded. His gaze swung back to Woodrow, the bastard who had driven Andrew into madness and death. Lucas could scarcely wait to take the scoundrel into custody. It would be damned difficult not to beat him to a bloody pulp.

Yet he had to remember their audience. Jenny was too young, too sweet, to witness violence. He hadn't had the chance to save her mother from brutality, but he could at least spare Jenny.

His face drawn and his eyes lowered, Woodrow plodded out of the bedroom. Lucas motioned him ahead, and the baronet meekly obeyed. Midway down the passageway, he whirled around, his hand inside his coat. He whipped out something that glinted in the dim light.

Before he could take more than a step, Lucas found himself gazing into the steely eye of a pistol. A smooth-barreled cavalry sidearm.

''Don't be hasty,'' he said, cursing his stupidity. ''We must talk—''

''I'm afraid,'' Woodrow broke in, ''there's really nothing for us to say.''

And he pulled the trigger.

* * *

Emma was halfway up the stairs when she heard a man's guttural voice. A shot rang out. Followed by a crash and a thump.

She froze, her heart lurching madly. The noise had come from upstairs.

With a frenzied cry, Emma rushed up the steps. A light shone at the end of a dim passageway. It illuminated the man sprawled on the floor.

"Lucas," she whispered.

Somehow she found herself beside him, on her knees, cradling his bloodied head in her lap. His eyes were closed, his face abnormally pale. Warmth seeped into her skirt. Blood. Her husband's blood. It matted the side of his head and stained his blue robe.

Her own veins ran cold as ice as she moved her shaking hands over him. Was he breathing? Dear God. She couldn't detect the rise and fall of his chest.

"I'm sorry," Woodrow said. "Truly I am."

His voice came to her from afar, swimming through a thick sea of horror. She looked up to see him standing over her. His elegant features wore a look of abject shock. Her gaze widened on the smoking pistol in his quavering hand.

"You shot him," she said faintly.

"I had no choice. He wanted to take Lady Jenny from me."

His words broke through Emma's dazed senses. "Jenny. Where is she? What have you done with her?"

"She's in there," he said, pointing with the barrel of the pistol to a doorway. "She's perfectly fine. You surely don't think *I* would hurt her . . ."

Emma didn't hear the rest. Leaving Lucas, she stumbled into a bedroom lit by a pair of candles. The garter-blue walls showcased the grand, gilded furnishings. A valise stood open on a chair, surrounded by tidy piles of clothing—folded cravats, starched linen shirts, pressed suits. A movement caught Emma's attention. On the other side of the tester bed, two woeful pairs of eyes peeked out. Jenny, holding Sissy.

Emma ran and gathered them close, keenly aware of Jenny's precious little form. Hugging her made the wrenching pain inside Emma more bearable.

Teary-eyed, the girl clung to her, and the puppy licked the two of them. "What happened?" Jenny asked fearfully. "Me and Sissy heard a loud bang."

Her throat tight with anguish, Emma could only shake her head. How could she give her daughter nightmares by telling her the truth? "Shh. It was only a noise from the street. People are still celebrating."

"But where's Papa? He was just here."

Emma swallowed hard, resisting the blackness of grief. "I'm afraid he . . . he had to go away suddenly."

"I shall be your papa now," Woodrow said, appearing in the doorway. "Just as I was always meant to be."

His gaze met Emma's. His gray eyes held a dangerous determination, a warning to her not to resist. Lest she suffer the same fate as Lucas.

"Aren't we going to see the fireworks?" Jenny asked. Her lower lip quivered. "When you woke up me and Sissy, you promised we would."

"I'm afraid we're too late," he said gently. "The fireworks are over." He sat down at the dressing table and, with smooth efficiency, began to reload the pistol. "We must go on a long journey, dear child. We'll see sights far more exciting than fireworks. The pyramids of Egypt. The châteaus of France. You can swim in the ocean and climb to the top of a mountain. Perhaps we'll even buy a yacht, you and I. We'll sail the seven seas . . ."

As he rambled on, his plans growing more and more grandiose, he used a long ramrod to push the ball down the barrel of his pistol. The sight of the gun unnerved Emma. She picked up Jenny and held her tightly. Woodrow was a murderer. He had killed Lucas.

Lucas!

She swallowed again, struggling valiantly to keep panic at bay. There would be no reasoning with Woodrow, not in his maddened state of mind. She could never again allow him near her cherished little girl. Never.

Turning his back for a moment, Woodrow replaced the powder flask in his valise. Emma held her finger to her lips. Jenny's eyes rounded. She clutched the squirmy white dog and nodded. Praying her daughter would keep quiet, Emma edged past the bedpost. The doorway loomed two yards distant. She had a chance . . .

She caught his reflection in the dressing table mirror. For one dire instant, their eyes locked. Then she ran.

He reached the door first, spreading his arms out to stop her. Though not a large man, he posed a menacing barrier. He gripped the pistol, his forefinger caressing the trigger. Trembling, she pressed Jenny's face into the crook of her neck.

"Emma, you disappoint me," he said. "You've disappointed me too many times lately. Especially when I learned you're the Bond Street Burglar."

"How—?"

"I sought out that slimy creature—that Youngblood. He told me everything." Woodrow raised the pistol, aiming its cold round barrel at her. "Put her down now, Emma. You're not a proper mother. I can take far better care of Jenny—"

A bloodcurdling screech split the air. The cacophony came from the passageway outside the room.

Woodrow spun around. Looking past him, Emma saw the housekeeper standing over Lucas's body. Her nightdress was rumpled and her gray hair straggled to her waist. " 'E's bleedin'! Call a doctor! Call the Watch! Heeelllp!''

"Shut up, you stupid cow." Woodrow lunged toward her. "You'll awaken the neighborhood with your caterwauling."

"But 'e's been shot! I 'eard it meself. Woke me out of a sound sleep—"

"I was forced to shoot an intruder, that's all. Chances are, he's the Bond Street Burglar."

"The Burglar's retired. 'Twas writ in yesterday's paper." Her jowly features knotted with skepticism, she peered closely at Woodrow. ''And ye, sir, ye're supposed to be in Gloucester, ain't ye?''

As Woodrow concocted a lie, Emma inched out of the bedroom, her arms weighed down by Jenny. Woodrow blocked the way to the main staircase. But from nighttime forays into town houses much like this one, Emma knew another escape route. A far more dangerous one. And she had no alternative but to use it.

She edged toward a small door half-hidden in the paneling at the end of the corridor. Jenny uttered no sound, though her eyes were big and alert. She gripped Emma's neck with one hand and cuddled the puppy in her other arm. Bless her for a sensible child, Emma thought fervently.

She reached the door and struggled to open it without dropping her warm burden. Her fingers slipped and the brass knob rattled.

Woodrow wheeled around. Emma flung open the door. Hastening up the steep, dark stairs, she nearly tripped on the hem of her skirt. She set Jenny down at once. ''Run, darling. Ahead of me. Pretend we're in a race.''

Grasping Sissy, the little girl dashed upward, toward another door at the head of the steps. The heavy harshness of Woodrow's breaths resounded as he entered the stairwell. The housekeeper was screeching again, down in the corridor. Her pulse quickening, Emma lifted her skirt and went after Jenny, keeping a hand on her daughter's back so she wouldn't take fright.

Emma's own back crawled in anticipaton of a shot. He wouldn't dare fire, she told herself. Not when the bullet might hit Jenny.

Amazingly, a giggle pealed from Jenny as she burst through the upper doorway and into the gloom of the attic. ''I won, Mama. I beat you!''

''You did, indeed.''

A sinister black shape surged up after them. ''Emma, wait! You mustn't take Jenny away from me—''

Emma slammed the door shut. Frantically she searched for something to bar it. Scrabbling in the shadows, she brushed a hard wooden surface. A chair. She hooked the high back of it beneath the door handle.

Just in time. The knob rattled. Woodrow pounded on the panel. "Open at once. I'll let you go if you do. Just give me Jenny. Give her to me!"

He must be deranged to think she would hand over her daughter. Oh, God. *Oh, God.* He'd shot Lucas. And now he meant to shoot her.

"Mama?" Jenny's voice quavered as she tugged at Emma's sleeve. "What's the matter? Why is Uncle Woodrow shouting?"

Taking a deep breath, Emma subdued her terror. "It's part of the game, darling. We must escape before he catches us."

"But how? It's too dark and scary in here."

"We'll pretend we're burglars and steal out the window. Come."

Grasping Jenny's hand, Emma headed toward a square of starlight beneath the eaves. Dull thuds resounded through the attic. Woodrow was trying to batter down the door. She heard the ominous creaking of wood.

Shaking, she thrust open the casement and peered out. Beyond the eave, the steep, tiled roof glinted in the moonlight. A thin lip of stone led to the roof, where a short iron railing encompassed the base of the chimney.

She hiked up Jenny's nightgown around her waist. Then she boosted the girl onto the windowsill. "You must crawl very carefully to the chimney pot. Wait there for me. I'll carry Sissy."

Emma took the wriggling puppy as Jenny clambered onto the ledge. "Ooh, Mama," she said in awe. "It's way far down to the ground."

The sight of the darkened yard dizzied Emma. Each breath felt like ice as she imagined her daughter's small, broken body lying in the bushes below. What was she thinking? Jenny was no Bond Street Burglar.

With a loud crash, the door splintered. Woodrow grunted like a bull as he charged into the attic.

Clasping Sissy, Emma scrambled over the windowsill. Her

skirts tangled her legs. Holding the puppy, she had only one free hand.

Before she could clamber onto the ledge, powerful fingers clamped around her hips and jerked hard. She gasped, losing her balance. As she grabbed desperately at the stone coping, Sissy sprang free. The puppy bounded down the ledge toward Jenny.

Hanging halfway out the window, Emma struggled against Woodrow's grip. Slowly, inexorably, he pulled her back inside. He slammed her facefirst against the wall. The painful impact wrested a cry from her. Then she felt the cold circle of the gun barrel against her cheek.

"I'm sorry to kill you, my dear," he said, breathing heavily in her ear. "But you'll keep me from Andrew's daughter."

Panic surged in Emma. She fought blindly, jabbing him with her elbows, twisting and turning against his thickly muscled form. She expected the world to explode with pain at any instant. But suddenly she was free.

Gasping, she spun around, her hands tensed to fight. She stopped short. Her breath caught in disbelieving wonder. A man grappled with Woodrow, a tall man. His bright blue robe flashed in the gloom of the attic.

Lucas. He was alive. Alive!

Even as her heart soared, she remembered Jenny, alone on the roof. Emma climbed out the window and onto the ledge.

A few yards ahead, Jenny crouched by the chimney, the puppy in her arms. Her eyes looked big and scared in the moonlight. "Mama."

"Hold tight," Emma called. "I'm coming for you."

As she glanced downward, her vision swayed dizzyingly. Dear God. It was a long, long way to the ground. The stone projection seemed impossibly narrow. Her nerve threatened to fail her. Forcing herself to concentrate, she inched onward, hampered by her skirts.

She worked her way along the expanse of tiled roof. She had almost reached the chimney when Jenny cried out, "Mama! Uncle Woodrow is coming out the window."

Emma turned. Her heart nearly stopped. Brandishing the pistol, he stood up and then walked the ledge with frightening speed.

Dear God. Where was Lucas?

He was weak from loss of blood. Woodrow must have overpowered him. At least she had heard no gunshot.

But Woodrow could fire at her. The bullet might hit Jenny.

Emma hurried to shield her daughter. She took firm hold of the little girl, guiding her past the chimney. If only they could reach the adjoining house, they could climb through the window. She lifted Jenny over the railing that divided the two residences.

As Emma hastened to clamber over, her gown caught on one of the decorative iron spindles. Tugging to no avail, she cast a frantic glance backward.

Woodrow was nearly upon them. He pointed the pistol straight at her. Her blood ran cold. *Please, God, no!*

Jenny's scream pierced Emma. Sissy dangled by her front paws below the ledge. The puppy must have slipped, catching her claws in the soft tar that affixed the drainpipe, else she would have fallen. Trying to reach the dog, Jenny leaned precariously over the edge of the roof.

"Jenny, no!" Emma cried.

She yanked desperately, ripping the fabric free.

At the same instant, Woodrow barreled past her, knocking her down against the railing as he sped toward Jenny. "Don't move, dear! You'll fall."

She already had her little hands around the puppy. But in the doing, she teetered on the edge of the roof. Her squeal of fright chilled Emma to the core. In a flash of movement, Woodrow flung away the pistol, scooped up the girl and puppy, and planted them securely on the ledge.

Momentum caused his feet to slip out from under him. Arms wheeling, Woodrow tumbled off the roof. His startled cry ended with sickening abruptness.

Emma didn't need to look down. No one could survive such a fall.

Dear God. It could have been Jenny. *Jenny.*

Swallowing bile, Emma crawled toward her daughter. The girl huddled her small body around Sissy. Emma gathered them close and clung tightly, treasuring the warmth of her precious Jenny.

"Emma! Are you all right?"

At the shout, she lifted her head to see Lucas gingerly making his way toward them along the ledge. A second wave of relief poured through her, bringing a heartfelt smile to her lips. "I'm fine," she called. "We all are."

Jenny squirmed against her. "That was a scary game, Mama. Sissy and I don't think we want to play it anymore."

Her gaze on Lucas, Emma laughed from pure joy. "We won't, darling, I promise. Never again will I scramble around on rooftops."

⤷ Epilogue ⤶

*E*very fashionable person who lingered in London over the holidays thronged St. George's Church in Hanover Square. The *ton* was abuzz with the excitement of witnessing an unprecedented event. On this, the Eve of Christmas, with all the pomp and circumstance of a formal wedding, Lord and Lady Wortham were to renew their marriage vows.

Sporting a rakish scar from the bullet wound on his temple, Lucas stood near the altar and awaited his bride. Scarcely able to suppress a wicked smile, he strove for an expression suitable to the solemn occasion. But he couldn't help remembering the pleasure of loving Emma. Seldom did a gentleman enjoy the privilege of being awakened at dawn on his wedding day by the sensual caresses of his bride.

The morning shone bright and crisp and cold. Snow had fallen during the night, veiling the city in white. Now, sunlight through the stained-glass windows scattered brilliant color over the guests. Lucas recognized so many smiling faces—his mother, his sisters with their husbands and children. And even those members of the *ton* who had once shunned Emma—Lord Gerald Mannering, Miss Pomfret, Lord Jasper Putney.

The bishop of London took his place before the altar. A string orchestra played a joyous melody from the choir loft.

The stately stone columns, the arched ceiling, the sense of anticipation—all these reminded Lucas of his first wedding day. Yet today was vastly different. And the distinction was more than the crisp chill in the air or the holiday greenery festooning the pews and chandeliers. It was the keen sense of rightness.

Back then, he had been a blushing lad wont to stutter at a smile from Emma. The loss of her for so many years had devastated him. But without the pain of the past, he could not savor the richness of the present. Sorrow and tragedy had matured him, expanded his capacity for love.

Gowned in green satin with perky red bows, Lady Jenny Coulter skipped down the aisle, strewing crimson rose petals from the basket in her little gloved hands. She spied Lucas and grinned, displaying a set of brand-new front teeth. Then she slipped into the front pew and perched beside the dowager marchioness, who hugged her granddaughter without restraint.

A momentary pensiveness struck Lucas. His mother would never know that Jenny had been conceived in violence. Nor would she ever know the truth about her beloved Andrew. There was no need. The past didn't matter to Lucas—only his future with Emma.

The music swelled. And then he could see no one but Emma. As always, the sight of her rendered him thunderstruck.

On her grandfather's arm, she entered the church. A circlet of tiny red rosebuds crowned her upswept moonbeam curls. Slim and radiant in a gown of spun gold, she looked like a goddess come down from the heavens. His body tightened with unholy longing. How well he knew she was a woman. Very much a woman.

Jeweled light streamed over her. The slight rounding of her belly did not yet show. It was their precious secret—it would be their gift to the family on Christmas Day.

A collective sigh swept the congregation as Emma glided up the aisle. Briggs winked as he passed his granddaughter to her husband. Aware of a sense of awe, Lucas took her kid-gloved hand and brought her to the altar.

The rich voice of the bishop intoned the movingly familiar words of the marriage service. Lucas listened to Emma speaking her vows without the hesitation he remembered from the first ceremony. Then it was his turn.

" 'Lucas James Coulter, Marquess of Wortham and Earl of Kendall, wilt thou have this woman to be thy wedded wife, to live together with her after God's ordinance in the holy estate of matrimony? Wilt thou love her, comfort her, honor and keep her, in sickness and in health, and forsaking all others, keep thee only unto her, as long as ye both shall live?' "

Scarcely able to contain the joy that leapt inside him, he gazed down at Emma. "I most certainly will."

As his voice rang out, her fingers tightened around his. Her blue eyes shone as brightly as stars. Her soft mouth curved into a familiar smile, the smile that stole his breath away. The sweet but sensual smile that required him to sternly remind himself of their sacred surroundings and the watchful audience.

Then it was time to seal their vows with a tender kiss. As the orchestra launched into the closing march and they turned to face their guests, Emma clung to his arm and demurely whispered, "How soon can we start our honeymoon?"

He choked back a laugh. "Wicked woman, always mad about sex. We've a lifetime ahead of us."

"A rich and exciting life," she murmured, a glint of deviltry in her eyes. "And when we're in our dotage, we can remember that once upon a time, we created a scandal."

DON'T MISS BARBARA DAWSON SMITH'S
EXCITING NEW HISTORICAL ROMANCE

The Venus Touch

COMING FROM ST. MARTIN'S PAPERBACKS IN
SPRING 1998

Turn the page for a sneak preview . . .

London, 1821

He would teach her a lesson she would never forget.

Standing in the gloom beneath a plane tree, he scrutinized her house. It didn't look like a brothel. Situated on a quiet street, the town house was built of the same pale stone as its neighbors. Rain scoured the tall windows and sluiced down the fluted columns that flanked the porch. Three granite steps led up to a discreet white door, its brass knocker gleaming in the twilight. From time to time, the lace curtains gave a glimpse of shadowy people moving inside the lighted, ground-floor rooms.

According to his spy, the harlots would be eating dinner before commencing their nightly activities. Upstairs, the closed draperies shut out all but a glimmering of candlelight in one room.

Her room.

A cold sense of purpose consumed him. He wanted no witness to their meeting. He would wait in her boudoir and use the element of surprise. . . .

He pivoted on his bootheel and crossed the wet cobblestones. Raindrops flew from his caped overcoat. A carriage rattled past, harness jingling and wheels clattering. He averted his face, then ducked into the mews behind the row of town houses.

Shadows darkened the narrow passage, and the odors of rubbish and droppings tainted the damp air. The stamping of a hoof came from inside a stable. At the third house, he spied the plain wooden door that marked the servants' entrance.

The knob turned easily and he stepped inside. He paused, orienting himself in the murky corridor. A faint, musky aroma hinted at decadent pleasures. From the front of the house came the clink of cutlery and the whining complaint of a woman, the shrill laughter of another. To his left lay the door to the basement kitchen; he could smell the stench of boiled cabbage and fried fish. The door to his right hid the stairwell, and he mounted the steep steps in the unlit shaft.

In the second-floor passageway, lewd paintings cluttered the walls. A golden arm of light beckoned him toward an opened doorway.

He walked quickly, quietly. He would take her unawares when she returned from dinner. He would put an end to her plans once and for all.

Stepping through the portal, he stopped dead.

She was *here*.

At the dressing table, his quarry sat on a gold-fringed stool. The hissing of the coal fire must have masked his footfalls, for she did not notice his presence. Or perhaps she was too absorbed in grooming her hair.

She looked young, no more than eighteen. Not that her age mattered; she was old enough in the ways of corruption. And like others of her calling, Miss Isabel Darling was an expert at controlling men.

But for once she had met her match.

She admired herself in the oval mirror, turning her head this way and that, her eyes half-closed as if she were entranced by her own beauty. Russet strands blazed amid the rich brown mass that curled down past her waist. Each stroke of the brush lifted her hair, teasing him with glimpses of a curvaceous form clad in a copper silk wrapper.

His body responded with untimely appetite. His blood

heated and his loins tightened. With senseless greed, he wanted to abandon his mission, to avail himself of her services instead.

Damn her.

He flexed his fingers and walked into the boudoir, his boots making no sound on the plush pink carpet. An opened door in the far wall revealed a room with a four-poster bed draped in gaudy gold hangings. The bed where she serviced her customers.

He stopped directly behind her. His black-gloved hands descended to her shoulders, his fingers curling lightly into her tender flesh. Her skin felt like a babe's, warm and satiny and unblemished.

Her brush froze in mid-stroke and her startled gaze flew to his in the gilt-framed mirror. Her eyes were wide and sherry-brown, fringed by thick lashes.

She gasped, her bosom lifting, luring his attention downward. He leaned closer, drawn to the feast of her cleavage. Though it might earn him a place in hell, he wanted to taste her—

With a wild cry, she pivoted on the stool. The hairbrush flashed out and whacked him in the ribs. The blow thundered through his chest. Her face fierce with savagery, she whipped her arm back for another strike.

He seized her wrist. "I wouldn't do that, Miss Darling."

"Who are you?" she demanded. "Who let you in here?"

"I showed myself in."

She jerked against his grip. "Get out. Before I scream."

"Go ahead. The other women are too far away to hear."

He could sense her fear. It was there in the flaring of her slim nose and the trembling of her lips. He relished his power over her. One sharp twist and he could break the fragile bones of her wrist. He could punish her for what she had done. For what she intended to do.

He pried the brush from her fingers and set it down on the dressing table. Then he planted his hands on either side of her and murmured into her ear, "That's no way to treat a guest. It's bad for business."

Isabel Darling reared back and blinked warily. "I don't know who you are, but I did not invite you here. This house is closed."

"Not to the Duke of Lynwood."

"The duke—?" Brazenly direct, she looked him up and down, white cravat and caped greatcoat, tan breeches, polished Hessians. She gave a toss of her head, causing her long wavy hair to shift around her shapely figure, brushing places that iron control denied him. "You're too young to be His Grace. Too . . . too . . ."

"Civilized," he said on a note of derision. She couldn't begin to fathom how different he and his sire were.

Isabel Darling sat watching him. "You're Lynwood's son," she said slowly. "You're Justin Culver. The Earl of Kern."

He stood back, acknowledging her words with a mocking bow. "I see you've done your research."

She looked into the mirror and deftly wound her hair into a loose topknot, securing the luxuriant dark curls with tortoiseshell pins. The utter femininity of her action bewitched him. The urge to press his lips to her soft skin warred with his sense of purpose. "Go away," she said. "My business is with Lynwood."

"Your business is with me. My father is indisposed, and I am handling his affairs."

"This is a matter of some delicacy," she said, clasping her hands on the dressing table. "I'm willing to wait until I can speak to the duke."

"No. We'll settle things now."

"On the contrary, I must insist—"

"Insist all you like, Miss Darling. It will do you no good." Kern spoke in an uncompromising tone. "I've read those bogus memoirs—or at least the portion you sent to him."

She countered his gaze with a frigid glare of her own. "Do you always open letters marked 'Private and Confidential'? It is not the honorable thing to do." Turning from him, she fussed with her hair again. "Now go away."

Kern's chest throbbed with bottled-up rage. She would

never see his father. Nor would anyone outside his family.

Controlling his temper, he leaned down, scowling at her in the mirror. "Heed me well," he stated. "You'll deal with me, and me alone. I'll wager you didn't bargain on *that* when you put together your vicious little scheme."

For the length of several heartbeats, Isabel Darling stared at his reflection. An aura of startled purity haloed her. Then a sultry smile transformed her face, banishing the illusion of innocence.

She rose gracefully from the stool, a dainty woman who barely reached his collarbone. As she walked away from him, her hips undulated with subtle sensuality. The coppery sheath did not reveal so much of her slim figure as he'd expected. Yet Isabel Darling embodied male fantasy.

His fantasies.

"Say what you have come here to say, then," she murmured.

"You are in possession of an obscene work involving my father. If you dare to publish it, I shall see you arrested for libel."

"Prove the memoirs false, then. That will make for a lively court case indeed, m'lord."

He stood very still, hating her audacity and hating even more to admit she was right. Isabel Darling possessed the means to sully his good name, to make his father a laughingstock, to subject his family to gossip and ostracism. And her proposition could not have come at a worse time.

"His Grace misused my mother," Miss Darling went on, picking up a pink feather boa from the chaise and caressing the plumage. "Everyone shall know of his vile behavior. Unless, of course, you comply with my request."

"Request." Kern let out a harsh laugh. "Extortion is more the word."

"*Is* that the word?" She tapped her forefinger against her dainty chin. "Hmm. I should call it justice."

"Justice? You think to coerce my father into sponsoring you. To pass off *you* as a lady. To present a strumpet's bastard to the *ton*."

Her gaze was unwavering, shameless. "Yes."

Kern paced the over-furnished boudoir, loathing the dissipated life it represented. The carnality *she* represented—the pain of broken lives, the stigma of degradation and dishonor. "That is ludicrous. You have no breeding. You don't belong in polite society."

"It is no more ludicrous than *your* father mincing about at the royal court, pretending to be respectable."

"His Grace of Lynwood has the blood of kings flowing through his veins."

"And the lust of a lecher flowing through his . . ."—she paused delicately—"well, you know what."

Her reproachful demeanor angered him. She acted as if she—and her mother—had been wronged. Kern slashed his hand downward. "Your mother was a whore. She did what whores are paid to do."

Miss Darling paled, but held her chin high. Her small white fingers gripped the feather boa. "And who pays *you* to be a self-righteous snob, sir?"

"Very amusing. How much gold will it take to buy your silence?"

"I do not want your money. *Entre* to society will suffice."

"Where you can dupe some rich fool into marrying you? I think not."

"I want the life that was denied to my mother. She was a penniless gentlewoman seduced by Lynwood. And then abandoned to her fate."

"Melodramatic nonsense," Kern said dismissingly. "She moved on to another customer quickly enough. In fact, I would venture to say she was servicing a procession of men even while she and my father were involved."

Miss Darling's gaze wavered, and he knew in cold triumph that he'd surmised correctly. There *had* been other men. Many of them.

And how many gentlemen had Isabel Darling beguiled? How many customers had run their hands down that exquisite body? How many men had shared her bed?

And for God's sake, why did *he* want to share it, too?

He strode toward her. "Don't pretend ignorance, Miss Darling. You doxies are all alike. You entertain whomever is willing to pay your price."

"Oh? No amount of money could induce me to have *you*."

"Suppose I were to agree to sponsor you. What would you give me in return?"

He saw her eyes round as he stopped before her, mere inches away. She seemed not to notice that the boa slipped from her fingers and pooled at her feet. The air felt charged as if he'd been struck by lightning. He'd come here expecting to confront a coarse, well-seasoned strumpet, not this dainty girl with huge dark eyes and fine features. As much as her scheme enraged him, he had to admire her pluck. She did not cower, not even now.

His body was on fire for her. But he kept his hands at his sides, even when her lashes fluttered slightly, a sign of submissiveness. She had a soft, willing mouth, and her lips were parted, revealing the gleam of pearly white teeth and the dark promise of pleasure.

Never in his life had Kern propositioned a common whore. Yet she goaded him beyond control. He recklessly bent his head to her, tilting up her chin with one fingertip. "Witch," he muttered. "You've gone about this all wrong. It would be far more profitable for you to seek my favor."

Sparks of gold glittered in her brown eyes. He could feel her quivering like a mare scenting her mate. Then she spun away from him.

She took up a position behind a gilt chair. Her rigid stance conveyed anger, yet when she spoke, her voice was calm. "You're as disgusting as your father," she said. "You'll introduce me to society—or I shall publish the memoirs within one month's time."

Kern clenched his teeth. What a bloody fool he was for letting her charms distract him. There would be the devil to pay if his father's randy exploits were printed for all the world to read. The scandal would taint his entire family, including his fiancée, the naïve Lady Helen Jeffries. God knew, the disgrace might destroy their betrothal.

Yet he would not—could not—succumb to this blackmail. It went against every principle he held dear.

Kern stalked toward Isabel Darling. She held her ground like a defiant martyr standing up to a lion. No, like an amoral bitch. Her physical beauty masked the ugliness of her character.

This time, he gave rein to his fury. He encircled her delicate neck with his hands. Through his thin gloves, he could feel the swift beating of her pulse. "You play a dangerous game, Miss Darling. But you'll have to find yourself another dupe."

"You daren't refuse me," she said in a low tone.

"On the contrary." He scanned her in contempt. "It would be easier to turn a leper into a lady than you."

A hiss of displeasure escaped her. She stared boldly up at him, impervious to his insult. Even now he was seduced by the softness of her flesh. He was disgusted by his urge to bear her down to the floor and take the release she sold to other men. . . .

Only in his dreams has Burke Grisham, the once-dissolute Earl of Thornwald, seen a lady as exquisite as Catherine Snow. Now, standing before him at last is the mysterious beauty whose life he has glimpsed in strange visions—whose voice called him back from death, and the shimmering radiance beyond, on the bloody field of Waterloo. But she is also the widow of the friend he destroyed: the one woman who scorns him; the one woman he must possess...

A Glimpse of Heaven

Barbara Dawson Smith

"An excellent reading experience from a master writer. A triumphant and extraordinary success!"
—*Affaire de Coeur*

A vision brought traveling preacher's daughter Mary Sheppard to the wicked city of London—she saw the image of her runaway identical twin Josephine, bloodstained and begging for help. But Josephine has vanished and is wanted for the murder of her nobleman lover. And his brother Adam, the haughtily elegant Duke of St. Chaldon, has sworn to see her hang.

The only way to clear Josephine's name is to find the real culprit, so shy Mary devises a scandalous ruse. Dressed as a courtesan, wearing gems as heavy as sin, and tutored in the arts of a temptress by the duke, she will enter the gilded salons of Regency society.

But soon Mary's passion and spirit arouse in Adam the dark heat of desire. And as he coaxes her to delicious abandon in a decadent game of deception, Mary finds herself living the life and the lie of a privileged lady—the lady she knows she can never be . . .

Never A Lady

BARBARA DAWSON SMITH

"A brilliant and daring tale . . . Barbara Dawson Smith provides a great reading experience."—*Affaire de Coeur*